Street Wolf: The Black Mask Stories
of Frederick Nebel

Frederick Nebel

STREET WOLF: THE
BLACK MASK

STORIES OF
FREDERICK NEBEL

PRIMARY ILLUSTRATOR
ARTHUR RODMAN BOWKER

INTRODUCTION BY
ROB PRESTON

SERIES EDITOR
KEITH ALAN DEUTSCH

ANOTHER VOLUME IN THE BLACK MASK LIBRARY

BOSTON • PHILADELPHIA • NEW YORK
2014

© 2014 Altus Press • First Edition—2014

DESIGNED AND PUBLISHED BY
Matthew Moring

BLACK MASK SERIES EDITOR
Keith Alan Deutsch

PUBLISHING HISTORY
"Introduction" appears here for the first time. Copyright © 2014 Rob Preston. All Rights Reserved.

Owing to limitations of space, permissions to reprint previously published material appear on pages 461–464.

Published by arrangement with Black Mask Press/Keith Alan Deutsch (keithdeutsch@mac.com).

THANKS TO
John Benson, Boris Dralyuk, John Locke, Rob Preston & Ray Riethmeier.

Visit altuspress.com for more books like this.
Printed in the United States of America.

Another volume in the BLACK MASK LIBRARY.

Table of

CONTENTS

Introduction

ROB PRESTON

DUE TO a whim of fate, Frederick Nebel (1903–1967) is one of the lesser known writers in the field of vintage hard-boiled crime literature. Hammett and Chandler get the accolades while so many others have been forgotten in the dust of time. This is mostly due to the simple fact that the bulk of his fictional output never received book publication. Nebel excelled at the novelette length and wrote no serial novels that were ever reprinted during his lifetime. With the exception of one collection and a handful of anthology appearances his stories were rarely reprinted. Few of his stories were made into film, none of which are widely remembered, with just a few available for modern viewers to re-examine. With the exception of some excellent dialogue even these films barely resemble a Nebel story. Fortunately 2012 ushered in a new era in Nebel publishing history that to date has seen ten volumes collecting the bulk of his crime stories.

This volume (number six in The Black Mask Library from Altus Press) collects the last remaining tales Frederick Nebel wrote for *Black Mask* beyond the series characters MacBride & Kennedy and Donahue. Petty crooks, gangsters, rum runners, hi-jackers, jewel smugglers, Chinatown tongs, hard-boiled cops, tramp gunmen, a prize fighter, and a private dick. These are just a few of the characters found within the pages of this collection. For the most in-depth examination (to date) of the life and career of Nebel, readers are encouraged to seek the introduction

by Evan Lewis in *Raw Law: The Complete Cases of MacBride &*
Kennedy Volume 1.

The first dozen stories in this collection constitute his earliest stories for *Black Mask* until the appearance of MacBride &
Kennedy in September 1928. They also constitute the earliest
known examples of his crime fiction, though the slightly earlier
series character, Canadian Northwoods RCMP Corporal Chet
Tyson, could ostensibly be called a detective. These stories and
others are reprinted in *Defiance Valley: The Complete Northwoods*
Stories of Frederick Nebel Volume 1. Most interestingly, with the
exception of the three Buck Jason tales contained herein, all of
the remaining 13 stories that make up this collection are stand-
alone non-recurring characters, several of which touch upon
themes that Nebel rarely if ever returns to in his writing career.

Nebel is essentially a Fiction House writer for the first three
years of his writing career, writing northwest, adventure and
western stories for their line of pulps. The Fiction House motto
was "action stripped to the bone" and Nebel delivered stories
to them up through 1932, coinciding with the death of editor
J.B. Kelly. Prior to this first *Black Mask* appearance in March
1926 he had only nine known stories appear in print, all from
Fiction House. These early stories, while competently told by
a beginning pulp writer, bear only a few of the marks of style
for which he is recognized today.

With his first *Black Mask* story, accepted by Philip C. Cody,
Nebel appeared side by side with Dashiell Hammett and Raoul
Whitfield, the two *Black Mask* authors that he is known to have
drank and socialized with in the early days. Coincidentally,
Whitfield's first appearance in *Black Mask* appears in this same
issue. "The Breaks of the Game" from March 1926 introduces
the character "Shrimp Darcey," small-time burglar. This tale is
competently told with a fairly obvious ending. It has the tale-tell
makings of a beginning writer with some clumsy bits of dialogue,
but does show his knack for putting the reader firmly in the
scene until the end. The hallmark of a Nebel tale is dialogue
and even in this first story it is present and effective.

After an eight-month gap appeared "Grain to Grain" in the November 1926 issue, possibly accepted by Shaw as this is the date Shaw assumed editorship of the magazine. Another first, the story has a detective duo working their way through the yarn to solve a crime. A minor weakness in this early yarn is apparent in the explanation of how "hard-boiled" one of the characters is, instead of showing this evolution through action. A dockyard setting shows how Nebel was quite familiar with this environment. Throughout this solid little murder mystery are yet more fine examples of effective dialogue, setting this early story apart from some of the other authors in the same issue, though right at home with Whitfield, Gardner and Daly.

The third story, "Dumb Luck," opened the January 1927 issue. A rather pedestrian story of double-cross, though competently told. Small-time criminal envious for the cash and the woman of another crook conspires to take both. Even in this story we see the mastery of dialogue and a marked improvement in setting the scene.

In December 1926 Nebel embarked on a 3½ month trip to the Caribbean on a tramp steamer. This atmosphere certainly affected his stories, as he immediately began to pen stories garnered from this experience. In "China Silk," his fourth story from March 1927, he introduced Buck Jason, one of his earliest series characters, a hard bitten adventuring rum runner in a New York waterfront setting. This is the first of his stories to really showcase the talent upon which his reputation rests. It displays his lead character's feelings with descriptions of action. Utilizing subtle knowledge of the waterfront gained from his time as a car checker on the wharfs, but more tellingly, atmosphere and dialogue picked up on this trip on a tramp steamer. Most importantly there is a shift in tone and improvement in ability and assuredness that is apparent from this story forward.

In the April 1933 issue of *Black Mask,* page seven, editor Joe Shaw penned the following in describing his mental equivalent of the readers of his magazine: "Vigorous minded; hard in a square man's hardness; hating unfairness, trickery, injustice, cowardly underhandedness; standing for a square deal and a fair show in little or big things, and willing to fight for them; not squeamish or prudish, but clean, admiring the good in man and woman; not sentimental in a gushing sort of way, but valuing true emotion, not hysterical, but responsive to the thrill of danger, the stirring exhilaration of clean, swift, hard action—and always pulling for the right guy to come out on top." In this description we see the summing up of values Shaw had been presenting to his authors and readers. In this description we can almost detect the exact template for these Buck Jason stories. Even as early as June 1927, seven months into his tenure as editor, Shaw wrote an editorial titled "The Aim of *Black Mask*" in which he presents a portion of this same editorial edict and ideal: "Its [*Black Mask*] chosen field—detective fiction—is the most absorbing of all literature. This subject embodies mental and physical conflict in man's most violent moods. Its stories are essentially stories of suspense and action, with the thrill of chasing, the terror of pursuit, the triumph of successful analysis and the dread of discovery. They touch at the very heart of human emotion. Therefore, word has gone out to all *Black Mask* writers of our requirements of plausibility, of truthfulness in details, of realism in the picturing of thought, the portrayal of action and emotion." Shaw had obviously been presenting these ideas from the beginning to his authors being groomed for his magazine. Though, in a letter to Ron Goulart, Nebel denied being editorially influenced by Shaw, the knowledge that he had to create a series character in *Black Mask* with the Shaw requirements in mind is clearly apparent.

The second and third Buck Jason tales, "Hounds of Darkness" (April 1927) and "Emeralds of Shade" (August 1927), continue along the lines of "China Silk." A solid pattern had been established for the total of three Buck Jason yarns. The scene is set and readers are plunged right into the action. Nautical lore is used to solid effect, these tense yarns grip from start to finish. By "Emeralds of Shade" Nebel had shaken off the few crudities of the earliest yarns and was using his abilities with dialogue to heighten the tension with great effect. These stories were published again side by side with *Black Mask* stalwarts Whitfield, Gardner and Daly. At this late date it is unknown the reason for the demise of this series, possibly it was simply a tepid reader response.

The July 1927 issue in which "A Man With Sand" was published also included a "Getting Personal" mini-biography page where we learn of his Caribbean jaunt mentioned earlier and learn some details about his own bent towards writing and work philosophy. These ideals were directly reflected in "A Man With Sand," a story of a human derelict and his attempt to score some quick and dirty cash. Set in a New York Chinatown opium den, it is another one-off yarn, as the hero, tough Skipper Lang of the *Pandora*, struggles to overcome the schemes of his adversaries. It is another solid action yarn with excellent hard-boiled dialogue.

OVER THE next six months Nebel settled into writing and seeing published a steady stream of crime yarns, all stellar examples. He was quite busy during this time period with the Fiction House market; a quick glance through his bibliography reveals a steady stream of tales during this same period. During this time appeared "A Grudge is a Grudge" from September 1927: a story of an Ex-pickpocket and a cut-rate killer who has a grudge against him. Then with a month break came "With Benefit of Law" in November 1927: Steve Ryan, hard-bitten police detective plays more on the sideline of the main story of prize fighter Jeff Young and his struggles to fight for the championship. Another month break saw "The Penalty of the Code," January 1928: a brutal thug frames an ex-partner and the action that results. Then a four-month gap sees "A Gun in the Dark," June 1928: two Chinatown police detectives go up against a chiseling dame and the grim outcome. All solid examples of Nebel crime yarns that *Black Mask* is still renowned for.

Then came "Hell to Pay" during August 1928, an unusual story for Nebel. First of only two known gangster stories he wrote, told in the first person as a confession. The story predates the first specialist gang pulps but coincided with massive public popularity of gangsters with films and newspapers promoting their exploits as heroes; also a unknown quantity of stories appeared throughout all of the crime fiction pulp markets and beyond. Crammed with hard-boiled dialogue and tough guy bravado from start to finish, Nebel struts his talents across these pages, though the plot is typical of many gang stories.

By the May 1930 appearance of "Street Wolf," Nebel was already ten stories into the MacBride & Kennedy series. This, his second (and only novelette length) gangster story, is without a doubt the *pièce de résistance* of this collection. The markers of style and dialogue that characterize a classic Nebel story really shine, here he had reached full maturity in his writing skills. Atypical of a standard crime tale, he was trying to do something a little different here. Typical of the many gangster stories hitting the newsstands of the day, though obviously in his own style. One thing that is very different from much of his *Black Mask* output is the description of the thoughts and feelings of the characters, whereas this would usually be told through action. Not to say there isn't action, and delivered in spades, in this tale of "a gangster who might have been a poet." With this yarn Nebel delved deep into the hopes and dreams of Napo, tough gang overlord and booze hi-jacker.

"The Kill," March 1931, the first of two stories published under the pseudonym "Grimes Hill," appeared in the same issue as "Junk," which was a MacBride & Kennedy story. Initially identified as Nebel from the papers at the University of Oregon, with the pseudonym crossed out and his own name appended, the name "Grimes Hill" derives from a hill on Staten Island near where he was born. Tougher than usual stylistically, this is a story of a private dick and his job to clean up a hick midwest town. Seen in hindsight it is easily detected as a Nebel tale, though at this point he was deep into writing his series characters, so no reader during 1931 was likely to have guessed. Two months later appeared "The Spot and the Lady," the second

"Grimes Hill" yarn from May 1931. This short little tale of a crook hiding out from the law, in the same issue as "Beat the Rap," a MacBride & Kennedy story, almost reads like a short filler piece done at request to flesh out an issue. Or just maybe a little idea that was fleshed out as an alternate take on an oft drama of cop versus crook.

And for the finale, "It's the Live Ones That Talk" from the November 1931 issue. Published smack dab during the peak of MacBride & Kennedy (and Donahue) yarns is this solitary story of the Eastern States Detective Service. Set in Maine, this tautly woven tale mixes up all of the elements that are expected from Nebel plus the added features of the Maine back-country atmosphere that filled reams of tales in his work over at Fiction House.

So grab a drink, relax in your easy-chair and enjoy these never before reprinted and very rare tales of murder and mayhem, gangsters and gun-molls, penned by this master of hard-boiled literature.

The Breaks
of the Game

"SHRIMP" DARCEY lingered for a moment at Canal and Essex Streets, tapping his foot on the curb, darting his little ferret eyes about searchingly. A little, scrawny man, the Shrimp, with the body of an underfed boy and the face of a sage. He looked anywhere between twenty and forty and no one, not even the police, knew his exact age.

Presently he hitched one shoulder, a habit of his, and drifted westward along Canal with a shuffling, dragging gait. This was a habit, too, for the Shrimp was a fast man when the occasion called. At Forsyth a spare, medium-sized, commonplace man eased around the corner and fell in step beside him. Under the low-set visor of his cap the Shrimp scowled. This was not without just cause—for the commonplace man was Detective Bill Baker, himself in person.

"Hello, Shrimp," said Baker casually.

" 'Lo, Bill," muttered the Shrimp.

"Nice day, eh?"

"Uh-huh."

"What you doing downtown, Shrimp?"

The Shrimp made a sour face, "Cripes, Bill, can't a guy go where he likes!"

"Some guys—yes. But when I see you this side of Times Square I'm always on the lookout for a loft job or something." Pause; then, "H'm. Maybe you've turned lush-worker, eh?"

The Shrimp made a rasping noise through his nose. "Lush-working" is the gentle art of frisking a drunk. The Shrimp was indignant. His playground was the Eighties, and his admirable

1

vocation was scaling fire-escapes and looting top-floor apartments from the roofs. A flat-worker, the Shrimp, and no pickpocket. *That* was a Jew's job.

"Cripes, Bill, you get a guy sore," he said.

He took a cigarette from a pack, passed Baker one, and they paused at Third Avenue to get a light.

Baker said, "Well, Shrimp, I've got a job down at Pell. Better get uptown again. See you again—eh?" with a whimsical wink.

"S'long, Bill."

The Shrimp was glad to get away. That Baker guy was a nuisance, anyhow, always snooping around where he wasn't wanted. Always trying to crack wise, too. Huh! A buddy couldn't come downtown without 'em trying to hang something on him.

The Shrimp left Chatham Square behind, carefully avoided the old Elizabeth Street Police Station and turned south into Mulberry. He was looking for someone. His furtive little eyes kept jumping about. He stopped at Bayard to buy a bag of peanuts and then idly wound his way through Columbus Park, hitching his shoulder, flipping the shells away deftly. He drifted west to Lafayette and then north to Canal again, nodding curtly now and then to some hard-eyed, silent gentlemen of his profession, or to a cop who said, "How's things, Shrimp?" and then stroked his jaw thoughtfully as the Shrimp passed by. Three or four years back the Shrimp used to work the lofts between Third and Sixth Avenues, and policemen have good memories where old, familiar faces are concerned.

After a while the Shrimp found himself in a speakeasy off Canal. Tony Ciani, the proprietor, whistled softly and arched his eyebrows.

"Ah-ha, Shrimp, whassa da mat'?"

"Shut up, you bonehead!" cut in the Shrimp. "Wanna let the hull world know I'm not s'posed t'be down here. Cut it, bud.—Give us a drink."

Tony tried to look intelligent after that and slid a glass of "ginger-ale" across the bar. Tony had a sad story to tell.

"Shrimp, deses eesa wan—watcha call—tough worl'—f'r da beezness man, lak me. Paya da bulls—paya da bulls—paya da bulls. Las' week two-hun'red, dese week wan hun'red so soon. 'S wan dam' tough worl', I tella you, Shrimp.—Ah, watcha doin' down dese way—hey, Shrimp?"

Shrimp slapped down fifty cents on the bar and lit a cigarette. "Slummin', Tony," he said shortly and strode out.

Outside, he started west, then hesitated, squinted, and quickly but inconspicuously darted to cover in the nearest hallway. From this point of view he followed the movements of a man moving west on the other side of the street. When the man swung north into the next block the Shrimp strolled casually from the doorway for a few yards, then began to quicken his pace, crossed the street, and soon had the man in sight again.

He followed him along Sullivan, around Broome into Clark and then up Macdougal, watching but not watched. In a back alley near Washington Square the man entered a dilapidated old house. The Shrimp slowed down to his shuffling stroll, looked the place over sidewise as he went by and, from force of habit, circumnavigated the block. Without a moment's hesitation, then, he pushed open the door and closed it with his heel.

Dark, the interior was, not inviting to the nostrils, though the Shrimp didn't mind. There was nothing furtive about his movements here. He went up the shoe-worn stairs in no great haste, reached the first landing, pulled his cap lower over his eyes and rapped on the first door he came to. It opened on a crack a moment later. A slatternly woman asked, "Huh? Whatcha want?"

The Shrimp, inclining his head so that the woman could not see his face, replied, "Ikey Silverstein live here?"

"No, he don't, he don't. T'ink he's on de nex' floor, end o' de hall."

The Shrimp grunted, hitched his shoulder and climbed the next flight of stairs. The door slammed behind him. Here a single gas jet burned and gave out a feeble yellow light. The Shrimp moved down the corridor silently as a ghost, one hand shoved in a coat pocket.

He stopped before the door in the rear, listened. No sound within—Yes, there was a sound, some movement that he could not place. Then there was a faint noise as of a bed-spring creaking under a sudden weight. Probably Ikey had just lain down. The Shrimp let a hand close over the knob. Softly, ever so softly, he turned it as far as it would go, eased the door open a fraction of an inch, then swung it wide and whisked in, the hand in his pocket tensing.

"Easy, Ikey!" he whispered harshly, closing the door behind him.

The man on the little bed had jerked himself to a sitting posture and was trying to reach a gun in his hip-pocket.

"Easy, Ikey!" repeated the Shrimp, leaning insolently against the door.

Ikey, a slim, sallow youth, bit his nether lip and frowned for a brief instant. Then he chuckled, got up and ran his hands through his tousled hair with a yawn.

"Hell, Shrimp," he said. "I thought you was a dick. What's the idea of the soft pedal visit and the gat? Sit down and take the load off your feet."

The Shrimp continued to lean against the door and eye Ikey solemnly. Then, after a long moment, he shuffled over to a chair and sat down. His hand came out of his pocket and with it came a stubby, nasty-looking automatic. Ikey made an impatient gesture with his hand.

"For the love o' Mike, Shrimp, bury it. Put it away. What's the big idea anyway." Ikey sat down again.

The Shrimp moistened his lips but did not put away the gun. "Say, Ikey," he said finally, "do I look like a hick? D'yuh see any green on me?"

The expression on Ikey's face was exceedingly painful. "Why, Shrimp—"

"Wasn't I borned in Hester Street?" went on the Shrimp. "Didn't I useter pal wit' de Paper Box Kid 'fore he was bumped off?"

"I don't see—"

"An' since when, huh, didja t'ink yuh could pull de merry wool over me eyes like yuh did, huh? Listen, yuh damn kike; come clean. I gave yuh dat job in Seventy-ninth 'cause I had a tougher one in de Nineties. I tol' you how t' pull it an' I made it clear I wanted a fifty-fifty split. What de hell d' yuh tell me yuh had t' skin out wit' out de ice for? Huh? Why?"

"Shrimp, s' help me God, I didn't lift a damn thing! S' help me, Shrimp!"

"Can it, bud. I know yuh did—see? De cops 'a' got some Wop from First avenue f'r dat job. Guess de Wop was about to haul off an' do his stuff when dey nabbed him. Caught him on de fire-escape. But you was on de roof an' yuh got in dat Missus Randolph's bedroom an' lifted a hunk o' ice worth five thousand. Ah-r-r! How do I know, eh?"

Ikey was beginning to turn pale. His thick upper lip fluttered.

"Where is it?" the Shrimp lashed out.

"I—I got it," stammered Ikey.

"Let's see it."

His eyes darting nervously, Ikey fumbled in his vest pocket and drew out a ladies' diamond. He held it out hesitantly. The Shrimp took it, palmed it and said, "Take dat gat out o' yuh pants an' let's have it while I look dis over."

Reluctantly Ikey obeyed. After which the Shrimp fitted a small glass to his eye and inspected the ring. A moment later he flipped it back to Ikey.

"Where'd yuh t'ink I was borned!" he snarled. "I never knew yuh lifted glass in Woolworth's. Listen, yuh damn kike: I know where de real ice is. Max bought it off yuh last night."

Ikey gasped.

"Sure; Max," repeated the Shrimp. "So dat's yuh fence, is it? Max useter help me out five 'r six years ago. When yuh blew uptown an' hid down here I figured yuh'd pull a stunt like dat. I tried Max 's mornin'. Sure 'nough, he'd picked it up. An' he gave yuh a cold t'ousand on it, didn't he?"

"Y-yes, b-b-but—"

"An' you are gonna gimme dat cold t'ousand instead o' splittin' fifty-fifty, like I planned first. Ain't yuh, Ikey?"

"Aw, Shrimp, have a heart! Let's split it two ways. I didn't mean t' do you. Honest, Shrimp; no kiddin'. I meant t' give you half first chance I got."

"Ras'berry, bud! Dat's old stuff. Just act natheral an' slide out de hull t'ousand."

"Wel—well, Shrimp, I ain't got it all now. I—I gave half it to me ailin' mother. S' help me, Shrimp."

The Shrimp's face took on a weary expression. He got to his feet and regarded Ikey with a blank detached stare. Ikey knew instinctively that that stare was the prologue to a possible murder. The Shrimp's forefinger kept twining carelessly around his gun-trigger.

"S' help me—" began Ikey, squirming.

"Don't yuh know, dope, yuh mudder's been dead five years?"

"I—I gave it—honest t' God, Shrimp—I gave it t' my woman. You—"

"S'nough! Dat's about what yuh did do, yuh damn sap. But dat don't let yuh out by a long shot."

With a sudden deft movement that even surprised Ikey the

Shrimp reversed his gun and leaped forward. He brought it down murderously upon Ikey's forehead. Ikey slumped back upon the bed. The Shrimp wielded it again and again, then, panting, lurched back. There had been no noise, no scream—nothing. Ikey had taken the first blow with gritted teeth. He knew nothing about the rest.

Gloating, the Shrimp bent over the blood smeared face, knitted his brows, then stood up with a hissing intake of breath. *Ikey was dead.* The Shrimp muttered something between his teeth, stood in the middle of the floor considering the situation. Then abruptly he went through Ikey's pockets, found only a dollar and a half. Then he searched every nook and cranny of the room. He found nothing. He rasped out an oath.

He took out a handkerchief, wiped his finger marks from Ikey's gun, smeared the gun with Ikey's blood and laid it on the floor. His own gun he dropped into his pocket wrapped in newspaper. He dried the blood from his hands with his handkerchief and, wrapping this in paper also, stuffed it into a pocket. He wanted no blood-stains on his person.

For a moment he reflected. No one had seen him enter. The woman on the floor below had not seen his face, and the hallway there was very dim. So far so good.

A moment later he closed the door noiselessly behind him. No less noiselessly did he descend the rickety old stairs. He reached the street without being seen, passed out and retraced his steps towards Canal Street. It was growing dusk. He kept his now dry but still stained hands in his pockets. Casually, as if nothing unusual had happened, he passed through the swing doors into Tony Ciani's place, nodded curtly to Tony and passed to a little room at the rear, where there were running water and a basin. First he cleaned his gun, inside and out, dried it and returned it to his pocket. Instead of washing out the handkerchief he burned it along with the paper in which he had wrapped it and the gun. His own hands now washed, he lit a cigarette to kill any odor the burned bloody paper might have left, and strolled out to the bar. He asked Tony to give him a room for the night.

An hour later he went up to his room with a package under his arm. From this he took a new gray fedora and a high, stiff collar. It is remarkable how a stiff collar will set a man up and a fedora make him seem taller if he ordinarily wears a cap. So with the Shrimp. He regarded himself in the cracked mirror over the washstand, nodded with satisfaction, took one of two cigars from his vest pocket and, lighting it, went downstairs.

He knew that if Ikey's body had been found by this time, Bill Baker would be nosing around. Of course, Baker had nothing on him. But it was out of the ordinary for him, the Shrimp, to be wandering around downtown. Ikey, they'd find out, was an uptown man too, and finding him murdered down near Washington Square would start Baker putting two and two together.

After he pulled off a job the Shrimp never tried to look innocent. Perhaps he couldn't if he tried. The innocent-looking crooks are always picked up first. But the Shrimp always appeared at ease, a little sour, perhaps, for that was his natural manner, and always ready to parry words with any dick.

He was not standing at the bar five minutes when Detective Bill Baker, himself in person, breezed in and nodded genially.

"See you're still hanging around, Shrimp," he observed, poking the Shrimp in the ribs. To Tony in undertone, "Yes, Tony, make it Scotch."

"Ain't been around here in some time," said the Shrimp. "Old town don't change much."

"No, Shrimp; guess it doesn't. Well, here goes."

They downed their drinks simultaneously. The Shrimp passed Baker a cigar, held a light to it. Over the light Baker looked at him whimsically.

"Tastes good," the detective remarked.

"Oughter. Two f'r a quarter."

A little later they went out into the street side by side.

"I don't like Ciani's hootch," grimaced Baker, "Let's go over to a good joint."

"Sure," agreed the Shrimp.

Baker was in good humor tonight. He'd stay that way so long as you humored him, reflected the Shrimp. They turned from Canal into Wooster Street, made some detours and entered a dark, dismal place near Prince Street. Baker led the way through a dark hall at the end of which was a door that, after the necessary raps, opened to admit them.

IT WAS a hidden cabaret, with many tables at which sat men and women drinking. A girl was singing. In the rear of this room was a small, glassed partition with gauzy curtains, so arranged that anyone sitting behind it could see out but not be seen. It was an accommodation installed by the Indian proprietor for the convenience of plainclothes men and their friends. A moment later the Shrimp and Baker were seated comfortably at a table behind this partition and sipping the real stuff.

Perhaps half-an-hour later or thereabouts, one of the waiters beckoned to Baker and the detective, with a brief apology to the Shrimp, went out into the main room, saying he'd be right back.

The Shrimp toying with his empty glass, sighed complacently. When Baker came back he wore a perplexed frown.

"Say Shrimp, there's some guy wants to see you outside."

"Me, Bill?"

"Yeh. Young bum, I think, pale and fagged-out kind of. Gave me his name but I can't—oh, yes, Ikey—Ikey Silverstein, he said his name was."

The Shrimp's teeth cliked shut with a snap. That was the only emotion he displayed. He had his nerves under rein in a flash. His face still wore that sour look.

"Oh—Ikey?" he said, disinterestly. "What's he want? Sure, let him come in. He downtown too?"

For a brief instant Baker's eyes showed that he was baffled.

He stepped out, came back a moment later and said that Ikey had left, gone home.

The Shrimp knew that he was under suspicion. He'd have to play a careful game now. Thus far the breaks of the situation were with himself.

"Guess I'll run along, Bill, an' see what the kike wants," he announced, with a yawn, getting up.

Baker's eyes were twinkling again. "Mind if I join in?" he asked. "Nothin' doin' much to-night."

After a pause the Shrimp said, "Sure, Bill. Come on."

Baker's brows bent downward quizzically. Together they went out and walked north, keeping in step, the Shrimp passing an idle remark now and then, Baker silent. When the Shrimp swung into the house where Ikey's room was located Baker tagged behind, looking more perplexed. The Shrimp felt that the possibility of the slatternly woman recognizing him, if she came out, was scant, for he had prepared for just this thing by donning a stiff collar and a light gray fedora hat.

The stairway was almost pitch dark. The gas jets here and there burned faintly. They reached Ikey's door without an interruption. The Shrimp knocked.

"Hey, Ikey, the Shrimp," he called softly. "Open up."

"Come in," said a heavy drowsy voice.

Knowing not what to expect, the Shrimp pushed open the door. A policeman, sleepy-eyed, twisted his head and stared at him interrogatively. Then Baker pushed by and entered.

"Hello Mike," said Baker.

"Hello Bill," said the policeman.

Said the Shrimp, "Huh! What happened to Ikey?"

"Murdered, Shrimp," offered Baker with a drawl.

It was not the Shrimp's way to evince awe at such an every day occurrence. "Humph. How?" he grunted, looking about the room. The body had been removed.

"Wish we knew," droned Baker thoughtfully; then to the

policeman, "Mike, go down and ask Mrs. O'Toole to come up a minute. Sit down, Shrimp. Take life easy."

Some minutes later Mike came up with Mrs. O'Toole, a large melodramatic woman.

"Gawd, some more 'bout dis turrible moider!" she panted.

The Shrimp stood by the window, erect, with his hat on. He must keep the hat on. His face was still sour. There was no outward show of emotion.

"Have you seen this man before, Mrs. O'Toole?" queried Baker.

Mrs. O'Toole looked the Shrimp over from several angles, at long distance and then at close range. Squinting, screwing up her fat, shapeless mouth, stroking her chin, she gave him a thorough examination.

"Off hand, mister, can't say I do now. H'm. Nope. He don't look like him as asked me where Ikey lived." Her face dropped. If she had discovered the murderer her name would be in the papers. "No, mister, can't say I do." Inwardly the Shrimp gloated. With a firm step he moved toward the center of the room, hitching his one shoulder, a habit of his.

Then Mrs. O'Toole let out a scream. "Oh, Gawd! Mister, it's him. I tell yuh, it's him. Grab him. Sure, now I remember. See de way he jerks up his shoulder—like he just did, I mean. De guy dat asked me for Ikey jerked his shoulder like dat. Grab, mister. He's de moiderer!"

Baker had his gun out. The Shrimp was reaching for his own.

"Stay put!" lashed out the detective. "Give us the gun. Lively!"

His little eyes darting about, a mutter in his throat, the Shrimp passed over his gun. At the same time Baker grasped his hand.

"Shrimp," he said, "I knew you weren't downtown for the scenery. Ikey was an uptown man, you're an uptown man. You've been seen with Ikey already around Columbus Circle. I figured you did the Jew in. The hat and the collar! Pretty good idea. But that shoulder gets away from you.

"And here. I was sure you were the man we wanted when you lit my cigar in Tony Ciani's. Know why?"

The Shrimp did not answer. Baker held the Shrimp's hand up to the light.

"Shrimp," he said, "you never were clean about your fingernails. You scrubbed your gun, you scrubbed your hands, but the dried blood stayed under your fingernails! See? You can't beat us, bud. In the end the breaks are with the law."

Grain to Grain

An ex-gangster and an ex-prizefighter, now detectives, are given a vicious murder to solve.

IN THE back room of a police station near the lower East River, two detectives were playing penny-ante to kill the dull, dragging hours of the graveyard watch.

A cold November drizzle encrusted the window-pane; the rumble of an "L" train a few blocks away penetrated the room with the startling clarity peculiar to wet city nights. This died away presently, and was replaced by the deep, monotonous voice of the desk lieutenant doing telephone routine with Headquarters.

The two men played under a cloud of tobacco smoke. One was tall, angular, lantern-jawed. His derby rested on an eyebrow. He looked hard-boiled. He was hard-boiled. Before his attachment to the Force, he had run the streets with a notorious gang of roughnecks and answered to the name of "Legs" Corson. Destiny—or something vague like that—had made him into a good dick instead of a bad gangster.

The other man was small, slight, but muscular, clean-cut in the face and neatly dressed. Not many years back he had been "Flash" Sullivan, likely contender for the lightweight title. Now he was Jimmy Gleason, plainclothes man.

At the moment, he copped a pot on three ladies.

"Remember the time," he remarked, shuffling the cards, "when I bet my head off on four queens. Know what the other guy had?"

"What?"

"Four queens."

"Huh?"

"Yeah."

"How come?"

"Some wiseguy's idea of a practical joke. Slipped in a pinochle deck."

Corson grinned—one of those ear to ear affairs. "Yeah? Open, Jim, f'r two. Gimme three cards."

Talk dwindled again. The game became listless, dull. No life in a two-handed game anyhow. Again the monotonous voice of the lieutenant… questions, grunts. Then the phone at Corson's elbow rang, and above it the booming voice of the lieutenant.

"Something doing, Corson. Better get it from this guy straight and we'll check up."

Corson took down the receiver, clamped it to his ear and played out his hand before speaking. He listened, jotting down notes on a piece of paper before him, interjecting brief questions, leaning aside to take a tobacco shot at the cuspidor. A final "Uhuh. Be right over," and he hung up the receiver, rubbed his square, under-slung jaw, stared at the notes he had made, crammed the paper into his pocket and unraveled his elongated body.

"Let's go, Jimmy. Swede done in down by the river."

"Killed?"

"Murdered. Sounds messy."

They got into their topcoats and stopped for a few words with the lieutenant, comparing notes. A few minutes later they were out in the damp, dismal street, pulling up their coat collars against the penetrating November chill. Corson craned his neck, squinted up and down for an auto, cursed under his breath when he found none in sight. They breezed along toward Chambers Street, and Gleason spotted a nighthawk taxi parked at the intersection. He knew the driver, and they got a lift riverwards, hitting James Street and then spinning up South for a couple of blocks.

"Get out here," clipped Corson, and with muttered thanks, they sent the chauffeur on his way.

The river sounds were subdued. Lights—green, red, white—moved or remained motionless in the gray-black murk. The muffled, heavy throb of a tug's engines drifted in. Up ahead the black bulk and network of the Brooklyn Bridge loomed vastly. Steamships bulked huge and black, moored against broad, squat pier-sheds, where the jetty water sloshed heavily, like thick oil. Rows of open barges and box-like river lighters hugged a weather-scarred dock, creaking at their hawsers, thumping dully against the dock or one another.

"This is it, I guess," said Gleason.

"This is it," said Corson.

They left the waterfront street and met a man with a lantern at the entrance to the dock.

"'Lo. You guys cops?"

"Yeah. Who are you?" was Corson's shot.

"Watchman. Guess you're the man I was speakin' to. Was me called up. Looked around for a cop, but not one in sight, so I called the station. No p'lice protection at all," complained the man.

"'S tough," clipped Corson. "Lead on. What's your name?"

"Connor. Been watchin' docks around here for twel' years."

They were hurrying along the dock.

"The guy was bumped off—what's his name? Didn't get it over the wire."

"Svensen—Alf Svensen; big Swede—barge captain. Here we are!"

The watchman nodded to a covered lighter that looked like a huge red box. At one end was the tiny cabin, with its four little window frames painted white. Atop this was a white pole with a metal pennant bearing the lighter's number—9. Two dark figures stood on the small deck space—a voice hailed a " 'Lo, there," hoarsely, and Connor took the short leap from the dock. Corson and Gleason were right behind him.

The little deck was wet, slippery. The two waiting men wore rubber coats and hats, and the lantern that Connor carried gleamed on them—gleamed on the swarthy, salt-seamed faces, too. Corson gave them a brief scrutiny. Connor explained that they were barge captains also, that they had been sitting with him in the little shanty on the pier-head.

"We heard a scream," he went on. "Terrible scream. Thought at first some guy'd fell overboard, didn't we? Uhuh. Ran out, we did, but didn't see nothin' of any feller in the water. Then we noticed Number 9's door swingin' open an' we jumped her an' found Svensen.… Here, take a took, if you got a good stomach." He pushed open the door.

Corson didn't hesitate a minute. Gleason trailed him hesitantly, hung in the doorway. One look and he grimaced. The sight of a man mashed up was something his stomach rebelled at; but for that, he might still have been in the ring. When he looked again Corson was spreading a sheet over the man. He moistened his lips and went in.

"Messy, eh?"

"Kind of, Jimmy—kind of," droned his partner musingly. "Swede sure got dented in, what I mean. Want a peek?"

"Don't rub it in, Legs."

Corson chuckled dryly. He bent down and picked up a piece of pine kindling wood a foot-and-a-half in length. It had been split at an angle, so that one end was considerably heavier than the other, making an effective weapon. The heavier end was smeared with blood. He dangled it in his hand, squinting about the room.

"This did it, Jimmy."

"S' I see."

"Guy that hefted it did a complete job, too. Wonder what for?"

"Search me."

Corson had taken a couple of keys from Svensen's pocket, and one of these fitted the locker in a corner. He found there a suit of rough black cloth, a black fedora, a pair of heavy, yellow shoes, some shirts and underwear. In an old cigar-box were some odds and ends; a pocket knife, a few foreign coins, a pack of cards, a few vile picture postcards, a couple of burlesque theatre stubs. These, in addition to twenty-eight dollars he had found on the dead man's person, constituted Svensen's entire immediate belongings.

"Mustn't have wanted money," he remarked, standing over the body. Then, to the three men grouped at the doorway: "Know if Svensen's got any relatives?"

The watchman said, "Guess not. Lived right here. Never heard him tell of any. Use t' be in sailin' ships, I think. Leastwise he use t' tell us tales o' foreign places an' talk a lot about ships an' sails an' such. Eh, boys?"

The other two nodded.

Corson scratched his chin and looked at Gleason. "Well, Jimmy, for the time being this bird 'll have to go to the morgue, I guess. We'll trot this young club up to Headquarters and see if any fingerprints are on it. Maybe there's something big behind this; maybe not. These big Swedes run amuck over almost nothin' sometimes. Might have been they started off to have a sociable evenin', got to arguin' over, say, the speed of ships between certain ports, and settled the argument this way. Or maybe it wasn't about ships at all. Don't know yet. Maybe the guy that beaned the Swede wasn't a waterfront man at all. Don't know. Can't say."

He turned to the watchman. "Say, was this Svensen a wiseguy? I mean, did he mind his own business as a rule or did he go huntin' trouble an' pickin' on little guys?"

"Svensen was all right. Quiet sort, I thought. Use to stop in at my shanty for a chat sometimes. Kept to himself mostly— didn't mix in much, eh, boys?"

"Alf was all right," said one of the barge captains.

"Never saw him pick a fight," added the other.

"Worked here long?" Corson plied.

" 'Bout six months," from Connor. "Six or seven."

"Know any guy had a grudge against him?"

No, they didn't—couldn't call to mind even one man.

Corson lit a cigarette and snapped the match through the doorway overside.

"Well," he told the watchman, "you make your report to the dock people and to the owners of the lighter. We'll see them later and I'll be around first thing tomorrow to go over this thing again. We'll shoot down the morgue bus. Jimmy, you skip along an' get the cop on the beat. Maloney's on, I think, an' you know where he hangs out. He'll have to stand guard here, an', anyhow, if he didn't show his mug around he'd have some tall explainin' to do."

"Sure," said Gleason. "Give us a butt and I'll drift."

A REPORTER from a local press syndicate, dropping in at the precinct at two in the morning, got the gist of the story from the man at the desk. The first edition of the yellow sheets gave it a big spread, and the later editions carried pictures of the barge. Hence it didn't take a great while for the morbidly curious to come nosing down around the scene of last night's tragedy.

Corson had taken the death club to Headquarters, but the expert there failed to find any fingerprints.

"Was pretty cold, anyhow, Legs. Guess he wore gloves."

Corson had expected this much, but he held on to the club, at any rate, wrapping it in a piece of newspaper and sticking it in the desk in the back room at the precinct. A little later he ran into Gleason in a one-arm restaurant, grabbed a meal, and they went down to the waterfront. Going straight to the dock office, they learned that Svensen had been in the employ of the Harbor Lighterage and Dock Company for exactly six months and ten days. The company did not own that particular lighter, but had leased it for a year's term, due to the increase in business. Svensen had come with the lighter; he had captained it previously and had been hired along with it. He had been steady, never called on the carpet once.

Corson got the address of the owners of the lighter, and the two sleuths sought them out, gleaning the information that Svensen had been with that firm for three years, with a good, clean record to boot. Before that time he had been on sea-going vessels.

"Looks like the Swede was fouled sure enough, huh?" ventured Gleason as they headed back for the dock.

"Don't know, Jimmy—don't know— can't say," said Corson. "At present I'm just followin' my nose. Told the reporters we were workin' on several clues, but I ain't got a damn one yet. You?"

"Not much."

When they reached the dock the day watchman said: "Say, somebody from the p'lice station called up—said one o' you guys should call up soon as I see you. Here's the phone. You got t' get the dock operator first, see?"

It took Corson but a few minutes to get in connection with his boss. When he hung up the phone, he looked at Gleason and grinned from ear to ear. He got up and led his partner out to a secluded part of the dock.

"Good news?" was Gleason's question.

"Little. Listen. Savings bank just got in touch with the chief. Teller says Svensen drew out five thousand he had in the bank.

Left a balance of two-hundred-and-ten. But here's the rub. He drew it out at nine-ten this morning—was one of the first customers—about nine hours after he croaked. Teller hadn't read the paper yet. Was a substitute, anyhow; the regular guy's laid up with the flu. Read it at noon, though, an' told the cashier, an' so on. Now, Jimmy, we've got a motive."

Gleason said: "Sure. The guy that beamed him swiped his bankbook and cleaned up. The balance in the bank was just a bluff—wouldn't arouse ready suspicion. The motive, then—robbery. Good enough, Legs. But, say, not ordinary robbery, eh? What I mean is, the bum didn't just drop in by chance an' croak him. He'd been there before. Him an' the Swede were kinder, well, acquainted, say. Look here. There's a lunch-wagon up near the foot o' the dock. Strikes me the dock men eat there some-times. Let's go up a minute."

"Got somethin', Jimmy?"

"Not much. Just a hunch."

They breezed off the dock and a little later were parked on high stools in the stuffy, greasy interior of a waterfront lunch-room. Each ordered coffee and pie.

"Say," Gleason sprung on the counter man, "s'pose you knew the Swede who was bumped off last night—this Svensen guy—huh?"

"Used t' drop in sometimes t' eat or just get a pail o' coffee—yeah. Damn shame, wasn't it?"

"Uh-uh. D'he drop in alone as a rule or with a friend?"

"Sometimes alone—sometimes with a friend."

"Men like himself, I s'pose—dockers, barge captains, steve-dores, an' the like, huh?"

"Yeah. Chummed a bit with a little Portuguese barge captain. Little runt, loud-mouthed as hell. Used t' bawl the big Swede out, call him names 'at I'd paste a guy for, strut around like a little fightin' cock. They'd get on, though. Svensen'd just sit back and grin at the runt. Easy-goin' slob, the Swede."

"This runt's name?"

"Pete Branco."

"That the only guy the Swede used to come in with?"

"Yeah— Well, no—not exactly. Once in a while, when I used t' be on the night shift, 'bout two months ago, I remember he came in twice with a kinder dressed-up guy. They'd sit way down the end o' the counter an' the dressed-up guy 'd do most o' the gabbin'. Came in about ten, I'd judge."

"Dressed-up guy, huh?"

"Yeah. No water man."

"Know his name?"

"Nope."

"Know him if you'd see him again?"

"Guess so; sure."

"Seen him lately?"

"Nope. Been on days right along. Might ask Joe, the night man. Joe comes on at six."

"Good. What's this guy look like—the Swede's friend— besides bein' dressed up?"

"Well, take me. I'm short an' skinny kinder, though not just a shrimp. This guy was maybe a inch or two bigger 'an me but built about the same, see? Judge him about thirty or so, with thin blond hair. Talks an' acts quick an' snappy-like, but pretty quiet an' wise-lookin'."

Gleason nodded. "I see. All right, bud; thanks for the dope. See you again. An', say, don't forget to tell this Joe party we'll be around. An' get Joe to be able to place this guy. O.K.?"

"O.K. by me. Two coffee an' pie; thirty cents. Right. S'long."

Outside, the two sleuths fell in step beside each other and headed for their precinct. Throughout the recent quizzing, Corson hadn't popped a question or interrupted his partner once.

Now he ventured. "Think you got somethin', Jimmy?"

"If I have, Legs, it's in the bud. This unidentified guy is worth payin' attention to. He wasn't the Swede's kind. I mean, he wasn't the kind of guy the Swede would chum with."

"Not like this little Portuguese, for instance?"

Gleason slowed down and shot his partner a sidelong look.

Corson grinned and said: "Forgot all about him, Jimmy, huh, when the hash slinger popped about the dressed-up guy?"

"No, not exactly, Legs. But this other guy sounds like a better bet to me? How about you?"

"Don't know, Jimmy. Can't say. Maybe you hooked on to somethin' hot, maybe. But listen. Just struck me we'd better see if Pete Branco is still hangin' round the docks. No, I don't expect much there, but we got to salt this Spic in case the papers start to blab about us gettin' no suspects. You might just as well ankle right along. The chief 'll want to know what we're doin'. It's three now. Drift down this way about six an' we'll eat at the wagon an' quiz this Joe guy. I'll be hangin' around."

They parted and Corson retraced his steps toward the dock. The din and clamor of river and pier commerce were in mid-career. Derricks swung back and forth from dock to ship. Steam engines puffed and hissed. Hand trucks, pushed by swarthy men, rumbled and clattered in the great warehouses and along the runways. Labor bosses swore in three languages. Checkers hurried back and forth with tally sheets. The day watchman leaned with his elbows on the window sill of his shanty and spat regularly into the oily water.

Corson approached him and asked where he might find Pete Branco.

"Oh, Pete? Pete's on a railroad lighter. Number 10. Ain't here now. Was towed some time this mornin'. Tell you what. Go up to the float bridge an' ask the despatcher. He'll tell you where Number 10's bound."

At the float bridge Corson secured the desired information. Number 10, loaded with barrels of sugar, was in a tow of three barges bound for a pier on the North River.

"Ought to be there now," remarked the despatcher. "Quick job. Export stuff for a ship leaving tomorrow."

Corson walked as far as Chambers Street and hopped a crosstown bus. After this short ride he hiked several blocks north on West Street until he came to the pier the despatcher had mentioned. Number 10 was a lighter with a steam hoist, and the shipment was being transferred from it to the ship direct, without the usual routine of first passing over a dock—this was evidence enough of the rush movement.

He found Branco leaning in the little cabin doorway, with a greasy black pipe between his teeth. Branco was, indeed, a mite of a man, brown and muscular in a miniature way, with a wide, straight mouth and restless black eyes.

"H'lo," clipped Corson. "You Pete Branco?"

The man nodded, took his pipe from between his teeth.

Corson flashed his badge and went on, "Knew Alf Svensen quite well, didn't you?"

"Sure t'ing."

"You an' him chummed together a bit, eh?"

"Sometams, yes."

"Got along well?"

"Sometams, yes. Alf was good faller. Mebbe sometam we have de leetle argument—but not mooch. Me, I'm—whatcha call—keed Alf, an' sometam Alf he get mad, but mos' tam he jus' mak de laugh. Alf was ver' good faller, though. Find de man what keel Alf yet?"

"No. Got an idea, though, followin' it up. Maybe you can help. Ever see Svensen hangin' around with a stranger? I mean, a guy that didn't mix as a rule with you barge men?"

"No-o. Alf he keep pretty mooch wit' de waterfron' men."

"Didn't see him last night before he was killed, eh?"

"Yes. 'Bout eight o'clock jus' stop on de dock to have de leetle chat wit' Alf."

"H'm. Where were you about one this mornin'—time Svensen was killed? Hear him yell or anything?"

"No-o." Branco shifted on his foot and the ghost of a grin flickered across his face. "Playeeng poker."

"Yeah? Play myself sometimes. Where were you playin'?"

"Nex' dock from where Alf was. Me an' Johnson an' Burke an' Nelson. Me I'm ween, too." He chuckled.

"What time 'd you leave?"

" 'Bout half-past de one."

"Playin' on a barge?"

"On de barge, yes—Nelson's."

"He still over there?"

"Yes. Was dere when I'm leave dese morneeng."

"That's enough. Just checkin' up, see? We got to do this. Well, maybe I'll see you again before we land the guy we're lookin' for. By the way, got a drink handy?"

"Water?"

"Well…" Corson grinned.

"Oh, sure t'ing. Come in."

Branco brought a dark bottle from a locker and poured two drinks. Corson, looking about the little cabin, touched his glass to Branco's and then downed the drink neat.

"Good stuff," he said. Nice place you have here."

He surveyed it again casually, with mild interest. It was cosy and neat and the little stove threw off a comfortable warmth. Then he lit a fresh cigarette, buttoned up his coat, and whisked back across several adjoining barges until he finally gained the pier. Here he paused, looked back and studied Number 10 thoughtfully for a long minute. He chuckled briefly, then, snapped his butt overside and hustled for the street.

Back again on the East River, he sought out the barge captain named Nelson. A tug was warping in and lines were being made ready to tow the barge along with several others. Nelson was short, gray-haired, genial, and pretty well on in years.

"Just a question or two, Mr. Nelson, in connection with that Svensen killing," said Corson.

"Oh, yes? Sure. Lucky you got here. Just ready to tow. What can I do for you?"

"Played cards last night, did you? You an' a couple of other gents. What time did the game break up?"

They were standing in the little cabin. Nelson looked across at an alarm clock on a washstand.

"Oh, 'tween one an' two sometime, I guess."

"Can't say exactly, eh?"

"Um. Lemme think. Oh, yes. Come to think of it, now, Pete—Pete Branco was playin' with us—Pete nodded to my clock an' said it was time we broke up—was half-past one."

"That's all I want to know. Thanks." Nelson's clock now showed a quarter to six and Corson was to meet Gleason at six. He regained the dock and reached the vicinity of the lunch-wagon in ten minutes. As he arrived there Gleason swung up from another direction.

"Oh-ho!" exclaimed the ex-pug. "Thought I'd have to wait for you, Legs."

"Said six, didn't we?"

"Yeah, but it ain't quite five-thirty yet."

Corson grunted. "Huh? What time you got? My watch's gettin' fixed."

Gleason dragged out his timepiece. "Exactly five-twenty-seven. How's that? Right, too. Just set it at City Hall."

Corson said, "Jimmy, you still strong for your lead?"

"Am I? Bet your life, bud. Listen. I been checkin' up at the bank, an' that Swede's been used to puttin' three hundred in the bank at a clip. Toward the end his deposits were five hundred. Say, guy, there ain't no barge captain sinkin' so much that frequent! There's been some kind of a game goin' on around here in the dark. If I can locate this mysterious dressed-up guy I think we got somethin' pretty."

"Good stuff, Jim. I got a hunch myself. Not much. Guess you're on a hot trail, but meantime I got to satisfy the streak of curiosity that's in me. You go on in an' quiz the hash slinger. Bleed all the info you can out of him. I'm goin' to see if there's anything in this hunch of mine."

"Sure. But let's snap some grub together. I won't be long. Go along with you."

"Got to follow this while it's hot, Jimmy, else it'll get cold before I know it. Run into you at the house this evenin'. Got to get some sleep tonight. Go to it, now, Jim. Follow your lead. Between the two of us we get somethin' out of this or I blow in my week's salary on drinks. See you later."

Mildly perplexed, Gleason watched his lank partner rock away. Then he continued on toward the lunch-wagon, entered and parked on a stool at one end. The counter man, with whom he and Corson had talked earlier in the day, was just removing his apron. He nodded to Gleason and said:

"Joe's due any minute now. Where's your partner?"

"Takin' a snooze. Slide me out some ham an' eggs an' a cup of coffee, will you? Fry the eggs on both sides."

He was half-way through the meal when Joe came in, hung up his coat and put on his apron. At a word or two from the day man, he looked at Gleason, nodded, and came down the counter toward him.

"Want me, mister?" he asked.

Gleason jerked his thumb toward the day man, who was getting into his street clothes. "He tell you what I wanted?"

"Yeah. Kinder. 'Bout this guy used to come in with the Swede who was croaked last night."

"Uh-uh." Gleason swallowed a chunk of bread. "Say, happen to know when him an' the Swede last stopped in here?"

"Sure. Last night."

"Last night!"

"Yeah. Sure. Last night."

Gleason lost all interest in what remained of the ham and eggs.

"What time?"

"Dunno exactly. 'Bout ten, I guess."

"Didn't hear what they talked about?"

"Nope. The other guy did most of the talkin'. The Swede listened."

"Just talkin'—or arguin', maybe?"

"Well, I guess the other guy wanted the Swede to agree to somethin', an' the Swede was holdin' back. Just my idea, that's all. I remember the dressed up guy got kinda sore an' took a crack at the counter an' I think I ketched his words; somethin' like, 'Where d' you get that stuff, buddy? What the hell do I look like?' Well, the Swede just grinned an' rubbed his hands an' looked around an' made a motion for his friend to go easy— put on the soft pedal. After a few minutes they got up an' went out."

"That's all, huh?"

"Yeah; that's all."

"Know this strange guy if you saw him again?"

"Sure."

Gleason thought for a moment.

Then— "Say, I'd like to take you along with me for about half an' hour."

"Kinda busy now, mister…."

"Ask the day man if he'll hang around till you come back."

Joe hesitated, scratched his head, and shuffled off to speak a few words with the other. A minute or two, and the day man agreed.

"But don't get lost, Joe. I got a date at eight an' I gotta get shaved," he added.

Outside, Joe asked: "Where to, mister?"

"P'lice Headquarters."

"Huh?"

"Don't get scared. Want to show you somethin'."

At Police Headquarters they passed through a high, wide corridor and ascended to what is familiarly known as Rogues Gallery. Hinged on to the wall were the metal files, arranged like big books, so that each section swung to and fro like a page.

"Look 'em over," said Gleason, standing back.

In silent awe Joe scrutinized each photograph, turned one metal "page" after another, almost pointed one out, but shook his head and continued his search. Finally his head jerked up and he jammed a grimy finger against a photograph near the middle of the file.

"That's the guy," he said.

"Sure?"

"Yup. That's him."

Gleason got the file data from the photograph, walked to another part of the big chamber and searched through a vast card index. He did not have to search long.

"Ah-ha!" he exclaimed softly, reading half-aloud. "James Sydney, alias 'Kid' Sydney, alias Sydney James, alias Sydney J. Jameson. Confidence man. Indicted May 3, 192.., for criminal assault against Ruby Sanders. Acquitted June 3, 192.., lack of evidence. Indicted January 8, 192.., for implication in the Gotham Bond Fraud. Convicted March 5, 192... Sentenced March 10. Two years. Indicted August 22, 192.., for illicit drug traffic, with Yut Sing. Acquitted September 15. Lack of evidence."

Gleason whistled, slammed shut the file cabinet and rubbed his hands in joyful anticipation.

"Better than I expected," he said, and then turned to Joe. "All right, buddy, you can breeze now. Thanks for comin'. See you again sometime. S' long."

Gleason remembered this Syd James now. He remembered Yut Sing, too. In fact, he knew Yut Sing—knew he lived over a shop around near Pell Street. On the way over from Spring, he stopped in at the precinct to break the good news to Corson, but his partner hadn't shown up yet, nor had he telephoned in. Hence Gleason wasted no time there, but continued on his way toward Pell Street and found Yut Sing at home.

"H'lo, Yut, old timer," he greeted. "Say, I'm lookin' for a one-time friend of yours. Syd James. Where is he, huh?"

Yut Sing was short and round as a barrel and liked peace. He shrugged his shoulders.

"Me don't know."

"Come on, Yut."

Yut squirmed. "Me don't know. Velly solly."

"Aw, applesauce! He tried to flimflam you in that deal three years ago an' it wouldn't be like you to forget him an' lose track of him. Spill it, Yut, else I can be damned nasty. I been keepin' my eyes closed lately to some of your monkey business, but I can open 'em any minute. Now come across."

Yut Sing blinked and sighed. "Him stlay uptown. Lots money."

"Whereabouts?"

Yut hesitated, sighed, and finally named a first-class hotel in the West Forties.

Gleason left him, hurried west and caught a northbound sub at Canal Street. He got off at Times Square and struggled through the early theatre crowds. At the desk of a well-known hotel he asked if Mr. S.J. Jameson were in—the name James was using at the time according to Yut Sing. Yes, he was in.

"Never mind callin' him," said Gleason, and drifted away, taking up a position in front of the elevators.

At the end of a half-hour he saw James emerge from one of the lifts. Spic and span, dressed according to the prevailing mode, affecting an easy manner, the man sauntered into the lobby, paused to light a slim panatela. Gleason fished a cigarette from his pocket and edged over.

"Mind holdin' the light, mister?"

"Surely."

Gleason got his cigarette going and said, "Now, say, let's go downtown, you and me."

"Beg pardon!"

"Take off the high hat. I'm bein' as pleasant as I know how, but I can be nasty too. No use stagin' a melodrama here. Just let's walk out as if we were old friends, grab a sub an' get off at Canal an' go around to the E. Street Station, where it's nice an' warm an' cosy in the back room. Then let's chat, Mr. James."

"Oh… I see. Quite right. Let's go, old man."

"You're sensible."

"Quite," nodded James, and they passed out.

WHEN THEY arrived at the station-house there was some little excitement there. Three reporters were hanging around, drifting back and forth between the desk and the detectives' room. The lieutenant was doing a lot of talking on the telephone, and so was the sergeant behind him. When the reporters saw Gleason and his man enter, they followed him into the rear room.

Corson was there, sprawled in a swivel-chair. The captain of detectives sat on the desk dangling his fat legs. Two other sleuths stood nearby. Beside Corson sat the little Portuguese barge captain, Pete Branco.

"Been waitin' for you, Jimmy," grinned Corson. "Got your man?"

"Guess I have, Legs. Got yours?"

"Guess I have, Jimmy."

The captain grunted, "Huh!" and spat into the cuspidor between his feet

Gleason looked at him, "Know this guy, boss?" indicating James.

"Sure. Was me nabbed him in that drug running. H'lo, Syd. How's tricks?"

"So-so. How have you been feeling?"

"Pretty fair, thanks. Little liver trouble lately, but nothing of much account." He turned to Gleason. "All right, Jimmy. Shoot the works. Do we send Syd up for life or does he get the chair?"

"I've got a man," explained Gleason, "who'll swear James, here, was around the docks the night Svensen was murdered. This same man—also another guy—will swear James has been meetin' Svensen now and then at night, in a lunch-wagon near that dock. Last night—night of the murder—about ten o'clock, Svensen and James, here, had words together."

"Damned lie," put in James, coolly.

Gleason looked at him. "Didn't you say to the Swede, kinda hot?—'Where d'you get that stuff, buddy? What the hell do I look like?'"

James shrugged. "Might have said that. Little difficulty; that's all. Was smoothed over before we left."

"All right. Where were you between one an' two this mornin'?"

"Nighthawk club. Left there at three."

Gleason reached for the phone, got in touch with the head waiter of the club. Yes, Mr. Jameson had been there up until three a.m. The headwaiter would swear to that. So would the waiter that had served Mr. Jameson. Gleason hung up.

Corson, who had been talking in low tones with Pete Branco, looked up and asked, "Mind if I talk a bit, Jimmy?"

"Sure; go to it, Legs."

"Between us, Jimmy, we've made a haul," said Corson, tipping his derby over one eyebrow. "Before we met at the dock I had a bit of a clue—crazy one, at that. When we met an' you told me the time, I got another clue. Branco, here, was supposed to be playin' cards with three buddies when the Swede was done in. Told me he quit at one-thirty. I went around to the barge him an' his buddies played on, to check up, an' a guy named Nelson said, yes, it was about one-thirty when they broke up, an' nodded to the alarm clock on his washstand. That was all right by me, an' for a while I began to think I was on a blind lead. Nelson's clock showed a quarter to six when I left the barge, an' when I met you, you said it wasn't quite half-past five. In other words, *Nelson's alarm clock was a half-hour fast.*

"All right. When we parted at the lunch-wagon I went back. Nelson was bein' towed away—was in the clear already. There was a guy nearby monkeyin' with a motorboat, an' I made him shoot me out after the barge, tellin' him to tag along behind. Then I told Nelson about his clock. We verified it, an' sure enough it was almost thirty-five minutes fast. Nelson said it was O.K. just before the game started. He'd gone out for some tobacco an' Branco was there alone when he came back, so Branco must have set the clock ahead while Nelson was away.

"That done, I got back in the motor-boat an' had the guy shoot me over to the North River, where Branco's barge was layin'. I found Branco all right, an' again took up my first clue—the one that seemed kinda crazy to me at first. There was a box of wood by Branco's stove an' I took possession of this. Then me an' Branco, with the box of wood, hopped a taxi an' come over here."

He paused, looked at James. "Branco's confessed, James, an' dragged you into the net."

James tried to smile. It was a remarkable effort, but his lower lip quivered—ever so slightly. "Go on," he said, casually.

"Sure," nodded Corson. "In plain words, *you hired Branco to kill the Swede.*"

"Yes."

"Yup. I'll explain. You were pretty clever, James, in your rum runnin'. You gave up the opium game, eh, because there's more money in booze now an' besides, it's a real he-man's game? All right. Svensen was your waterfront contact man. Nice, quiet guy that you was sure wouldn't blabber too much. He didn't mix with the boys much. Was too busy nights slippin' in the goods. You paid him three hundred bucks every time he did a job. Then he jumped you to five hundred. Last night, eh, he maybe wanted more, eh? That's why you said, 'Where d'you get that stuff, buddy? What the hell do I look like?

"All right. You'd met Branco before. You hunted him up. You told him Svensen had a bank account an' it might be easy to bump him off, swipe the book an' draw the money. Then, if he wanted to make more money, you'd give him Svensen's job. This looked good to Branco, an' he sure had gall to walk into the bank, an' a hell of a lot of luck to walk out again. Oh, yes, Branco's come clean."

James sat down, stared at the floor, then stared at Branco.

"My God, you're dumb!" he snapped.

Gleason, smiling, said, "But the clue, Legs?"

"Oh, the clue—the crazy clue," Corson chuckled. "You see, it was this way. The first trip I made to Branco's barge I saw this box of kindlin' wood I was tellin' you about. Well, it struck me it looked mighty like the piece that had done for Svensen. I was thinkin' about it all the way over to Nelson's barge, an' when the clock business popped up, I began to think more about it an' it didn't seem so crazy after all."

He paused and picked up a log lying beside the chair. This log had been carefully pieced together and wrapped around with pieces of string to hold the sections in place. One of these sections was the blood-stained death club.

"You see," explained Corson. "The club fits right in. But that's not all. You might say this club could fit in accidentally. But here's the point. Not only does the club fit in, *but it runs grain to grain with the rest of the wood.* That's somethin' you can't fake. Branco had found the log layin' around the dock, chopped it up to use in his little stove in case the coal burnt out, an' took this piece to bash in the Swede's head. An' that's that."

"An' me ready to bet my last dollar that James, here, did the job," said Gleason.

"Well, didn't he… in a way?" Corson shot at him.

"Well… in a way…."

"Sure he did. Gimme a butt an' shut up," chuckled Corson.

Dumb Luck

A crook, with all his cunning craft, sets out to get another crook. But on two things he fails to reckon—that sentiment which often survives in most sordid conditions, which men call love, and—dumb luck.

A **CERTAIN** detective once remarked that "Whitey" Fleer was the most innocent-looking crook between the Battery and the Bronx. This same detective also said many things about Whitey that would make a blue police blotter blush for shame. On one occasion he had remarked to his chief that he hoped some fine day Whitey would make the mistake of killing somebody, so that they could ticket him to Sing Sing for good. You gather from this that Whitey was no dub in his chosen profession; that as a crook he was really a crook, and no false alarm.

Whitey was. He had crossed the sea when all the world was in chaos and had done most of his fighting in crap games behind the lines. He had earned himself no glory, and after the Armistice he had drifted to London's East End and run with the gutter-snipes there. He knew the dank alleys of Montmartre, too, and he had killed a man in Barcelona. Mexico City had claimed him for a while, and a Creole woman in New Orleans had slipped a knife between his ribs in a shady dive down near the river. More than one crooked deal he had engineered in Chicago, and finally had skipped to New York in the nick of time.

Perhaps Whitey was thinking of his colorful past as he sat in Nickie Lombardi's restaurant near Chatham Square, idly stirring a mug of dark-brown coffee. Perhaps not. Anyhow, you couldn't say for sure. Whitey had such a guileless face, such gentle blue eyes, such a wistful smile. His hair was blond and silky, very much unlike the waitress's in Nickie Lombardi's place; her hair was coarse and dull like old straw. With a detached air he watched her gather up an armful of dishes and breeze into the rear, her high heels rapping the floor resolutely, her starched apron swishing. Then his eyes drifted back to his coffee and he drank it slowly.

A few moments later he sauntered out into the street, with a fresh cigarette between his lips, pulling his hat well down over his eyes against the bright morning sun. He was not good-looking, yet there was something subtly engaging about his pale, thin face. His chin and his forehead seemed to retreat from his long nose, and a perpetual smile—that wistful smile of his—always held his mouth a trifle askew.

He drifted down the Bowery to Pell Street. He turned into a crooked Chinatown alley and slowed down when he saw up ahead a crowd of people gathered on the street and sidewalk. He caught sight of a policeman or two, stopped in his tracks with intention of turning back, but after a moment's hesitation moved on. He stopped and lingered at the outer edge of the mob, which consisted for the greater part of jabbering Chinese.

Presently a tall, rangy man, inconspicuously clad in dark clothes, with a cigarette butt drooping from one corner of his mouth, appeared in the doorway of that building that seemed to be the center of interest. Under the low-slung visor of his cap a pair of cold agate eyes glinted aggressively, and his mouth was wide and hard. The agate eyes, sweeping the crowd like an icy winter's blast, froze on Whitey. The hard mouth bent down at the corners. He spat away the cigarette and elbowed his way through the crowd.

"Hello, Whitey," he bit off, his eyes narrowing.

"Why, hello there, Barney! Gee, I'm glad to see you!"

"Yeah, is that so? Well, listen, guy, I'm glad to see you, too. I'm lookin' for 'Dapper Lew' Brant. Wise me up as to where I can lay hands on him."

Whitey's innocent blue eyes dilated. "How should I know where he's hangin' out, Barney? You know as well as me I got no use for Dapper, same as Dapper has no use for me. We hates each other like poison, Barney. You know that."

"I know—I know," went on Barney a little impatiently. "But that ain't preventin' you from knowin' where Dapper hangs his hat. Come on, Whitey, open up. Come across. Be decent. Ain't us guys at the precinct been treatin' you decent right along?"

"Sure, Barney—sure thing. I ain't kickin', but I don't know where Dapper is, so help me. We don't travel in the same comp'ny. You know how high hat Dapper has got recent. I hates him, Barney, an' I wouldn't mind seein' him get plugged some night, or sent to the chair. Now, if I knowed where he is, wouldn't I tell you?"

Barney jammed his fists against his hips and rocked on his feet. "I don't know whether you would or not. With that there pious mug o' yourn, a man never knows when you're lyin' an' when you ain't. Yes, I know you hate Dapper like poison, an' that's why I figure you're keepin' tabs on him."

"But, Barney, now listen. If I knowed where he was, me havin' a grudge against him, like I said before, wouldn't I tell you?"

Barney snorted. "That's just it—I don't know! Y' see, guy, you're such a lousy liar, I sometimes feel like takin' a poke out o' you. Well, never mind, then. Better drift, though, because this here street ain't no healthy place for a guy like you."

"Sure. But what's up, Barney?"

"Yut Wong was found this mornin' with a knife in his guts."

"An Dapper Lew?"

"Seen beatin' it down Doyer Street at one this mornin'. Aw, say, come on now, Whitey, an' tell your boy friend Barney what you know about this here Dapper Lew."

"Barney, will you listen t' reason? I tell you I don't know a damn thing—"

Barney made a rasping noise in his throat. "Drift, Whitey! Breeze. Scat. Blow. Get the hell out of here before I get sore. Hey, wait a minute! Got a butt?"

Whitey proffered his pack and Barney took a cigarette, lit it and plowed his way back into the crowd. Whitey did not linger there for long. He retraced his steps to Pell Street and then up the Bowery to Canal, in no great hurry, ruminating meanwhile that Barney Doyle was a tough dick. Barney had tried to plant something on him more than once. Yeah, he was some go-getter, this here Barney, with a record at Headquarters for doing his stuff. He'd like to get somethin' on Whitey—yes, sir! But Whitey was no sap—not by a long shot. It would take a better guy than Barney Doyle to give him a one-way ticket to Sing Sing. Betcha life!

He headed westward on Canal and after a while slipped into a speakeasy near West Broadway. Mike Masella sold fruits and vegetables in the front and red ink in the back. Upstairs were a dozen or more rooms with dubious reputations. Mike was a pretty good sort, though, take him by and large. Whitey passed the time of day with him, went into the rear and then climbed a flight of stairs. He walked down a narrow, gloomy hallway where the floorboards creaked under a worn carpet. He stopped before a door and rapped it lightly with his knuckles. After a moment it opened on a crack, then swung wide, and Whitey entered.

" 'Lo, Tess," he said, with his most wistful smile.

Tess stifled a yawn. "Oh, it's you. Park yourself."

She dropped to a rumpled cot, drawing her stockinged feet up and leaning back against the wall. "Gimme a butt." She wore a cheap Chinese kimono. Her hair was jet black, bobbed, disheveled. She was pretty in the way that glass may be pretty, and her eyes were lazy. Her mouth was insolent.

She was saying, "Well?"

Whitey held a match to her cigarette. He blew the match out, leaned back in his chair and rubbed his hands together musingly. Then he looked up at Tess gently, and his soft, liquid eyes wandered over her face. She frowned, shuddered a trifle.

"Get it off your chest!" she snapped. "An' for God's sake, don't look at me that way!"

Whitey smiled sweetly—just that—sweetly.

"The cops is after Dapper," he said.

Tess held her breath for a moment, staring blankly at Whitey. Then she exhaled a stream of smoke and chuckled sardonically. "What's that to me, huh?"

"Maybe nothin'," he shrugged, clasping his skeleton hands between his knees and regarding the ceiling. "Just thought I'd tell you, Tess."

There was a long silence during which Whitey continued to gaze at the ceiling and Tess gazed moodily at Whitey. Then a cloud surged up in the woman's eyes, and she sat erect.

"What are you drivin' at?" she gave him harshly.

Whitey looked around the room, wagging his head sorrowfully. "Rotten dump you got here, ain't it, Tess? H'm. Kinder rotten of Dapper, the way he gave you the cold shoulder."

Tess half snarled, jerked to her feet and stood before the window, gazing out bitterly. After a moment she swiveled about, her hands clenched, her bosom heaving, dark fires in her eyes.

"What do I care!" she flung at him savagely. "What did you have to come here and tell me for? What do I care! I wish they'd get him—I wish they would!"

Whitey stood up, his hands and eyebrows raised in a gentle plea for silence. "Don't yell like that, Tess. You'll get yourself all unstrung." He went over and put his hands on her shoulders, but she shrugged them off. "Take it easy, Tess," he went on, unabashed. "I like you, Tess. I ain't what you could call a handsome guy, but me heart's in the right place. I know you're heart-broken."

"Aw, cut the sob-stuff!"

"Now it ain't sob-stuff a-tall, Tess. I mean it—honest. It wasn't right for Dapper to treat you mean for Birdie Doroski. She's a gold-digger, Tess, an' you know it. Why, hell, I don't know what he seen in her, though, because she ain't half as good-lookin' as you are. But what I was goin' to say. Barney Doyle—you know that tough dick—well, Barney's got a hunch Dapper knifed Yut Wong last night. Barney tried to pump me before, but I acted dumb."

"Yut Wong," echoed Tess in a flat voice.

"Yeah. Well, you know as well as me, Tess, that Dapper's been runnin' dope to a high-class dump uptown paternized by, you know, the idle rich. Yut was supplyin' it to Dapper an' Dapper was sellin' it to the swells at a fancy price. Dapper always had too much temper to do him any good, an' I ain't su'prised if he got in a row with Yut an' stuck him. Maybe the Chink wanted more money or somepin'. Anyways, I got an' idea Barney's hunch ain't wrong."

"You got a grudge against Dapper," she said, half rebellious.

"I ain't denyin' that, Tess, but it ain't that I'm thinkin' of—honest. Dapper did you dirt. You got a chancet to do him dirt. Me, I got a bright idea. You ain't ought to live in a dump like this. Dapper's got money. You work with me, Tess, an' we'll fleece Dapper an' split it two ways."

She lowered her head, brushed by him and sat down on the cot, placing her elbows on her knees and her chin in her hands.

After a while she said, "Well, what's your bright idea?"

She did not see Whitey smile covertly and moisten his lips. He sat down and regarded her bowed head, and the ghost of a twinkle flickered through his blue eyes.

"Dapper is layin' low in a hotel uptown," he explained. "An' Birdie is livin' with him."

"Ancient history!" muttered Tess ironically.

"I got some dough," Whitey continued. "You go an' take a couple o' rooms in a place I'll tell you about later. You get Dapper on the wire—he's registered at this swell dump as John Patterson—you get him on the wire. Tell him you got somepin' important to tell him, an' have him meet you on a street corner. Then take him to your rooms an' keep him there, sayin' you got tipped the cops is after him an' they're on the way to nab him at the hotel. Keep him with you, Tess, an' I'll give you a number you can get me at from a public phone, an' I'll hand you more instructions. Does that much listen good to you, Tess?"

"It sounds interestin'," she admitted in a muffled voice.

"Then we'll see about them rooms," he told her. "Nice rooms, Tess, an' I'll get you some glad rags. You look mighty nifty when you're dolled up a bit. We'll fleece Dapper, eh, Tess?"

She nodded but did not raise her head. Hence Whitey did not see the soft, warm look that came into her eyes, the color that mounted to her cheeks, and he did not see the way the hardness faded magically from her lips.

WHITEY WAS finishing another breakfast at Nickie Lombardi's restaurant. He had placed Tess in a couple of furnished rooms uptown, and he was complimenting himself on having thus far succeeded in his plan to fleece Dapper Lew. Everything had gone along smoothly, and in an hour or so he would tell Tess to start the ball rolling.

Strolling along Canal Street a little later, he almost ran into Barney Doyle as the latter came out of Elizabeth Street at a brisk walk. As usual, Barney wore a dark frown on his forehead, as though some weighty business rested heavily on his mind; and as usual, he asked Whitey for a cigarette.

"Left mine at the precinct," he explained.

"Nice day," offered Whitey.

"Yeah, if it don't rain. How's tricks?"

"So-so; can't complain, Barney. How's everything by you?"

"Rotten! That Dapper Lew case. The papers are on our neck, Whitey. I've turned this damned town inside out for Dapper, an' I ain't even warm yet. It's the bunk—we got a lot of snow in Yut's joint. Now if you was a real friend of mine, Whitey, like I am to you, you'd put me on the right track."

"Barney, you know me, an' you know if I knowed anything about Dapper I'd be only too willin' to tip you off. Cripes, I'd like to see Dapper get his. He's pretty high-hat now, but some day some guy's gonna plug him, an' I won't be sorry none. Where you headed?"

"Mike Masella's."

"Huh?"

"Yeah. There was a frail Dapper used to trot around with. Might know her—Tess Brady. I was just wised, an' I'm gonna see if she'll open up."

"Mind if I go along, Barney? I'm just out for a walk, anyhow."

"Sure. Come on."

Barney led the way into Mike's, nodded toward the back room, and Mike, grinning and rubbing his hands, showed them through the door and waved them to a table, with a grand Sicilian gesture.

"Bring your best, Mike," clipped Barney, "an' then squat."

Mike brought his best and took a seat at the table.

Barney said, "There's a dame livin' upstairs I'd like to have a chat with, Mike. Tess Brady. Know if she's alone now?"

"Ah, Barney, Tess she go away," replied Mike.

"Away? When did this happen?"

"Tess she go yes'day mornin'."

Barney snorted, "Another bum break! Where'd she go, Mike, d'you know?"

"Ah, dunno, Barn. Mebbe Whitey know, eh, Whitey?"

Barney shot a fast glance at Whitey.

"Don't know, Barney. I was speakin' to Tess a couple a days ago but she didn't say nothin' about movin'."

"Didn't know you was hangin' around her, Whitey."

"I wasn't, Barney; just dropped in, you know, to say hello."

"Sure that's all you said?"

"Sure, Barney. Now what else would I say?"

"Lots of things. Now look here, guy. You an' me ain't goin' to get along so good if you keep on bein' so tight-mouthed. I happen to know that Dapper chucked this here now Tess frail for a Polack blonde a year or so ago. I understand Tess was head-over-heels in love with Dapper, an' it's natural that, bein' given the air, she'd ache to get back at Dapper somehow. All right. You got a grudge against Dapper. Tess is got a love grudge. Now, tell me, guy, what the hell's preventin' you two from joinin' and playin' a two-handed game against Dapper?"

Whitey smiled peacefully. "Nothin' preventin' us, Barney—nothing a-tall. Only thing is, you're way off your track."

"Oh, I am, am I?" rolled out Barney. "Maybe I am—maybe I ain't. Anyhow, I got a hunch that you're the lousiest liar on the face o' the earth. From now on, Whitey, you want to watch your step. I'm goin' to get this here now Dapper, but it would give me a lot more satisfaction if I could land you. Huh, a guy can't be decent with you bums. Why, last night I read in a letter in the newspaper from some shocked reader—says us cops aren't gentlemen, because we handle a suspect too rough. I'd just like to take that guy on a stroll some night an' show him the kind of boy scouts we gotta handle. He'd damned soon change his mind. Well, here's how."

He downed his drink straight and got up. "Remember, Whitey," he said. "I've declared war on you, an' in war everything's fair." With that he turned and strode out.

Mike leaned over and said, "Dis is won tough worl', Whitey."

"Oh, it ain't so bad," Whitey replied softly. "Barney? He'll get over it. Barney thinks he's a good dick, Mike, but he's awful dumb—terrible dumb."

"Ah, dat is wan question! Allah tam it ain' tah de wise cop

make-ah de big haul. Some tam de dumb cop make-ah de big haul by—whatcha call—dumb luck."

"Dumb luck is right, Mike—if Barney ever nabs his guy. Well, I guess I'll be gettin' along."

Calm, unruffled, benign, Whitey made his way to the street. Inwardly he was amused. Barney always amused him. Barney always took himself so seriously—he wasted so much energy dashing around on blind leads. Yes, he had a record at Headquarters, but…dumb luck.

Whitey entered a cigar store and closed himself in a telephone booth. Soon he had Tess on the wire.

"Hello, Tess. This is Whitey. Say, it's O.K. to call Dapper now." He gave her the phone number of the hotel where Dapper was registered as John Patterson. "Get him to meet you, Tess, an' get him in your rooms an' keep him there. An' instead of you callin' me at that number I gave you, I'll call you when it's time for you to breeze. If I say, 'O.K.,' you'll meet me at Times Square, north side o' the Times Buildin'. That's all I'll say, an' you hang up an' remark to Dapper someone had the wrong number. I'll pass your place in a couple o' hours. If you got Dapper, open one o' your windows; if you ain't, leave 'em closed. All right, then, Tess, start in an do your best."

Leaving the cigar store, Whitey smiled to himself. To kill some time, he took a subway down to Courtlandt Street and hung around in the Hudson Tubes station. A small, commonplace, inconspicuous figure he made, looking for all the world like a stranger in the big city—and a forlorn one at that, with his clothes, decent enough though they were, hanging from his narrow shoulders like the rags of a scarecrow.

The time dragged by until finally he went outside and took the Sixth Avenue "L" uptown. He got off at Herald Square and drifted west at a leisurely pace, circling a few blocks, pausing to look idly in some store windows, and to glance at his watch. Finally he entered a street where traffic was light, gazing obliquely at a row of buildings across the way. Then he stopped, scratched his chin and smiled, nodding his head thoughtfully as, after a moment, he turned about and retraced his steps at a somewhat faster gait. The window in Tess's room was open!

ON THE following day, after a luncheon at Nickie Lombardi's that consisted of a Spanish omelet, French frieds, raspberry pie and dark coffee, Whitey, permitting himself the infrequent luxury of a twenty-five-cent cigar, strolled along Canal Street in his most benign manner.

He was about to enter the West Side Subway kiosk when someone yelled, "Hey, Whitey!"

He stopped, turned about slowly and saw Detective Barney Doyle crossing the square. Barney's frown was more important than ever, and he had never walked more briskly. Barney was indeed a human dynamo. Whitey wondered what he would be wanting, and even as he wondered Barney reached him and asked:

"Got a butt, Whitey?"

"Sure. How about a cigar?"

"Well, now, don't ask foolish questions."

Barney clamped the cigar between strong teeth and Whitey held a match to it.

"Ah, some smoke, Whitey! How do you do it? Some day you'll be in Dapper Lew's class."

"How's the case comin' along, Barney?"

Barney spat sharply. "Rotten! I can't seem to get me mitts on it. If I could get a hold of this here now Tess frail, I might be able to do somethin'. But I been gettin' so many bum breaks, it gets me sore. Well, thanks for the cheroot."

" 'S all right, Barney. So-long."

"G'bye, An, say, don't forget."

"What?"

"Our little war is still on."

Whitey descended into the subway, mildly amused, and caught a north-bound local. He left the train at Pennsylvania

Station and walked through Thirty-third Street to Broadway. Soon he was in the ornate lobby of a pretentious hotel. He found the hotel switchboard and asked the operator for Mr. John Patterson. A moment later she indicated a booth and Whitey entered, closed the door and put the receiver to his ear. A woman's voice floated over the wire, and Whitey smiled.

"Is this you, Birdie?" he asked.

"Yes—ah—who—who is this?"

"An old friend of yours, Whitey Fleer."

"Oh, for cryin' out loud! Where are you, anyhow?"

"Downstairs, an' I got somepin' to tell you, Birdie, if you'll come down an' meet me in the lobby."

"What about?"

"Somepin' *very* important, Birdie. When will you be down?"

"I—ah—in about ten minutes, Whitey. But, say, listen—"

"I'll be waitin', Birdie."

He hung up and drifted back into the lobby, leaning against one of the marble columns near the row of six elevators that were forever in motion. Birdie appeared quite on time. She was a small, chic blonde, with a doll-like face and rosebud lips; and your average cosmopolitan would label her, "beautiful but dumb." She walked with her nose and chin elevated at a rather snobbish angle—as though the humanity about her was as dust beneath her feet. However, Whitey knew her of old.

"Come down to earth, Birdie," he said genially.

"Never mind any wisecracks, an' lets get into the writin' room, where it's darker an' not so public."

In a secluded corner they found a divan and sat down. Birdie was restless and kept tucking strands of hair under her black turban.

"Well, Whitey, what's so important, huh? You got me all worked up. I been awake most of the night besides an' even a Bromo Seltzer this mornin' didn't do me no good."

Whitey smiled gently, inclining his head on one shoulder. "Yeah, Birdie, I s'pose it's Dapper you're thinkin' of."

"Huh?" With a rapid glance.

"Yeah. I seen Dapper last night."

"You did! Now, where?"

Whitey clasped his hands together between his knees. "Well, now, Birdie, maybe I oughtn't tell you."

She leaned forward grasping his coat sleeve. "Is—is Dapper pinched—is he?"

"Pinched? What for?"

She sat back, holding her breath. "Oh—nothin'. I—I—well, Whitey, you know how it is. You never knew when they might frame him for somethin' he didn't do. But you saw him, Whitey? Tell me where."

"I—well, Birdie, I seen him on Broadway with Tess Brady."

"Tess Brady!" she gasped.

"Yeah. You know, Birdie, I always liked you like a sister. When you went wit' Dapper I says to meself: 'He'll chuck her over just like he's chucked the rest.' Dapper's that kind of a guy. It's only because I like you, Birdie, that I'm tellin' you. An' it looks like he's keepin' Tess on the side now."

Birdie pursed her lips. "Whitey, you're lyin'!"

"Honest t' Gawd, Birdie, I ain't. I seen 'em together, an' I know where they're stayin'. They got a couple rooms over near Eight' Avenue. It ain't fair by you, Birdie. Hell, I don't know what he sees in Tess. She ain't nowhere near as classy as you are, Birdie."

Birdie put her hands on her hips. "Say, listen, Whitey, lay off the applesauce. You got to show me—see? You got to prove that Dapper is stayin' with Tess."

"Gee, Bird, don't treat me so rough. I'm only tryin' to be your friend. Guess I shouldn't ha' told you in the first place. Well, anyhow, I told you, an' I can prove what I say, if you don't want to take my word for it."

"Well, if you can, then begin struttin' your stuff."

"All right. But you got to promise to hold your head an' not start any fireworks."

"All I want is to see Dapper where you say he is. I got a better idea than startin' fireworks."

"Let's go, Birdie," said Whitey.

They went. Whitey even went so far as to hire a taxi, and this gave Birdie plenty of opportunity to powder her nose and primp up generally. They alighted a few blocks away from the apartment house and walked the remainder of the distance, and Whitey motioned Birdie to precede him through the entrance. Then he led the way up two short flights, turning at the top to put a finger to his lips. Birdie nodded understandingly and followed him down the corridor. He stopped before a door near the end, and Birdie put her ear against it. After a few moments she stood erect and whispered in Whitey's ear:

"I can't make them voices out."

Whitey looked around, then clasped his hands in front of him and braced one shoulder against the door frame. He nodded to Birdie, and she put one foot in his clasped hands, grasped his shoulders and raised herself up to the level of the transom above the door. Whitey held his breath. He sensed rather than felt that a tremor ran through Birdie. She almost lost her balance and might have fallen had not Whitey unclasped his hands and flung his arms about her as she toppled. Still holding her, he ran down the hall to the staircase and did not set her down until he was on the floor below.

"They might ha' heard us," he told her.

She was busy with her pocket mirror, adjusting her hat, which had been knocked on one ear in the scuffle.

"But I seen them, so I don't care," she retorted.

"Don't talk foolish, Birdie. We got to get out o' here." He grasped her hand and pulled her down to the street door. "Keep close to the buildin's," he warned. "They might be lookin' out."

At the next corner they entered a taxi. Birdie was quite breathless and in a state of nervous excitement.

"I seen them all right," she said. "My Gawd, she was layin' in his arms like the fade-out scene in a bum movie. Well, he won't kid me any longer. I been gettin' tired o' him, anyhow, lately. Some nights he didn't come home at all. So that's where he was hangin' out! He must think I'm a fool. I'll fool him!"

" 'Tain't right, him treatin' you like that," Whitey reflected with a sad smile. "That's why I told you. I always liked you, Birdie. I ain't good-lookin' like Dapper, but me heart's in the right place. Maybe I can do somepin' for you, Birdie, huh?"

"You can come right up to my apartment an' help me pack. I'm givin' this here burg the air an' I'm leavin' Dapper flatter than a flat tire. When I get through with that guy he won't have a cent to his name."

Birdie's three-room suit was a comfortable affair. Whitey followed her in and closed the door softly, scanning the appointments with an appreciative eye. Birdie had flung her hat across the room and was now hauling her array of clothing from the closet. She pointed to a wardrobe trunk and told Whitey to get busy.

"You help me, Whitey, an' I'll slip you five grand," she said.

"Aw, gee, Birdie, I wasn't thinkin' o' that. I was just doin' you a friendly turn, for old times' sake."

"Well, anyhow, shake a leg, Whitey, will you?"

Whitey smiled behind bony fingers and opened the wardrobe trunk, but he kept his eyes on Birdie. He saw her go into the next room and unscrew the knob from one of the brass bed-posts. He nodded to himself and smiled his crooked smile. Everything was working out as he had hoped it would. He saw Birdie draw several rolls of bills from the hollow bed-post.

He was about to thrust a long white silk scarf into the trunk, but hesitated, looking from the scarf to Birdie. Holding the scarf before him with both hands, he tiptoed across the soft carpet, and with a quick, deft movement clapped it over Birdie's mouth. The only sound was a muffled gasp. He twisted her arms behind her back until she dropped the packets of money. Then he bound her hands and feet with a convenient pair of silk stockings. He lifted her in his arms and carried her into the closet, where he left her half-unconscious. Closing the door, he went back into the bedroom and gathered up the money; three compact rolls of yellow bills which he flipped hastily.

"Easy ten thousand," he told himself.

Dapper would feel this blow. But that wasn't all. There was more to come. It all had been carefully planned, carefully thought out, and the black conscience of Whitey had not felt a qualm in considering the human pawns that would unwittingly serve his own ends. He stuffed the money in his pockets.

Now for the culmination of his old grudge against Dapper. He would never have planned all this for the grudge alone, for he was quite incapable of an emotion strong enough to warrant a grudge for the grudge alone. But now he would wipe clean the slate with one vast flourish. He had Dapper's money, and now he would get Dapper out of the way.

He picked up the telephone, clearing his throat. His voice was naturally soft, and with a little effort he could make it sound like a woman's. He called his number, and in a few moments was connected with a downtown police station.

He said, in his most feminine voice, "Tell Barney Doyle that he'll find Dapper Lew in an apartment house at number — Eight' Avenue—apartment 34."

He hung up, rubbing his hands together, smiling wistfully. The police might trace the call, and if they did they would find Birdie bound and gagged. Now to get away. He would not hurry. He had plenty of time. He would drop down to Pennsylvania Station and hop an outbound train for—anywhere. Birdie—Tess? Pawns—nothing more. And to look at him, with that sad, gentle smile, you would have thought him the embodiment of all that was good and benevolent.

He put on his hat, buttoned his coat and, with a last look at the room, opened the door to go out. He walked straight into the muzzle of a blunt automatic pistol.

"Back up!" bit off the man behind the gun.

He was a tall, slim man, immaculately dressed from gray spats to kid gloves. He had a small, well-groomed mustache and piercing black eyes. He shoved Whitey back into the room, closed and locked the door behind him, removing the key. His white teeth glittered in an uncanny smile.

"The elevator boy, a kind of friend of mine, casually remarked that I had a visitor," he explained. "I suspected who the visitor was. Surprised, Whitey?"

"Aw, now, look here, Dapper, put away the cannon," whined Whitey. "I just come up to tip you off the cops was after you."

Dapper Lew chucked dryly. "Is that so? Come out of your shell, buddy. Tess told me everything."

Whitey blanched.

"She told me everything because, you poor fool, she loves me. She can't help loving me. Why, you dirty little shrimp, you should have known that much. No, I don't love her, but that doesn't stop her from loving me. Huh, and you thought you could make her work with you! I love Birdie. I don't know why, but I do, and I only wish she'd love me the way Tess does. Where is she?"

Whitey was almost speechless. He kept moistening his lips, shrinking from the man with the gun.

Dapper's face went dark. "Damn you, where is she? If you so much as harmed a hair on her head—"

There was a groan from the closet, and for a split-second Dapper's eyes left Whitey. Whitey saw it was his only chance, and he flung himself at Dapper's legs. They crashed to the floor, knocking over a pedestal, and Dapper snapped out a warm oath.

At that instant the closet door swung open and Birdie, still bound and gagged, fell into the room. Through much effort she apparently had managed to open the door, and now she lay there, watching with wide eyes the two struggling men.

Whitey was small but unbelievably quick, and he knew a dirty trick or two about the rough-and-tumble game. Dapper, taller and heavier, had his hands full. They rolled back and forth across the floor striving frantically to break each other's grip, and a hand-painted floor-lamp crashed down in ruin. Dapper had lost his gun, and now it lay in the center of the floor.

By sheer superior strength he succeeded in heaving himself to his feet, with Whitey still clinging to him like a leech. He then tore about the room in an effort to fling Whitey loose and, losing his balance, tumbled over a chair. This broke Whitey's hold, though Dapper found himself in a bad way with the chair on top of him. Whitey had landed on the back of his head and twisted about with startling agility. Though a bit stunned, instinct prompted him to struggle to his feet, and, swaying, he saw Dapper shove aside the chair and try to get up.

At the same instant his foot kicked something. He looked down and saw Dapper's revolver lying at his feet. With a sweep of his arm he snatched it up, even as Dapper, with a snarl on his lips, picked up a chair.

"You damn pup, drop that gun!" roared Dapper.

Whitey crouched, the revolver pressed along his hip, a weird smile twisting his mouth. Dapper, instead of raising the chair above his head, swung it at arm's length as he lunged and let it skim along the floor. Ten to one, Whitey had no intention of shooting at that moment. He had killed a man or two before, but the acts had been done under circumstances favorable to Whitey's subsequent freedom as far as the law was concerned. But now he realized that it would be suicidal plain and simple to do any killing, and he yelled:

"Put up your hands, Dapper!"

However, the heavy chair had already been flung and it struck him a cruel blow across the legs. He hit the floor on his elbows and the shock caused his finger to yank the trigger. The gun boomed with a deafening roar.

Dapper buckled to his knees and fell heavily on his face,

groaning between clenched teeth. He twisted around on his back, clutching at his chest, gasping spasmodically. His body heaved with a jerk, rolled over, shuddered and then lay very still.

Birdie was trying frantically to free herself.

There were loud knocks on the door.

Whitey, his face pale with a ghastly pallor, the revolver still clutched in his hand, shrank away from the door. He turned and looked out the window. Below—far below—a dozen stories or more—was the street. He grimaced, brushing a hand across his face. He ran into another room, looked out. No fire-escape there either. It must be in the hall. Then—then he was trapped!

There was the sound of splintering wood—and a crash. Whitey spun about, crouching with his back against the wall. There were voices—hoarse shouts—running feet. Whitey felt his heart pounding against his ribs like a sledge-hammer. His hand shook. Perspiration poured down his face and made his clothes cling to his body. He felt very weak, very small, very much alone.

Never before had he been in a tight corner like this. Never before had he been trapped. He had never known what it was to be afraid. But he was afraid now. He was lost—irrevocably lost. Tess had turned on him. Birdie had seen him shoot Dapper. He could not have foreseen this. He would have sworn by Tess. Damn Tess… damn all women!… He had not meant to shoot Dapper… he had not….

Two men rushed through the door from the other room. He saw them through a mist…house detectives. One ripped the gun from his hand; the other held him in a grip of steel. He did not struggle. Hot sweat enveloped him and made him very weak. He was half-dragged, half-carried into the other room. There was a crowd there. He saw Birdie, flushed and wild-eyed, fixing her hair with one hand and pointing at him with the other. And she was talking—he didn't care about what. It all seemed like a dream—a horrible nightmare. He had been tricked. He had not meant to kill Dapper….

Later he saw Barney Doyle come in and take command of the situation. Barney was brisk as ever, so sure of himself.

He was saying, "Hell, Whitey, I never expected a haul like this. Trailed that phone call here after I looked up that tip. Yeah, I found Tess—found her *dead!* Poisoned herself! Yeah. I don't know, but there's a sob artist from one of the yellow sheets swears it's a case o' love spurned—somethin' like that. An' I find Dapper here killed, an' *you* killed him! Baby! Say, you got a butt handy? Thanks."

Whitey lit one himself and smiled wistfully at the match until it burned out. "You just got me, Barney, by—well, dumb luck," he said.

"Sure," clipped Barney. "But I *got* you. An' you'll get the chair. So what about it, huh?—what about it?"

Whitey hadn't a chance in the world. Nor can it be said that he deserved one. Birdie testified heavily against him. She was grief-stricken—or so it seemed—over the loss of Dapper. At any rate, she made a pathetic picture on the stand, and that was that.

When the judge decreed that he must die in the chair, Whitey swayed a little on his feet and then dropped back into his seat. He clasped his skeleton hands between his knees and stared at the floor. But now not even a ghost of a smile was on his face. His counsel, leaning over, heard him mutter:

"Dumb…luck…."

China Silk

A man—a great hulk of a man who will run the blockade in defiance of the law and the bullets of the harbor-patrol, but who scorns the petty thief and the sly killer—Buck Jason.

IT WAS a mean room, in a mean house, in a mean street. There was a single gas-jet by the door. Its flame was yellow, unsteady, and hissed shrilly. The walls were scarred and dirty; a wedge-shaped gash was in the ceiling, revealing half a dozen laths of a mouldy gray color. Snow formed a white frame around an otherwise grimy and disreputable window. A rusty oil-stove burned in one corner.

In the center of the room was a small table, coverless, stained, warped with age and dampness. On this table stood a bottle of square-face gin and two glasses. Dust lay thick and heavy about the room; on the table, on the floor, on the rumpled cot against the wall—so much so that you could smell it. Mixed with it, too, were the smells of the oil-stove and stale gin and the almost indescribable smell of decrepit age.

It was a hovel, a den. There was something subtly sinister and oddly vicious about its dank, repulsive atmosphere. The incessant hissing sound of the gas-jet injected a note of uncanniness into the whole, and the occasional rattle of the window in the grip of the wind, was heart-chilling.

Abruptly, then, upon this scene of passive, brooding malevolence, the door banged open and a huge, rough rock of a man surged in. Behind him, with much less dash of manner, came a shriveled, pale-eyed man who seemed to be nothing more than a bundle of uncontrollable nerves.

The big man, a mountain of vigor, settled himself on one of the two chairs by the table and rumbled, "For the love 'o Mike, Shifty, close the door! It's cold."

The little man kicked the door shut with his heel, rubbed his hands together nervously and by fits and starts reached the table and sat down. The giant poured out two stiff drinks from the bottle of square-face and threw his own down with a sweeping movement of his steel-thewed arm, rasping his throat with vast satisfaction. The little man bolted his after the fashion of a mongrel dog stealing a chop. He jerked a cigarette to his colorless lips. The big man crammed tobacco into an ancient pipe.

"Well, what's on your mind, Shifty," he asked. "Spill it fast. I've got to run some booze tonight and I can't spare more than half an hour. But before you begin, get me straight. I'm not your kind. Get that, boy friend, and get it right! I run booze, which to my way of thinking is a man's game. I supply, among others, a judge who privately considers it a lawful business. Of course, when he's on the bench, it's different. But you can't blame him for that. It's his business, just like mine is selling him good Scotch at a hundred bucks a case. Understand, now. If it's dirty work you've got me up your sleeve, save your breath—save your breath. Do you get me?"

"Yeah—sure, Buck. But you shouldn't go now gettin' me wrong like that. I'm just goin' t' ask you t' do somet'in' an' I'm goin' t' pay you."

"Well, I should hope so! Shoot!"

"Yeah." Shifty's lips twitched nervously. "It's this way, Buck. I'm workin' f'r a man higher up, o' course, but his name don't make no difference t' you. We'll let that part go. There's a little no-account steamer due outside the Hook in about two nights from now—little freighter from the Orient. The boss I'm workin' for an' this here skipper o' the steamer has been speakin' t'gether by code or somet'in'. The skipper is bringin' a big case o' Oriental rugs an' silks an' such, an' you know as well as me there'd be an awful lot o' duty t' pay on 'em.

"All right. Now. You got a pretty good sea-boat in that there launch o' yourn, an' I'm puttin' you in the way o' some easy money. You just poke your nose t' sea when I get word from the boss. This here freighter is goin' t' heave to over night outside the

Hook. Is all you have t' do is slide up alongside her under cover o' darkness an' the skipper will have the case lowered into your boat. There needn't be no words. You just get the case an' plug back. I'll meet you at the dock where we can figure on the watchman bein' asleep."

"I haven't heard a word, Shifty, unless you mention what *I* get out o' this," put in the big man.

Shifty pecked at his chin for a moment. "The boss says I should give three-hundred bucks."

"He did, eh?" The big man chuckled harshly. "That's his lowest offer, isn't it, Shifty? Now forget that and pop me his limit."

"Why, now, Buck, three hundred is pretty good—"

"Cut it, you runt! I've got an idea what's going to be made on a case load of silks and rugs, and I'm not working for charity. Five hundred in cold cash hires me and my launch for one night."

"But Buck, I—"

The big man took a crack at the table with his fist. "Don't go giving me any buts! Five hundred! Get me, Shifty? Five hundred—*before I start for the Hook!*"

Shifty sat erect with a start and began tearing apart his cigarette with shaking fingers. He feared this big rough adventurer—this man who called a spade a spade and was afraid of nobody. He admired, feared and hated Buck Jason. Yet he realized that if any man along New York's waterfront was capable of pulling off the job he had in mind, Buck was that man.

"Well, Buck, it ain't fair, it ain't, but I s'pose I'll have t' come across," he gave away reluctantly, his eyes darting about erratically. "But, say, now, half when you leave f'r the Hook an' t' other half when you get back wit' the case."

Jason stood up, pushing the tobacco farther into his pipe-bowl with a rigid finger. He regarded Shifty for a long moment, then suddenly pointed the pipe-stem at him. "I said the whole five hundred when I leave for the Hook. Take it or leave it." There was crisp finality in his tone. He started for the door.

"Wait a second, Buck," clucked Shifty, hopping to his feet and gesturing aimlessly with his hands. "All right, then. I c'n depend on you, Buck, I know. You ain't the kind t' frame a guy. Five hundred when you leave the dock. Gee, it—it's kinder tough—"

"Quit your crabbing!" Jason flung at him.

Shifty swallowed hard and said, "It's all fixed then, huh? We'll meet here day after t'morrer, 'bout five in the evenin', an' I'll give you the dope."

"Suits me," clipped the big man, and he rocked out without another word.

Shifty blinked at the closed door for a moment and then twisted his face in a hateful grimace. In a sudden fit of futile rage he beat his hands together and muttered rasping, incoherent sounds. Then he jerked himself to a chair, poured a tot of gin and downed it at a gulp, almost choking. He snorted, hurled the glass against the wall spitefully and glared at the broken fragments.

Damn Buck Jason! Buck had pressed him to the limit. Yes, the "boss" had authorized him to pay five hundred dollars, but Shifty had hoped to close the deal for less and pocket the difference in his own jeans. It seemed that Buck had read his mind perfectly. He hated Buck, hated him because he was big, because he was fearless, because he talked plain and to the point. He was everything that Shifty was not, and the realization of this gnawed insidiously at the little man's brain. He would never have approached Buck but for the fact that Buck was the only man capable of such a daring move. Not only that. Buck was also a man of his word. He did not run with the pack. He scorned the common criminal. He found adventure by night on the rivers that flow into New York Bay, pitting his brains, his brawn and his swift, powerful launch against the law and against the criminal element as well.

Shifty, finally quieting down somewhat, buttoned his overcoat, put out the oil-stove and the gas-jet and locked the door after him as he went out. He descended two flights of narrow, creaking stairs. He emerged upon a narrow, dimly-lighted street, where old tenement houses rose in a world of winter gloom. Snow lay in big dirty heaps in the gutters. Brown slush cluttered the street and sidewalks, beginning now to freeze again after a day of warm fog. The air was cold and brittle, whining plaintively among the house-tops.

Shifty, his hands jammed deep into his overcoat pockets, his meager shoulders hunched till they touched his ears, crunched along with short, nervous steps. His was a nervous, spiteful, petulant nature, given to quick, unreasonable rages which, however, he could hold in check if he were facing someone whom he feared. With those weaker than himself—with women particularly—he was infinitely cruel.

He wound his way through a maze of cross streets and finally reached Chatham Square. His shoes were soggy and he drummed them on the curb for a few moments before proceeding. A taxi tore by and splashed slush all over his overcoat. He swore a dark blue streak until the words choked him and made him gasp for breath.

Presently he moved on along Canal Street and after a few more blocks turned south toward the Chinese quarter. Fifteen minutes later he stopped before a quaint Oriental building, looked up and down the street a few times, then ducked into a narrow, dark hallway. He went up a short flight of stairs, knocked at a door three times, and whispered his name. There followed a faint click. The door opened on a crack, an eye regarded him for a moment, and then the door swung open noiselessly.

Shifty entered a room lavishly appointed after the Chinese manner; surely the retreat of a man of means and not any ordinary, peaceful work-a-day Chinaman. The Celestial who had admitted him now stepped to one side, while from an adjoining room there entered a large, fleshy Chinese attired in garments that reeked of luxury. His face was fat and oily, heavy-lipped, with lazy, inscrutable eyes. With a movement of his finger he indicated for the servant to leave the room. Then he folded his well-kept hands on his round paunch and regarded Shifty mutely.

Shifty said, "It's all fixed, Yung."

Yung Chau nodded his head slowly and a crafty smile suddenly came to his face. "Excellent! I will give you further details regarding the position of the ship two nights hence."

Yung Chau suddenly put a finger to his lips, and his eyes darkened. With a rapid movement he stepped to the curtain leading into the adjoining chamber, grasped it and flung it back with a great show of violence. The young Chinese servant almost toppled into the room.

Yung Chau straightened up, his pulpy lips fluttered with suppressed rage, his eyes dilated and shot with hot fires. His hand went out and caught the servant by the throat.

There followed harsh accusation on the part of the master, in Cantonese—sharp and sibilant; whining protestation from the cringing servant.

Yung Chau hurled the man to the floor, bent low to the cowering form and hissed a threat into his ear. Then he flung up his hand and the servant scurried from the room.

Yung Chau slowly turned narrowed slits of eyes upon his

visitor, and Shifty shuddered at the pitiless menace in their black impenetrable depths.

"Gee!" croaked Shifty. "You sure know how t' handle him. But, say, don't you t'ink he's a kinder dangerous guy t' have in the house?"

"He dare not let his tongue wag, friend of mine. I am not always gentle. I would have his tongue and his heart if he talked."

"But we got t' be careful, Yung," he persisted, "else those other guys'll get wise an' ball up the whole works. This is a damn ticklish bizness."

Yung pawed his chin musingly. "Ah—by the way, you found a reliable man?"

"Yeah, I got the man all right. If any man c'n pull this here stunt, he c'n, an' I don't mean maybe. But, listen, if Chen Tsung gets wind of this—"

"Be at ease," interrupted Yung Chau quietly. "Chen Tsung must, of course, be considered an enemy, but do not let thoughts of him interfere with your digestion. You have made arrangements with your man, so let me worry over Chen Tsung."

"Yeah, but looka here," complained Shifty. "I gotta drive that truck an' if anyt'ing happens I'm the guy gets hurt."

"Ah, I see now," purred Yung. "You are, in a word, afraid."

"N-n-no; not that," stammered Shifty, feeling ill at ease.

Yung Chau murmured, "H'm," and stared at the floor like a man who suddenly begins to wonder if he has erred in judgment.

AGAIN THE mean room, in the mean house, in the mean street. Again the hissing gas-jet and on the table the bottle of square-faced gin. Shifty alone, huddled in his overcoat, with an empty glass in one hand and a cigarette in the other, feeling miserably cold. For there was no heat in that bare room, and a bitter winter rain was roaring against the window.

Presently heavy footsteps sounded in the hall outside and then a rough hand jerked at the knob. Shifty got up and shot back the bolt. The door flew open and Jason heaved in, a whale of a man in a black rubber coat with a battered seaman's cap slanted low over his forehead. The huge rubber coat gleamed under the gas light and rain dripped from the big, clean-clipped face.

"All set," he bit off shortly, making for the bottle.

A flurry of enthusiasm mounted in Shifty's voice. "Glad you come, Buck. You know—you know, I t'ought maybe you wouldn't go."

Jason, with the glass of gin at his lips, paused to cut Shifty with a black, derisive look. "Wouldn't go? And why not?"

"Well, you know, Buck, the rain—"

"Rain never stops me. Nor snow. Nor anything. I've made up my mind to pull this stunt for a little diversion and I'd like to see the man what's going to stop me. Throw a jolt under your belt, Shifty, and be yourself." He laughed lustily and put away his drink neat; then went on, in a new tone: "Say, do you know I've never been drunk in my life? Funny, eh? Never drink this stuff except to warm me up. Funny, I mean, being that I handle it in boatloads. Well, let's get down to brass tacks."

They sat down and Shifty brought from his pocket a packet of bills. Very reluctantly he counted out the entire amount of five hundred.

"There you are, Buck, the whole shootin' match," he said.

Jason counted the bills himself, gave a satisfied grunt and stowed them away. "Now about this tub."

"Yeah—about the steamer," explained Shifty, bringing out a sheet of paper with figures on it. "She's layin' to now. Here's her position off the coast, due east o' Sandy Hook. An' here's her name—*Lady Fair*. Somet'in' else, Buck. When you come alongside her an' get the hail, just yell, 'From the city.' That's so the skipper'll know you're O.K."

"All right that far," nodded Jason, taking the paper. "Now about the dock."

"Yeah—I was comin' t' that. Biddle's Pier, Buck. I know the watchman there. He's an old soak an' I'll get him drunk. Biddle's

Pier. I'll be there wit' a flivver delivery truck. You'll have t' help me carry the case t' the truck. Then you just drift away wherever you want t'. That's all."

"All set, then." Jason got up, yanking his cap farther down across his level dark eyes.

"Now be careful, Buck," whimpered Shifty.

Jason grinned. "What's the matter? You're more scared than I am, and I'm the one ought to be scared. Does it mean that if I flop this job you don't get your share? Well, Shifty, you're afraid of your own shadow anyway. If you wasn't you'd be doing the whole job instead of letting me get a share. But you haven't got the guts to run the rum blockade and take a chance of being blown to hell by a raking fire. It means hard lines out on the bay and around the Narrows these nights. Say, why don't you go washing dishes in a Greek all-American restaurant? Ho! Ho! So long, Shifty. See you at Biddle's Pier later."

With a sweep of his arm he swung out of the room. Shifty rushed at the closed door, snarling at it, raising clenched fists and shaking like a leaf in the throes of an unutterable rage. Jason's words bit deep, and they bit deep because they were true, every one of them. In short, Shifty hadn't the "guts" to play a man's game, to fight alone and win all or lose all. He was a miserable go-between. When he lost, he lost all; when he won, he won only half.

Jason rolled along toward the waterfront with long, powerful strides. The rain drove against him in solid sheets and rolled from his rubber coat in streams. It was dusk now and growing dark very quickly. He was a rough-and-ready, devil-may-care man, blunt of speech and capable of action, entertaining a monumental disregard for harbor patrol boats, and, on the other hand, holding in black contempt petty thieves and killers. He had never found it necessary to use a gun himself; in truth, he never carried a gun—a strange fact for a man of his precarious calling.

Half an hour after leaving Shifty's retreat, he was aboard his motor launch, tuning up the powerful engine. The craft was about forty feet over all, painted black, with a trunk cabin covering that part forward of the waist and also the engine. The cockpit was rather roomy and the wheel was at the left against the rear of the cabin.

Darkness had settled completely when he backed away from the little East River dock, turned about and pointed his bow into the rain-drenched murk that hung over the river. The engine chugged lazily for a little while as he oozed out past a string of barges; then, getting well beyond the pierhead line, he advanced speed until the engine was running smoothly, and the craft now slid through the water like a black shadow.

Jason stood in the open at the wheel, a sou'wester having replaced his battered seaman's cap. The rain cut down on him out of the black void above, lashing at his face. Once or twice he grinned, his teeth flashing, a deep chuckle in his throat. He did not mind the rain, so long as it did not interfere with the perfect rhythm of his motor.

He passed under the broad expanse of the Brooklyn Bridge, cut sharply across the bow of a cautious ferry. He pounded against a strong current in the Buttermilk Channel and soon was running in the lee of Governor's Island. To his right the Statue of Liberty showed pale and wraith-like. Dead ahead one of the swift Municipal ferries was legging it beautifully for St. George.

Steadily he drove his craft across the beshrouded bay in the teeth of the heavy downpour. Scattered lights began to blink in the gloom on his right, and he knew that he was now running off the Staten Island shore, heading for the Narrows. Presently he passed Fort Wadsworth and began to nose into rougher water. A swell broke over the bow and the salt spray swept over him. He shook himself vigorously. He kept to a southeasterly course, finding the sea rough but not troublesome. He had the Sandy Hook Light in view now, and tucked away in his mind the position of the *Lady Fair*.

He passed a huge ocean palace with its tiers of bright lights and heard faintly the strains of an orchestra. Time passed while he urged his sturdy little boat through the heaving sea, and soon he spotted the riding lights of a ship that he judged should be the *Lady Fair*. He proceeded at reduced speed, endeavoring to get in the lee of what he could now make out as a black, rakish vessel with a single "cigarette" funnel, clipper bows and a low well-deck amidships. This tallied with the description on the slip of paper Shifty had given him. He reached for his megaphone.

"Ahoy!" he bawled in a deep voice. "What ship?"

A voice floated out to him—"*Lady Fair*... Shanghai."

Jason again put the megaphone to his mouth. "From the city," he shouted.

"Aye, from the city," came the voice from the ship. "Will you lay alongside under our lee bow? We'll lower the box with our derrick."

"I'll lay alongside," shouted Jason.

It was ticklish work maneuvering up to the scarred side of the black sea-tramp that came from the other side of the world. No doubt everything was in readiness on board to lower the case of contraband, for the derrick began to creak, and finally swung out over the rail. Below, Jason kept his engine running slowly while the case was being lowered bit by bit. In one hand he held a pocket knife, ready to cut away the line as soon as the case settled. It came down slowly, while two men leaned over the rail, one of them calling orders to the man who controlled the derrick. Now the case was swinging just over Jason's head, and as he advanced the boat a trifle, it hung directly over the cockpit within easy reach.

"Let her go!" he shouted.

The case fell with a slight thump. For a brief moment he let go the wheel, jumped over and with two slashes released the line from the derrick. Then he dived for the wheel, spun it over and began to swing away from the ship.

"Good work!" someone from the deck called to him.

"Better douse your lights on the way in!" yelled another.

Jason laughed and waved a hand, then turned his back on them and gave his entire attention to the course ahead. Several big waves caught him astern and the case thumped against his back. He saw the danger and, lashing the wheel, he went into the cabin and came out a few moments later with a coil of heavy rope which he wound about the case, securing the ends to deck-cleats. The case was pretty heavy, solidly built, about five feet long, four wide and four deep. A dangerous thing to have slamming about.

When he left the Sandy Hook Light on the port quarter and began heading into Lower New York Bay, Jason put out his lights. He did not believe in inviting any patrol boat to look over him. Without lights the chances of being spotted were few, and the beating rain drowned to a great extent the sound of his engine which, enclosed in the cabin, was muffled to begin with. As he plowed through the Narrows into the Upper Bay he caught sight of the lights of some swift-moving small craft on his starboard bow. Taking no chances, he slowed down the engine and threw out the clutch, rolling noiselessly in the trough.

The boat sped swiftly by on his starboard side and Jason marked it for a patrol, thanking his stars that he had doused his lights long before. He waited until it was well away before throwing in the clutch and gathering up speed. He plugged steadily across the bay, got his eye on the blinking Robbins Reef Light far ahead and began edging to the right until he picked up Governor's Island and Liberty to the left of it.

At four in the morning, with the rain easing up, he drove under the Brooklyn Bridge on his way back up the East River. He was dead-tired, for he had been under a tremendous mental and physical strain all night. But he was five hundred dollars to the good. Well, it was worth it—the risk, the danger of rough weather, the double peril of patrol boats and the sea; added to this the ever-possible menace of roving hi-jackers.

He flexed his muscles, shook himself, and flakes of ice fell from his rubber coat. A covering of thin ice lay over the boat. Jason was running at low speed now, searching the pierheads on his left. Presently he edged in closer, slowed down still more, then swung in sharply, running between two groups of barges. He saw a lantern swinging on the dock and recognized Shifty's face in its glow. He let out a vast, healthy sigh of relief and shut off the engine, gliding smoothly up along the dock.

"YOU GOT it, huh?" Shifty called in a muffled whisper.

"Looks that way," said Jason. "Here! Get this rope and wind it around that bitt."

When the launch was made fast, Jason unlashed the case from the deck and threw one end of the line up to Shifty. The other end he fastened securely about the case, then jumped up to the dock. In this way they hauled it up out of the cockpit and safely on to the dock.

"How's the watchman—potted?" asked Jason.

"Yeah—stewed t' the ears an' sound asleep."

"Well, you keep moving ahead to see if the way's clear. I'll carry this box out on my back. Here—just give me a lift; jack it up so I can get under it." Jason bent, swayed for a moment under the huge case but steadied himself and began moving carefully along the pier. Without any mishap he reached the light truck.

"Easy, now," cautioned Shifty, jumping about excitedly.

With a grunt Jason slid the huge box into the rear of the truck and stood up, brushing his hands together.

"Well, there you are, boy friend," he said. "Take your silks and rugs and beat it. That five hundred was well earned, unlike the dough that you'll get."

Shifty almost broke into a snarl, but checked himself, looking about furtively.

"Did you say anything?" Jason put to him.

"N-no. You goin' back t' your own dock now?"

"Yup. Got to take the bus back. See you again maybe. Don't take any wooden money."

Shifty leered, and Jason, returning along the dock to his boat, reflected that he did not like that smile. He had never seen Shifty smile in quite that manner before.

"Somehow or other—I don't know—I'd like to wring that bird's neck," he mused. "He's such a sniveling hunk of humanity—absolutely no guts at all. Well…."

He shrugged his broad shoulders and jumped down into his boat. As he bent down to look at his engine a flashlight snapped on and a short, blunt automatic was shoved in his face. He fell back with a start and a sharp intake of breath. He could see the man behind the gun wore a mask.

"Shell out, bud!" snapped a hoarse voice.

"Nothing on me, stranger," bit off Jason, his fists clenched.

"Think again. Back up." The man emerged from the cabin as Jason dragged his feet backward.

"No, sir," chuckled Jason harshly, "You're out of luck. I'm dead broke."

"Want me t' pot you?"

"That's up to you."

The stranger ripped out, "No wisecracks! Reach in through your raincoat and fish that jack out of your inside pocket!"

"How do you know what's in my inside pocket?"

"Listen! I'm not stagin' a play, guy!" He stepped forward and jammed his automatic against Jason's chest. "Over your head, those hands."

"You've got me, I guess," drawled Jason.

"Don't I know it!" With his free hand he reached inside Jason's coat and pulled out the packet of bills.

"Where do you buy your masks?" inquired Jason irreverently.

"Don't be funny!" snapped the stranger, backing away. "Now get down in your cabin and stay there till I'm out of sight."

"Look out when you hop to the dock; it's slippery."

"You ain't funny. Down in the cabin. Fast!"

Jason bounded down into the cabin with more speed than the stranger had anticipated. And as he landed he jammed his foot on the self-starter, with the gas well advanced. The engine, still hot from its recent long duty, started with a roar. Quick as a flash Jason threw in the clutch.

The boat lunged ahead, swung away from the dock, lunged back and forth at its hawsers. The stranger was caught midway between the deck and the dock. He missed his jump, clawed wildly, losing his gun, and rebounded back into the cockpit, landing on the back of his head.

Jason shut off the motor and leaped from the cabin as the man was rising, caught him in a terrific jolt on the side of the jaw and sent him sprawling to the deck. He went right after him, caught him by the throat and heaved him erect with one hand. With the other hand he tore away the mask. The man struggled and Jason again flung him savagely to the deck, lunged after him and bent down with doubled fists.

"Get up again, you bum, and I'll knock you into the river!" he hurled at him. "Pass back that money!"

The man thrust the packet of bills back into Jason's hands.

"Now," went on Jason menacingly, "how did you know I had any money on me?"

"Just—just took a chance."

"You're a damned liar!" He gripped the man by the throat. "I know you now. 'Skeets' Sleary, eh? Cough up, boy, or I'll break your neck! Didn't that rotten runt Shifty tell you?"

"Ouch! Leggo! F'r Gawd's sake, you're chok—chok—"

"Who told you? Spit it out!"

"Y-yes—Shifty—"

"He did, eh? Where'd he go with that flivver?"

"Don't—don't know—"

Jason pulled Sleary to his feet and shook him violently. "Yes, you know, and I'll shake hell out of you if you don't spout!"

"S-s-say, y-you're killin' me!"

"Killing you! So you're another yellow rat just like Shifty! Brave as a bulldog when you've got a gun—None of that stuff. I'll shake you apart if you don't tell me where that runt went!"

"Yung's—Chinatown—"

"So-o! All right!"

Jason flung Sleary up on to the dock and leaped after him. He trotted him out to the street.

"Now drop out of sight," he flung at him, and Sleary scuttled off.

Jason ran across the street as a nighthawk taxi drifted out of a dark alley. He hailed it and jumped to the running-board.

"Step on it and drop me at Mott and Pell!" he clipped.

The taxi shot off, swung into Oliver Street, tore through to the New Bowery and then into Mott and skidded to a stop at Pell. Jason jumped out, thrust a bill into the chauffeur's hand and told him to disappear. He was about to dash down Pell Street when he saw a familiar delivery truck turn slowly from Bayard into Mott Street. It was spitting at the exhaust and acting cranky. Jason ran toward it and leaped inside beside Shifty.

"Well, what happened?" he asked.

"Engine trouble. Was stopped back there on East Broadway." Shifty was so nervous he stalled the engine.

"Hurry up and get it started," rumbled Jason. "Tried to double-cross me, eh? Got Sleary to hold me up and then you'd split with him. I'll double-cross you, you dirty little rat! I'll show you just what it means to monkey with me. I still got my five hundred, and you don't get a cent of it. What's more, just for playing that trick on me, you're going to lose whatever else you might have got. *We'll drive back to the river and pitch this damned box overboard!*"

"Oh, no, Buck! Oh-oh-oh, no! You—you don't—don't know—"

"Shut up!" Jason gripped him by the back of the neck and shook him till his teeth rattled.

"I—I can't drive. My nerves is—is unstrung."

"Then I'll drive," asserted Jason.

"But Buck, s"elp me Gawd, you don't—"

"Get out of my way!" barked Jason.

Shifty almost fell to the street. He pranced about, waving his hands frantically, gurgling incoherently.

"Damn you, shut up!" Jason flung at him savagely. "D' you want to wake up the town?"

"Buck—Buck—oh, my Gawd Awmighty—!"

Jason had the motor going and now the truck began to move.

Shifty beat his hands together, jumped up and down, then broke into a run and jumped to the footboard of the moving truck, clutching and striking at the big man's arm, begging him to stop, with prayers and curses. But Jason held him at arm's length. Shifty had tried to double-cross him, and he would make Shifty pay pound for pound. He would get no satisfaction out of battering the little man to a pulp. He weighed twice as much as Shifty and he could break the man's back with one arm if he chose. Jason was one of those raw elemental men who love a fight only when the odds are against themselves. Hence, although he had often remarked a desire to break Shifty's neck, a certain code of ethics, rough but reliable, prevented him from actually committing the act.

Small though Shifty was, he was slippery and troublesome to handle. And Jason, holding him with one hand and the wheel with the other, encountered a little difficulty in turning a corner and jammed the front wheels against the curb. He threw out the clutch and yanked on the brake.

"Listen, Shifty, I might hurt you!" he threatened. "Close your jaw and stop jumping at me like a damned idiot!"

"But Buck, please, f'r Gawd's sake, don't go pitch—"

"Pitch it I am going to, Shifty, right off the nearest dock, and if you don't clamp your face I'll pitch you with it."

There was a sudden commotion in the narrow street. Shifty gasped and held his breath. Jason raised an ear and frowned perplexedly. In a flash he realized that something disastrous was impending. He flung a glance at Shifty, whose face had paled till it was deathly white.

There was the sound of running feet on the soft slush that cluttered the streets and sidewalks.

Jason heaved himself out of the driver's seat and landed in a puddle ankle-deep, his fists clenched, his broad shoulders dropping, his legs spread wide.

From three different directions a gang of men materialized out of the gloom and darkness in this mysterious back-pocket of a great city. Muffled, clipped commands shot back and forth. One man stumbled, plowed headlong into a mound of snow, came up snorting and shaking himself.

Jason's stubborn fighting spirit, never far below the surface, now welled up and asserted itself. He divined that these men had come to take possession of the case of silks. They seemed determined about it, but Jason was just as determined to keep it out of their hands, and he welcomed the brawl with that grand carelessness of odds that so typifies men of his self-willed type. He counted six in all, and he marked them for Chinese gunmen. Ordinarily Chinatown is a peaceful quarter, but things break loose on occasion. And they were breaking wide open now.

Three made a combined rush for Jason. They were armed with short clubs, but he was sure they carried guns, too, to be used as a last resort. Spread-legged, he met the onslaught. He knocked down a hard-driven club with his left arm, and with his right fist, a lump comparable to a chunk of granite, he drove a terrific blow to the nearest man's jaw that carried more sleep-inducing ingredients than an all-night opium party. This man was hit so hard that the back of his head was the first part to strike the ground after his feet left it.

Then the other two were upon Jason, trying to club him on the head. He warded off these blows with his arms, gritting his teeth at the pain, and at the same time began rushing the men backward. From now on he carried the fight. His big hands shot out. He caught one man by the throat, lifted him easily and then with a mighty effort hurled him ten feet away. At the same time he took a glancing blow above the left ear that made his head hum. Instinctively he backed away till his head cleared, knocked away the next blow, and in a new devastating attack tore into his adversary with a crushing array of short-arm jabs that a moment later had the unfortunate man sprawled on his back, senseless.

Jason jumped over him and made for the other three who were trying to start the machine and get away. He was warmed to his task now, just as a motor runs better and smoother after it has been in motion for a while. He wondered only vaguely where Shifty was, what had happened to him. Probably hiding. No matter. He didn't need the yellow-backed rat. He'd smear these birds alone on general principles.

He was essentially a fearless man, a bulldog of a man, disregardful of the odds against him. He packed the kick of a mule in both fists, and he descended upon the remaining trio with such demoralizing aggressiveness that he struck sheer horror to their hearts. They hesitated, helpless, for a brief second, and in that brief second one was draped over the front mudguard, screaming his lungs out. Another fell back, at last drawing his gun. Jason dived for him and pinned his gun-hand as the weapon was half-drawn. With the same movement he picked the man up and heaved him at the other, who had pulled a gun also. Both crashed to the street, groping feebly for their senses.

"Scum!" he spat out, throwing his eyes about.

Then his muscles tautened, and his square, cleft jaw went hard.

ANOTHER GANG was coming pell-mell down the street, and at the head of it he could make out the scrawny figure of Shifty. So the runt had sneaked away for reinforcements! He counted five in all, and he flexed his arms. Let them come. He was in top shape now. He'd fought so long for that case of silks, and he could fight longer still—he felt he could fight till dawn!

Shifty did not lead the attack right up to Jason. He stopped about ten yards away and shouted encouragement to the four Chinese he had recruited from some dark alley.

"Get him, boys! Lam the big stiff! He's got five hundred berries on him. Ha! Ha! I'll fix you, Buck!" snarled Shifty, hopping around with Satanic glee.

One of the men who for five minutes had been lying in a puddle, sat up, blinked, then scampered to his feet and set a wobbly course away from the mêlée.

Jason, instead of waiting for the four men to reach him, bent his shoulders and sailed into them like a battering ram. He was a fighter at heart, and a fighter at heart doesn't wait to be hit. So with Jason. He took the offensive immediately, weaving in, and dropped one man with a right smash between the eyes.

Chinatown certainly was breaking loose. Men came running from all directions, singly or in pairs. Shouts went up, ringing through the crooked, shadowy streets. A police whistle blew shrilly. Black gaping hall doors, disembodied muffled figures. Men met, spoke hurriedly to one another and flew to the center of the activity.

Somehow Jason now found himself standing to one side, unmolested, while a seething mass of yellow men were lambasting one another, screaming, roaring, kicking, clawing. The police whistle blew again, this time imperatively. The mob was deaf to it. The men fought like wildcats, and now knives began to flash and slash with murderous intent. It was a peaceful community gone mad!

"There's only one way I can figure this out," Jason told himself. "It's a Tong war, sure as hell. The first gang that popped up were enemies of the guy that hired Shifty. While I was laying them flat Shifty skint out for *his* bunch. Then one of the guys I pasted must have sneaked off for recruits—and there you are. Boy, oh, boy, what a carnival!"

From the direction of Bayard Street three uniformed policemen came tearing along with drawn clubs. They skidded through the slush into the midst of the brawl and began pounding away with their nightsticks, seeming to enjoy their task immensely. The job was growing in numbers and a split head or two did not seem to damp the general uproar. One of the bluecoats took time to blow his whistle for reinforcements, then promptly felled a boy of China with a neat crack on the point of the chin.

Jason judged that now was the time for him to get away with the truck. The fight had shifted up the street a bit, and no one would pay any particular attention to him. He could not afford to hang around and get in any tangle with the police. He crossed the street boldly, got into the truck, started the engine, backed up a few feet, then made off.

He drove for the dock where he had left his motorboat, and as he drew up before it he heard a quavering voice at hand. He jumped out, went around and found Shifty peering from under the tarpaulin that covered the case of China silk. One of Shifty's eyes was a beautiful shade of blue-black, and his jaw was swollen and somewhat out of true.

Jason jammed his hands to his hips. "Well, what the hell are you doing here?" he bit off.

"I—I—they were stampin' all over me, Buck. I crawled away an' hid here."

"A fine mess you are! A fine figure of a man! Tell the truth, Shifty, I don't know what to do with you. Honest, I don't. I feel like taking you in my hands and breaking you in two. But hell, it would be cruelty to animals. You're yellow; you haven't guts enough to fill a thimble! And you're the dirtiest double-cross artist I ever run across. Shifty, will you for God's sake fade away before I *do* accidentally twist your head off!"

Shifty crawled painfully out of the truck, dropped to the street and shrank back, fidgeting with his fingers and grimacing grotesquely as he struggled for words.

Jason made a gesture of profound disgust and threw the tarpaulin clear of the case.

"Buck," croaked Shifty. "Buck, you ain't goin' t' pitch it overboard!"

"You heard me the first time, little one."

"Buck, f'r Gawd's sake, listen t' reason—"

Jason swiveled about savagely, doubling a fist. "Damn you, get out of here! Get out before I poke you so hard—"

"But, Buck, you can't pitch it over! You can't—can't! There ain't no silks in it, Buck, there ain't no silks!"

"What? What's that?" He had Shifty by the collar in a vice-like grip.

"There—there ain't no—no silks, Buck. There's a man—a man—a high-caste Chink. That fight—Yung Chau's boy must ha' squealed t' the other Tong."

Jason shook him violently. "What! There is a Chink in this case! Good Lord! A Chink! I've smuggled in a Chink!" He held Shifty at arm's length, and his eyes narrowed. "All right, I won't pitch it overboard. I've got a better idea. Now you blow and don't show your face around me again. You've double-crossed me all around, and you've lost everything. I'm not heavy on smuggling Chinks—don't cotton to the idea at all. But it's done now and I'm not going to yap about it. Get!" He spun Shifty away, and the little man, catching his balance with an effort, took to his heels and disappeared in the graying dusk of early dawn.

Jason, muttering to himself, got the big case on his back and made his cautious way out on the pier to his launch. He tied a rope about it and lowered it into the cockpit, then jumped down and started the engine.

Slowly he oozed away from the dock, passed between two rows of barges and, clearing the pierhead line, pointed the boat's

nose upstream. Fifteen minutes later he tied up at an unfrequented jetty.

Satisfied that no one was in sight, he brought a handful of
tools from the cabin and attacked the lid on the case. Only now
did he notice a number of holes bored in the sides. He worked
quickly, fighting against time.

When the lid finally came off there was a huddled, blanket-
swathed form that immediately began to utter sounds which
Jason did not understand. However, he leaned down and pulled
out a very cold, very cramped, very voluble man of China, and
carried him hastily down into the cabin, blanket and all. He
propped him on one of two bunks and gave him a stimulant,
took one himself and chafed his hands vigorously.

"Well, everybody's had a fine time but you, China Silk," he
chuckled. He chuckled again, repeating, humorously, "China
Silk!"

Then by gestures he indicated that China Silk was to remain
on the bunk and be very quiet. Following this bit of pantomime
he removed his raincoat, took another drink, locked China Silk
in the cabin and left the boat.

Half an hour later he left a taxi near Pell Street and strode
vigorously for a short block. Here he entered a narrow hallway,
went up a staircase two steps at a time and pounded on a door
at the top. The door opened on a crack, and before the person
on the other side could make a sound Jason heaved his way in
after the manner of a steam-roller and booted it shut with a
heel. The servant was just regaining his balance.

Jason clipped, "Where's Yung Chau? Trot him out till I talk
business with him."

"No home," clicked the servant.

"Can that chatter! I'm not a dick. I want to do business with
the boss. Mention silk to him—tell him I've got it."

The boy hesitated for a moment, then padded away into
another room. Jason meanwhile parked himself in a luxurious
chair, stuffed his pipe and smoked hungrily.

A few moments later the curtains parted and Yung Chau, an impassive hulk of Oriental guile, entered. He stood just inside the doorway with his hands folded on his paunch and stared dispassionately at his visitor.

Jason, taking his pipe from his mouth, surged to his feet and stood spread-legged, his level eyes cutting into Yung Chau's.

"Listen," he said. "I've got the Chink I smuggled in last night under the impression I was handling silks and rugs. I've got him and I've got to do something with him. I can't throw him overboard. I can't run him back to the *Lady Fair* in broad daylight. So I've got to hand him over to you."

Yung's eyes brightened. "Ah, yes! It is good of you."

"But wait a minute. I'm not Santa Claus. I want five hundred spot cash for my trouble."

"But sir, did you not receive—"

"I did. But that was for shooting in silks. *This* is for saving the neck of your boy friend. Come across or I'll draw the last straw by shipping him to the Immigration Office."

Yung Chau seemed in distress. He tapped his lip meditatively with an immaculate finger. Then he sighed.

"Well, there is no alternative for me," he admitted. "Five hundred upon delivery."

"Five hundred right now!" corrected Jason. "And another thing. I don't bring him here. I've got him safe and sound. You give me one of your men. We'll take a taxi to this place. I'll hand over your world traveler to this man and they'll shoot back in another taxi. That, mister, or nothing."

"But—"

"Save your breath. Do I or do I not get the five hundred now?"

"Um— You are sure the man is safe?"

"I told you that once. Why go over it? Snap to life!"

"I must submit to your plans," bowed Yung Chau with gleaming eyes. He left the room for a few moments and returned with a packet of bills. Jason counted them and stowed them away. Another Chinese, dressed for the street, entered.

"This man will go with you," said Yung Chau.

"Come on, then," clipped Jason, and rolled out without another word.

Back on his boat, he unlocked the cabin and hauled out the contraband Chinese. The man he had brought along immediately took the stranger's hand and began to get off a clacking line of talk. The stranger gasped, grinned, and then started to out-talk the other so much that Jason, standing to one side, stepped over and tapped him on the shoulder.

"Shut up!" he said; and to the other, "All right, boy, don't hang around here. Be on your way. Talk it over with little China Silk when you get home. Savvy? All right, then shuffle along!"

They hurried off, still clacking excitedly.

Jason swung down into his cabin, chuckling in his deep throat. He sat down on one of the bunks, pulled out the two packets of five hundred each and smacked them across his knee, breaking into a broad grin.

"Ho! Ho! China Silk at a thousand a case!" he exclaimed to himself. "Not so bad. But, fact is, I think I'll stick to Scotch at a hundred a case hereafter. But a thousand a case! Baby!..."

He shook with silent mirth.

WHILE IN a mean room, in a mean house, in a mean street, a scrawny wisp of a man sat hunched at a dirty table. He reached for the gin bottle, tilted it over a glass, but not a drop flowed out. It was empty.

With a savage, petulant snarl, he gripped the bottle by the neck and smashed it to smithereens against the wall. Then he beat on the table with meager, puny fists.

"Damn Buck Jason!" he choked, and buried his face in his arms on the rum-stained table.

Hounds of Darkness

The New York waterfront—a no-man's land between the city's teeming streets and the twin rivers, the harbor, the lower bays, the broad Atlantic beyond. It is a setting for rough, strong men of the sea, for the scum of many lands, for slinking hounds of darkness.

OUTSIDE IT was cold, bitter, cheerless. Rain and sleet whipped vindictively out of the black void, roaring against the huge metal warehouses. Box-like lighters lunged about drunkenly, bludgeoning one another with dull, groaning blows, while the water, lashed to a white froth, snarled and bellowed among the piles that supported the long, dark piers.

At one of the pierheads was a window frame of yellow light, and clouds of dark smoke issuing from a lean pipe-like chimney were caught up and gobbled by the wind and the rain. Inside there was warmth, for a small, potbellied stove glowed cheerily. The room was small, square, with a battered roll-top desk against one wall, several scarred chairs, and an array of time-yellowed harbor maps on the walls.

Two men sat facing each other. Between them was an up-ended box, and on this box was a faded checker-board. Both smoked pipes, and both appeared deep in thought. One was an old man badly in need of a shave, with a straggly mustache that hid his mouth. His eyes were pale, washed-out, kindly; his nose was a weather-beaten beak.

The other man was younger—say thirty-odd—and gazed intently at the few remaining checkers with eyes that glinted under the light like chips of blue steel. A whale of a man, too, big and thick in the shoulders, straight-necked, firm-mouthed, aggressive, with bulging muscle-thews on his lower jaw. The blue woolen shirt he wore was open at the throat, and the sleeves were rolled up, revealing corded but quite hairless arms.

Taking his pipe from his mouth, he scratched his chin musingly with the stem, then placed it between his teeth again and grunted. He puffed slowly, thoughtfully, letting the smoke drift lazily from his wide nostrils. Presently, after another grunt, he sat back and slapped his palms to his knees.

"Well, Danny, I guess you pick up the marbles," he said, with a slow grin. "You win again, dammit!"

"Why, sure," droned Old Danny, chuckling through his pipe. "Take ye that long t' find out?"

"Well, you see, old timer, I was trying to think of a way to flimflam you."

"Aw, go 'way wit' ye! Ye may be able to flimflam the harbor patrol an' hi-jackers an' sich, but when it comes t' playin' checkers, why, Lor' bless my soul, I never did see such a gosh-awful rotten player."

Buck Jason laughed with rough good nature. "Now, I guess you're right there, Danny. But, then, you've been playing checkers for fifty years or more. Now when it comes to playing hide-and-seek with wise-acting hi-jackers—"

"Like I says, there ain't none like ye, Buck," cut in Old Danny, as he took a tobacco shot at the coal-scuttle and missed by a foot. "Like I says many times, when it comes t' such tricks why, man, ye're a cross between a slipp'ry eel an' a—a—a—well, a ghost or so'thin'. Um—how about another, game?"

"No, Danny. I've had enough. I'm licked." He put up his hands. Then he rose and went to the window, looking out. "Some night, old timer! Baby! Look at those barges clout each other! Ho! Bet you don't see any harbor patrol out tonight. No hi-jackers, either."

"Um. 'S funny y' ain't out yerself, Buck. Gettin' cold feet, maybe, huh?"

" 'S I suppose… *not!*" chortled Jason. "Say, old timer, the only time you'll find my feet cold is when the rest of me is cold. You know, when I'm the sole occupant of a box six feet long. Cripes. I don't suppose I'd be cold for long at that. All depends on how long it takes a chum to navigate the crooked road from here to hell. Ho!"

Old Danny raised his hand. "Sh! Such talk, Buck!"

"What do you mean—talk?" came back Jason. "You don't think for a moment that I've got any chance of getting booked for the pearly gates, do you? Ho! I should say not. Old boy, my outbound ticket'll read like this: 'Hell; one way trip.' I've got no illusions—not a damned one."

"Ah-r-r, ye talk like an idjit! Only thing, Buck, I wish ye'd be leavin' the river soon. Some one o' these nights a gang o' hi-jacks is goin' t' get ye in a corner an' riddle ye clean."

"You think so, eh? Think again, old timer. The hi-jack that monkeys with me generally gets the dirty end of the situation. Why, I'm not afraid of any blue-blazin' son of a hi-jacking pup that ever lived."

"Anyhow, Buck, if I was you I'd be packin' a gun," said Danny.

"Gun me eye! I never carry arms, Danny, and that's just why I'm ahead of the game. Shoot one of those birds and get sent up the river? I should say not! I'm not so dumb. They're not worth it."

"Well..." Old Danny shrugged his shoulders and got up. "Guess I'll be makin' the rounds." He took down his black raincoat from a peg on the wall and put it on slowly. Pretty old, Danny, and not as fast as he used to be. He was one of the very few men whom Jason called friend, for Jason was primarily a lone wolf, playing a lone hand, and careful of whom he trusted. And though they were vastly dissimilar, the two men, one an old watchman, the other owner of a sleek black motorboat whose actions were not entirely within the law as it is written, had come to understand each other.

"Won't be long, Buck," said Old Danny. "Keep an eye on that there fire till I get back."

Time-clock in hand, he shuffled across the room, opened the door and went out slowly.

"Getting slower on his feet every day," Jason mused, standing spread-legged before the stove. "H'm."

He went over to the window again. The storm was still in mid-career. The barges still rocked and thumped; the derrick of a steam lighter swayed back and forth mightily. Sleet cut down through the darkness, gleaming under the few dock-lights. The tortured water rumbled among the barges and beneath the piers like a restless giant. Ice formed everywhere—on the docks, on the barges, on the cables. A bitter, brutal night, dangerous for nocturnal tugs and the men who worked them. Sleet that rasped and clawed at a man's face. Frozen, ice-caked hawsers that tore at a man's hands. Slippery decks. Slippery docks.

"Wonder if my boat's all right," thought Jason. "Better take a look, anyhow."

Suiting the action to the thought, he shrugged into a heavy blue sweater, over which he drew his black rubber coat. Taking a look at the fire, he threw in a few lumps of soft coal, slapped on his sou'wester and rolled out. Walking across the huge warehouse, he reached a door which he slid open, and then stood on the open pier where the wind and sleet clattered and whistled against his big bulk.

He lowered his head and strode out on the open extension, a narrow dock lined on either side with thumping barges that strained at their hawsers. He found his motorboat tossing and dipping but still safe at her lines. At intervals on her black hull he had fastened old automobile tires, to save her planks from unnecessary scars and possible injury that might result from too severe contact with the dock. The sleek little craft, veteran of many a dark night on the East or the North River, or perhaps on New York Bay, still appeared shipshape. The trunk-cabin protected her powerful engine and a tarpaulin kept her cockpit dry.

"Guess she'll weather it," Jason remarked half aloud.

He flung his gaze out at the beshrouded river. Faintly he could see the riverfront lights of New Jersey. A few green and red lights marked the passage of cautious, slow-moving tugs or ferries. Not much traffic, though. Probably a few railroad floats, carrying carloads of express freight, forced to make a schedule despite the wrath of the night. And then an indomitable ferryboat—probably a West Shore tub, bound to make train connections.

After a moment Jason turned and hurried back toward the watchman's cubby-hole. It would be warm and cheerful there. Come to think of it, maybe he *would* play another game of checkers with Old Danny. Maybe he'd trim the old boy this time. The wind was at his rear, flapping and clapping the wide skirts of his coat, rattling the harsh sleet against his back.

He slid open the door leading into the warehouse, closed it securely and, shaking the ice from his coat, strode across to the room. He thrust open the door, chuckling to himself at thought of trimming Old Danny, and walked straight into the muzzle of an automatic held in the hand of a masked man.

"Up, buddy!" snarled the stranger.

Jason's eyes turned to steel and an oath snapped through his teeth before he clenched them. But his hands went up—slowly.

"Now boot that door shut," added the man with the gun.

Jason kicked shut the door.

The man took a few steps backward and waved his gun toward one of the chairs. "Now you can park for a while."

"I'll stand," bit off Jason.

"Suit yourself. Only keep your hands up."

"If you think I'm the watchman—"

"Nobody thinks you're a watchman, guy. I know who you are. Never mind poppin' off."

Jason's eyes narrowed, and one corner of his mouth bent down harshly. "What's your game, Bat?"

The other drew in his breath sharply.

Jason said, "Sure, I know you. Take off the rag."

"Take off hell!" rasped the gunman. "And close your face."

"Make me, you bum!" Jason came back with a growl.

"Cut that stuff, guy! Kinder sore because somebody else horned in on your game, eh?"

"Listen to me, you dirty louse! Don't try to class me with the crowd you run with. The whole damned lot of you are rotten. I'd sure like to know what you're up to. But I'm running no game here and you're not horning in on me. Somebody's been giving you a bum steer, Bat."

"That so? Nemmine, though. Watch what happens after."

"You're dumb, Bat! You're not playing wise by rubbing me on the wrong side at all. I don't care what happens."

"You talk big for a man with a gun in his mug."

There were three raps on the door. Bat, tensing, waved Jason to the other side of the room and edged sidewise to the door.

"All right, come in," he said.

The door opened, and two masked men, each carrying a revolver equipped with a silencer, entered. They wore mackinaws, soggy and dripping, and pools of water formed where they stood.

"O.K.," muttered one.

"Everyt'ing worked out neat so far, boss," supplemented the other.

Bat, with his eyes and gun still on Jason, spoke to his men in sotto voce. "Where's the rest o' the gang?"

"All waitin' ready," replied the first speaker. "Watchman put up a fight an' we hadder give him the works. Tried t' blow his whistle, too."

"What's that?" barked Jason, his hands knotting.

Bat said, "Nothing much. They just tell me the watchman fell on the ice an' rolled overboard. Tough on the watchman, ain't it?"

"Damn your souls!" swore Jason, starting forward.

Three guns swung in line for his chest and he brought up sharply, his eyes burning with a cold, deadly fire.

"You dirty, filthy, lousy bilge-rats!" he rasped. "That old man was a friend of mine."

"Can it!" barked Bat. "And get a move on! We ain't got all night."

One of the trio got behind Jason and jabbed a gun in the small of his back. Another stood by the door. Bat went out first, backward, with his automatic leveled at Jason's heart. Jason, muttering in the depths of his throat, scowling his black hatred of these raw killers, was none the less forced, in the name of common sense, to put up no physical argument—for the present, at least.

He knew the leader, if not the rest of the wolves. Bat Shane, river pirate, hi-jacker extraordinary, with several prison sentences behind him and a certain municipal judge aching to send him to the chair on his next offense. This Shane possessed no super-intelligence. He had nerve of a kind engendered by drugs. He was a "cokey," and had killed more men than he could remember. He had collected into his fold the scum of the city streets and the jetsam of the waterfront, and every man obeyed him or was dropped into the river with a stone tied to his neck. He sent one of his gang to bump off a man, and if the man he sent contracted cold feet or a weak heart another of the gang was sent to get *him*. The method was simple, fiendish and yet effective. A man who squealed was riddled in some dark alley in less time than it takes to tell it. The law of the gun and of Bat Shane were one and the same.

Jason had crossed him before, but for some singular reason Shane had not elected to do away with him. Whatever he was up to now, mused Jason, was something on a large scale. Else why all the men? Besides the two roughnecks who had joined Shane in the watchman's room, there were six more who joined them as they, along with Jason and Bat, crossed the dim interior of the warehouse.

A sliding door was open, and through this they all passed out on to an open passageway that ran alongside the huge building. Other forms, wrapped in overcoats or shining raincoats, materialized out of the gloom, and muffled questions and answers went around. The gang hurried along the passageway out to the open pierhead, where a steam lighter hissed mildly and groaned at her hawsers. Moving shapes were on this, too.

Jason frowned perplexedly. Revolvers poked constantly in his ribs. The men began hopping from the dock to the lighter. He himself was thrust forward and had to jump quickly to prevent a bad tumble. Ice crackled under his boots. Sleet drove down at a slant, swishing against the rubber coats of the men who moved hurriedly, with drawn guns. The big derricks swayed and pulleys clanked, and ice-caked cables crackled.

The pilot-house and engine room were well aft, leaving a long broad sweep of deck for cargo. This deck, however, was empty of any cargo at present. Muffled figures, masked or with handkerchiefs across their faces, stood here and there singly or in groups. One or two carried sawed-off shotguns. Bat Shane, who now stood facing Jason, motioned four men to draw closer.

"Now get me, you guys," he rasped, shaking his pistol at them. "You four keep close t' this bird. The four o' you are detailed to watch him. I'll be near most o' the time, but if I happen t' stroll away, it ain't a sign for you t' follow. If this guy escapes or bulls things, I'll pot you guys personally. Get me?"

"We got yuh, boss," came the muttered reply.

Bat Shane looked at Jason. "An' you do as you're told or you'll get the works. There's nineteen men here, an' none o' them was raised in a boy scout camp. The first bum move you make you get a bad case o' blood poison by lead. Follow me."

Jason was prodded aft by the four who had been detailed to guard him with their own lives at stake if he got away. At the foot of the ladder leading to the pilot-house, he caught a glimpse of the engine room, with a gray-haired engineer getting up steam while three masked men covered him with guns.

Bat Shane, cackling at the sight, continued past and led the way up the ladder to the pilot-house. Jason, following, caught a fleeting glimpse of the craft's name as he entered the house. It was *Josephine Lee*, and, knowing what he did of river shipping, he placed it as one of three such craft, half-lighter, half-tug, that belonged to the William C. Lee Lighterage Company.

Then Bat Shane and his hounds of darkness were stealing it for—what purpose? Something big, to be sure; something, some venture, that Shane's fleet of motorboats could not handle. In the pilot-house there was a man bound and gagged and lying on the floor. He was a deckhand of the tug and Jason gathered from the brief remarks among the river pirates that he and the engineer had been playing a game of two-handed pinochle below, and were the only men of the crew aboard.

Bat Shane was saying: "Here's the idea, Jason. I know that some years ago you uster work on a tug. Well, scrape your memory an' see how good you can handle this bathtub. I know too that you're pretty well acquainted with the channels and the creeks clean out to Montauk Point. You'll need t' know tonight or get a slug in your guts."

"D' you expect to get away with a job like this, Bat?" Jason put to him. "You'll have every patrol boat in the harbor on you."

"That's my business, guy. Just you take that wheel. The course until further notice is the Statue of Liberty. Now strut your stuff."

Jason looked around him. There was Shane with a gun. There were four others surrounding him, and each had a gun, and each was a deadly gun, with a deadly man behind it. He could do nothing yet but obey. Old Danny had met with sudden death, brutally and mercilessly dealt, and was now deep in the icy waters of the river. And he had intended playing another game of checkers with Old Danny! By running amuck and getting his own body riddled he would not avenge Danny. These hounds must pay pound for pound, not only for their raw, wanton slaughter of the feeble old man, but for getting Jason into a hole like this.

Jason was not a sentimental man. The rough, risky life he led would not allow it. He was made of tough fibre. Stealing a tugboat did not shock him in the least. Hi-jackers as hi-jackers alone were to be expected. But what made him boil inwardly was the rank brutality and lack of sportsmanship that existed among these river pirates. They never attacked unless they were perfectly sure of outnumbering their prey two to one or more. They shot to kill on sight and caught a man from behind every time and always in the dark.

"Well, you bums have got me this time," Jason admitted.

"Sure we have," said Bat Shane, "Now git goin'. Lights are up for a while. We'll douse 'em later. The engineer is ready."

Jason took the wheel and gave brief instructions to the engineer through the speaking tube. After a moment he gave the bells and the propeller began to churn the water. The boat, her hawsers cast loose, began to move out into the channel.

Rain and sleet encrusted the pilot-house windows so thickly that visibility became impossible, and Jason had to drop one window. The wind rushed into the little house, and the men behind him grumbled and stamped their feet to keep warm. Down on the deck below he could see groups of rivermen huddled against the bulwarks. The tide was almost at high-water mark and still coming in, and as the boat headed south white spume broke over her blunt bow and foamed on the deck.

He had orders to make for the Statue of Liberty. What wild scheme was under way he did not know. But somehow, some time later, he must turn the tables on these hounds. He knew very well that his life was at stake; divined, too, that when his services as pilot were no longer required he would be done away with—murdered, thrown overside. For Bat Shane knew that if Jason were to go free he would stage a comeback at a later date.

Jason was pounding thought upon thought through his brain as he guided the broad, ungainly boat down the river. A squat tug with a tow of two railroad floats passed him on the way north. Whistles blew here and there in the stormy murk, some shrill and petulant, others deep and peremptory. He peered intently ahead, trying to place the various warnings, answering blasts from the darkness with his own deep-toned whistle. Once he slowed down, to reassure himself of his own position and that of another craft that was blowing almost continuously. Finally a tug with a tow appeared on his starboard bow, whistles were exchanged satisfactorily, and Jason rang for more speed.

Soon Liberty's light shone dead ahead, and a little later Jason could make out its dim, shadowy form.

"Keep headin' like you are till I say different," ordered Shane.

Jason made no reply, but kept on his course. Ice covered his raincoat, and his face gleamed wet with ice-particles. Wave after wave broke over the bow, slithering across the deck like froth and then freezing.

"Now," said Shane, "we douse the lights. You know about 'em more than these guys, Jason, so you go out an' douse them. Slow down an' I'll take the wheel. An' remember. These four guys go out with you, an' their guns ain't carried for show, if you don't know."

Jason rang for reduced speed and, with the four guards surrounding him, went out and extinguished the running lights and lowered the single white light from aloft, all of which were old-fashioned oil-burners. This done, he was steered back into the pilot-house, where he again took the wheel and rang for more speed.

"Now you c'n see a ship's riding lights," went on Shane. "You can't see the ship yet but you see her lights. Well, sneak up under her lee bow."

Jason kept on, and soon he could make out vaguely the black hull of a low, rakish vessel riding at anchor. On such a night there doubtlessly would be no one on deck, and if there was a man stationed on the bridge he would, probably, be having a pipe or a snooze in the warmth of the chart-room.

Now Jason began to see what Bat Shane and his crew were up to. Piracy—nothing less. The fact that the lights had been doused was indication enough that the tug's mission was not by any chance a friendly one.

Jason was not appalled at this. Shady deeds under cover of darkness were not new to him. He even went so far as to regard this venture with mild amusement. No one but that drug-soaked assassin Bat Shane, could have concocted such a wild scheme. There would be blood shed here tonight, he guessed. Looking again at the knot of men by the hoisting mechanism, he saw that individual lengths of rope, each with a loop at the loose end, were being fastened to the hook on the derrick-cable. Of these ropes he counted six, and even as he looked he saw that the men were fitting their feet in the loops.

Meanwhile he was drawing nearer to the anchored ship, and soon he was in the shadow of her clipper bow. He could see no signs of life aboard the vessel, and now he heard below him the steam-winch in action and the cable of the derrick snapping and clanking as it grew taut.

"Not too close," came Shane's voice. "Just so we can raise that line aboard."

Jason saw the idea now. The steam-winch began to labor. Six men, all armed, had placed their feet in the rope-loops suspended from the hook at the end of the cable and gripped with gloved hands the cable itself. Now suddenly the winch labored under a strain, the boom lifted and the six men, holding on grimly, were hoisted from the deck of the tug, swung high and then over the bulwarks of the vessel, where they were lowered upon the forward well-deck. A moment later the boom swung back, and dropped its hook and rope lengths back aboard the tug.

"Ha!" chuckled Bat Shane. "This is easy. All with silencers."

Six more men, attaching themselves to the end of the cable, were lifted up and swung aboard the vessel.

"Now," said Shane, "I'll leave you with these four guys. Watch this, big boy, and learn a lesson from a man that knows. And don't get ambitious."

With that Bat Shane laughed hollowly and left the pilot-house.

Jason chuckled—an intimate sort of chuckle—and looked up at the vessel. He could not, of course, see what was taking place on her decks. But he heard a fusillade of shots—these apparently from the officers of the vessel, for the pirates carried guns equipped with silencers. Mingled with the noises of wind and sleet and sloshing waves, he heard hoarse shouts. No blast of distress had yet been sounded by the vessel, and Jason concluded that Shane's men had things well in hand.

Ten minutes passed quickly, and now there were no more shots, no more cries. Presently one of the pirates, now possessed of a megaphone, appeared at the rail and shouted down to Shane, who was by the winch.

"O.K., boss. We got the hull damn crew locked in the fo'c's'le, an' the skipper an' officers are bottled up in the skipper's room. We got possession of the engine room an' the wireless right off, so no call f'r help's been sent. Two-hundred-fifty cases in the for'ard hold. We'll pitch down two lines f'r you t' make fast while we unload. We only lost one guy. Ship here lost three. Let's have the derrick."

Bat Shane shouted: "All right," and turned to the man at the winch. The boom swung up and the cable was dropped aboard the vessel. Shane left the deck and came into the pilot-house.

Meanwhile two lines were cast from the ship and made fast to a forward and after bitt aboard the tug.

Shane said: "Just keep your engine goin' slow now so we stand off a little from that scow. There y' are! Easy, huh? Pretty work, huh? Now we unload two-hundred-fifty cases o' rye, Scotch, champagne, an' what have you. Rum f'r St. Johns! Ha-ha! She had t' get a Customs permit to stay in port until she's unloaded a shipment o' sugar from Matanzas. Y' see, I got a friend in the Customs, an' I was wised about the whole business. Pays, huh, t' know. Was wised when the permit was issued. Mull over that, big boy, an' grow small."

"Yes, Bat, you sure are top-dog right now," admitted Jason.

"An' I'm always top-dog, guy. You'll find out before the night's through. I got you just where I want you."

Jason looked around at his guardians. "Huh, I don't doubt that. But I notice you need four armed bums to do it."

"That's all right. Why, say, if you was wise you'd have tried to hook up with me instead of lone-wolfin' in your dinky little tub."

"Bat, I'd much prefer hooking up with a snake. What you make you've got to split with your men. I split with nobody and I trust nobody. Hook up with you? Not by a damned sight. What's more, I'm no killer. There's no blood on my hands. In my eyes, Bat, you're nothing but a hunk of scum on the river."

Shane leaned forward, baring yellow teeth. "You'll eat them words, big boy, an' they'll choke you!"

Jason gave a short, grim laugh and spat out through the window.

Bat Shane banged out of the pilot-house and went down to watch the first load come aboard. Ten cases came down in the first batch, and two men with them. Working quickly, these two stacked the cases and the boom swung up and back aboard the vessel.

Jason leaned out of the window, smoking his pipe and watching with mild interest the unlawful proceedings. The men worked quickly, frantically, and the derrick creaked, rattled, and swayed, and the steam-winch snorted, pounded and roared. Meanwhile the wind still whistled and flung sheets of lacerating sleet out of the gloom above, and the deck below was coated with ice upon which a man trod at his peril.

An hour passed, and then another hour, and Jason saw by his watch that it was half-past one in the morning. Ten or fifteen minutes later the last of the cases was lowered, and then the cable returned to the vessel twice to bring back the men that had boarded her. They returned chuckling and boisterous, but Shane silenced them with a few crisp words. Following this he came up to the pilot-house.

"Now, *captain*," he sneered, "you can pull away. You hit for the Narrows, an' stay to windward of Governor's Island. Then you make for Sheepshead Bay, keepin' well off the point, go down past Coney an' raise Canarsie. An' the first hint I get of you tryin' to hit a rock I'll blow your brains out!"

"Be right in your line, wouldn't it?"

"No wise-cracks, either. Get goin'."

Jason chuckled briefly and signaled the engine room. The boat began to move off away from the ransacked vessel, and Jason, once clear, swung the wheel over and plowed into the wind and waves that pounded in from the sea.

Circumstances had indeed placed him in a grave situation. His only salvation now would be an inquisitive patrol boat. On other nights, and under other circumstances, a patrol boat would have meant just the opposite to him. But circumstances alter cases, and tonight he was hoping for, instead of against, the appearance of a patrol.

Tonight he was a champion of the law. Tonight he would help the law if he had the chance. This was not because he held any great affection for it. Necessity demanded that for one night he uphold the law. It was, to say the least, ironical. Buck Jason ready to join arms with the harbor police! But he had not forgotten Old Danny, and the watchman's cruel end. He was, in spite of himself, bound to stick on the side of the law for tonight at least.

Steadily he drove the tug toward the Narrows, while the waves became rougher and broke regularly over the blunt prow. Dimly on his left now he could see the lights of Bay Ridge, and presently these passed from sight over the port quarter, and he was plugging through the Narrows.

Now the boat pitched and lunged and swayed from side to side, shipping sea after sea as she plunged stubbornly into the bigger rollers that rumbled in from Sandy Hook. All the men left the deck and crowded into the engine room or any available space below. Jason, rocking on his feet easily with the motion, was still thinking hard. Somehow he must turn the tables, and turn them before he brought this boat to anchor off the Canarsie marshes. To wreck it would be foolhardy. Neither he nor Old Danny would be revenged. These wolves must be made to pay pound for pound, not only for Danny's death, but for trying to make a fall guy out of himself.

Jason was a man who usually relied on brute strength to carry him through. But he had brains, too, and resourcefulness, and tonight brains and resourcefulness must take the place of brute strength. Though he relished a brawl now and then, he knew when a brawl would be futile. Tonight it was—above all other nights. With five guns at his back and a dozen or more of cutthroats below, not even a giant could win out. And he must win.

Bat Shane spoke again: "Keep well off the point, remember. Stay out in the channel. An' no monkey-business when you go in Jamaica Bay. We're goin' to run into a creek near Sands Bay, and there'll be trucks to cart away the stuff. When the tide goes out this dreadnaught 'll be high an' dry. You know Sands Bay? Well, that's where you head for."

Jason thought for a moment, then leaned out of the pilot window and looked about.

"Look here," he said. "If I'm going to run broad in the channel I want some lights up. We'll be right in the path of the coast boats, and those babies travel fast."

"Lights me eye!" clipped Shane.

"You poor fool!" came back Jason. "We'll be cut down in no time. What's more, if a spotlight picks you up out here without lights you'll have the whole dry navy on you. What do you think wireless was invented for?"

"Well, I'm damned sure *I'm* not goin' to go out an' bother with the lights," replied Shane. "An' those guys I got below don't know the first thing about them. An' these four ain't ever seen a ship until last week. They're gentlemen from the wide open spaces o' the West."

Jason grumbled and took a few turns on the wheel, peering ahead cautiously. "Soon now you'll see those sea flyers coming up out of nowhere. Well, you'll lose your rum, mister, so it'll be your own little swan song if we're hit."

Bat Shane peered ahead too, and then said, "Well, if you know so much, put 'em out yourself. But these four guys go out with you an' watch you. Guess I can hold the wheel till you come in. But make it snappy."

"Why the hell don't you truck a couple of sailors with you?" muttered Jason. Then: "Well, I guess I'll have to. Here, take the wheel, then, and keep bearing gently to the right till I get back. If you don't you'll get the drift and come inshore too close for comfort." He swung around and looked at the inevitable four. "Come on, you gunmen. Maybe Bat thinks I'll jump overboard. What a chance!"

One of the gunmen went out first and the other three crowded close behind Jason as he left the pilot-house and gathered up the lanterns. It was too windy there in the open to strike a match, so Jason carried the lamps back into the pilot-house while the four gunmen watched him like so many hawks.

Jason worked quickly, and a few minutes later went out again with the lighted lanterns. Hard at his heels hung the four. Running up the white light, he stood for a moment braced against the driving wind and peering ahead. Sure enough, one of the speedy express steamers was plowing out of the murk beyond. He'd have to hurry and get back at the wheel. Picking up the port and starboard lights, he hustled to the port box and, leaning down, fastened one of the lights in place. This done, he hastily ran over to the starboard box and clamped the remaining light there.

Standing up, he looked quizzically at his four guards for a brief moment, then strode back for the pilot-house and entered.

"Cripes, you took long enough!" snapped Bat Shane. "Look at that ship zoomin' down—"

"Yes, look at it," rumbled Jason, taking the wheel. "See her giving us a little room now. Without those lights we'd be knocked clear to Coney Island."

He gripped the wheel with rugged hands, leaning forward while the swift vessel loomed on his starboard bow, flinging away fountains of spray as her sharp prow cleaved the dark, foam-flecked waters. She slid past the tug like a sleek white bird, a-glitter with many lights, with her green running light distinct from them all.

If she had come up out of the blackness rapidly, her departure into the blackness again was no less rapid. Jason threw a glance after her diminishing lights and then swung his eye across the channel to the distant lights of Manhattan Beach. Dead ahead, behind the wall of night, lay Rockaway Point, which he would raise before swinging in for Jamaica Bay.

The mournful voice of a channel buoy reached him dully from the gloom, and he slowed down, proceeding at a cautious rate of speed. Already the stacked cases of liquor were covered with ice, and the bulwarks were white and hoary. Presently Jason located the buoy and signaled the engine room for more speed. A little later a swift, racy white liner came tearing out of the night. She passed very close to the tug, and Jason, leaning out of the window and looking up, saw a man on the bridge motioning and shouting through a megaphone.

"What'd he say?" asked Bat Shane.

"Didn't get it," replied Jason. "Just saying hello, I guess."

The tug lumbered on, still shipping an occasional sea, still rolling and pitching. And presently Jason, peering intently ahead, raised Rockaway Point, and remarked it. Bat Shane cackled with delight and rubbed his chilled hands together. The inevitable four grunted among themselves. Jason, scanning the channel, seemed disappointed over something.

Swinging in now toward Jamaica Bay the waves broke less frequently over the bow, for the arm of land that extends peninsula-like from Far Rockaway Point, was presently to windward, breaking the force of the open sea. Still Jason kept peering about with restless eyes while he drove the tug farther into the bay, with little islands looming on either side.

"Ah," Bat Shane was gloating. "Some trick, I'll say. Soon we'll have this old barge up a creek where nobody ever goes. Yes, big boy, you may know how to steer a tub around these parts, but when it comes to brains, a clever trick, an' strategy, you got to admit you ain't in it with yours truly."

Jason made no reply; he was too busy navigating through a narrow channel.

Shane was about to continue enumerating his qualities when a blinding searchlight suddenly appeared on the starboard bow. It had flashed on so suddenly, so mysteriously, that Shane almost choked with surprise. The four guards swore loudly, and Jason clamped his jaw. Below there was a stir among the men and some ran out on deck. Stark and naked the tug moved under the blinding glare of the searchlight. And now the searchlight began to move, growing larger, sweeping back and forth and settling again on the tug.

"What the hell can that be?" bit off Bat Shane.

"Bearin' down on us," offered one of the men.

Shane spun on Jason. "You drive her, guy! Don't stop for anything! If you do...." He jabbed a gun against Jason's back.

The tug lunged on. The craft with the searchlight drew nearer, and all in the pilot-house of the tug could now see that it was a low, gray rum-chaser. A hail, shouted through a megaphone, commanded the tug to heave to.

"Don't you dare!" Shane muttered near Jason's ear.

Jason smiled to himself.

A shot was sent across the tug's bow, but Jason kept at full speed ahead. The searchlight raked back and forth and another shot crossed the bow. Still Jason made no attempt to stop. Followed a third shot, fair and last warning to heave to. The fleet little chaser raced nimbly for the tug's quarter and sent a fusillade of shots rattling through her pilot-house.

One of the four guards pitched down, while another swayed back and forth drunkenly and then slumped to his knees. Jason ducked down, still holding the wheel, while another bunch of shots shattered the pilot-house windows.

"Keep driving her!" snarled Shane.

Jason smiled to himself. He knew where he was, knew the channel. He knew that a hundred yards ahead, a little to the left of the channel, was a sand bar. By keeping straight ahead he would avoid it. By turning the wheel a few spokes he would plow into sand and come to a dead stop. And now he began to turn the wheel over slowly. When the jolt came it would be sudden, unexpected by any but himself, and if he acted quickly he would be master of the situation in the pilot-house. He tensed as the tug drew near the bar, for he knew by heart where that bar was, and had been driving for it. Now he let go of the wheel with one hand, bracing himself with the other. Now—in an instant—she should strike the bar.

She did. At full speed ahead the tug ran on the bar, and every man in the pilot-house with the exception of Jason piled into a heap. Bat Shane would have fallen from the pilot-house window had not one of the men grabbed his coat tails; and Jason, taking advantage of the mix-up, pounced on a revolver which one of the gang had dropped and clubbed it over the nearest head. The man that owned that head reeled, smashed against the door, which opened, and disappeared. In a flash

Jason was on the man who was drawing Shane back into the pilot-house. This man he grabbed by the coat collar and the back of the pants and with a mighty effort sent him crashing through the door and down to the deck below.

Shane, gaining his balance, let out a wolfish, yellow-fanged snarl, and swung up his automatic. A dagger of flame cut the gloom even as Jason was upon the man, wresting the automatic from his hand and flinging it away. That shot had gone wild, and now Shane was unarmed, clawing wildly, snarling fiendishly.

"Damn you, Jason, you ain't got me yet!" he screamed.

"Haven't I?" roared Jason. "Got you just where I want you. Tables are turned now, you lousy rat! I laugh last, Bat—and best."

"It was chance—this. A bum break—"

"Can that stuff! That chaser was laying for us. I had an idea it was. I was looking for it. Expected it at the Point. Bat, you monkeyed with the wrong man tonight. And you're going to pay for it. And you're going to pay for murdering Old Danny."

"It wasn't me. It was Ike—"

"But under your orders. He fell overboard, eh? Thought that was a wise-crack, didn't you. You're in a tight corner now, you bum, and you can thank me for putting you there."

"You—you'll be in deep as me. You run the tug. You was at the wheel. Engineer 'll swear t' that—so 'll this trussed-up deckhand."

"You poor sap, the engineer hasn't seen me, and that deckhand is blindfolded. You'll pay now, Bat! You'll pay for the killing of Old Danny, and you'll pay for making a fall guy out of me. There's the chaser coming alongside. Try to explain to them."

"You—you'll do some explainin' too!"

"Me? Ho! Not me. I'm leaving this battleship right now. I'm satisfied. The whole damn lot of you are bottled pretty. That's what you get for monkeying with the wrong man. Well—tell it to the judge!"

Jason flung him across the pilot-house and lunged for the door. But Bat Shane was on his feet in a flash.

"No—you won't—get away—damn you!" he choked.

There was a knife in his hand, and he hurled himself for the door and landed on Jason's shoulder, hissing between clenched teeth. The knife-point which was headed for Jason's throat jammed miraculously in one of the metal clips that held shut his raincoat. In that split second Jason twisted around, and with a terrific effort heaved Bat Shane over his shoulder.

The killer landed just outside the pilot-house door, slid on the ice, pitched over and struck head-first on the deck below. Thus he escaped the law once more. The law has nothing to do with a dead man. Indeed, Bat Shane was dead—quite dead.

Jason saw the men all huddled aft, watching the chaser draw alongside. They did not know that by jumping off the lee bow they would land in only three feet of water, where they might follow the sand-bar to the mainland. Jason knew, and while the sleek gray chaser was hooking on to the tug's windward side, he quietly slipped along the lee rail to the bow, pulled up his hip boots and inconspicuously went overside.

Unobserved, he plodded almost hip-deep in the icy water for the not so distant shore. Looking back once he saw uniformed men aboard the tug disarming the river pirates under the glare of the powerful searchlight. Chuckling to himself, he turned his back on the scene, plodded on, and a little later walked out upon a sandy beach. Here he paused to cram tobacco into his pipe and chuckle again—an intimate, satisfied sort of chuckle. Then lighting his pipe under a cupped hand, he spun away the match, jammed his hands in his pockets and rocked off into the darkness.

In most of the newspapers the following morning the story of the stolen tug, the rank piracy, and the subsequent capture, was a prominent feature. There was mention made also of the finding of a body in the North River—the body of the ancient watchman at the pier from which the tug had been stolen.

Before that same day was out the officials at the morgue received three hundred dollars with instructions to give the old man decent burial. The contributor elected to remain anonymous.

Buck Jason was that kind of a man. What is more, it was politic to remain anonymous. The rest of the newspaper story he found sometimes amusing, and there was a paragraph near the end that made him actually laugh out loud. It ran like this:

The whereabouts and general course of this piratical tugboat, without which information the patrol boat on duty might have remained ignorant until a general alarm was spread from the plundered vessel, were given by Captain George Stern, of the S.S. Whitewing, who at the time was on the bridge. Noticing that the tug's running lights were in improper position, i.e., the red being to starboard instead of the green, and the green to port instead of the red, he immediately went into wireless communication with the patrol on duty in those waters, recommending that this craft be located, hailed and warned of her improper running lights, so that a possible collision might be avoided.

It is believed that whoever affixed the lights was either intoxicated or ignorant of the nautical rule governing * * *

Buck Jason rumbled with deep, healthy laughter.

"Wrong, Mr. Editor, on each guess," he addressed the sheet. "The man that fixed those lights switched them for a reason. He switched them to draw the attention of any ships that passed. And it worked! Ho! I'll tell the merry world it worked!"

A Man
With Sand

*A man of the sea runs
afoul of city slime.*

THE DOOR opened noiselessly, and Canton Joe oozed into the room as silently as a ghost. Turning to ease the door shut as soundlessly as he had opened it, he looked over his shoulder and smiled crookedly at the averted head of "Ruby" Jessup.

Then he swivelled quietly on his toes, placed his finger tips lightly on his meager hips and glided with cat-like grace and ease across the thick rug to the heavy mahogany table upon which there were a decanter and glasses. With another of his slow, crooked smiles, which revealed yellow, chalk-like teeth, he poured out a drink and downed it meditatively. Setting the glass back on the tray he again placed his finger tips on his hips and regarded the man who reclined in an easy-chair reading a newspaper.

Ruby Jessup read on as though Canton Joe did not exist. His fat, soft hulk was wrapped in a maroon lounging-robe. His pale, moist, bulging eyes followed the small print intently. His big, white face, upon which there was not the faintest touch of color, was immobile. His broad, bald head was lustreless under the glow of the reading lamp. He had thick, pale lips and the nether one drooped out and downward, allowing a glimpse of his lower teeth. The hands that held the paper were fat and smooth and white, and afire with a galaxy of four rubies. His chin merged into a short, fleshy neck.

Canton Joe arched his eyebrows and smiled his crooked smile. His jet eyes glittered behind narrow, oblique lids, and his black, oiled hair shone like polished onyx. What mongrel strains coursed through his blood it would be difficult to say, but there was at least the unmistakable slant-eyes of the Oriental, and the yellow skin, while the general mold of his face seemed more or less a Caucasian legacy. He was Western, too, from the patent leather shoes to the wasp-waisted blue suit and the fawn-colored vest.

"Well... Ruby," he purred through lips that scarcely moved.

Jessup turned a few sheets of his newspaper and, without looking up, grunted, "Well?"

Canton Joe inclined his head toward the floor. "There's a fellow downstairs wants to see you."

"Yeah? Who is he?"

"I don't know."

"Well, why the hell don't you? What's he want?"

"I don't know. He wants to see you."

Jessup snorted. "You dope, what do you know? Um—who sent him here?"

"I don't know," murmured Canton Joe, eyelids drowsing.

Jessup crashed his paper and smacked it down on the table, his big eyes glaring. "My God, ain't you got no tongue to ask questions?"

"I asked," replied Joe, tapping a yawn lightly with two fingers. "I asked, but he said it was none of my business. He wants to see you."

"Oh, so that's the kind of a guy he is!" Ruby Jessup sat up with an effort, his lower lip gleaming with moisture, and took a revolver from a rosewood box on the table. Shoving it into the pocket of his robe, he said, "Well, I might see him, Joe. I'm curious, anyhow. Never saw him before, huh?"

"No. Send him up, you say?"

"Sure. Then you go into the next room and watch. If the breaks go against me— Well, you ain't dumb. You know what to do."

Canton Joe's sardonic smile shone for a brief instant, and his jet eyes glittered. Taking a long ivory cigarette-holder from his vest pocket, he screwed it over a cigarette, lighted up and held the match aloft until the flame licked at his finger. Then he dropped it into a receptacle and let a cloud of purple smoke wander indolently from his nostrils.

"Ruby," he purred softly, "I think this fellow will prove interesting—and—well—profitable."

"What makes you think so?" flung out Ruby Jessup, his lower lip hanging expectantly.

Canton Joe put his hands on his hips, smiled and glided toward the door. With his hand on the knob, he half-turned, still smiling, and said, "I don't know." Then he vanished.

Ruby Jessup muttered thickly in his throat and stuck a cigar between his teeth. Then he got up and stood reflecting for a moment. The back of his neck was white and soft, and corrugated with rolls of flesh. He was a veritable mountain of soft, formless flesh of the paleness of milk. He moved the chair he had been sitting in to a new position, and shifted another to face it about eight feet away. Then, snapping on the electric lights in the chandelier that hung from the ceiling, he settled down into his favorite easy-chair and kept one hand in the pocket of his lounging-robe, where his revolver nestled.

Faintly there came to the room the rumble and then the screech of an elevated train rounding a sharp curve.

Presently the door opened and Canton Joe stood ushering a stranger into the retreat of Ruby Jessup. When the man entered Canton Joe gave Jessup another of his crooked smiles and stepped back into the hallway, pulling the door quietly after him.

This stranger was a lank, rangy man, with a bronzed, clean-clipped face and keen blue eyes. He stood now with his hands jammed solidly into his dark gray jacket, and a half-smoked cigar jutting rigidly from a wide, firm mouth. His gaze swept about the room with a sort of aggressive inquisitiveness, and finally settled on Ruby Jessup with a penetrating directness.

"Your name Jessup?" he asked brusquely.

"Yes," nodded Jessup, eying the stranger speculatively.

"Well, mine's Lang."

"Yes," said Jessup. "Have a seat."

"Thanks," was the clipped retort, as Lang rolled across the room and dropped into the chair facing Jessup.

For a long moment the two men studied each other.

Finally Lang said, "I've just come in from Seattle on the *Pandora.* I own her. Incidentally I'm her skipper. Does my name mean anything to you?"

"Not a thing."

"All right. Have you any idea why I came here?"

"No."

"Then I'll tell you. I'm here looking for a man whom you may know as Jack Brown."

Ruby Jessup's big eyes grew bigger, and his nether lip hung lower than ever. "Oh," he breathed out, nodding his grotesque head. "Jack Brown—Jack Brown?"

"Right. I've reason to believe you know of his whereabouts, and I'm going to take him out of New York."

Ruby Jessup thought over this for a moment, rubbing the ash from his cigar against a bronze tray. Then, "You're his friend?"

"On the contrary, I'm his enemy. But never mind that. I've made arrangements to sail at noon tomorrow and I don't intend to break them. I'll thank you very much if you'll tell me where I can lay hands on this man who calls himself Jack Brown."

"What makes you think I know where he is?" dragged out Jessup heavily.

"I don't see why all the details are necessary," came back Lang with a bit of steel in his gaze. "Can you or can't you tell me where this man is?"

Ruby Jessup crossed one fat leg over the other and closed his eyes while he drew thoughtfully on his cigar; and without opening them he said, "It all depends."

Lang clipped, "What do you mean by that?"

"Oh, I mean it ought to be worth something to me—or to you—to know where Jack Brown is. How much is the information worth to you?"

Lang leaned forward and his lips curled above his lean jaw. "What," he asked bitingly, "is it worth to you?"

"Um—are you talking business?" inquired Jessup, opening his eyes half-way.

"I'm asking you a question."

"Oh," sighed out Jessup. "Well, how does ten thousand sound to you, stranger?"

"Your price?"

"Why… yes."

Lang chuckled dryly. "Do you think I'd pay ten thousand for that miserable hunk of scum?"

"His—wife—might," said Jessup.

"What the hell do you know about his wife?" ripped out Lang, clenching a fist.

"I simply know that she's worth about a hundred thousand dollars. I've been—well—expecting her."

"And you're rather disappointed to find me instead, aren't you? Now get me straight, mister. Don't try to pull any stunt like that. You're not getting away with anything on this sailor. So you thought you'd have a woman to face, eh? Well, you haven't, and don't forget it, either."

Ruby Jessup sat up in his chair and a hint of challenge rose in his bulging eyes. "You're a pretty tough guy, aren't you?"

"That's just your point of view. Tough? I don't know. I guess I am—in a way. But that has nothing to do with this. I get tough, though, when a bird like you tries to take me for a damned fool. I want to know where Jack Brown is, and as for that ten-thousand-dollar proposition, try to pull it on some greenhorn and not a West Coast sailor."

"They must boil you fellows hard out that way," sneered Jessup.

"Eh? Hard? Seattle sailing men are *born* hard-boiled. But lay off the stalling chatter. I'm sailing at noon tomorrow, and Jack Brown is going with me whether he likes it or not. And I'd like to see you or any other damned crook try to stop me."

"That kind of talk might go out on the West Coast, stranger, but here in New York it's just a lot of hot air. You got to act here—"

"Oh, do I?" With a brittle chuckle Lang catapulted from the chair and drove straight into Jessup's paunch, pinning the latter's hand as he strove to pull his gun from the lounging-robe pocket. With a terrific jerk he tore the gun from the fat, soft hand and leaped back. A cold blue fire was in his eyes, and there was a jut to his wind-tanned jaw as he stood spread-legged and menacing.

"So you think I'm full of hot air, do you?" he bit off. "You'll get over that, mister."

With his eyes riveted on Ruby Jessup, he did not see a picture above the moulding on the wall behind him swing outward on a noiseless hinge. But a moment later his rangy body stiffened, the revolver dropped from his hand, and his knees buckled. He twisted down to the floor and lay in a huddled heap.

Ruby Jessup grunted and rubbed his pudgy hands together slowly. He looked up and nodded to Canton Joe, who smirked from the opening in the wall as he drew back a revolver equipped with a silencer. Then the picture swung into place noiselessly.

Jessup moved over to the huddled body and planted a slippered foot in Lang's ribs.

"Huh," he grunted. "Not so tough after all."

IN ANOTHER room in this same house of shade, this honeycomb of crime, a man lounged at full length on a cheap sofa, with his hands clasped behind his head, and stared vacantly at the cracked, spotted ceiling.

Nearby a woman, a peroxide blonde, with full red lips—the pouting kind of lips—sat curled up in an over-stuffed chair, smoking a cigarette and reading a tabloid newspaper. She was pretty, but there was something peculiarly tattered about that beauty. Yet she did not look so old—in her middle twenties, say. A gaudy kind of beauty—cheap like tinsel, that shows up best under the glitter of lights.

The man was tall and thin, with a pale, emaciated face that contrasted sharply with the large, midnight eyes. His nose was a beak, and his lips were small, colorless and weak, and always a trifle parted. There was a vague hint that once on a time he might have been good-looking, but now it all seemed long ago and far away. There was no resolve in that face, no shadow of firmness, or of purposeful character. It was a washed-out spectre of a face.

The woman suddenly scaled the newspaper across the room, stretched her arms over her head and yawned. Then she dropped them suddenly and regarded the man with something akin to disgust.

"You make me sick!" she growled, half to herself, and chewed sullenly on a fingernail.

The man continued to stare vacantly at the ceiling.

"You make me sick!" she rasped, this time aloud, in a voice barbed with acid.

The man's eyes came to life. He turned his head on one ear and his dark eyes flickered at her.

"Well, why don't you say somethin'?" she flung at him.

"What'll I say?" he clicked.

She grumbled impatiently. "You're a dope! I never seen a guy like you. Honest t' Gawd! You mope around like a funeral on the way to the cemetery. You ain't got the spine you was borned with, s' help me!"

The man raised himself to one elbow and moistened his lips. "What's eating you, Mabel?" he asked.

"What's eating me!" she jerked erect and regarded him frigidly. "You poor sap, it's you gettin' on my nerves. It's because I got a lemon on my hands like you—a sour lemon. Because you ain't got the guts to break away from the boss so's we can sock away all the dough we make."

"You wait," he gave her suddenly, his lower lip quivering. "I'll get enough money soon. I'm expecting it any day now. You wait! Just wait! The sun 'll shine for me—"

"Can that po'try garbage! It gives me indigestion awful!"

He swung his feet to the floor and pointed a bony, unsteady forefinger at her.

"Oh, it does, does it? Well, when I get my ten thousand you'll see. I'll get away. And if you don't cut out that kind o' talk you'll be sorry. I'll leave you flat. See if I won't!"

"Leave me flat! Ha-ha!" she laughed lightly, throwing back her head. "No you won't. Not you. Why, say, Jack, old boy, you're in a rut so deep you can't see over the top. You ain't got the guts to skin out on the boss. For one thing, he's got the goods on you, and if he passes on what he knows to Flannigan, that cheap dick from Headquarters, you'll have about as much chance as a snowball in hell. 'Nother thing: So long as the boss keeps you in 'snow,' you're anchored here like a ship. Oh, don't tell me! I know you."

"I notice you can't get along without your 'snow'."

"I ain't a man. I'm only a woman. An' I ain't as crazy for it as you are. When did you have that bad dream about ten thousand dollars?"

"Not a dream—it's not!" he cried, beating a meager fist against a no less meager knee, his eyes burning. "You're always pickin' on me. It's not fair. Everybody picks on me. You can't let a poor guy alone. Shut up! Leave me alone!"

"Anything gives me indigestion is a bimbo that's always pityin' himself."

"Suppose my ten thousand 'll give you indigestion too!" he flung at her, shaking like a leaf. "Just wait and see. I'll get it. I'll show you. Sure as my name's Jack Brown—"

"Pretty good joke!" she chortled. "Sure as your name's Jack Brown. Ha! Well, your name ain't Brown. Keep makin' cracks like that an' I'll get indigest—"

"My God, will you shut up!" he exploded, leaping to his feet and shaking his fists at her threatingly. "I'll—I'll—"

She waved a hand at him. "Go sit down. Take a shot of dope else you'll shake apart."

"Then shut up!" he cried in a high-pitched voice. "If you don't I'll choke you. I'll—"

"Say, listen, guy!" she drawled, getting up and laying her hand on a heavy plate. "Pull another song-and-dance like that an' I'll bounce something off that thing you call a head. You couldn't choke a mosquito. Ease up, Jackie—take it easy or you'll do a fade-out."

He stood with his hands half-raised, struggling for breath, wild fires in his eyes, and a feverish blotch of crimson on either pallid cheek. Then he withered and went limp, falling back to the sofa and dropping down.

"You—you're always picking on me," he breathed out hoarse-ly.

"So is your old man," she gave him, and turned casually to a mirror, admiring herself.

An electric bell rang twice—sharply.

The man looked up. "The boss," he muttered.

"Better take a shot before you go down," she advised, penciling an eyebrow.

"Yes… I better," he replied.

Rising on unsteady feet, he dragged himself into an adjoining room.

The woman yawned, drew her negligée tighter about her, and again curled up in the easy-chair and picked a dog-eared magazine from the table.

A little later the man re-entered the room, put on a jacket and brushed back his sleek hair.

"Wonder what he wants," he ventured.

"Got me. Don't be long, Jack."

"All right, Mabel."

These two were linked to each other as irrevocably as day is linked to night. They lived in a world strangely all their own, a shadow world. Crime had welded them together—crime and the false goddess which they called "snow." Some day one might kill the other, because they were so close to each other and yet so far apart.

The man, leaving her, walked down to the end of a corridor, descended a stairway, and knocked at a door in the hall below. It opened after a moment, and Canton Joe ushered him in with a yellow smirk and mock obsequity. Closing the door softly, the mongrel stood there with one knee bent slightly, with one slim hand resting lightly on his hip, and a look of satanic amusement in his narrowed eyes.

Ruby Jessup sat in his favorite chair, chewing on a cigar and seeming very much at ease and satisfied with life.

"Hello, Jack," he rolled out.

"Hello, Ruby."

The sallow man was pretty steady now. He lit a cigarette in an offhand manner and flipped the match carelessly into the ash-tray.

"What's up?" he asked.

"Little game for you. There's a gambler downstairs who's roarin' for meat. You know the game."

"I know it, Ruby."

"Little pin money for you. Your nerves steady?"

"All right. But—but I'll need some—some—"

"I'll give you some more 'snow' tonight after the game," cut in Ruby. "Now go down. This guy comes from Chi, and ten to one he's crooked an' lookin' for gravy. We'll play a game he never heard of. An' yet our cards are on the level—eh?"

"Air-tight, so far as the cards are concerned," replied Jack. "What's his game?"

"Draw poker—table stakes—no limit. He's slick, I guess, an' has got a bag of tricks. But we have too, eh?" cackled Ruby.

He pulled open a drawer in the table and drew out a thick packet of bills.

"There you are, Jack, an' good luck," he grinned.

The sallow man picked up the bills, thrust them into an inside pocket and said:

"Leave it to me, Ruby." Then he moved over to the door, put his hand on the knob and turned to add: "You'll have that—that stuff—"

"Sure, come in after the game, Jack."

Canton Joe smiled his crooked smile behind a yellow hand.

The sallow man pulled open the door and strode out.

A few moments later he entered a large room filled with tobacco smoke. Half a dozen tables stood here and there, with bottles and glasses on them. At some of these tables sat rat-faced or belligerent-eyed men, and with them were tawdry women reeking of cheap powder and cheaper perfume—women of shade, most of them gold-toothed, hard-eyed, coarse-voiced.

A few were pretty, but all bore that indefinable stamp of their kind—that air, or demeanor, or whatever vague thing it is, that marks them for outcasts from the social and moral stratum which women of another kind hold sacred and inviolable.

Some waved to the sallow man called Jack. At one table were three men, and one of these motioned him over with a forefinger. He crossed the room and sat down. A big Negro lumbered through the clouds of smoke and asked about drinks.

"I don't drink," said the sallow man.

"This," put in one of the party, indicating a lean, heady-eyed giant who gnawed thoughtfully on a cigar, "is Mr. Houk, Jack. He's from the West. This is Jack Brown, Mr. Houk."

"Hello," grunted Houk. "Let's play."

A gruff, unfriendly, gray-eyed man.

A new deck of cards was broken, and all drew for the deal. Houk got the deal, and shuffled the cards with lightning-like swiftness. No less swift did he deal them; they shot from his deft fingers almost magically, it seemed. He knew cards, and knew how to juggle them. There was no doubt about that.

But nevertheless he started off on a losing streak, and lost steadily. He said nothing, and his face remained the same. He opened on a pair of kings and had a third on the draw, yet when the showdown came one of the others held three aces and raked in a huge pot.

The sallow man was deft with the cards, too. He knew every trick, every bluff worth knowing, and he knew when to boost and when to drop away. He won steadily, and looked bored when he drew in one pot after another. Mabel was right. He had needed a good shot, to brace him. He was braced now, sure of himself, basking in a peculiar kind of serenity.

The minutes wheeled by. The smoke grew denser. Somebody had started a phonograph, and a few couples were dancing. They reeled across the rough floor, laughing raucously. They exchanged repartee while they spun around—the coarse, vile witticisms of the gutter. The big Negro grinned and roared and rocked.

"Close your mug, you dinge!" barked one of the men.

A woman croaked a broken laugh that died on an asthmatic note.

Houk still lost. Still he shuffled the cards with amazing swiftness, dealt them with unfailing aim, and chewed on his dead cigar. The sallow man's luck was so great that as yet he had not drawn from the capital which Ruby Jessup had given him. An hour passed, and then another hour. The sallow man passed a deal and used the time to give most of the money he had won to the Negro waiter to put into the safe.

Presently Houk laid his hand flat on the table and said:

"I'm cleaned, guys, except for fifty bucks." He drew a cigar from a vest-pocket and at the same time casually, and no doubt intentionally, revealed a revolver under his arm. "I'll play the last fifty provided I play with one man. I'd like to play with you, Brown."

The men looked at one another. A wink or two were exchanged.

"All right, buddy," said Jack Brown.

The other two players dropped out and Houk called for a fresh deck. He seemed a deadly man. In a roundabout way he had practically said that he thought the game was crooked. Now he and the sallow man faced each other, and the latter drew a wad of bills from his inside pocket and laid them on the table.

He won the first hand on two pair, kings up. He lost the second hand when Houk called his bluff and beat his jacks with a pair of queens. He lost the third, and the fourth, won the fifth, and lost the next four straight running. Houk lit a fresh cigar and dealt in his whirlwind fashion.

Jack Brown lost steadily, but showed no discomfiture. At the end of an hour Houk had regained his original stakes, and now his eyes were boring into Brown's as the latter dallied with the cards.

"Well, deal, why don't you?" he grumbled.

"I think I'm through," said the sallow man.

"Not so easy when you're alone, huh?"

"Cards turned, that's all."

Houk looked about. "Anybody else wanter play?"

Nobody wanted to play.

"All right," grunted Houk, gathering up his pile. "Lucky I got what I started with. Lucky for *you* birds, I mean," he added with a deadly look.

He stood up, jamming his hand into his pocket and rolling his cigar from one side of his mouth to the other.

"Cheap sports," he snarled and strode across the room.

The big Negro shot back the bolt and let him out, chuckling liquidly as he closed the door and eased the bolt back into place. Then looked at Jack Brown, nodded, and brought from the safe the money which Brown had given him to lock up. The other players also handed over the money which they had won.

Brown pocketed it all and left the room. He went upstairs rapidly, knocked at Ruby Jessup's door, and Canton Joe, with another of his yellow, satanic smirks, admitted him and eyed him with a thin, mocking gaze. Brown crossed to the table and Ruby chafed his soft fat hands and rolled his huge eyes.

"Ah… Jack! O.K., is it?" he gurgled.

"Yes, Ruby. We got his money first, then let him stage a come-back. He wasn't crooked, though. A damned level player, and pretty fast. But what's that to us! We got all of his money first, and I had the nigger put it in the safe. When we let him make his comeback, I played with the money you gave me."

"The counterfeit money, eh?"

"Sure. He thinks he's got his stakes back, the poor sap!"

"Ha! An' he ain't!" laughed Jessup. "Gimme the dough. Ho! Ho!"

Even Canton Joe had to laugh aloud.

THE MAN from the sea—this Lang, captain of the *Pandora*—opened his eyes and saw nothing but Stygian darkness. For an incalculable time he had been buried in darkness—mental darkness. He was sprawled now upon a rickety couch, and as he moved, its springs creaked. His head pained; there was a stinging sensation at the back of his neck when he moved. Tentatively he felt it with his fingers—felt a raw gash that made him wince.

"Scraped by a bullet," he muttered.

He took a clean white handkerchief from his pocket and tied it carefully around his neck. Then he sat up, placing his feet on the floor. He sniffed. The atmosphere was damp, so he divined he was in the lower regions of the building, perhaps below the street level. Added to the smell of mouldy dampness was the odor of stale opium.

Grimacing with disgust, he got to his feet, put his hands out before him and groped in the darkness. He touched a wall, felt along it and came to another wall. Then he came to a door and searched for the knob, but the door was locked. He made a tour of the room, feeling his way, and came back to where he had started from. The room was small—perhaps ten by six feet.

Finally he sat down on the couch again, and started a fresh cigar to kill the unpleasant odor of stale opium. For a few moments he puffed furiously. Then he got up and made another try at the door. He lit a match and studied the lock. He tapped the panels, and found that they were old and warped. For a moment he stood pondering over the situation, while the match burned out. He lit another match and studied the door again, and saw that the hinges were on the inside; a type such as are on the outside of barn or stable doors.

Rummaging in his pockets, he found a clasp knife, and opened the heaviest of three blades. Catching this in the crevice between the door and the frame, he broke off about a quarter of an inch of the point. He picked up a bit of old newspaper from the floor, twisted it tightly and made of it a torch. Then, using his knife for a screw-driver, he went to work on the hinge screws.

The screws were rusty and stubborn, and he continually broke off bits of the blade. The improvised torch went out and he was forced to stop and relight it. Back at the hinges again, he worked with renewed vigor, and presently removed the hinge that was attached to the door on top. Following this he went to work on the lower hinge, and after ruining two blades and part of the third, and spending almost half an hour, it swung loose and he eased in the door cautiously.

Now he looked into a narrow corridor, dimly lighted at the farther end by one sputtering gas-jet. The walls were drab and dirty, splotched with dampness that exuded an odor of decay. The floor was made of rough, wide planks that bulged and receded. A clammy coolness stirred here but could not entirely subdue the persistent smell of stale opium. Globules of moisture stood out from the ceiling.

Lang left the cubbyhole in which he had been imprisoned. He passed three doors on his way to the other end of the corridor. Here he found a staircase and ascended eight steps to a small landing, where the stairway reversed its direction and led up eight steps to another corridor. Through a hall window he could see the lights of a tenement house across a back lot, and he knew, then, that he was on the main floor. Two lights burned in this hall, and the walls were in somewhat better condition than those below.

As he started along the corridor, a door opened and a shoddily dressed man, small, bent-shouldered, insignificant, lurched out of a door, cackling raucously, and steered a crooked course away from Lang. The man from the sea waited until he had disappeared around a corner, then followed. When he came abreast of the door from which the stranger had lurched, a woman looked out and grinned.

"Hello, big boy," she greeted, with a brazen grin.

Lang started to go on, but hesitated and turned about to face her, boring her with a keen blue gaze.

She leaned in the doorway, chewing gum and regarding him whimsically. "Sure, come on in, boy friend," she invited, showing her teeth.

With a sudden movement Lang entered, and she closed the door with a kick from her heel. Again he smelled the breath of opium. He stood spread-legged, with his hands jammed firmly into his coat pockets, and his back to the woman. However, after looking him over with approving eyes, she snapped her gum and sauntered around to face him.

"Well, take the load off your feet." She indicated a shabby sofa. "Sit down, honey."

Lang spun on her and bit her with his keen eyes. "Stow that stuff, sister. Sit down yourself. I want to talk to you."

She arched her dark eyebrows and said out of the corner of her mouth, "Cripes, what are you—one of these damn reformers?"

"Not on your natural, Susie—"

"My name ain't Susie. It's—"

"I don't give a rap what it is. Sit down and peel your ears."

She shrugged her shoulders, sat down and looked bored.

Lang said, crisply, "I want the lay of this dump. Give me my bearings and I'll slip you a twenty-spot."

"You a dick?"

"No. I'm not a dick, nor do I belong to any uplift society."

"Well, who or what are you, then?"

"Never mind that. Listen. I'm looking for a man who calls himself Jack Brown."

The woman chuckled harshly. "Oh, that guy!"

"Yes. Maybe you know where he hangs out."

"He hangs out with a doll called Mabel Halsey. They work the badger game and split with the boss. Brown's a hop-head."

"Who's the boss?"

"Say, feller, let's see the twenty-spot," she said suddenly.

Lang pulled a yellow-back from his wallet and dropped it in her lap. "Go ahead, now," he suggested.

"Well, the boss owns this joint. It's an old loft buildin', an' you can get anything here. Protection, y'know—Brown works for the boss because the boss supplies him with dope an' I guess the boss has got a lot on him. This guy Brown is the bunk, though. He gives me a pain in the eye."

"But where does he hang out?"

"Well, him an' his jane ha' got a couple rooms upstairs. Two flights up from here, in the front o' the hall on the left."

"That's all," clipped Lang, and started for the door. He paused, however, with his foot on the threshold. "And who's the boss?" he asked her.

"That's tellin's, feller," she gave him.

"I think I know," was Lang's shot, and then he stepped out, pulling the door shut behind him.

Hurrying to the stairway, he went up two steps at a time to the next corridor, paused to look and listen, and then ascended the staircase leading to the floor above. Remembering the woman's directions, he tiptoed to the front of the corridor and listened at the door on the left. For a long minute there was no sound. Then he heard a low cough. Straightening up, he rapped briefly on the door with his knuckles, and placed one foot against the bottom so that he could jam it between the door and the frame as soon as the door was opened.

There was a stir inside, and then Lang heard the click of a key in the lock. After another long moment the knob turned slowly and the door was eased open. An eye appeared at the crack, and as it did Lang thrust his weight forward and crashed in. A slim, sallow man recoiled and clutched at his hip pocket apparently for a gun. Lang clamped his jaw and attacked the man in whirlwind fashion, grabbing his gun-hand and twisting it with a sudden savageness that brought a scream of pain from his victim. The gun clattered to the floor. Lang, with a grim little chuckle, spun the man around and flung him across the room. The man careened over a chair, toppled with it awkwardly, and landed on the back of his head. Lang picked up the revolver and dropped it into his pocket. Then he stood spread-legged, with his hands jammed solidly into his pockets, and there was a curl to his wide lips and a look of disdain in his sea-blue eyes.

"At last, you scum!" he ground out bitterly.

The man on the floor drew up his knees and writhed in mental, not physical, pain. His frail hands straggled aimlessly over his face and his eyes stared horror-stricken from their sockets. His mouth hung open and the stringy cords on his neck stood out as he struggled for breath. His lower lip began to tremble and he drew it under his upper teeth with a faint groan.

"Oh... *you!*" he choked, raising a hand as if to ward off a blow.

Lang stood rooted to the floor as immovably as a great tree. "Get on your feet!" he spat out suddenly.

The sallow man, grimacing, got to his feet by fits and starts and backed away with stark fear burning in his eyes.

"Sit down!" clipped Lang.

The man, quavering, sat down on the edge of a chair, wringing his hands, shifting his feet nervously, and sucking on his lower lip.

Lang said, "A helluva looking man you are, you miserable swine! You didn't expect me, did you? Rather expected some money from Alice, didn't you? Ha! You'll get it—*not!* My ship's anchored in the harbor and I'm going to take you aboard and back to Seattle."

The sallow man cringed. "N-no... n-no!"

"But yes!" clipped Lang. "So raw it hurts—that vengeance, eh?"

"Y-you can't do that. N-no you can't."

"Who," inquired Lang acidly, "is going to stop me?"

"I—I tell you, you can't take me back. Won't go—no I won't. See if I will. There! See if I will! Humph!"

"Listen, Jack Brown, as you call yourself, or Jack Bronson, as you were christened—listen! You're going aboard the *Pandora* with me and I'll take you if it's by the slack of your pants."

"Will you?—will you? Ha! Ha!" cackled the sallow man. "I just have to yell and you'll never get out of here alive."

"Yell, mister, and neither of us will go out alive!" Lang told him bluntly, and then leveled a finger at him. "You're the lowest example of a man I've ever seen, and I've banged into a good many ports in this world. You always were low—as far back as I can remember. Optimists say a man may be changed. It's a damned lie. Alice never loved you. She pitied you, and you begged her to marry you because you said if she didn't you would go to the dogs.

"You? You never loved her. You're too weak to even love—unless it's yourself. You were always jealous of me, and you took advantage of my absence. You dodged the draft, while a lot of us poor suckers joined up the first week. I was first officer on a ship running contraband to France, and we got blown up and I was put down for lost. You tricked Alice—and me. You said you were going to war and begged her to marry you before you went. All the time you knew you didn't have the guts to get into a man's game. And Alice—married you. Thought I was gone, and that she could save a wreck—you! Ah-r-r, you dirty scum!"

"What—what can you do?" cried Bronson, half-defiant.

"What can I do? I'm taking you back and your marriage to Alice, now, five years old, is going to be broken!"

"You're what!" exclaimed Bronson, his eyes flaming feverishly.

"You heard me," was the reply.

"And you—you—"

"I'm going to marry her!"

Bronson sprang to his feet, quivering in every limb. "Marry

her? Ha! Ha! You're after her money. You can't fool me. I know she inherited almost a hundred thousand from a distant uncle. I read the item in the newspaper. Ha! That's what you're after. You—you—you—ha!—you…." He found himself groping for words and breath.

It was because Lang regarded him with eyes that cut into his shriveled soul like rapier points. The man from the sea stood rigid as a rock, with his feet planted wide and a dangerous jut to his cleft jaw.

"Easy, Bronson, or I'll spread you over the floor," he warned quietly. "Thought you were in for some easy money, eh? It's more than four years now since you left your wife. She supported you from the time you were married, and then she went down with the flu, and instead of sticking by her, you beat it and left her half-dead. Oh, I know."

"She—she told me the week after we were married she—she didn't love me," cried Bronson, alias Brown.

"She only told the truth. Yet she worked to support you, until her health was ruined. She never knew you were a dope fiend. I did—but I—never told her. I'll spare her that. I love her, and she loves me. We always have loved each other. And now, you scum, you are coming back to Seattle. For three years she's advertised in every paper for you, and so have I. You saw those ads, don't tell me different. But not until the piece telling of an inheritance did you answer—and then you had the gall to ask her to send you ten thousand. Said you were in debt and all that. Bah! You are rotten to the core!"

"Yeah? You think so? Suppose you think you'll get that money. You won't! By God, you won't! The boss will help me."

"The boss," said Lang, "knows about that money, too. He must have intercepted your mail. At any rate, he was ready to pinch your ten thousand."

Bronson blanched. "It's a lie! He doesn't know! He—"

"Shut up! He does. And as for that item in the paper—"

At this juncture there were footsteps outside in the hall, and before Lang could reach the door it opened and a blonde woman sauntered in. She stopped short and dilated her eyes in surprise, looking from Lang to Bronson quizzically.

"Who's your friend?" she flung at Bronson.

"He—he's no friend, Mabel," replied Bronson. "Quick! Call for help!"

Lang started for the woman, but she dodged back into the hall and shouted at the top of her voice. Lang clenched his fists and whirled on Bronson.

"Damn you!" he rapped out, and leaped for the man.

He caught him by the throat and Bronson went down to his knees. Lang snarled and dragged him toward the door, kicked it open and plunged with him into the hallway. The woman called Mabel sprang for him and clawed cat-like at his face. With one free hand he brushed her roughly aside. She tripped and sprawled to the floor, and Lang, still gripping his man grimly, lugged him down the hall to the head of the staircase.

He descended the stairs in leaps, pulling Bronson after him with no gentleness, and as he was about to go down the next stairway Ruby Jessup and Canton Joe burst out of a doorway midway down the hall and came after him. Lang stopped, seeing that he must leave his man and run or remain and fight. He chose to stand, and to insure Bronson's staying where he put him, he knocked the man unconscious with a short-arm jab to the jaw.

Then he dropped him and, disdaining to wait till the other two reached him, charged down the hall to meet them, at the same time drawing the revolver he had taken from Bronson. Jessup carried an automatic, and Canton Joe gripped a knife. Jessup fired and the shot clipped Lang's hat from his head. Lang fired almost at the same instant, and Jessup stumbled and fell headlong.

Before Lang could fire again Canton Joe, grinning fiendishly, was upon him, and his knife came in an upward thrust so favored by the cutthroats of the China coast. Lang blocked it, and grasped the brown wrist and at the same time Canton Joe, his eyes glittering, caught Lang's gun-hand and, with unexpected strength, raised it above his head. They both spun around, as Lang bent back the hand that held the deadly knife even as Canton Joe was striving to keep the gun on high.

They struggled silently, Lang grim-lipped, Canton Joe baring his yellow teeth in a mirthless grin as his sinewy body twisted and swayed in an effort to upset the white man. But Lang was rangy and heavy-boned, with seasoned muscles, and thwarted every trick, at the same time forcing Canton Joe's knife-hand behind his back.

And Canton Joe, whose grin began to pale, realized that his arm would snap if he did not shift and shift quickly. So he abruptly let go Lang's gun-hand and spun around in an attempt to throw Lang over his shoulders. Lang must have anticipated this move, for he shifted even as Canton Joe shifted, and before the latter knew what it was all about he was hurtling through space.

He landed hard on his face, turned heels over head and came up on his feet with fine grace. Meanwhile Bronson had come to his senses, tottered to his feet and with a shrill scream, threw himself on Lang's back. Lang squirmed about and was grappling face to face with him when Canton Joe rose to his toes, grinned his satanic grin, and leaped for Lang's back with his knife poised.

With a sweeping movement he brought it up and outward just as Lang, with his free hand spun Bronson around clear off his feet. Canton Joe's stroke was in mid-career; the flashing knife grazed Lang's cheek and imbedded itself in Bronson's neck. Lang dropped him with a grimace, turned and brought his revolver down on Canton Joe's head. The mongrel dropped like a log over the newly dead body of Bronson, and Lang staggered away.

He never could recollect how he escaped from that honeycomb of crime that was disguised as an ancient loft building. He remembered vaguely that he dashed down several staircases, bounded along dimly-lighted hallways, bowled over several men who appeared mysteriously from the depths. He remembered smashing headlong into a policeman and both of them tumbling down a flight of stairs. He heard a whistle blow, and hoarse shouts.

Somehow he reached the lower hall and felt a gust of fresh air, and the next moment he was in a narrow street, shadowy and deserted, and the first wan streaks of dawn were climbing out of the East. He ran on in the dim half-light, and heard milk trucks banging along somewhere not far distant.

Eventually he reached the waterfront, and found a motor launch ready to put off. He jumped down into it and paid the grizzled junkman five dollars to run him out to the *Pandora*. When the red sun was flaming just above the jagged skyline of Brooklyn, he went up the Jacob's ladder and one of his mates greeted him at the forward welldeck.

Late that night, while his ship was plowing southward, he sat in his stateroom under the lower bridge and stared at the picture of a young woman with raven hair and soft, dark eyes. In one hand he held a newspaper clipping, and presently he began to tear this to bits.

It had been his own idea—this insertion in the paper of Alice's inheritance. He had known it would draw word from Bronson. There was no legacy at all. Alice was poor. But soon all would be well.

Four bells—ten o'clock—rang from the bridge.

Emeralds of Shade

Big Buck Jason finds himself in embarrassing circumstances, on a mysterious mission of unknown danger, because a woman has sought his aid.

DETECTIVE LUKE TRASK sat with his chair tipped back against the wall and his heels hooked on a front rung. A pearl-gray fedora was slanted down across his eyebrows, and a dead cigar jutted from one corner of his drooping, sardonic mouth. He had pink cheeks, a bulbous nose, and damp, glassy eyes. The black suit he wore was of modish pattern and clung tightly to his rather adipose and shapeless form. A diamond sparkled on a white, soft finger, and another shone from his black, knitted silk cravat. Something of a dandified sleuth, this Luke Trask, from his soft patent-leather shoes to his eight-dollar Stetson. Highly polished, like cheap jewelry. Yet you did not have to look very sharply to see the innate coarseness oozing through the brittle veneer.

"Buck, I can make the river damn uncomfortable for you," he was saying out of the side of his mouth.

Buck Jason, standing at the little gas-range, split two eggs on the edge of the fry-pan and snapped the shells into a refuse box that stood nearby.

"That's up to you, Luke," he replied, without looking up.

"Course it's up to me, and it ain't goin' to take an awful lot to make me do it."

"You mean to make you *try* to do it," corrected Jason, sprinkling salt on the sizzling eggs.

"Think I can't, eh?"

"Better men than you have tried. Have an egg?"

Trask frowned. "T''ell with your eggs. I'm talkin' business."

"Illegitimate business." Jason looked in the coffee pot and

shut off the light under it. Then: "I'm not talking business tonight, Luke, so you might just as well ankle along and see if you can arrest some kids on Grand Street for pitching pennies. That's about your speed."

"No wisecracks," grumbled Trask. "You think you're sittin' on the top o' the world, don't you? Keep thinkin' that way an' you'll fall so damn hard it'll jar out your wisdom teeth."

Jason slid his eggs from the pan on to a plate and banged the empty pan back to the range.

"Listen, you cheap gumshoe," he rapped out, cutting Trask

with a rapier stare. "Don't try to pull any of that folderol here. It's birds like you that make the police a laughing stock. You're getting no graft out of me, understand? I'm paying it to a man bigger than you, and if you take it into your head to knock the props from under me you'll get so almighty tangled up in the wreckage you'll never get over it. I'm no greenhorn, Trask, and if you take me for one you're blind in one eye and crossed in the other. If you're looking for graft go over and pinch some poor Jew storekeeper for selling bread on Sundays. But don't try it where you're known."

"Tall talk, guy, tall talk," dragged out Trask with a sneer. "Stick a pin in a gas-bag and it'll explode. Tall talk, tall talk."

Jason sat down to his homemade meal of eggs, potatoes and warmed-over rolls. He picked up a fork and pointed it at Trask.

"Try your dirtiest; try it," he challenged. "But don't wear out shoe-leather coming here. If you want any booze from me, mister, you're going to pay for it in cold cash. I sure do take a fit over your gall, all right. Will I shoot you over three cases of Scotch and three cases of Bacardi? Huh! Crust is one thing you haven't got anything else but! If you want six cases of booze, you're going to pay me. If you want graft, go down to Canal Street and hound the Wops, but don't mistake me for Santa Claus. There's a man a damned sight higher up than you getting all the graft that's coming from this boy, so if you mess around in my bed of roses you'll get more than one thorn in your hide. If you think that's a lot of applesauce, you're dumber than I've always said you were. The door's to your left, and don't fall over the bundle of wash on the way to the stairs."

Trask, his damp eyes narrowing, rolled his stub of a cigar back and forth between his thick lips, brought his chair down to all fours, and stood up.

"I hope we meet again, rum runner," he droned, adding after a momentary pause, "under other conditions."

"Look out for the wash on the way down," advised Jason.

Trask lifted his lip in a sneer and put his hand on the knob. He was about to say something when a light, hesitant knock sounded on the door. He took his hand off the knob and stepped back, shooting Jason a sidelong glance.

"Go ahead and open it," said Jason, and then swallowed some coffee.

Trask thought for a moment and then, with another sidelong, quizzical look at the big man, turned the knob and opened the door.

A young woman looked in, half-smiling. She wore a gray silk dress and a small turban to match, with a light summer fur about her neck.

"Mr. Jason?" she asked in a soft contralto.

"Umph!" grunted Trask.

Jason put down the chunk of bread with which he had been wiping his plate, kicked back his chair and stood up to his full six feet of muscle and rock-like bone. A frown of mild perplexity corrugated his high, broad forehead.

"I'm Jason," he said simply.

She bowed her head, smiled and stood for a moment in perplexed indecision. Then: "May I come in?"

"Well—um—sure," he gave her, still frowning his puzzlement.

The young woman entered and Jason mumbled something and motioned to his old Morris chair. The woman sat down and for the next moment seemed interested in drawing off one of her long gray silk gloves. A pretty woman, expensively clothed, smart-looking, attractive. Then she brought up a curious stare to Trask and shifted it to Jason after a brief instant.

"May I speak to you alone, Mr. Jason?" was her inquiry.

Jason stroked his jaw, regarding her levelly and perplexedly. Then he looked at Trask, and with a careless fling of his hand indicated the door. The detective smirked behind a white hand as he pulled open the door and went out.

Jason sat down at the table and brought his steady eyes back to the woman.

"Well?" he said.

"I—I've come here, Mr. Jason, with a rather strange purpose in mind. I—"

Jason touched a finger to his lips, got up and moved across noiselessly to the door. With a sudden movement he jerked it open just in time to see Trask straightening up.

"Key-hole's plugged," he clipped shortly. "There's the stairway. Look out for the wash on the way down."

Trask leered. "Some new game, eh?"

"Wouldn't you wish you knew?"

"I might find out—later."

"You couldn't find the nose on your face without looking in a mirror. So long."

Trask swore silently and headed for the stairway.

Jason closed the door and went back to his chair by the table.

"All right now," he told the woman.

"Well, as I said, I am here for a rather strange purpose. I understand you have a large motor launch?"

Jason nodded while he stuffed his pipe. "Who told you?" he asked.

"A very prominent lawyer for whom you have—er—well, worked at times."

"Corson?"

"Is it necessary that we indulge in names, Mr. Jason?"

"No—not at all. Go ahead."

"This lawyer told me you are a dependable man willing to take chances on ventures not entirely within the law as it is written."

Jason chuckled deep in his throat. "Did he add that my prices are not cut-rate?"

"He did. But before we continue, can you arrange to be out with your launch most of tomorrow night? And are you willing to do me a service which is outside of the law?"

"I don't know whether to answer that or not. There is no detail yet! It all depends. If this lawyer gave you the impression that I am a common gunman—"

She raised a hand. "Oh, no, he didn't, else I should not have come here. He said you never carry a gun, and he also said you're not a man who bothers much about minor details."

"But you haven't even given me the main ones."

"I can't do that now," she said.

Jason was about to strike a match, but paused.

"What's that?"

"I—I said—"

"I heard you," he broke in. "But to tell you the truth I don't go in for this mystery stuff. If you're looking for a hero, miss, you certainly have got the wrong number. Mind a pipe?"

"No—not a bit," she hastened to assure him, and then stared at the floor.

After a moment she stood up, drawing on her glove.

"Well, I'm sorry to have annoyed you," she told him, smiling. "I'll have to try someone else."

"If you're looking for a gunman, I know a Greek—"

"No—no, thank you."

She moved over to the door, and Jason, getting up, crossed to open it. A pretty woman, he mused, eying her sidewise. Twenty-eight or so. Soft-spoken, steady-eyed, capable. Apparently a woman of means; at least she gave that impression.

"Good-night," she was saying.

"Night," he said, holding open the door.

She went out, and Jason, closing the door softly, stood for a long moment stroking his jaw ruminatively and staring at the knob. Then he crossed to his Morris chair, sprawled at length in it and relit his pipe. He wondered if maybe he hadn't acted too quickly, been too blunt and to the point. He wasn't used to dealing with women. Men were mostly his associates, and the men he did business with were hard-heads like himself. He began to wish he had talked a little longer with her. Maybe he might have got some inkling of what was in the wind.

His train of thought was suddenly shattered by a medley of sounds outside his door—scuffling feet, a low, rasping voice, and a woman's half-stifled cry. In a flash he was out of his chair. He lunged for the door, whipped it open, and poised on the threshold for a brief moment as he peered into the darkened hall. Then he heaved out and over to the head of the staircase, and saw vaguely two forms swaying half-way down the stairs.

Again he heard the half-choked cry of a woman. He went down the steps in bounds, and a split-second later had his big hands clamped about a thick, muscled neck. Dimly he could make out the woman who but a few moments back had talked with him in his room. She was gasping for breath.

The man who had been struggling with her, swore under his breath as he exerted a great effort in his attempt to break away from Jason. The woman, coughing as she strove to regain her breath, stumbled down the stairs, clutching at the banister, and disappeared in the thick gloom below.

The two men rocked back and forth in a silent, tense struggle. Jason found no weakling in his hands, but a broad hulk of bone and solid flesh, almost as tall as himself, who knew a dirty trick or two about wrestling in close quarters. But Jason was no novice himself in that ungentle art. He matched the stranger trick for trick, and ground out, with a grim chuckle:

"Try your dirtiest, mister!"

"Leggo, you!" grunted the stranger. "I've got no argument with you."

"Ho! You're acting that way, aren't you?"

The man snarled and heaved his full weight against Jason. Jason blocked it as a deep-rooted rock blocks a vicious current of water. Then he bored in with his own weight, and they skidded down four steps, brought up short, and crashed against the rickety banister. There was the creak of straining wood, then the crackling sound of it giving away, followed a split-second later by a sharp, staccato crack as the banister broke off. Still locked they pitched down to the lower hall.

Jason was on the bottom when they landed. He hit flat on his back, and his head banged solidly against the floor. The stranger's elbow dug brutally into the pit of his stomach, and Jason choked for his wind while his head spun and a darkness that was not natural swept over him.

The stranger tore away, tottered to his feet, and reeled down the corridor. He reached the front door, ripped it open in panicky haste, and lunged out.

Jason groaned deep in his throat and rolled over on his stomach as his knees buckled in a vast effort to regain his breath.

A door opened and a stream of yellow light leaped out. Two men, one of them half-dressed, peered out cautiously and saw him toiling to his knees, with his hands braced against the floor. After a brief moment they rushed over to him and dragged him to his feet.

"What the hell happened, Buddy?" asked one.

"Oh… I must have… fell," gasped the big man hoarsely.

"I'll say you must have. Here, we'll give you a hand."

"No. I'll be… all right."

"But let's give you a hand."

Jason shrugged them off. "Dammit, let go! I can walk."

He reeled away, found the staircase and climbed it slowly. He sagged into his room, kicked shut the door and dropped down into the Morris chair. Ten minutes later he was breathing normally. He reached for his pipe and began stuffing it thoughtfully.

An hour later the telephone rang, and he stared at the instrument absently for a moment before rising to detach the receiver. A voice at the other end said:

"Listen, Buck, what the devil do you mean by treating a friend and client of mine like that?"

"Oh, hello, Phil," grumbled Jason.

"Honest, Buck, it rather stunned me," said Philip Corson, attorney-at-law. "I send a friend to engage your services and you treat her as if—"

"Lady didn't mention your name," was Jason's lame excuse.

"Oh, pshaw, you knew who sent her! Now see here, Buck. Take my word that it's not riskier than any other stunt you've pulled—"

"Hold on," interrupted Jason. "You're speaking over a telephone wire."

"Well, I'll run down, then, and have a chat with you," suggests Corson.

"Come on. But I wish to hell you wouldn't be sending any

more women around. It's kind of out o' my line, and I don't like it. You ought to know that."

"Oh, stop your growling, you old bear!" chuckled Corson, and hung up.

Jason put down the telephone, still frowning. He had not told Corson of the fight on the stairs, nor was he of a mind to—not yet, at least.

Corson breezed in half an hour later. He was a tall, spare, intense man, graying slightly at the temples. He again took Jason to task for being so short with the woman, and the big man sat in his old Morris chair puffing out clouds of tobacco smoke and saying nothing until the lawyer had concluded.

"Finished, Phil?" was what Jason said then, and continued with—"All your fault for not warning me. You know that in my game women don't go. And you know that if I went putting my face as blindly into something dark as this client of yours wants me to, you wouldn't be getting as good liquor as you've been getting lately from yours truly. I'll admit she's a damned fine-looking lady, and that I'm a pretty low animal not to work for her in this mystery. But you know me. You should have known better, sending her here."

"Well, Buck, take my word for it that she's all right," pleaded Corson. "I don't know what it is, but she is probably making more mystery out of it than is really necessary. It's river work, or harbor work, and you know your ground. She swears to me there's no gun work."

"And another thing," broke in Jason. "I'm not used to dickering with women on money matters."

"You don't have to. I'll act as her agent and pay you, and you know I wouldn't be doing that if I wasn't sure of things. I told her you'd probably consent—"

"Who told you to tell her that?"

"Now, Buck—now, Buck!" grinned Corson. "The orders so far are for you to be at an unfrequented pier on the East River at ten-thirty tomorrow night. Somebody will meet you there and board your launch. What pier would you suggest, Buck?"

Jason was scowling to himself, and two impulses were fighting within him. One was his innate shrewdness that balked at flighty ideas, that sensed a trap at every turn—this rare impulse that made it possible for him to ply his shadow-trade in New York waters. The other impulse was one quite human in the healthy male—the impulse to serve this woman who had come seeking his aid for some mission of the night. She was, he mused, fighting against odds. There was the man whom he had fought in the hallway, the man who for some reason had attacked her. By gad, he would like to meet that bird again!

It came hard, but it came— "Farley's Pier, I guess."

"Good!" exclaimed Corson.

Jason leveled a finger at him. "Now get me straight, Phil. You send any more women to get me mixed up with and you'll get no more liquor."

"All right, Buck, old boy," put in Corson, clapping him on the back. "Well, I must get along. Awfully busy, y' know."

"Humph!" Jason got to his feet and crossed to the sideboard. "Have a drink before you go," he rumbled—an amiable rumble.

II

I T WAS ten of a hot and moonless summer night when Jason boarded his motorboat at a North River pier. Night gangs were at work unloading sugar from a big tramp steamer, and steam winches were clanging and rattling. Starting the motor, he let it run for a few minutes before casting off. In order to reach the stream he had to pass between a row of lighters and the big tramp steamer, and as he was gliding cautiously alongside the black hull a man looked over the rail on the after well-deck, grinned and emptied a bucket of refuse that landed full on the small boat's cabin.

Jason stopped and raised a fist. "You mutt-faced dock-rat, I'll come up there and cave in your jaw!" he roared.

"So'll yer old man, matey," cackled the sailor. "Maybe ye like this better." A moment later something solid hurtled down and landed with a muffled thud in a coil of hawse-line in the cockpit. It was a rock-like lump of sugar big as a man's head, and it was fortunate that Jason had ducked it.

Cackling, the man left the rail and Jason, after a moment, threw his engine into speed and drove on. It took him about twenty minutes to reach Farley's Pier, which is on South Street not far from the Seamen's Institute. Looping a line about a bitt on the dock, he saw that the place was deserted, silent, and he nodded his satisfaction as he bent to wind the line tighter about the bow bitt. Then he rolled into the small cabin, took a bottle of beer from a metal tub in which there was a small cake of ice to keep the drinks cool, and yanked off the cap on the rim of the brass porthole. He swallowed half of the contents in three huge gulps, then set the bottle down, rasped his throat, and crammed fresh tobacco in his briar.

"Too warm down here," he muttered half aloud, and went up on the dock.

The river—the river he knew so well—rolled by in the humid darkness. Lights shone upon its black bosom—lights that moved, red lights, green lights, white lights. The many lights of Brooklyn Bridge arched across the dark river. Pompous little tugs strutted by puffing importantly. One, with two white lights at its masthead, groaned under the burden of a heavy tow that sloshed behind at the end of a fifty-foot line.

Jason stood with his feet planted wide, with his steel-thewed arms crossed on his great chest, and a ribbon of smoke drifting slowly from his pipe. And he stared out across the beshrouded river, wondering what strange mission lay before him. He was not worried; he was not the man to worry. He merely was curious concerning the vague undertaking to which he was to be a party; a perfectly natural curiosity, considering his precarious position in the enterprise.

After a while he jumped down on to the roof of his cabin,

took a glance at the clock inside, and then sat on the seat in the stern sheets, watching the dock. Presently he heard footsteps that walked slower as they approached, and after a moment he saw a face, shaded by a low-pulled hat, regarding him.

"O.K.," he called in a low voice.

A small figure in a loose-fitting coat and baggy trousers came down awkwardly from the dock, stepped cautiously across the roof of the cabin and then down into the cockpit.

"You were sent by—" began Jason; then he rasped: "Good Lord!"

It was the woman in man's clothing.

"Am I on time?" she inquired simply.

Jason was standing by this time, with his fists jammed solidly against his hips.

"Yes, you are on time all right, but where do you think you're going? I didn't contract to carry a woman."

"But I'm here now," she stated quietly.

"Lord, if I had Corson here now I'd push in his face for playing a trick like this on me!"

"Oh, no, Mr. Corson didn't know I was coming," she explained.

"Well, if he hadn't sent you in the first place—"

"Oh, please, Mr. Jason, don't be angry. You'll be paid well—"

"Bah! I'm not thinking about money. But I don't like the idea of sailing around with a woman in man's clothing on a wild-goose chase I know nothing about. It's crazy. I've never done anything like it before. It's out of my line."

"But we've gotten so far we may as well go through with it."

"Oh, *we* may as well go through with it! You talk as if I know what it is all about."

She stood silent for a long moment, fumbling with a button on her coat. Then she asked a point-blank question: "Are you going or aren't you?"

Jason muttered impatiently, stormed below, drank another bottle of beer and sat for a whole minute glaring at the empty bottle. Then he chopped off a silent oath, reached over and jammed the heel of his hand against the self-starter. The motor started with a roar, and Jason, after casting off, climbed back to the cockpit and sat down by the wheel. He threw the motor into reverse, released the clutch and backed out into the stream.

"Oh, you—you're going?" the woman ventured tentatively.

"What's the course?" he flung at her.

"Up through Hell Gate to Long Island Sound."

Once clear of the pierhead, Jason spun the wheel savagely and headed upriver. Looking back, he saw three dim shapes standing at the end of the dock, and he thought he saw one of them studying his craft with a pair of night glasses.

"I don't like that," he clipped.

"What's that?" asked the woman.

"Oh, nothing," he lied gruffly.

They drove northward on the dark river, passed beneath the Brooklyn Bridge.

"I don't blame you for being a little angry," began the woman. "It seems awfully absurd, this role I'm playing. I'd explain everything to you, only it's of such a personal nature.... You know how it is."

"Um," murmured Jason through his pipe, toying with the wheel. Then: "At least I ought to know what I'm to do when we reach Long Island Sound."

"There is a yacht lying off Westchester Creek," she said.

"And?—"

"I'm going to board it and I should like you to wait for me."

"I suppose that's all I'm supposed to know."

"Ye—es, please."

Jason took his pipe from his mouth and looked across at her piercingly. "Honest, I can't understand you at all. You're harder to figure out than a Chinese puzzle."

"You," she smiled, her white teeth gleaming in the darkness, "are just as much of a puzzle to me."

"Rats!" scoffed Jason, as he chugged beneath Manhattan Bridge.

He stood up, then, and with a pair of binoculars peered downriver.

"Someone following us?" queried the woman.

"Pretty black. Can't see much." He sat down by the wheel again and put the binoculars into the small box screwed to the back of the little cabin.

Steadily he drove his fast black craft upriver, up past Blackwell's Island and Long Island City, where he was almost run down by a railroad tug hauling two loaded steel car floats, in his attempt to race across its bow before it blocked the narrow passage. He made it, but not by a very large margin, and the tugboat's captain, who was leaning out of the pilot-house window, unleashed a tobacco shot and a stream of waterfront oaths that made the woman blush and turn away.

Strangely Jason held his tongue. He knew that if he returned some of his own abuse it would only bring warmer and more colorful curses from the man on the tug. So he turned his back to the man and soon was out of earshot. He kept turning the wheel slowly and a little later passed between Astoria and Ward's Island, plugging through Hell Gate passage.

He did not say much to the woman. He had nothing to say—nothing, he reasoned, that would be of any interest to her. She was sitting on the bench that covered the gasoline tanks on the starboard side of the cockpit, and she was silent, too. Time and again Jason stood up to sweep the darkness behind with his glasses, and when they were passing between Riker's Island and the Brother Islands, he strained his ears.

"What?" asked the woman.

"Oh, nothing, I guess," he muttered slowly.

Big railroad yards were off to their left, and they could see many lights and hear the sudden, explosive exhausts of switching engines. But Jason wasn't paying any attention to those

sounds. He thought he had heard the low put-a-put of a motorboat somewhere behind in the gloom, but he wasn't sure.

He drove on through the darkness, wishing this strange
venture was over. Not that strange ventures worried him much.
But this woman. What a mess there would be if they got tangled
up with the law! Alone, he wouldn't care. But the woman would
cause a lot of explaining on his part.

Damn Phil Corson! Well, if they got into trouble he'd make
Corson work his head off to get them out again, and there
would be no fee either. Of course, he mused, on second thought,
Corson would do that without being prompted. But why the
devil had Corson picked on him to aid the woman? Blast the
fool!

"It's off to the right more," the woman was saying, "farther
away from the mouth. I think I see its lights."

They were off Pugsley's Creek now and beginning to plow
across the mouth of Westchester Creek. Jason spun the wheel
and swung his bow to starboard.

"I shan't be on board more than five minutes," the woman
explained.

He could see the riding lights of a fair-sized craft up ahead
in the murk, and soon he could make out the vague lines of a
white schooner yacht. Looking across at the woman, he saw
that she was tying a black silk handkerchief about her face just
below the eyes. He frowned.

"What's the idea of the rag?" he bit off.

"I mustn't be recognized," she replied.

He thought for a moment, still frowning. Finally—"Listen.
You're going to make a mess of things, I'll bet. You're not the
kind to pull whatever you're going to attempt. Dammit, I've
come this far, and if there's anything aboard that yacht you
want, tell me where it is and I'll go and get it."

"Oh, it's so awfully good of you," she told him warmly, "but
it is better that I go."

"It's this," clipped Jason. "What do you know about dirty

work after dark? What good d' you suppose that masquerade is going to do you? Your hands are shaking as it is. If it— Say, speaking frank, is it letters you're after—old love letters?" he asked abruptly.

"No; oh, no," she hastened to deny.

"Humph! This is a fine fix," muttered Jason. "Blind leading the blind. I know blamed well I shouldn't have come on this skylark in the first place. I—"

"Oh, please, we are so near there now." Her voice came muffled through the black silk handkerchief.

Jason clamped his teeth harder on the stem of his pipe and said nothing. The dusky white schooner yacht was looming larger, and he could see a few lighted portholes, and distinguish her rigging in detail. She was bow on to him now, and he maneuvered so that he could slide up alongside her 'midships without any waste motion. The water was calm here, and black as ink, and he shut his engine down to low speed, moving along with the least noise possible. He slid past her graceful prow, shut off the motor, and let his sleek black craft drift with the momentum. There was scarcely any noise at all as he grazed the white hull, his launch's rubber bumpers deadening what little sound there was.

The woman was already standing on the roof of the trunk cabin, with a hand outstretched to catch one of the upright steel bars that supported the rail. Then, with a quick movement, she leaped, caught on with both hands and swung up aboard the yacht. In another moment she had disappeared from Jason's sight.

The tide kept Jason's boat against the yacht's hull, and he stood in the cockpit with his hands thrust deep in his pockets and his eyes glued on the beshrouded yacht. His head was cocked a little on one side, his ears tuned to catch the first indication of danger. Oddly enough he found himself worrying more over the strange woman's safety than was customary for him to worry even over his own. Rounding thirty, he was old in the ways of the world—that is, in the world of give and take—and he was one of that hard-headed company of men that believes in the slogan, every man for himself. This same slogan becomes a puzzle difficult to solve when there is a woman in the case.

Thus with Jason who ever since the strange woman had first visited him and made her enigmatic request, had found himself in a tangled dilemma. Optimists may talk a lot about man sacrificing for man, depriving himself of this, that and the other thing to benefit another; but optimists in human character are usually men who do not go out and down into the world and meet life raw and unadorned, fighting their fight alone, working out their own salvation. Jason was not an optimist. The existence he lived would not allow of it. Close contact with the ragged edge of humanity had moulded him into a man who stood alone, fought alone, worked out his own salvation alone, asking no counsel but his own. He was hard-headed because only in that, considering his precarious calling, lay his scheme of self-preservation; which scheme, when you get right down to bed-rock, is a driving force, vast and elemental, a legacy from the stone age, an inheritance of every man, optimists to the contrary notwithstanding.

Jason had no illusions of heroism and valor. Yet there was something vague and unaccountable working within him, something that caused him no little anxiety over the woman's safety, that welled up gradually and made him want to help her in whatever strange undertaking she was engaged. Impatient now, peculiarly on edge, he stepped to the roof of the cabin just as a door on the yacht opened and a man in shirtsleeves, with a peaked officer's cap on the back of his head, strolled out upon the deck, puffing a cigarette. At sight of Jason on the launch he stopped short and squinted.

"What are you doing there?" he asked promptly.

Jason thought for a moment, undecided just what excuse to make. Then:

"Oh, I just slid up alongside thinking you might want—"

The man chuckled; then said:

"Nope, I don't. We've got a case of Old Taylor can beat any of your bootleg. Just up from the tropics."

"Oh, I see. H'm. You the captain?"

"Nope. One of the officers." He leaned on the rail. "Skipper got a brain-storm in Algiers. He's here in a hospital now. How's business?"

"Not so bad. Pretty nice yacht you've got."

"Yeah, not so bad. Been on better ones, though. Still, she's all right. Can do twelve easy, only she's jumpy in dirty weather."

Jason was satisfied that as yet the woman's presence aboard the yacht was not known, but this was her only line of escape and somehow he must get rid of the man before he himself was invited to move along. He said:

"Dark night out."

"Yeah, ain't it though?" He chuckled intimately. "Good for your kind of business, huh?"

"Kind of. Riding pretty short, aren't—?"

His question was interrupted by the sudden slam of a door aft.

"What th' hell was that!" snapped the officer, and darted off.

Jason stood for a moment considering, then swung up aboard the yacht and crouched spread-legged in an attentive attitude.

III

THE WOMAN came tearing toward him. The black handkerchief had fallen down about her neck and she was extending a hand before her as she ran, as if mutely imploring his assistance. In that hand, he noticed, she gripped a small leather pouch.

Two men gained the deck and raced for her. One was the officer with whom Jason had been talking, and the other was a huge, broad man whom he instantly recognized as the man who had fought him last night in the hallway. He noticed the gold braid on the cap pulled low on the man's head.

"Behind me—then jump to the boat!" he flung at the woman.

His shoulders drooped a bit, and his fists rolled into two hummocky chunks of flesh and bone. In the beam of light thrown from the nearest porthole a lump of muscle showed at the corner of his mouth, and there was a jut to his teak-hard jaw.

The younger officer, who reached him first, struck at him with a wrench, and Jason stopped the blow in mid-career with a bare, rugged forearm. His other fist swept in a short arc and crunched with terrific force against the man's chin. The young officer keeled over, crashed against the wall of the deckhouse and slid down in a huddled, motionless heap.

Jason rushed to meet the chief officer. The two men, both big and tough in the framework, met as two bulls might meet. There was no parrying for an opening. They plowed into each other with fists driving hard, and both took blows that would have dropped a smaller man. They locked and wheeled across the deck, every muscle in their bodies bulging and straining.

With a huge effort Jason tore loose, reeled back sharply and then stopped short, standing spread-legged with his head thrust forward. The mate lunged for him, let go with an overhead swing that missed Jason's cheek by a hair and thudded against his shoulder. Jason laughed in his face and ripped up a short, stiff jab that snapped back the mate's head. He followed with a straight blow to the stomach, and then a well-timed, thundering shot flush on the iron jaw. The mate sagged, his head rolled, his knees buckled, and he pitched forward on his face. But he came up again, rushing before he was fully erect. Jason laughed and crashed to the button again. The mate stopped short, wobbled, and began falling back until he hit the deck on the back of his head, where he rolled over, groaning in his arms which covered his face.

Jason leaped for the rail and saw the woman standing on the

roof of the launch's cabin, clutching the leather pouch in hands that moved up and down nervously. He landed beside her with a thud.

"Down in the cockpit—fast!" he clipped over his shoulder as he dived below.

The engine started with a roar, and the timbers vibrated. Leaping up to the wheel, he spun it hard over even as he released the clutch. The propeller churned the calm water, the boat rocked a bit and then curved away from the white yacht, plugging hard into the darkness that lay thick upon the darker Sound.

The yacht faded gradually, until soon it lay pale and scarce discernible in the black murk. Only then did Jason relax and sit back with one hand resting carelessly on the wheel. And only then did he look across at the woman, who was sitting opposite him on the other side of the cockpit, silent and tense and white-faced.

"Well," he dragged out, "now what?"

She exhaled a long breath and her shoulders drooped. "Oh, I don't know how I can ever thank you," she said throatily.

"H'm. You got what you came for?"

She looked down at the pouch still grasped in her hands.

"Yes," she nodded, though it seemed her thoughts were elsewhere. After a moment she went on: "Yes, I have them, thanks to you. You were wonderful. You didn't even ask about things. What made you help me?"

Jason frowned. "Only thing there was to do."

"Oh, no," she argued softly, and sighed. "You might have stood by and—"

"Rats!" he grumbled.

She smiled at him in the darkness, as if amused, perhaps oddly pleased, at his gruffness.

"You know," she said, "I ought to tell you—now—why I came."

"I don't care a rap why you came," he gave her. "Only thing I'm interested in now, is getting you back ashore and dodging whatever patrol boats are out."

"But I'll tell you," she insisted softly, "because I was so pig-headed about it before. I know I can trust you now—"

"Don't be too sure. You never know who you can trust. Take it from me."

"But I trust you. Listen!" She raised the pouch. "There are six emeralds in here."

Jason showed no interest.

"Six emeralds," she repeated. "My father's. He was captain of that yacht, which has just returned from the Near East. In Algiers he got a touch of sun—was out of his mind till day before yesterday, when he told me about the emeralds. He came by them in Constantinople. He was taking a stroll one night when he saw two men attacking another with knives. He intervened, and the man whom he saved turned out to be a wealthy Turk. These emeralds came from the Turk in a plain box just at sailing time, and he did not open the box until they were well under way. When he did open it, it was in his cabin, and his chief officer, whom you fought with in your hall last night, and whom you knocked out on the yacht, saw them. He tried to buy some from dad so that he might sell them in this country at a great profit, but dad refused to sell. He asked dad many times, and became ugly when he did not succeed. So my father, playing safe, hid them in the oil lamp in his cabin. This lamp was rarely used, and was there in case the electric system broke down. He merely dropped them in the oil well, and I thought it was a novel idea.

"The chief officer became bitter, and he and dad came to words. Then dad got a touch of sun in Algiers. He recovered, or thought he had, but somehow or other, while they were at sea on the way over, he collapsed on the bridge, and was half-unconscious all the way over. He has been in the hospital since the yacht arrived.

"The night before last someone broke into my apartment and ransacked the place while I was out. I told father about it when he was able to sit up, and he swore it must have been his chief officer who, failing to find the emeralds on the ship, had looked for them in my apartment. He didn't want to have the mate arrested, because the emeralds were shady to begin with. It was necessary to smuggle them in, for the duty would have been more than we could pay. I begged him to let me get them, somehow or other, and finally he gave me a spare key to his stateroom. It had to be done quickly, for the yacht is leaving tomorrow morning to meet the owner at Bar Harbor, and the mate is in command till dad returns, though he still keeps his own quarters.

"Well, the emeralds were in the lamp. I got them and was just closing the door when the mate happened to come out of his room. He's a brutal man. That night he trailed me to your place and when he caught me in the hall he almost choked me because I wouldn't tell what I knew about them. Tonight he actually struck at me with his fist, but I dodged—" She stopped short, catching her breath.

Out of the darkness a long shaft of dazzling light had suddenly leaped upon the boat. Jason crouched instinctively, gripping the wheel hard.

"What?" cried the woman.

"Patrol, damn them!" barked Jason. "Get below. Get!"

The woman leaped into the cabin, and Jason threw a quick glance over his shoulder, saw vaguely a low black shape racing after him, while the glaring white eye regarded him unwaveringly. His big engine roared and pounded, and every timber in the sleek little craft vibrated. He was driving it for all it was worth, with everything open wide, with the propeller churning the water at top speed and leaving behind a sudsy white wake.

This running away from the law was not new to him. He had done it time and time again on other black, moonless nights, and lady luck had run beside him. He had a fast boat, and on those other occasions the law had had slower boats, or he had lost them among the maze of islands and creeks round about New York and New Jersey.

But it did not take him long to see that tonight the situation was reversed, that, of all nights, this was one when the law had a boat just a little faster than his own. Yes, that searchlight was gaining slowly but steadily, and eventually he would be overtaken, his boat would be searched, and they would come upon the emeralds.

This seemed inevitable. Under the circumstances they would mistake the woman for his woman and treat her accordingly. Indeed, he mused, it would not be a very pleasant experience for her, and he swore under his breath on general principles.

He racked his brain for some method of eluding that persistent patrol boat, for some method of keeping those emeralds out of the hands of the law. Once in such hands, the woman would lose them forever.

Above the roar of his motor he heard a bull voice roaring through the gloom for him to stop. A shot spat in the darkness and lead buried itself in the back of the cabin. Jason bent lower and drove steadily for a creek he knew was dead ahead. Perhaps if he could run in there, beach his boat and get the woman ashore....

Another slug rapped against the cabin, splintering the wood. The light was drawing nearer. Still another jet of gun-fire slashed through the darkness, and the slug ricochetted off the roof of the cabin.

The woman called to him— "They're shooting! You'll get hit! Hadn't we better give up? Oh, I never thought—"

"Lay low!" he flung down to her.

Again the bull voice came roaring through a megaphone.

Jason rasped back: "Come and get me, you bums!"

The mouth of the creek now spread before him, and the water lay inky and smooth as a mill-pond. Faintly there came to him the dank, sweet smell of the marshes. Not much water here; a little shallower and that patrol boat could not follow him. But as it was....

Another shot, dangerously close that time.

Jason certainly was in a pinch, and he was thinking hard. It seems that when big, capable men are in a bad way, hard-pressed with the last vestige of hope apparently flown—it seems that at such a time strange ideas rebound through the brain, and out of the hodge-podge of it all one is drawn and used to stave off what a moment ago appeared to be inevitable.

Jason bent down suddenly and called to the woman. "Give me that bag of emeralds." Even as he yelled this he left the wheel and dived into the cabin.

THE PATROL boat pressed on, with a group of men bunched in the bow. One of these men was Detective Luke Trask. He leaned on the rail, his wet eyes glaring, a smoking revolver in his hand, and oath after oath rolling from his lips.

"I'd go easy with the gun, Luke," counseled one in the group. "The guy might get sore and fire back."

Trask rasped: "He don't use a gun—not if you paid him."

"Anyhow, I'd go easy—"

"Shut your trap!" snapped Trask, and, aiming, took another shot.

After a moment a new figure came out of the cabin—a capable looking woman well in her thirties, apparently, with keen, shrewd eyes and a firm, almost masculine mouth.

"I shouldn't go firing that thing like that, detective," she said, moving up among the group in the bow.

"But we got to get that guy, Miss Tait," argued Trask.

"Nevertheless," she clipped tartly, "I have no desire to see the woman hit by a stray shot. You're interested in this Buck Jason individual, but my game is the woman."

"But I tell you it's a man with Jason."

"No. A woman in man's clothing," corrected Miss Tait. "I trailed her from her apartment. And as a conscientious federal agent, I'm not eager to see her killed. At first I thought the man who tipped us off was just sore over something. He's a mate or something. Came in first thing this morning, told us some precious emeralds were being smuggled in, and pointed out to me where the woman lived."

"Look, guys!" cried one of the men. "He's swingin' around."

"Maybe Luke hit him," volunteered another.

"No such luck!" snarled Trask.

But the boat ahead was indeed turning about and in short time was bow on to them, and motionless.

Trask stood erect and spun his gun on his finger. "Finally got wise to himself. We got a faster boat than him tonight. Watch me take the big boob down a peg."

The patrol boat bore down on the black launch, and her propeller stopped presently as she nosed alongside.

Trask, chuckling thickly, leaped across with his gun drawn, while three men followed close at his heels, and the woman brought up the rear.

Jason stood in the cockpit with his hands in his pockets and his pipe in his mouth.

"Oh, it's you, Trask," he rumbled with disapproval.

"Yeah, it's me. Take a good look if y' ain't sure. Kinder spoiled your game tonight, huh?"

"No game at all, you ham gumshoe."

"Oh, so! Ha! Ha! Know any more jokes?"

"Only the one I'm looking at."

Trask scowled and turned to his men.

"Search this tub, boys, for liquor," he snapped.

The men jumped to their task, and Miss Tait, who had remained in the background, came forward and regarded the woman in man's clothing.

"I want to search you," she said crisply. "As soon as the men get out of the cabin, we'll go in there."

"Who are you?" Jason put to her.

"Tait, federal agent."

The men came out of the cabin and one said:

"Nothin' doin', boss."

"Told you it wasn't liquor," Miss Tait gave Trask. "You search the man for the emeralds and I'll search the woman. Come, miss," she said to the other woman, who by this time was pale, nervous and very much embarrassed.

The federal agent took the young woman into the cabin while Trask and one of his men went through Jason. They found nothing. As they finished, Miss Tait came out with the girl.

"Nothing on her," she reported. "Now make a systematic search of the boat, will you, detective?"

The search began. They ransacked every inch of the boat, ripped open the leather seats in the cabin, tore up the boards. Cans of motor oil were drained. They left nothing unturned, and ruined everything they put their hands on.

Trask perspired in the stuffy cabin, muttering through twisted lips as he bored into every dark nook. Finally he came out mopping his face, which was crimson with chagrin. For want of something better to do, he again searched Jason, and finding nothing, snarled:

"Where's them jewels?"

"Pipe down!" chuckled Jason. "You make me laugh, you're so dumb. Who ever said anything about jewels?"

Miss Tait put in: "Have a man walk around the boat and see if there is anything hanging overside."

Trask grunted and passed the order on to one of his men. The man came back a moment later and shook his head.

"Nothin' doin', boss," he said.

"You must ha' got a bum steer," Trask said to Miss Tait.

"I don't know," replied Miss Tait. "Anyhow, I've searched this woman, you've searched the man and the boat. It's strange, though, that she should be dressed like a man."

"Not at all," broke in Jason. "She intends to write some articles on New York, and she's seeing life from the bottom up."

"Um," mused Miss Tait.

Jason said, "Now, Trask, you'd better drift. You've just about torn my boat to pieces and you've found nothing."

Trask pursed his lips and eyed Jason damply.

"Just been givin' us a chase, eh?" he droned.

"Sure. Try laughing it off, gumshoe," was Jason's shot.

"All right, big boy. I'll laugh it off. Pull another one like that, though, an' a stray bullet's liable to cook your goose. An' remember! We got our eyes on you—ev'ry night. Park that in your head an' don't let it get away."

"Better use the best glasses you can get," said Jason. "You'll need 'em."

Trask chopped off an oath, swung about and climbed back aboard the patrol boat. Miss Tait and the men followed. The searchlight swept away, and the patrol boat, its engines roaring, slid by, turned around and headed out of the creek.

The woman relaxed. "Thank the Lord that's over," she murmured. "Look what they've done to your boat. Oh, it's awful of me, causing you all this trouble. That Miss Tait was a woman who followed me from my apartment—I should have told you—only I thought I had lost her and I had to take the chance. But now I guess they're gone. You had to throw them away, didn't you?"

"Um," muttered Jason through his pipe, and turned to stare overside at the water. "We ought to have 'em back pretty soon now."

"But how? You can't dive down and find them in the dark."

Jason pointed at the water, close to the side. "Just keep watching there."

They both watched, sitting side by side, saying little. And before very long there was a ripple on the smooth surface as some object broke slowly from beneath. Jason reached out with a boat-hook and pulled it closer, then leaned over and lifted from the water a gallon-size tin can that once had contained lubricating oil. Attached to this was a short length of line and at the other end of the line was a rope sling. Chuckling, Jason unscrewed the cap and poured out six emeralds into the woman's hands.

"Thank you—oh, I don't know what I can ever do—" she began.

"Wait," put in Jason. "Thank a sailor on a dirty old tramp steamer."

"I don't understand," she said.

"Before I reached that pier on the East River I had an argument with a sailor who heaved a big hunk of sugar at me. Maybe you saw it on that coil of rope. Well, the idea just popped. I shoved it in this sling, tied it to the can with the emeralds and pitched the whole-shooting match overside. It was heavy enough then to drag down the can, but the water broke it up gradually and, well, you saw how the can just came up again. Funny, eh, how a guy thinks of things like that?"

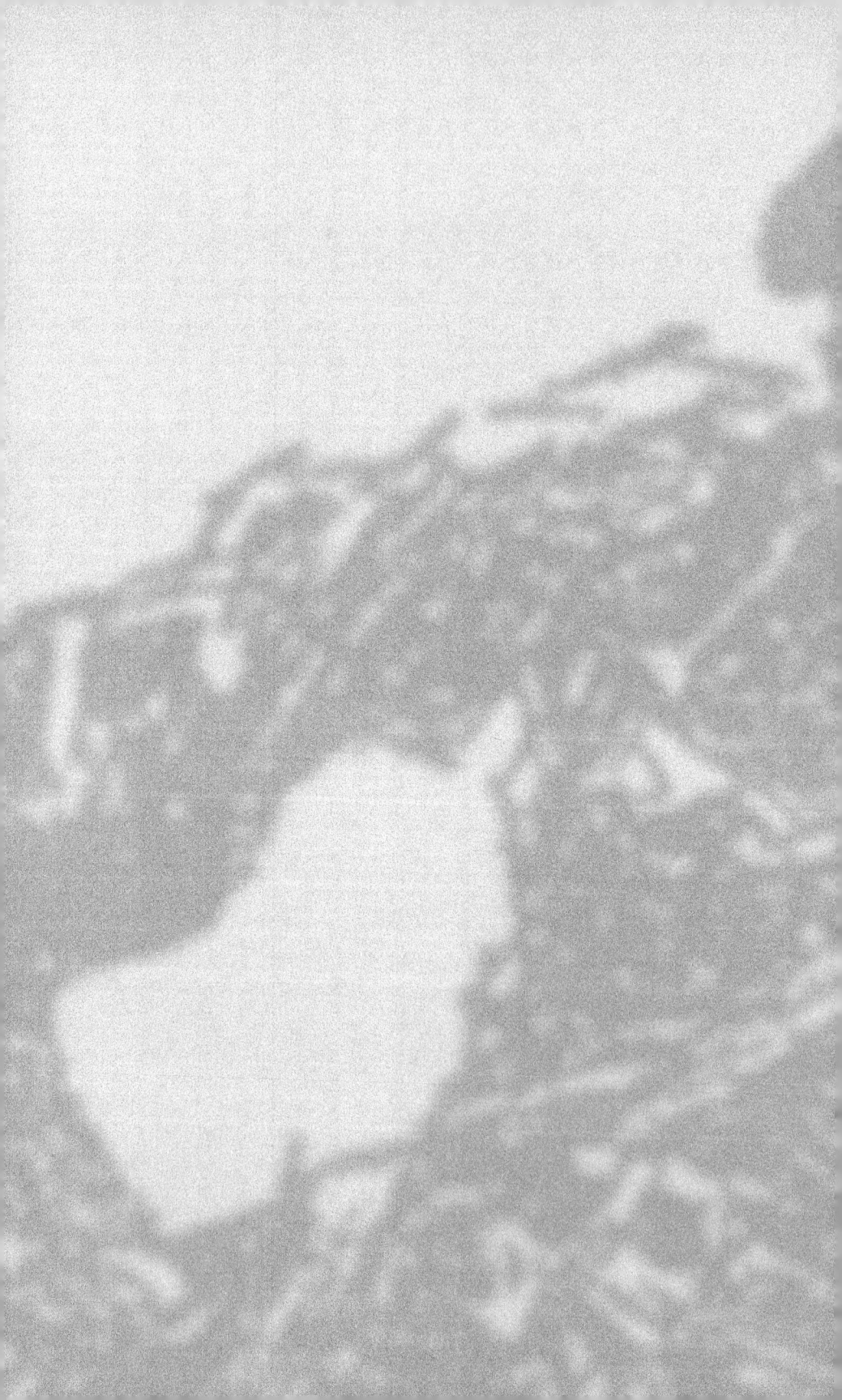

A Grudge is a Grudge

And it is a strong one when a crook has it in for a former pal.

TWO MEN faced each other across a bare table in the back room of a Greek speakeasy near Madison Street. One was Eddie Winstrom, who once on a time had done a short stretch for getting his hand caught in somebody else's pocket. The other was "Chick" Cronin, who had killed four men in as many years and done no stretch at all.

Winstrom seemed nervous and ill at ease. There was a hunted look in his troubled blue eyes, and he was tearing a half-smoked cigarette to shreds. He kept biting his under lip. He was a rather good-looking young man, clean-cut and neatly dressed.

Cronin was older—say in his late thirties. His mouth was wide and hard, with a sardonic twist at the corners. Big eyes, dark and malignant, flanked a beak of a nose. There was a jut to his jaw, and the cicatrix of an old wound gleamed just under his right cheek-bone. He was lean and wiry, a little above medium height, and hard as nails. The well-made clothes he wore offered sufficient evidence of the fact that he was not by any chance a tramp gunman who went in for cut-rate killings.

He took a long pull on his cigar and let the smoke drift lazily from his nostrils. His lips parted crookedly in what was intended for a smile.

"Cripes, Eddie, I never thought I'd meet you in New York," he said. "When did you leave 'Frisco?"

"Three years ago."

"Just after you got out o' jail, eh?"

Winstrom dug his fingernails in his palm. "Yes," he replied in a muffled voice.

"That's great," chuckled Cronin, and regarded his hands for a moment. Then: "Guess you been finding pickings pretty good, eh? You look like it."

"I'm working—have been since I came here."

"What are you working, Eddie?"

Winstrom shot him a fast look. "I'm working! Don't you understand? I've gone straight since that job in 'Frisco, and I'm going straight as long as I live, so help me!" He hit the table a crack with the flat of his hand.

Cronin sat back and made a round "o" of surprise with his mouth. His eyebrows arched, and his big eyes seemed ready to pop from their sockets.

"So-o!" he exclaimed in a soft whisper.

Winstrom looked away, muttering behind clenched teeth, tapping nervously on the table with his fingers.

Then Cronin dropped his chin to his chest and chuckled softly, liquidly, as though he were musing over an enormous joke.

"You're funny, Eddie," he drawled. "Cripes, you're funny! Suppose you've joined a Bowery mission an' all. Makes me laugh, the way them bums get up there on Sundays an' pull the sob stuff."

"Oh, shut up!" Winstrom flung at him. "I'm not that kind. But I'm straight now."

"No wonder you tried to duck me, eh? Putting on the high hat and all, ain't you?"

"No, not a bit of it. But there's no use in you and me hanging around together."

"Oh, ain't there? Ain't there, now?" Cronin smiled thinly.

Winstrom sat erect and cut the man with a black stare. "See here, Chick. If you're trying to get me into the old game you're all wet. I'm through, I tell you—through! You half dragged me in here, but I'm leaving now, and you're only wasting your time."

"I got plenty o' that to waste. Now listen, you boy scout." He braced his elbow on the table, leaned forward, and wagged a forefinger slowly. "I've been watching you for the past week. I know where you work. I know you're keeping company with a broad in the Bronx, and I know where you live. Guy, we can do business."

"No, we can't," Winstrom bit off.

"Oh, but yes we can. And we're going to."

"The hell we are!"

"For Gawd's sake, pipe down! I said we're going to do business, and I don't mean maybe. As a bank guard, you fit in my plans like a glove. You just have to let me in late some night—"

"Nothing doing!" snapped Winstrom. He jumped to his feet, his fists clenched and his jaw clamped hard.

"Wait, you!" ground out Cronin, a heavy, portentous look in his big eyes. "You'll play with me or I'll spit everything I know about you. You'll lose your job and your girl and before long you'll be frisking pockets on the subway. Get that, boy friend, and hang on to it!"

Winstrom fell back a step, and the old hunted look welled in his eyes, while he ground fist into palm and strove to keep his lips steady.

"Chick, you wouldn't do that!" he cried brokenly.

"Wouldn't I? Wouldn't I, now?" leered Cronin.

"Have a heart, Chick. Give me a decent break. I've been making good. I've been straight right along. That job in 'Frisco was the first I ever tried. I was hard up, hungry, and sick, and at the end of things. You told me it would be easy, and I took a chance. I was clumsy. I—"

"Quit your crabbing!"

"I'm not crabbing, Chick. But lay off me. I don't want to play your game. I don't—"

"Rats! I got you where I want you, an' you got to come across. If you stall, I'll just drop a mysterious message to your boss and one to your sweet mama."

"Damn you, Chick, you're black! You're—"

"Easy, guy, easy, now! I've talked cold turkey. You play with me or your goose is cooked. You get me in that bank somehow—either at night, or some time during the afternoon, when you get me a place to hide. You do that or I spit." His lower lip drooped out and downward when he finished, motionless and wet, repulsive and sullen. His big eyes rested on Winstrom with a dull, dismal stare.

"But, Chick, it's not fair," pleaded Winstrom. "I want to keep straight. It's not fair, the way you—"

"I'm not saying it's fair, am I?" Cronin put in.

Winstrom crouched, his fists knotted so rigidly that the knuckles paled. A lump of muscle quivered at either corner of his mouth, and anguish burned in his eyes, flickered across his face.

"Chick, I won't! I can't!"

"Damn you, you will! I'll squeal on you—tell your boss and the frail you're trotting around with."

"You don't have to!" cried Winstrom suddenly, shaking a fist at him. "I'll tell them. I've been wanting to all along. It's hell keeping a secret like that. I'll tell them. If I get fired, I've got enough money for a while. If my girl sticks by me, we'll take a ship and go somewheres. She'll stick. I know she will. But you can't drag me back. Chick—you can't!"

"I will, damme, or—"

"You won't. If you keep on dogging me, I'll tell the police here about my 'Frisco record and tell 'em you're trying to get me in with you. I will. It might be dirty, but not half as dirty as what you're trying to do." His eyes were blazing now, and he was towering over Cronin.

Cronin got up, a dark frown on his forehead, a deadly look in his malignant eyes.

"You will, will you?" he dragged out menacingly.

"You bet your sweet life I will!"

Cronin's hand moved toward his pocket. Winstrom, tingling all over, with his nerves on edge, did not stop to consider whether the man was reaching for a gun or not. He was all primed, and instinct prompted him to lash out with a terrific blow that crashed on the point of Cronin's jaw and sent him toppling backward over a chair.

Without lingering to ascertain the amount of damage done by his punch, Winstrom leaped for the door, bowled over the Greek bootlegger who was on the run to investigate, and sped on into the street. He hurried along Madison Street, went through Rutgers to Canal and did not stop until he was seated, breathless, in a Second Avenue "L" bound uptown.

"I'll tell Elsie," he kept repeating over and over to himself. "I'll tell the bank people. It'll come out some day. I'll take a chance. I can't keep it to myself any longer."

And he took the chance.

He met Elsie at noon and took her to lunch. He was silent all through the meal, and this caused her to look askance at him, though she asked no questions. Afterward they strolled down to Battery Park and sat there. He kept patting her hand and remarking about the traffic on New York Bay in a jerky, strained voice. His face was flushed, and a troubled look was in his eyes.

Finally, curiosity getting the better of her, she asked, "Eddie, what's the matter? You're—you're—"

He turned to her abruptly, then, biting his lip and meeting her quizzical gaze with a brave effort, he told her. He didn't take long. There was no self-pity. She watched him without the flicker of an eyelash, and when he concluded and bowed his head, she bowed hers, too, and both remained silent for a long minute.

"Eddie," she said at last, "I'm sorry."

He didn't look up. He wasn't sure yet what she was sorry about—sorry for him, or sorry because, perhaps, they must break off relationship. Then she sighed, and pressed his hand, smiling wanly.

"Eddie, you'll be coming up to see me Wednesday, as usual, won't you?" she put to him gently.

He shivered, and almost raised her hand to his lips, but there were too many people about. Yes, he would be there, as usual, for it was his night off.

When he left her, he went directly to the bank where he was guard. To the manager he told his story, told of his three months' imprisonment in California, and of his subsequent three years of silence. The manager listened attentively, showing no surprise, and when the story was finished he sat staring moodily at the desk for a long minute.

Then he took Winstrom into the office of the president, sat down and, after a few preliminary words with the head official, told Winstrom to repeat his story. Winstrom did, in a low, steady voice, and the president, a large, leathery-faced man with a keen, gray eye, puffed slowly on his cigar and listened.

In the end he said, "Well, Winstrom, my boy, you've come clean. Take the load off your feet. Sit down. And listen. I knew all about you a week after you were hired. I'm something of an optimist. You do not know it, but for a solid year after you were hired there was a man watching you every night while you watched the bank. You've been here two and a half years, and you've made good. What made you come clean?"

"Oh, I just couldn't hold in any longer," Winstrom replied.

"I see," nodded the president, then pondered for a moment. "Are you sure," he went on, "that somebody hasn't threatened to expose you?"

Winstrom shook his head negatively, but said nothing. The president looked at the manager, and the manager looked at the president. Then the latter said, "All right, Winstrom. Now that we understand each other, I guess you are safer than ever. When there's an opening in the office, you may find it more pleasant than your night job. Good luck, my boy."

Winstrom went out with a lump in his throat—a lump of pure happiness.

II

IN A dusty room in a police precinct south of Union Square and east of Broadway, Detective Jake Sleary sat on the small of his back in a rickety swivel-chair, with his feet perched atop a desk littered with reward notices, newspaper clippings and tobacco ashes.

The afternoon was warm and drowsy. A bar of rare sunlight streamed through the one dirty window, half raised, and, falling just short of the swivel-chair, shone upon a portion of the floor generously sprinkled with ground-out cigarette butts. The high drab walls were pasted with the likenesses of various men wanted for various crimes, ranging from murder to grand larceny.

Sleary, finding the atmosphere of the day contagious, was likewise warm and drowsy. He reclined in shirtsleeves, with his collar open and his unfastened tie straggling over his shoulders. He was a lank, gaunt man with sandy hair and gentle blue eyes that at times seemed melancholy. He had a wife and two youngsters in a flat in West Eighteenth Street, and throughout the underworld he was known for a man who yanked his gun at

the drop of a hat. His gentle, strangely sad blue eyes had perplexed many a promiscuous gunman.

Presently a large, heavy-set man, with a black mustache and
a serious frown, appeared in the doorway, mopping his sweaty
forehead. He said:

"Hello, Jake. You busy?"

"Yeah," drawled Sleary with a yawn, "Come in and park."

"Thanks. It's hot, ain't it?" The large man settled into an
armchair with a sigh of relief.

"Yeah," agreed Sleary, twisting a little to face his visitor.
"How's tricks, Henry?"

"So-so. How's things by you?"

"Fair. The wife ain't feeling so good, and one o' my kids has
been troubled awful with prickly heat."

"It's the heat, Jake," sympathized the other. "Why don't you
buy a little place in the country—over in Jersey somewheres?
Like me. I got a garden and a flivver and all, only a mile from
the station. The missus meets me at the station with the car.
Nothing like the country, Jake."

"Yeah, I guess you're right, Henry. That's what my wife was
saying. That's what I been thinking about so much lately—I
want to buy a house on time, but the thing is a guy like me
never knows when one o' these hop-heads is going to take a
shot at him. Then where'd the wife be?"

"It's tough, Jake. But what I come about now. The boss at
the bank had a little chin with me, and I guess you're the man
I want to see 'cause me and you are old friends and you can
keep a thing under your hat."

"Sure, Henry."

"Well, it's this, Jake: We got a young bank guard over at the
place who is kind of in trouble, if you know what I mean. I tell
you frank, Jake, he done a three months' stretch about three
years ago in 'Frisco for snooping in somebody's pocket. He's
just told the boss about it, and the boss thinks some mutt is
riding him. The thing is, Jake, we know all about this guy and

his little stretch. The boss is one o' these gents they call optimists. When he first hired this guard he trailed down his record, but instead of giving him the merry air, he has me trail him and keep tabs on him for damn near a year. And I tell you, Jake, the guy's on the level, a square shooter, what I mean. See?"

"Sure, Henry."

"Well," proceeded Henry, scratching his ear, "between you and me, like old friends, I'd like you to look into it. I'll give you the bank guard's address, and when he works, and kind of look after him, Jake, what I mean, in your spare time. Kind of see if any mutt's riding him, and what's what. Will you, Jake, for my sake, like old friends?"

"Yeah, Henry," drawled Sleary. "Why, sure. If some egg's riding your man, why we'll see who the egg is, and maybe we'll do some riding ourself. How about a butt, Henry?"

"Have a cigar. Here."

"Thanks. I ain't been able to buy so many cigars since the wife bought that new living-room set."

"And here's a photograph of the bank guard," went on Henry, passing over a snapshot. "Edward Winstrom. He's square, Jake, and trying hard, and the boss thinks some mutt's riding him ragged."

"I'll poke around first chance I get, Henry," said Sleary peacefully.

The bank detective gave him a few more details, and then rose to go. Looking about the room, his gaze rested on a photo of a particularly venomous-looking man, which was accompanied by a reward notice and a detailed statement of crimes committed.

"Ain't that 'Butch' Sorge, Jake?" he asked, pointing.

"Oh, that? Yeah. Will you tear it down, Henry? There ain't no system here at all. It should have been torn down long ago. But Ike, that Jew partner o' mine, is either out with the girls or taking in a ball game or something."

"Butch is off the slate then, hey, Jake?" asked Henry as he reached over and tore the paper from the wall.

"Yeah. Why, ain't you read the papers yet today?" inquired Sleary with mild surprise.

"No, Jake, I ain't, to tell the truth."

"Well, Henry, Butch is in the morgue. It was his own fault. I asked him in a nice way to keep his hands in the air, but he got nasty and pulled his gat. I just simply had to let daylight into him, that's all. One good thing, he wasn't married."

Henry said, "Oh-o-o!" softly, and then added, "I'll have to get a paper, all right."

When he left, Sleary slouched lower in his chair and drowsed serenely behind the screen of fragrant tobacco smoke which his cigar sent curling toward the ceiling.

"Henry was right," he soliloquized. "There's no place like the country, especially for kids. H'm. Now about this here bank guard...."

III

CHICK CRONIN, who had killed four men in as many years, was nursing a full-size grudge. Some there are in the underworld who claim that a professional killer should never stoop so low as to let a personal grudge drive him to distraction. From a strictly professional viewpoint there is, of course, no money in it, and more than enough danger.

But human nature is human nature, and a grudge is a grudge.

Now Cronin had done two things in an attempt to knock the props from under Eddie Winstrom. That same afternoon, from a telephone booth in the Pennsylvania Station, he had called the bank and, after having become connected with the president's private phone, had said:

"There's a man in your employ named Winstrom. Three years ago he was sentenced to jail for three months in California. You can check up by wiring the San Francisco police department."

That was all he had intended to say, and that was all he said.

He had started to hang up the receiver, but the voice at the other end held him on. It said:

"Thank you for the information. Fact is, we know all about what Winstrom *used* to be. At present, however, he is a very able guard...."

Cronin had slammed the receiver home with a savage gesture and, cursing under his breath, had banged out of the booth and taken the subway to Times Square. From a booth there he had called the office where Elsie Lane worked and said:

"Perhaps it'd interest you to know, miss, that the man you go with is an ex-jailbird. I happen—"

"I don't care," had been the prompt, slightly tremulous reply. "What he is now is what matters, and he is very good."

Again Cronin had slammed back the receiver, muttering:

"The damned skunk has beat me to it! All right, we'll see."

Cronin was black at heart. He was a confirmed crook and a cold-blooded killer, and it stung him to the core to see a one-time crook going straight and making a go of it. He had been quite certain, dead sure, that he could make Eddie Winstrom a pawn in his hands. He had always thought Winstrom a weak kid, and when he discovered that Winstrom had the sand to buck him and go straight in the face of his threats, a smouldering lust for revenge burned in his dark heart.

He sat now in a room in a dubious hotel that reared its six stories of sooty red brick among the other battered brick tenements that sprawl in squalor and disorder between lower Second Avenue and the East River. With him were three hard-eyed men who had a positive past and a rather uncertain future; "Slugs" Howard, "Squint" Daranzio, and "Soup" Dester. Slugs was an ex-pug and notorious bail-jumper; Squint was an out-and-out gunman; Soup knew more about safes than the men who made them.

"Well, you guys," Cronin was saying, "are you game?"

"We're always game," growled Slugs.

"Speak for yourself, big boy," cut in Soup.

Slugs turned a dismal stare on the speaker.

"Crackin' wise? Ever get socked in the nose?" was the frank question.

Soup leaned forward, tapping the table with a bony finger.

"Yes, an' by better men than you. You ain't spokesman here, bimbo. You're just strong-arm guy. An' don't forget who's the little doctor operates on these egg-shell safes."

"Aw, lay off, both o' you," snarled Squint.

"Now, listen," put in Cronin. "Just now I'm spokesman. Can the cheap talk. I asked you birds a question. Are you game?"

"Sure I'm game," replied Slugs.

"Me, too," nodded Squint.

And Soup snapped, "Ditto."

"All right then," went on Cronin. "That's settled. We blow the bank Friday night—night after tomorrow. How's your car running, Squint?"

"Aces up. Them eight cylinders can shove her eighty miles per an' I don't mean maybe."

"O.K. We'll use your car—"

"Say, listen," interrupted Soup. "I ain't heard nothin' yet about a split."

Cronin snapped: "Don't four ways suit you?"

"Sure it does."

"Then pipe down."

"I'm piped, boss."

"Now," went on Cronin, "as I said, we'll use Squint's car. Every guy carries his rod, and don't forget the silencers. I ain't aiming to pull this job bloodless, and if the breaks go against us, it's shoot, guys, and no stalling. After the bust we'll hit for Harlem. Remember, Squint, you want two sets of license plates. If there's a chase and it gets too hot, we switch cars—shake yours and swipe one uptown. All your tools in trim, Soup?"

"Always in trim, bud—like me," was the laconic reply.

"That's jake, then," said Cronin. "I'll be busy for a while now.

Got several other stunts up my sleeve. We'll meet here tomorrow night and I'll spin more details. And meantime you guys keep sober and steer clear of the frails."

"You sure we c'n get in this place?" asked Slugs.

"You leave that to me, boy friend. I'll give you more details tomorrow night, like I said. All right. Now we'll scatter till tomorrow night. Be here at eight."

IV

LIFE TO Eddie Winstrom was beginning to mean something again. Men trusted him; a girl trusted him—his California record notwithstanding. The three years behind represented a malignant sore that suddenly had been removed. In a way of speaking, he was sitting on top of the world.

Yet he somehow knew that he still had Chick Cronin to reckon with. Elsie, like the bank people, was keeping the phone call of the anonymous informer a secret. While with the bank people it might have been tact, with Elsie it was simply the gesture of a strong, deep-rooted love.

It was possibly a so-called sixth sense that made Winstrom believe he had not seen the last of Cronin. Since he had turned the killer's proposition down flat, called his bluff and wound up by taking a blow at his jaw, it was, to his way of thinking, logical that Cronin should try to smash him through another channel.

He knew Cronin pretty well. As a matter of fact, you did not have to study Cronin very long in order to come to the conclusion that he was deadly. It was in his eyes. The hallmark of his calling was stamped in his features.

Winstrom had no intention of looking for trouble. He merely wanted to be left alone by Cronin or anybody else connected with the life that moves in a world of incarnadined shadows. He was clean now—purged. He began to have illusions again—illusions of happiness—ideals. This in itself was a sign indicatory of a healthy mind.

It was Wednesday night, the one night each week he was granted freedom from his vigil in the corridors of marble in the bank. And it was the one night each week that he took Elsie to an unpretentious restaurant for dinner and afterward a movie show or a play, if it wasn't too warm.

Leaving his rooming-house on Twelfth Street at half-past six, he started west for the Fourteenth Street subway station. He did not see a lank, gaunt man step from a hallway in a house opposite and stroll casually after him. Winstrom, clad in a gray suit with a shining new straw hat contrasting well with his tanned, clean-clipped face, was the embodiment of youthful health and vigor.

He boarded an uptown train, and the lank, gaunt man, who had a singularly sad face, entered the car behind and took up a position in the forward vestibule, through the door of which he could look into the car ahead. When Winstrom left the train at Times Square the lank man also left.

He met Elsie at the Forty-second Street exit, and they went to a small restaurant on Thirty-ninth Street. Both were in high spirits. A certain ruddiness beamed through the tan on the man's cheeks, and his blue eyes shone with happiness. Elsie was radiant, and soft laughter rippled from her red lips.

At a table at the far end of the restaurant the gaunt, sad-looking man sat stirring a cup of coffee.

Following dinner, Winstrom and Elsie left the place and strolled up Broadway through the milling crowd. Yellow taxis weaved and honked and darted like things possessed. Newsboys shouted. Trolleys clanged incessantly. Traffic policemen blew shrilly on whistles. Brakes screamed. The surge and sweep and nerve-racking din of the most turbulent of cities was in full sway. To the stranger it is shocking, monstrous; to the cosmopolite it is vaguely monotonous.

Winstrom took Elsie to a moving picture theatre which was artificially cooled, and restful. An usher found them seats in the darkened interior, while the lank man found himself a seat two rows behind them.

After the show they boarded a Fifth Avenue bus and took a seat on top, while the lank man contented himself with a seat below. When they alighted at one of the Central Park byways, the lank man also alighted. And when they started walking uptown the man followed at a discreet distance.

They walked for an hour, slowly, arm in arm, and presently entered a house near One Hundred and Sixtieth Street. The gaunt man strolled by the house, and then stopped at the next corner. Looking over his shoulder, he saw a dark figure cross the street and enter the same house.

He slowly thrust his hand into his coat pocket, retraced his steps and casually entered the doorway. In the lower hall he saw a wiry, well-dressed man standing before a wall telephone and writing in a small book—possibly the telephone number.

The lank, sad-looking man showed no interest, while the other hastily thrust the book into his pocket and, lifting the receiver from the hook, put it to his ear. The lank man passed on, though out of the corner of his eye he did not fail to notice that the other man was holding down the hook. Wearily he began climbing the stairs, and as he reached the first landing he looked back cautiously and saw the man below making for the exit. With a sudden rapidity he descended the stairway, paused in the lobby and, peering out, saw the man hurrying down the street. He lit a cigarette and followed.

Meanwhile Eddie Winstrom was holding Elsie in his arms and kissing her, for Elsie had promised to marry him at the end of another month.

"I'm going to try hard, Elsie," he said earnestly. "I'm going to try hard as the devil to make you happy."

"Eddie, you couldn't try any harder than you have," she told him warmly. "You're wonderful."

"Gee, honey, you're wonderful, too. We'll try to get a little place out in the country—over in Jersey, maybe, huh?"

"Oh, I'd love that, Eddie!" she cried.

V

INTERMITTENT SHOWERS pelted the city on Friday, which dawned hot and sultry, with a bruised red sun that glowered sullenly behind the humid haze. After each shower the pavements steamed, and the thick breath of the city wilted the vitality of its dwellers.

With nightfall there came a steady downpour that drove with a dull rhythm through the motionless air. Uptown the millions of show lights glittered and sparkled and the sidewalks were roofed with the umbrellas of pedestrians. Downtown, way down below City Hall, the deserted canyons of the financial district, barred with black shadows, brooded in a silence that was only emphasized by the monotonous and peculiarly unhurried beat of the falling rain.

Winstrom strolled through the vaulted chambers of the silent bank. Little night-lights here and there shone with a quiet dignity among the marble columns, and a fretwork of vague shadows lay motionless upon the walls and floors. A footfall, a slight cough, reëchoed with startling clarity.

Winstrom wore a simple gray uniform with a visored cap of military design. On his hip was a heavy automatic pistol. He made his rounds slowly, peering into the private offices, looking out of the windows, listening with the involuntary attentiveness to which he had become accustomed.

Presently he reached a small cubbyhole, where he sat down, stuffed and lighted his pipe, and removed his cap, wiping his slightly moist forehead. Leaning back and puffing musingly on his pipe, he smiled to himself.

That afternoon he had bought a ring for Elsie. This time next month they would be married. He was happy—serenely happy. The world was a good place after all. He had spoken to the manager about a day job, and the manager had promised to do all in his power to get him one. There were a lot of good men in the world, Winstrom mused. Three years ago he had thought much differently.

He took a small black case from his pocket, opened it and stared at a small ring with meditative eyes. He hoped Elsie would like it. He was sure she would. Some day soon they would make a pilgrimage to the country and see about a cozy little bungalow. There was no place like the country. That's what Henry Trainor, the bank detective, always said.

His meditations were suddenly interrupted by an insistent pounding in some part of the building. He snapped the little black case shut and thrust it back into his pocket. He looked at the clock on the wall. It was twenty minutes shy of midnight.

He left the cubbyhole with rapid strides, drawing his pistol and releasing the safety catch. He strode down a wide corridor with his ears alert and his narrowed eyes peering intently. He crossed a domed rotunda and slowed down.

He placed the pounding at the front entrance. After a moment's hesitation he proceeded slowly, cautiously. Opening one of the two plate-glass doors that led into the lobby, he hesitated again before the huge, massive, intricately carved oak doors that led to the street. Someone was knocking on these doors.

With his gun leveled, he turned the lock and opened one of the doors on a crack, standing to one side, every nerve and muscle alert and primed.

"Oh, let me in!" panted a woman's voice.

"Elsie!" exclaimed Winstrom. "I—why, no...."

"Eddie!" she gasped; and then groaned, "Oh-o-o!" in sudden agony and pain.

Winstrom looked out to see her crumpling and rolling down the short flight of stone steps. Mystified, he stepped out, saw a big sedan, with a man standing on the running-board, roll to a stop at the curb. Something metallic glinted in this man's hand.

There was a sharp click, and Winstrom felt his left arm

suddenly paralyzed. He pitched down, and with a great effort reached back and pulled the big door shut. The lock clicked. The keys were on the inside.

Three men rushed from the sedan with drawn guns. One carried a small handbag. From where he lay Winstrom pulled his trigger and shot this man dead in his tracks.

"Cripes, there goes Soup!" snarled one.

"Hell!" rasped another. "Pot this bum. Give him the works!"

A revolver boomed a short distance down the street and the man who had swung his gun on Winstrom twisted and fell screaming to the sidewalk.

The man at the wheel of the car snapped: "Come on, Chick. It's the bulls! We gotta get outta here."

A police whistle blew.

"Chick Cronin!" Winstrom muttered under his breath, bitterly.

He slumped down beside Elsie, who lay white-faced and silent, with a crimson shoulder. His own left arm was bloody and throbbing with intense pain.

"Elsie," he groaned, "I'll get him—get him!"

The big sedan's engine roared. Gears crashed as it lunged away from the curb.

Winstrom, lying on his stomach, his eyes blurred, a sob in his throat, raised his pistol and emptied it at the car. The big machine swayed, lurched. It's engine roared as it swung sharply, tore across the opposite walk, and crashed head-on into a stone building that did not give an inch.

There was a burst of flame and a wild scream, while thick, oily smoke billowed from the shattered thing that once had been an automobile.

Police whistles were blowing.

Two patrolmen came running from opposite directions with drawn nightsticks and guns.

A gaunt, lank man in plainclothes was kneeling over the

prostrate form of the girl who lay on the sidewalk in front of the bank. As the first patrolman reached him he said:

"Go and get an ambulance, will you? There's been some dirty rod work here tonight. These mutts just let go with their popguns like they was at a carnival. Yeah, get an ambulance."

"Sure. Say, look—there's a guy crawlin'."

A man was crawling away from the burning wreck, clawing at the hard pavement and screaming his lungs out.

The lank man raised his gun, took aim, then, on second thought, lowered.

"I forgot," he said. "The wife asked me, it being her birthday, I should go easy on the crooks for once."

The patrolman ran off to call an ambulance. As the other patrolman reached the bank, the lanky man, pointing to the writhing, groaning figure in the street, said:

"See if you can handle that blistered snake."

VI

IT WAS some days later that Detective Jake Sleary, lounging on the small of his back in the battered swivel-chair in the dusty back room of the police precinct, looked up with his strangely sad blue eyes to find a large, heavy-set man standing in the doorway.

"Are you busy, Jake?" asked the large man.

Sleary shifted his gaunt, lank form a trifle and said:

"Yeah. Come in and park, Henry."

The large man parked and mopped his sweaty forehead.

"Well, Jake," he said presently, "the last one cashed in today, hey?"

"Yeah, that's right, Henry," nodded Sleary. "He got burnt proper when that machine hit the building. I was going to plug him when he was crawling from it, but I didn't. He was the guy had the grudge against Winstrom. Chick Cronin, one of these wiseguys from the Coast that think New York is a shooting gallery."

"He's the guy, Jake. But tell me, how did you hook on to that gang?"

"Well, Henry, it was this way," explained Sleary. "Wednesday night I trailed Winstrom and his lady friend all around the city. When he took her home, I seen a guy enter the building where she lived and mark down the number of the hall telephone. It was Cronin. I followed him downtown, spotted his hang-out in a dump hotel on Second Avenue, and kept my eye on him all next day. I seen him go in there again that night with Squint Daranzio, and later I seen Slugs Howard and Soup Dester go in. I figured these playmates was aiming to play something besides dominoes.

"Next night I watched this dump again and seen Squint pull up with his car. Later they all came out, piled in the car and snaked off, me hopping a taxi and following. The sedan stopped two blocks away from the street where Winstrom worked, and Cronin got out and walked alone them two blocks, stopping and waiting on the corner.

"Me, I shook my taxi in another block and sneaked around to watch Cronin from a nearby lobby. Twenty minutes later I seen a girl hurrying from the direction of Broadway. Cronin seen her, too, walked to the curb and lit a butt. It was the signal for them mutts in the machine to drift along and pick him up.

"The girl—Winstrom's girl, of course—went on toward the bank. The sedan picked up Cronin and they followed her. I had to sneak along slow, keeping close to the buildings.

"Well, you know how it happened. You know the girl got a phone call telling her to hurry to the bank, where her boy friend was dying. Cronin made that call, and him and his boy scouts was watching for her. It was their idea to have her get Winstrom to the door, then use their rods and bust in to blow the works. Well, they just didn't, that's all."

"Because you were in the neighborhood, Jake," said Henry. "I knew I could figure on you."

"Yeah? Thanks, Henry. I was just over to the hospital speaking to Winstrom and his lady friend. They'll pull through. And didja know they're going to get married? Why, yeah. And Winstrom was saying he's going to get a place in the country."

"Well, Jake, there's nothing like the country," replied Henry. "Especially for kids."

With Benefit of Law

*A prize-fighter, a crooked deal
and vengeance—with benefit
of the law.*

"WELL, DID you hear the announcement from the ring?... Here, I'll give it to you. Jeff Young knocked out 'Tiger' Dineen... one minute and twenty seconds of the fourth round of a scheduled fifteen-round bout. It was a great fight, folks, while it lasted. Young was in the pink of condition, and so was the Tiger. It was fast and furious, and the Tiger was simply outboxed by a man whose meteoric rise in the squared circle has been nothing short of phenomenal. The Tiger is still unconscious. Young is leaving the ring amid a shower of applause. He waves to all....

"This boxing program was broadcast by the makers of Old Pal Smoking Tobacco, through the courtesy of Station WMX...."

" 'S 'nough!" rumbled "Babe" Conroy good-naturedly as he pressed his thumb against the switch on the pretentious radio set in the private room of the Bat Wing Supper Club. Babe was the club's strong-arm man.

Mike Guatelli, owner of the Bat Wing, chafed his pink, bejeweled hands and rolled his big, glittering black eyes.

"A dreenk, let us all dreenk to ze success of Jeff Young. He ees wan dam' good box-fighter."

"Yeah, you mean he's one damn good customer of yours," chimed in Steve Ryan, two-fisted, hard-bitten detective from the nearby precinct.

Guatelli, small, slight, dapper in his well-fitting dinner suit, shrugged his shoulders and ran a hand across his bald head.

"Well, anyhow, Steve," he offered, "let us all have ze dreenk."

"Sure," chuckled Ryan, rolling a cigarette between his lips, "drag out your wood alcohol."

"You said somethin'—wood alcohol," nodded Arty Fink, a skinny, charred clinker of a runt, with shoe-button eyes and a pinched, twisted mouth, which gave a sense of incongruity to his rather smart attire.

Babe Conroy said:

"Clam yourself, wiseguy. You don't know good hooch when you taste it. If Jeff wasn't supportin' you I'm damn sure you wouldn't be sportin' a tux and travelin' in this crowd. The way you been shootin' off your jaw lately a guy'd think you was a big-timer. Take off the high hat an' come down t' earth."

Fink moistened his lips to get off a warm retort, but changed his mind. The gap was filled up by Kitty Davis, featured songbird of the club's midnight revue.

"Well, go ahead, Mike," she put to Guatelli, "give the boys a drink."

"What you drinkin', Kit?" asked Babe Conroy.

"Nix," she flung at him.

"That's a good girl," quoted Ryan from a popular song; and then earnestly: "I mean it, girlie. If Jeff wants you to stay off it, stay off it."

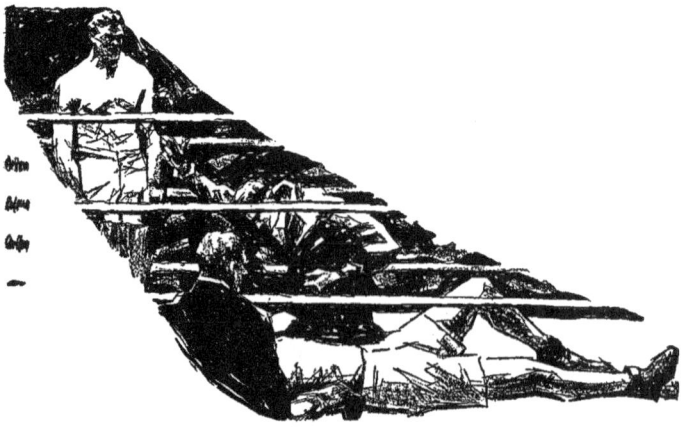

Fink smirked behind a hand that only recently had begun to know the care of a professional manicurist.

"I'll fix the drinks," said Babe Conroy.

Kitty curled up on a divan and mused over a cigarette. She was tall and sinuous, with shining, midnight hair and a warm, ivory complexion. Nightly she thrilled the patrons of the Bat Wing with her soft, haunting contralto. No jazz for Kitty. Arias silvered with romance, breathing the color of old Spanish gardens, sung in a voice scarcely above a whisper. She did her act along about two a.m., when most of the guests were genially drunk, sentimental and romantic. Some psychology in that! And she had fallen for Jeff—fallen hard.

At eleven sharp the big boy sailed in—lean-stomached, square-jawed, clean-cut and virile in his dinner suit; a towering, squint-eyed blond giant, with a slow, easy-going smile, and a deep, rolling voice. With him were two men from his camp; Ed O'Donnel, his manager, and Sam Hale, press agent.

"Hello, gang," greeted Young. "D'you all hear the fight?"

"Boy, it was a wow!" exclaimed Ryan. "Mitt a common, ordinary dick, Jeff!"

They shook, and the others crowded around to follow suit. Kitty stood aside, polishing the fingernails of one hand against the palm of the other. Fink kept his distance, drawing on a fresh cigar. Young shook himself free and started toward Kitty. On the way his gaze met Fink's and there was a brief moment during which the big man's lips tightened perceptibly. But Fink was saying out of the corner of his mouth:

"That's sockin' 'em, Jeff." Then he bent down to flick an imaginary speck of dust from his trousers.

Young reached Kitty and gripped her hands.

"Hello, Kit!"

"Hello, Jeff."

"Well, you heard it, eh? Gee, I'm glad it's over. I didn't think the Tiger'd flop so soon. He was out, though—cold. Now there's only one guy between me and the champ. I'm already signed to meet 'Slam' Cary. When I beat him the champ's got to meet me. Yes, Kit, Marty McCune'll *have* to meet me. How's the girl, anyhow?"

"Little headache."

"Too many butts."

"Maybe."

"Listen, Kit, why don't you marry me and shake this racket? I don't like to see you mixing with the bunch of eggs that drift through here. I'm headed high, and if I had you, why, hell, I'd wipe out all comers."

She was toying with one of his waistcoat buttons.

"Isn't my promise enough?"

"Sure, but what I mean—"

"Sh-h. We're drawing an audience."

Young flushed a little, then shrugged and turned to grin at the gathering. Babe Conroy said:

"Won't be long now, Jeff, till you're wearin' the crown. You can knock this Cary guy for a row of ashcans, an' you'll be a favorite over the champ."

There followed a rapid cross-fire of humorous repartee at the expense of the big boy, who took it all with a broad, embarrassed grin. Then the first number of the orchestra burst in from the adjoining cabaret.

"Well, Kit, about a dance now?" ventured Young.

"Let's," she smiled up at him.

But Fink, standing in a far corner, caught Young's eye and motioned him over with a slight jerk of the head. Young crossed the room and after a few low words both went out into the corridor.

Everyone in the gathering automatically became silent and, after a few sidelong glances at one another, shuffled about or looked around with affected nonchalance. In Kitty's eyes, as she stared at the door which had closed behind Young and Fink, there was a subtly mutinous expression.

Ryan, the hard-bitten detective, who could not occupy a chair without lounging all over it, studied Kitty discreetly and then swung his gaze toward the door. Guatelli kept tapping a sleek foot to the tune of "Barcelona," the orchestra's number, and regarding his hands. O'Donnel, the big boy's fatherly manager, bit his lower lip impatiently.

Most of them could not fathom Fink's connection with Young. But they knew that Fink was a leech and that Young's money kept him from the gutter. This much they knew, but why—there was the rub! Three months ago Fink had first appeared, and thenceforth was a fixture, idling about Broadway, smoking La Coronas, and living at an apartment in the West Seventies.

Ryan, whose business was mysteries, had seen the vague change in Young since the coming of the rat-faced runt. No one knew where Young came from. He just came, saw and conquered. In less than a year, with the aid of good management, he was among the top-notchers. No one knew where Fink came from, either.

But the change. Before Fink's coming Young had been a rollicking, boyish fellow, open-handed, big-hearted, always in a lively mood. Afterward he had seemed to throttle down, and an air of caution and reserve had enveloped him. Of course, he still had moments of sparkling good humor, as when he had sailed in a short time back. But the vague hint of reserve, of caution, or whatever it was, was none the less indubitable. And his squint, which almost hid his eyes, was more noticeable than ever before.

A few minutes, and the door opened. Young rolled in, a little grave, but with an apparent effort threw off the gravity and, clapping his manager on the back as he passed, went over and reminded Kitty about the dance.

Fink sauntered in after him, took his topcoat and hat from a clothes-tree in one corner, and said:

"Well, g'-night, boys."

"Drifting, too," announced Ryan shortly, unraveling his lank, bony body and coming to his feet.

They left the club together and Fink hailed a taxi.

"Goin' my way?" he asked.

"If it's past Times Square."

"Yeah. Hop in."

As the taxi started off, Fink drew a roll of crisp bills from his trousers pocket and transferred them to a wallet which he took from his coat pocket.

Alighting at Times Square, Ryan stood for a moment on the curb and watched the taxi crawl off into the congested traffic. Then he snapped a match to a fresh cigarette.

"What a guy!" he mused.

II

THREE MONTHS later, toward the end of April, Young met Slam Cary in a fifteen round bout at the Mid-Town Stadium. Cary was no set-up, and there were some who claimed that he was actually better than the present champion. In fact, there were many who claimed that Marty McCune, the boss of the heavies, was no champion at all but a false alarm and a mighty loud one at that.

The day before the fight, in his uptown apartment, Young was brooding. Something weighed heavily on his mind, and O'Donnel, his manager, knew it. These two men were very close to each other in some ways, yet in others they were leagues apart.

"Brace up, boy," O'Donnel urged, pacing the floor in carpet slippers. "What is it, the girl again, on your mind?"

"No, Ed."

"Then what? Hell, I wish I could understand you, boy, get under your skin. Sometimes, I tell you, you get me all worked up and sore as the devil. No foolin'."

"Listen, Ed. Go out and take a walk, will you?"

"Had my walk. Say, this Slam Cary ain't worryin' you, is he?"

"Cary? No, not much. I think I can beat him—sure I can. But...."

"But what?"

"Aw, hell, don't bother me!" Young slumped lower in his easy-chair and hid behind a copy of the afternoon paper.

O'Donnel stopped short in his pacing, jammed his hands to his hips and bent a dark, petulant stare on his "boy."

"Jeff, there's somethin' worryin' you. Since last October you've been a changed man. Ever since that runt— Say, what the hell *is* between that runt and you, anyhow?"

"Nothing."

"Apple gravy! All the boys know he's gettin' a slice out o' your bankroll."

"Who says so?" ripped out Young suddenly, crashing down the paper.

"Who says so! Don't make me laugh! When he came here he was down at the heels, lousy and half-starved. Then presto! Evenin' clothes, a classy apartment, night-clubs, a motor car, and who the hell knows what else. D' you think I'm blind? D' you think the rest o' the boys are blind? D' you—"

"Listen, Ed," cut in Young. "Is it any of your business, or anybody else's, what I do with my jack?"

O'Donnel flushed, a little hurt at the sharp incision.

"No, Jeff, o' course not, but—"

"Then lay off!"

The big boy heaved up, wrapped his bathrobe about his clean-limbed frame and banged out of the room.

O'Donnel shrugged hopelessly, sighed and sank into the nearest chair, biting his lip.

So Young met Slam Cary at the Mid-Town Stadium, a five to four favorite. The house was packed and eager for blood. The preliminaries passed quickly, and Slam Cary stalked to the ring under a thunderous barrage of applause. A minute later Young appeared, waving to right and left as the vast place trembled with shouts, hand-clapping and the rhythmic beat of feet on the floor.

You could see the big boy's chest swell, his face radiant with joy. It was great to hear that tremendous ovation, to know that thousands of fans were pulling for you, staking their money on you. Many reached out to shake his taped hands, to rap him on the shoulders.

" 'Ray f'r Jeff Young!"

"The next champ! And how!"

"Plant him quick, Jeff! I gotta make a train!"

Laughing, tingling all over, he clawed his way to the ring and climbed in through the ropes.

Among those present in the ringside seats were Babe Conroy, Sam Hale, and, in another section, Arty Fink. Fink did not applaud. He sat with his skinny arms folded on his meager chest, a thin, sardonic smile on his pinched, undersized face.

The fighters were in the center of the ring now, getting the formal instructions from the referee. Then they were in their respective corners, eying each other while their handlers worked over them and whispered quick, throaty words of encouragement.

Then the warning whistle, and a sudden hush in the audience. And then the bell!

In the back room of the Bat Wing, Kitty Davis and Detective Steve Ryan sat and listened to the graphic phrases of the seasoned radio announcer. Mike Guatelli was upstairs wrestling with his accounts.

"They're off! Slam leads with a right. Jeff blocks it and taps Slam high on the cheek with a straight left. He takes three rights in the stomach and ducks a sizzling uppercut. They tangle in a clinch and break before the referee reaches them. Slam lets loose with a storm of rights and lefts and drives Jeff against the ropes in a neutral corner. Jeff keeps his guard high and takes a pounding in the stomach. He must have a good stomach. Now they're tangled in a clinch. They weave to the center of the ring. The referee breaks them.

"Slam's on his toes. He comes in fast, trying a one-two punch, He walks into a wow of a right cross that rocks his head and knocks him off balance. Jeff follows up hard like a whirlwind. He shoots a left to Slam's jaw—a right—a left—another right. He's got Slam against the ropes. Another right—two lefts—a right. Oh, boy! The house is roaring! He doubles Slam with a sock to the stomach—straightens him up with a—oh, boy!—a beautiful crack on the jaw. D'you hear it? Another left—and a right—on the nose—wow!—and— There goes the bell!"

Kitty settled back in the divan and released a long-held breath.

"Jeff's round, girlie," said Ryan.

"He's on his toes tonight. Say, when's the wedding coming off?"

"Don't get personal, Steve."

"Aw, say, the boy's nuts about you."

Kitty seemed not to hear this. After a moment she said:

"Jeff was awful gloomy today. I never saw him so glum. He's been getting gloomier all the time."

"Marry him and cheer him up, girlie."

"Oh, it's not that. Something else. That Arty…."

"I wonder!" drawled Ryan.

"The damn runt!"

"You ought to find out what's between 'em."

"Oh, how many times have I tried! Nothing—that's what he says. Gets grumpy any time I bring up the subject."

Ryan leaned forward to say something, but the bell sounded from the ringside and the announcer was on the air. The round was Slam Cary's by a slight margin. Jeff started off well, timing his blows' carefully, rocking Slam more than once and drawing a roar of applause from the audience. But Slam connected toward the end of the round and sent Jeff sprawling. Jeff waited for the count of nine and then came up with a spring, but Slam walked all over him till the bell sounded.

The third round was Jeff's and the fourth was even. In the fifth Jeff came out to knock Slam on his back with the very first blow. There was a great howl from the fans, and when Slam came up at the count of nine he was shaky on his pins. He tried to take the offensive, weaving in trickily, and ran into a left cross that stopped him in his tracks. From that instant until the sound of the bell he took an unmerciful lacing. He was driven round the ring under a staggering fusillade of head and body blows that made him draw together and grit his teeth and try to hide behind his folded arms. He worked into a clinch, dazed, unsteady, his breath laboring. In the break the referee snapped:

"No back-handin', there!"

And then the clang of the bell.

Kitty sighed relievedly. Ryan squirmed lower in his chair, seeking a more comfortable position, and stuck a cigarette between his lips. Mike Guatelli came tripping down from upstairs, chafing his soft hands, showing his teeth in a wide, sparkling grin.

"Well, how eet goes now?"

"Pretty," grunted Ryan. "Listen."

Round six was on. Both fighters came out briskly, then became wary and sparred for an opening. Slam Cary rapped four blows against Jeff's stomach, and the announcer said:

"As always, Jeff keeps his guard high. Always protects his face at the cost of his stomach. There! He gets over a beautiful sock to Slam's jaw—another right in the same spot. Slam shakes his head and falls back quick. Jeff's after him—shoots over a high right that bounces off Slam's ear. No damage. But Jeff bores in, driving Slam to the ropes. Now! A right to the jaw—another right—and a left to the mouth. Think Slam just spit out a tooth. Crowd's yelling for a knockout.

"Baby! What a sock *that* was! A smashing right that almost took Slam's head from his shoulders. That hurt and I'm not

kidding. Slam folds into a clinch. Referee tells him to break—
has to tear 'em apart—warns Slam for back-handing on the
break. Lookit that! Wow! Jeff's at him again like a whirlwind.
Rights—lefts—crashing through to Slam's jaw. Slam reels and
wavers. The crowd's gone bug-house! Sock! A long, terrible
blow to Slam's mouth. He keels sidewise. Jeff straightens him
with one on the ear and follows up with a sizzling jab to the
point of the jaw.

"There! Slam's *down!* One—two—three—hear the crowd
going crazy?— five—six—Slam rolls over—eight—nine—the
crowd's surging to their feet, flinging up hats and yowling like
a pack of—*he's out!* Slam Cary is knocked out! Boy, what a
bedlam! Slam Cary's knocked out! Two minutes and fifty seconds
of the sixth round. Jeff is helping him to his feet. The camera-
men are storming the ring...."

"Well," said Steve Ryan, grinning, "*that* is that!"

Kitty settled back in the divan, her forehead moist with
perspiration. Her fingers shook as she lit a cigarette.

III

THERE WAS no evading the issue. The champion had to
meet Jeff Young. The newspapers said so. On the day after
Jeff's victory over Slam Cary the sport writers, dipping their
pens in the ink of subtle sarcasm, admitted that Marty McCune
was a splendid movie actor; but they went on to add that his
title called for doing his stuff in an honest-to-goodness squared
circle, and not on the silver screen.

Jeff's press agent had it published that the big boy was eager
for the match and chockful of pep and enthusiasm. As a matter
of fact, after the first flush of victory had petered out, Jeff again
sank into that brooding, meditative mood that so worried his
manager and those of his friends who were closest to him.

You see, Jeff was not an actor. The fundamental was strong
within him. When he was happy, he showed it to an almost
exaggerated degree. When he was depressed, he was the incar-

nation of gloom. Out of the ring, he was never known to pick a fight or wax belligerent. He was just a big, easy-going, overgrown kid, extremely sensitive yet quick to forgive a hurt. Once in the ring, he was a wary, calculating machine, asking no quarter and giving none; a colorful boxer, a hard-hitter, taking every advantage the rules allowed, yet never stepping beyond the pale.

That something was preying on his mind was obvious. Another man more finished in the art of masking his inner emotions and stifling his secret thoughts, might have got by without arousing any interest. But Jeff was simply not that kind of a man. His manager called him a stubborn fool for not confiding in him, but neither threats nor entreaties could move the big boy to reveal his secret.

The summer wore by, with the championship match hanging fire and the newspapers still razzing Marty McCune. But the sporting world was suddenly startled in late August by the announcement that Jeff would meet the champion in a fifteen-round bout on November thirtieth, at the Metro Boxing Club. The two men immediately went into training.

One of the most interested persons, perhaps, was Arty Fink. He received the news before it was published, and then he read the announcement in the papers and chuckled to himself. A few weeks later he went up to Harlem and sought out "Wash" Emmonds, a colored boxer. When they were seated alone in a dingy little room Fink said:

"Do it next month. Get a job as sparrin' partner for Jeff Young. He'll need 'em. He'll pay you pretty good and then I'll keep slippin' you some gravy on the side. He'll stop trainin' about a week before the bout. Two weeks before the bout we'll have a little chat, me an' you, an' I'll tell you what to do."

As a starter, he slipped Emmonds a few crisp bills, and departed. During those strenuous weeks before the bout, Jeff was not seen very often at the Bat Wing. He worked hard and earnestly and kept good hours. He saw Kitty a couple of times a week, and was still as much in love with her as ever. Still she balked at marriage. She gave no reason, but then a woman doesn't need a reason in such cases. Yet she loved him, in her strange, undemonstrative way, and had eyes for no one else.

In late October Wash Emmonds was added to Jeff's camp. He was a huge fellow, with a tremendous reach, who fought flat-footed. Jeff took him on because he thought Emmonds' style was somewhat like the champion's, and he promptly proceeded to make Emmonds earn his wages. But the Negro had a few tricks, and made Jeff step lively more than once.

Up until two weeks before the fight Jeff appeared to be in pretty good spirits. Then gradually they slumped. He became less buoyant, less communicative. He formed the habit of shutting himself up away from his manager and making no explanations.

One night Fink met Wash Emmonds in the latter's Harlem flat and gave him final instructions.

"Go after him hard this week," he explained. "Mess him up if you got to get knocked out to do it. Sock one of his eyes. Go after his right eye—yeah, his right one. That'll handicap him more. Close it or cut it or somethin'. You do that, fella, an' I slip you a thousand bucks, see."

"Ah's got yuh, boss, suah."

Fink left him, then. He took a taxi southward, drawing serenely on a fresh cigar. Witness the monumental gall of him when, alighting near Columbus Circle, he cut across to Jeff's apartment and found the big boy alone.

"Hello," he droned upon entering. "I need some dough, Jeff. Got a couple hundred handy?"

Jeff's jaw muscles tightened a bit, and he moistened his lips. A vague cloud of resentment brushed across his face.

"Hell, Arty," he drawled, "I've given you five hundred so far this week. Go easy, won't you?"

Fink smiled thinly behind a cloud of tobacco smoke and rocked on the balls of his feet. He seemed perfectly sure of himself.

"Too bad, Jeff, but my expenses keep mountin' awful. I gotta have a couple hundred. Then, y' know, I want t' have some dough t' lay on the fight. Ain't I always laid money on you? Come on, Jeff, open up."

Jeff took a step toward him, his hands knotting, then sagged to a standstill. His voice was husky.

"Arty, you're a damn little leech. You're bleeding me right and left. I'm willing to keep you—"

"Willin' you say? Ha, you gotta!"

Jeff turned away sharply, gritting his teeth. With one hand he could have broken Fink's body in two, yet he had never so much as laid a finger on the little man. He slouched across the room to a desk, unlocked a drawer and pulled out a roll of bills. He counted off ten twenties and flung them on the desk. Fink calmly gathered them up.

"Thanks," he said. "Well, in two weeks you'll be the champ."

"And then," muttered Jeff, "you'll be asking for a small fortune."

"Well, maybe," purred Fink, studying his cigar.

Then he looked up and grinned crookedly at the big boy. Jeff bit off a sharp oath and rolled into an adjoining room. Fink chuckled drily to himself and left the apartment.

The last week of training swung by. It was on the very last day that Emmonds, sparring with Jeff, tore loose with everything he had, and the big boy knocked Emmonds out for a solid hour, but not before the Negro had left a wide gash above Jeff's right eye.

O'Donnel, his manager, swore an indigo blue streak.

"Now that's pretty, ain't it? Like I said all along, you should have wore a headguard while sparrin'."

Jeff took the bawling out silently, while a doctor cleansed the gash and covered it with a strip of adhesive tape two inches long. In fact, it worried Jeff quite as much, if not more, than it worried O'Donnel.

That night, in his Harlem flat, Wash Emmonds received a

thousand dollars from Arty Fink. And on the following day Fink began placing his bets through an agent who asked no questions. By the middle of the week Jeff was a six to four favorite over the champion, and Fink had no trouble in placing his bets. He had no trouble, you understand, because he was betting that Marty McCune would *win!*

Two days before the fight he dropped an anonymous note to a man in McCune's camp.

He bled Jeff for every dollar possible, and then went off to lay that money against the big boy's victory.

On the evening before the battle Jeff blew into the Bat Wing.

"Where's Kitty?" he asked Mike Guatelli.

"Up in her room, Jeff."

Steve Ryan, who had just dropped in for a drink, said:

"I'm betting my last buck on you, Jeff. How's your eye?"

"Be all right, I guess, Steve." He was grave-faced, and touched the taped cut with a finger.

Guatelli drifted out to the cabaret and Jeff, after a moment of indecision, went upstairs to see Kitty.

Steve Ryan stroked his hard jaw musingly and stared obliquely at the ceiling. His eyes narrowed speculatively, and he moved toward the stairway. Then he went up quietly on tiptoes, reached a broad corridor, and listened. He heard voices and crept along toward a door a few yards distant. Here he paused, an unconscientious eavesdropper.

"You never told me… before," came Kitty's voice faintly.

"No… afraid to."

"You didn't trust me?"

"Of course I did, but… you know."

"Poor boy!"

Their voices dwindled at this point and Ryan strained his ears in vain. Then he heard Kitty's "damn… grafter!" and Jeff's, "Sh! Not so loud, Kit!" A moment later the big boy was saying, "Well, guess I'll go down."

Ryan spun silently, cat-footed along the corridor and descended the stairway. When Kitty and Jeff came down the detective was sprawled on the divan drowsing over a cigarette.

"Listen, Steve," called the big boy huskily. "Are you doing anything?"

"Nope. I should be shadowing a guy right now, but what the hell!"

"All right, then. Put on your hat. Kit and me are going to get married now. No noise, Steve. On the sly."

Ryan weaved to his feet, a little amazed. Then he thrust forth his hand.

"Boy, shake!"

To Kitty he said evenly, with the ghost of a smile:

"Girlie, you're the real goods."

IV

A T TEN p.m. on the night of November thirtieth Jeff Young stepped through the ropes at the Metro Boxing Club and heard the roar of the crowd acclaiming him. He gazed out over the vast field of bobbing heads and flashing hands that became murky and vague in the farther tiers. He brought his gaze down to the press box and waved to the boys there.

The din subsided for a moment and then broke anew as Marty McCune, the champion, swung into the ring and crossed to shake hands with his challenger. McCune had an inch or two on Jeff in height and quite as much in reach. Also, he was ten pounds heavier. He had never been a popular champion, and his title had always been subject for bitter controversy on the part of experts.

Jeff was very grave that night, eying his opponent steadily. His handlers were continually shooting words of encouragement at him, patting him on the back, telling him how he was going to knock the champ into the middle of next week. He nodded, smiled with an effort, and involuntarily brushed his gloved hand across the unhealed wound over his right eye.

He heard the warning gong and crouched on his stool, his hands resting on his knees, his toes gripping the floor. His mouth was a little hard, and he bored the champion with his calculating squint.

With the bell he was off like a shot. He met McCune in the center of the ring and sent a right hook to the champ's jaw. In return he took a glancing blow on the left ear. There was no stalling, and no time for warming up. Both men were hot at the start and went to it with plenty of heart and plenty of muscle. Jeff pounded his man around the ring with smashing rights and lefts, rocked him and made him clinch twice, and won the round by a wide margin.

McCune, however, came out in the second fresh and wary, and let Jeff take the offensive. The champ fought flat-footed, holding his head up and back, blocking with his long arms. Jeff broke through that guard twice, and McCune's lips began to puff up. Just before the bell the champ let drive with a terrific right cross that landed flush on Jeff's right eye. The wound was opened and blood gushed down across his eye. He covered up, missed six shots in a row, and was clinching at the bell.

Back in his corner, he was white-faced, tight-lipped. A man worked over his eye, but with little success.

He flung out for the third round and missed his first blow so wide that the momentum of it spun him to the floor. Refusing to wait out the count of nine, he sprang up and plunged for his opponent. McCune sidestepped deftly and made another try for the wounded eye, but the blow slid over Jeff's ear. A moment later, however, he connected squarely and fresh blood rolled down over the big boy's eye. Jeff fell back, covering up, and the champ came after him, pounding his stomach and trying to make him lower his guard. Jeff reeled and fell into a clinch. The referee broke them and McCune sent Jeff spinning to the canvas with a fast uppercut.

He waited out the count of nine and then came up. But he seemed to be unsteady and groping with his hands. He swung for the champ, missed and caught another terrific jolt on his wounded eye. The champ grinned and drove six more blows to that eye. Jeff stood spread-legged, turning his head back and forth slowly, panting hard.

McCune measured him and sent over a well-aimed blow to the big boy's jaw. Jeff went down like a log, rolled over, got to his knees and toiled up at the count of nine. Again a bone-crushing blow to the button sent him down with a crash. Again he rolled over, shaking his head as if to clear it, and struggled to his knees, then to his feet.

He stood in the center of the ring, his guard up, his whole body heaving and groaning for breath. It was a terrible sight, and yet one which many spectators would remember; the sight of Jeff coming up again and again, reeling, groping, practically out on his feet, but unwilling to stay down.

The champ, priming for another blow, looked sidewise at the referee. The referee, nodding, stepped between them and in a booming voice stopped the slaughter. Marty McCune was still champion, by a technical knockout. As a matter of form, he grabbed Jeff and dragged him to his corner, and the big boy sank down, bloody and beaten, muttering incoherently through bruised lips.

Back in the Bat Wing Supper Club Kitty Davis, who was not a very demonstrative girl, sobbed once and then caught herself. The color had drained from her face, and her hands were moist. She sat on the divan, stiff and straight and silent.

Mike Guatelli hung his head. Babe Conroy blinked his eyes and sighed vastly. Detective Steve Ryan did nothing but regard Kitty through slitted lids.

Then suddenly Kitty was on her feet. She flew across the floor and ran upstairs to her room.

"Cripes, it's tough!" rumbled Babe Conroy thickly.

"Ah, eet ees dat," agreed Guatelli.

Ryan looked from one to the other, frowned studiously, and said nothing.

An hour later Kitty came down, and then Arty Fink came in, looking very worn and desolate.

"Ain't it hell?" he asked dismally.

"Yeah," rumbled Babe Conroy. "You lose your meal ticket, don't you, huh?"

Fink seemed to be in mental pain.

"Aw, don't rub it in," he pleaded. "We was old friends. Sure, I'm on the rocks now. Lost all I bet. I'm leavin' tomorrow if I can't do anything for Jeff."

Kitty was staring vacantly at the carpet. Ryan seemed steeped in thought, with a dead cigarette drooping from his lips.

Fifteen minutes later the telephone rang. Guatelli, who was standing beside it, took off the receiver and placed it to his ear. As he listened his eyes dilated and his lips flexed. When he hung up he turned with bated breath.

"Jeff he ees dead!"

Kitty wilted on the divan, closing her eyes tight and sucking in her lower lip till it bled.

"What?" boomed Babe Conroy.

"Dead!" repeated Guatelli, spreading his hands. "He leaves his manager like he ees crazy—runs off. He can hardly see. He ees knock down by taxi and die twent' minutes after at de hospeetal."

"Good God!" groaned Babe Conroy.

Steve Ryan's gaze was riveted on Kitty. Fink said:

"I—I better go over t' see him. He—he was an old friend o' mine."

Kitty jumped to her feet.

"Take me with you!" she panted. "Oh… Jeff!"

She ran upstairs and came down a few minutes later wrapped in her furs. Fink already had his topcoat on, and they left the Bat Wing together.

Steve Ryan stood up and started a fresh cigarette.

"Gotta drift, too," he clipped, and banged out.

He saw Kitty getting into Fink's sport coupe, with Fink already at the wheel. When the coupe snaked off Ryan hailed a taxi and told the driver to follow. Soon the coupe was heading uptown. Ten minutes later it wound through Columbus Circle and went on toward Central Park.

"Hell," muttered Ryan, "that ain't bound for any hospital!"

The coupe entered one of the Park's drives, and five minutes later Ryan saw it glide to a stop. He had his driver pull up, paid him and told him to turn back. Then he crept along the deserted drive, his hand wound around the gun in his pocket.

Just as he reached the coupe he saw the door open. He stopped short and pulled his gun. It was Kitty who stepped out, and started to run off.

"Wait a minute!" he called sharply.

She spun about quietly, gasping.

"What's up?" clipped Ryan.

His hand touched her arm, and gripped it. She was holding her breath, her eyes wide, every muscle tense.

Ryan looked at the coupe and said:

"Come here a minute."

She held back, but he forced her along with gentle but firm persistence. He looked into the coupe and saw Fink slumped over the wheel.

"H'm," he mused.

"Yes, I did it!" Kitty exploded suddenly. "The damn runt! He was the one who ruined Jeff. It was his fault Jeff was killed. I tell you, he just the same as murdered him."

"How come?" asked Ryan quietly.

"Jeff told me something before the fight. I was the only one knew, besides the runt. Jeff was paying for his silence all along. You didn't know, did you, *that Jeff was blind in the left eye?*"

"Huh?"

"That's why I went with Fink tonight. I shoved a gun against his ribs and made him talk.

"Do you know what he did? Hired that nigger sparring partner, got him into Jeff's camp, and paid him to try and bruise Jeff's good eye. Then he dropped a hint to the champ's outfit that Jeff might be licked if the champ could spoil his right eye. See?

"Then he squeezed, stole, or borrowed all the money he could and bet against Jeff. Look in his pocket. He's got twenty thousand on him and claims for almost fifty thousand more. So I shot him, the dirty double-crossing runt!"

"Didn't hear any shot," said Ryan.

"Silencer." She drew a pistol from her pocket and showed it to him.

Ryan took the revolver and frowned over it studiously.

"Same calibre as mine," he observed, half to himself.

He turned and climbed into the coupe. Fink was very much dead. In his pockets Ryan found twenty thousand dollars and claims for approximately fifty thousand more. He grunted reflectively, turned his head a trifle and regarded the girl aslant. He thrust her gun into his pocket and got out of the coupe, standing spread-legged and staring at her now with almost provocative intensity. Suddenly he said, in a low, clipped voice:

"It was this way, wasn't it girlie? He attacked you while the car was parked. You screamed. I happened to be in the vicinity and heard you. All right. I ran up and found him tussling with you. I told him to lay off and pulled my rod. He pulled his, too—this one, with the silencer. He fired at me and missed. I fired and killed him. Wasn't that the way it all happened?"

Her brows bent in a puzzled frown. For a long moment her eyes roamed over his expressionless face. Then she leaned forward.

"You mean…?"

"Remember," he said, "how it happened. Now there's one more detail. There was my shot that killed him. Here it is." He raised his own gun, aimed at the nearby pond and pulled the trigger once. Then he shoved the gun into his pocket and asked, almost casually:

"Got a butt handy?"

Penalty of the Code

A strange thing is this code of silence; stranger still, when one reckons with the penalty it exacts.

"SHUT YOUR trap!"

Bull Callahan spun on the woman sharply. There was a hard, bitter twist to his mouth. His intense, agate-pale eyes lashed her to a momentary silence.

"And keep it shut!" he added brutally.

Nance lowered her cloudy-brown eyes and exhaled softly, almost tremulously. She was sitting in a cheap wicker easy-chair in a dingy room whose walls were covered with drab tan paper, faded and streaked with dampness. A woman in her middle twenties, she had about her a kind of soft, warm beauty and an easy, indolent charm which even under the tenseness of the moment seemed invulnerable.

Callahan flamed a match to a cigarette which drooped from one corner of his wide, cruel mouth. In the small, low-ceiled room he hulked like the bull he was—stocky, thick-shouldered, barrel-chested; a whale of a man.

"It's my business," he went on, "and you keep your lip out of it." He blew out the match and snapped it across the room. "If I want to drag this bird in, it's nothing to you. Hell, but you're getting pious all at once!"

"I'm not," she defended with gentle persistence. "Only it's not fair to pull him in when he's working and going straight where he is. You can pull the job yourself, if you try hard."

Callahan slashed a hand through the air in an impatient gesture. "Dan knows safes like you know your knitting. It's kinder born in him. The company he works for is paying him for what he knows. They're wise he's pulled a couple o' deals, but they're taking the chance. They keep building safes and Dan keeps opening 'em. That's why they've hired him. They know he's an expert, and they're trying to get up a small can that he *can't* open. Now why the holy hell shouldn't I take advantage of what he knows, if I can?"

"But he'll not do it," said Nance simply.

"Listen, kiddo!" He took a step nearer and stood over her threateningly. "When he comes here in a few minutes, you want to say as little as you know how. Remember, if you talk out of turn I'll bat the living hell outta you. Remember that. I'm getting sick and tired of your crossing me at every turn."

The woman raised her eyes, and there was in them now a subtly mutinous expression.

"You'll hit me once too often," she told him in a subdued voice.

"Is that a threat?" he grated.

"It's anything you want to make it."

His laugh was short and hard and brittle. He struck out viciously, and the back of his hand caught her across the right cheek. She winced, choked back a sob, sat rigid, with her hands folded in her lap and her eyes closed tight. Her lower lip was drawn in under her teeth. A dark welt was growing on the soft, tender skin which he had struck.

"That's just a sample," he ground out coarsely. "I'll learn you to crack wise, my little wife."

She said nothing. For a long moment she remained rigid, her eyes still closed, her lip still drawn in under her teeth. Then, quite suddenly, she relaxed, and her head drooped. Her hand crept up across her cheek and tentatively touched the darkening bruise.

Callahan grunted derisively, pivoted and crossed the room to a sideboard. He slopped whiskey into a glass and sank the contents neat. He smacked his lips loudly, shot the woman another black look and, snatching up a newspaper, dropped into a rocker.

Five minutes later there was a rap on the door. Callahan got up, crashed aside the paper and shot back the bolt. He opened the door on a crack, peered out, then swung it wide.

"Come in, Dan," he said.

Lean, clean-clipped, tawny-skinned, Dan Sanderson drifted in. He stood with his hands in his coat pockets, the ghost of an engaging smile flirting about his lips, a hint of easy, casual gayety in his clear blue eyes.

"Hello, Bull. Hello, Nance."

Nance sat with her bruised cheek away from him. She smiled bravely.

"Hello, Dan," she said.

"Have a seat," suggested Callahan, clicking shut the bolt.

Dan dropped his hat on the table, sat down with lazy grace and lit a cigarette. He was an easy-going young man of a mild and balmy temperament, with eyes that at times were provocatively whimsical. You somehow likened him to oil smoothing troubled, tempestuous waters. He knew more about safes than the men who made them.

He was saying: "They told me at the rooming-house that you'd called me up, Bull, and wanted to see me about something. I thought I'd just drop in and see what it was."

"Yeah, sure." Bull was standing by the sideboard. "Have a drink?"

"Thanks, no. I've been laying off the stuff lately. I guess I can't stand much liquor. Makes me feel dull next day always."

Callahan poured himself a drink, crossed with it to a chair and sat down with ponderous deliberation. He held the glass up to the light, started to take a drink, but changed his mind. He leaned forward, elbows on knees, forehead wrinkled in thought.

"You know, Dan," he began, and cleared his throat before proceeding. "You know, I have a job in mind, but I got to admit the safe has me stumped. It's one o' them little tricks put out by the company you work for."

"Oh, yes?" softly.

"Yeah. I was thinking you might want to try out your hand on it. I got the whole lay figured out to a T. I know the grounds, got a diagram of the house, and I know just how many servants are around and where they are. The place is up in Westchester. You know, my side line of electric wiring and repairing helps me out a lot. I managed to get a job there re-insulating, and I made good use of it. With you and me working this job it'd be a cinch. I had to wire the electric alarm attached to the safe, and the guy that owned the place was hanging around while I did it. We got gabbing, and he says: 'Of course, the safe is absolutely burglar-proof, but there's nothing like being cautious, especially when you've got a couple hundred thousand dollars' worth of jewels in it.' A cinch, eh? A dead cinch, if you ask me."

He paused to let this sink in and to see how Dan would take it. He downed his drink at a gulp and placed the empty glass on the table with exaggerated precision.

"It's a dead cinch," he repeated.

"Oh, yes?" softly.

"Yeah." He smacked fist to palm. "There'd be nothing to it, Dan, with all you know about the game. The only ones in the house are the butler, maid and cook. They all sleep way upstairs, in the left rear wing. We could run out there in my car in an hour and a half, easy, pull the job at one a.m. and be pounding our ear at three next morning."

Dan blew ash from his cigarette.

"I'm really out of the game, Bull," he said gently. "They're paying me good money where I work, and I'm learning a lot more about the business. They've put me on my honor, what little I have, and, anyhow, they've got me pretty well tied up. The police know the circumstances, and there's not a chance in the world for me to get away with anything."

"Aw, the hell there ain't!" argued Callahan. "I tell you, Dan, this is like taking pennies from kids."

"It may be, Bull, but, honest, I'm off the game for life. You shouldn't take me into your confidence like this. It's not fair by the company, and it's not fair by you. But you've told me, and for old sake's sake I'm mum, Bull. I'll stick by the code of silence."

"Then you won't throw in with me?"

"Sorry, Bull."

Nance was smiling wistfully. The sigh she exhaled was quite audible. Callahan looked at her, saw the expression, and cursed under his breath. He stood up, fumbled in his pockets for a cigarette.

"Try one of mine, Bull," offered Dan, and slid his silver case across the table.

Callahan lit up and paced the room in a black mood. He stopped short, his lips writhing against his teeth.

"Cripes, Dan, you're like blood turned to water!" he snapped. "You're a good man gone wrong!"

"I guess I am, Bull." He shrugged and rose to his feet. "But then I've been thinking it over. If I cracked safes I'd make a pile in a short time and then wind up in jail for a ten-year stretch. You can't beat the bulls in the end. By hook or crook they'll get you. I don't make money in piles here, but in the end I'll have more."

"Rats! You're talking like them bums at the Bowery Mission."

"Well, maybe I am. Anyhow, I'm practicing what I preach."

"I hate preachers! Damn all preachers!"

Dan shrugged, but offered no reply. He picked up his hat, stood creasing and re-creasing it and staring meditatively at the floor. Then he looked up, and the old gay twinkle grew in his eyes again.

"Guess I'll be getting along, then, Bull." He turned to the woman. " 'Bye, Nance. See you all again some time."

"Good-bye, Dan." She stood up, and the light revealed the blue bruise on her cheek.

She saw the sudden concentrated look in Dan's eyes, and turned away sharply, stifling an impulse to reach up and cover the mark with her hand. Callahan, too was conscious of the little by-play, and his hands knotted.

"Well, good luck," offered Dan, moving toward the door.

"G'-night," Callahan bit off brusquely.

Alone in the room, he set his back against the door and bit his wife with a cold, hard stare.

"I s'pose," he snarled, "you feel better now?"

"He's going straight, all right," she said.

"Bah! He's yellow!"

"Oh, I don't know. I feel glad, sometimes, to see a man throw over the old game and at least try."

Callahan closed his fist. His chest expanded and his iron jaw went low and rigid. He advanced on the woman with a slow, portentous tread.

Nance fell back a step, then stopped and remained stiff and straight, her chin raised, her eyes steady, her breath bated. The color, however, was ebbing from her face.

Callahan struck her savagely. His hummocky hand crashed against the bruise with a resounding smack. She reeled backward with a half-stifled scream of pain, toppled over a chair and sprawled to the floor, where she lay quivering and moaning.

"Damn your soul!" rasped Callahan.

There were quick footsteps in the hallway, a sudden rush against the door. Callahan had neglected to close the bolt, and the door, whipping open, revealed Sanderson poised on the threshold.

Nance was weaving to her feet, choking back sobs that wracked her throat.

Callahan swiveled abruptly, stood with his feet planted wide and his thick shoulders hunched belligerently.

"That's not right, Bull," drawled Dan in a flat voice.

"You mind your own lousy business!" barked Callahan.

Nance was between them.

"Don't—don't—don't!" she gasped. And to Dan, "Please—go away—go away!"

For a long moment they stood motionless—the three of them. Callahan had not budged from his crouch. Dan still stood in the doorway, his mouth a straight, tight line, his eyes unwavering, his fists clenched.

"Go—go!" Nance pleaded with him.

Dan relaxed. "All right," he nodded, and added, "All right, Nan." He backed out.

"Wait!" clipped Callahan, and took a step forward. "If you pop anything about this job I got in mind, I'll get you, if it takes me twenty years."

Dan smiled leisurely and shook his head.

"I stick by my codes, Bull, under all circumstances—even this."

An instant later he was gone.

Callahan swore bitterly and went over to pour himself another drink. On the table, half-hidden by a newspaper, he saw the silver cigarette case which Dan had forgotten. He picked it up, snapped it open and extracted a cigarette. His eyes narrowed. He peered closely at the inscription engraved on the inside:

DANIEL SANDERSON
With compliments from
THE COLUMBIAN SAFE COMPANY

Callahan's muscles tensed. His eyes narrowed speculatively. He snapped the case shut and slipped it into his pocket. A cunning smile crept slowly over his face.

"Bull!" gasped the woman.

"Shut your trap!" he snapped.

II

CALLAHAN WAS a bull in more ways than one. How Nance had managed to stand five years of his brutality is a mystery, but then women are mysterious, anyhow. How she succeeded in retaining her soft allure and sweet temperament under the existing conditions, offers further matter for conjecture. How she, a rare slip of intriguing femininity, had ever allowed herself to become married to this callous hunk of a brute, is for the gods to solve.

Three years back Callahan had brought Dan home one night. Dan, who had never pulled a job with the Bull, had, however, let the big man into the tempting art of working safe combinations. Callahan had worked safes before that, but as a neophyte, and with little or no success. In his time he had cracked many safes, and the patron saint of chance had flown with him and kept him from the clutches of the law.

On occasion the three of them had gone out to picture shows and dances, and in a vague way Dan and Nance had been drawn to each other, though their relations were entirely aboveboard. Often Dan, in his smooth, leisurely way had acted as a kind of a soothing balm to the Callahans' domestic troubles. His presence, the fact that he was merely about, served as a gentle sedative. It was a long while before he became cognizant of the fact that Callahan was used to beating his wife on the slightest provocation. Then he came around less, not that he was afraid of the Bull, but he knew that sooner or later he would interfere, and he was not the kind that ordinarily championed other men's wives. He well knew the indiscretion of it.

This was his first attempt at interference. He had heard Nance scream, and instinct had prompted him to act, because he was in such close proximity to the occurrence.

Now Callahan, besides being a bull of a man, was in his own crude way something of a schemer. He sat smoking for an hour after Dan's departure. Nance, weak from the blow he had dealt her, had gone off to her room and sobbed herself to sleep.

It was at about ten-thirty that Callahan got up and put on his coat. From a closet he drew a kit of burglar's tools and secreted them on various parts of his person. He did not take the black leather bag. He did take, however, a small black cotton bag that, when folded, fitted snugly in an inner pocket. On his hip he carried a stubby-nosed automatic pistol.

At ten-forty-five he left his rooms. He went around to the neighborhood garage, got into his roadster, and drove uptown. He cut across to the East Side at Herald Square, to avoid the after theatre traffic which, around eleven p.m., is nothing short of a nightmare, and continued north at a moderate pace. He crossed the Harlem River over the Third Avenue Bridge, and struck Westchester Avenue at One-Hundred-Fiftieth Street. When he passed the Bronx River he was doing forty-five an hour, but he cut the pace down soon afterward, in the name of caution.

Fifteen minutes later he left the main highway and rolled slowly south on an avenue that led toward the Sound. Presently he slowed down until the engine, still in high, began to jerk irregularly. He threw out the clutch, then shut off the ignition and allowed the car to roll to a stop. He looked up and down the road several times before getting out.

Under his seat was a pair of license plates—the original plates of the car. On front and rear was a pair of plates which he had taken from a parked car in Jersey a couple of nights back. Alighting, he left the parking lights on, but extinguished the dash light. He rolled down the side-curtain facing the roadway, so that a casual motorist passing by might suspect a couple of spooners, and think nothing of it.

A moment later he was slouching down a silent, deserted walk. A hundred yards beyond he turned into a driveway that led up to an imposing white house. The lower part of the house was immersed in darkness. In the upper regions—to be exact, in the upper left wing—was a solitary glow. After a long moment of consideration, he put it down as a corridor light, for he saw it through a French door which led out upon a balcony.

Moving from bush to bush, from hedge to hedge, he circum-navigated the house and wound up at the point from which he had started. There were no lights in the servants' quarters—no lights anywhere but in the corridor behind the French window, and that a dim, frosted night-light.

This time he crept in a straight line for the side of the house and hugged it around to the rear. He began working on a window that led into the cellar. He wore black cotton gloves and rubber soled shoes. It took him twenty minutes to break his way into the cellar. Once in, he waited for two solid minutes, motionless, intensely alert.

Then he snapped on his pocket flashlight. Its white wedge of light showed him a spacious cellar, with coal-bins to the right and a huge furnace to the left. Pipes formed a fretwork under the ceiling. He glided forward, a bulking, ape-like figure, one hand closed around the pistol which he shifted from his hip to his right coat pocket. He was ripe for anything, including murder.

He found a staircase leading to the first floor. He followed it, silent as a ghost, each step deliberately planned. He reached the door, eased the knob around, pushed in softly. A moment later he was in a roomy, well-stocked pantry. The beam of his flash probed the darkness and settled on another door. This led him into the kitchen. Again he paused to listen. The silence was sepulchral.

Moving on, he pushed aside the swing-door that led into a kind of breakfast alcove, then on down a short, broad corridor and into what apparently was the dining-room. He knew the lay-out from memory. Next he was in a wide drawing-room, creeping across a rug so soft that his feet seemed to sink into it as if it were snow. Followed a small reception chamber, appointed with a few rare pieces of Jacobean furniture. From this he slid into the library, and eased shut the sliding door behind him.

He knew where the switch in the safe alarm was. He reached up alongside a massive bookcase and pressed one of two buttons. The circuit was disconnected. Moving down the room, he stopped before another bookcase, slid back the glass door and pulled out half a dozen books. There was before him a small wall safe.

In the darkness, he smiled to himself. With this haul, he would drop out of sight—leave Nance and see the world. To hell with Nance! There were lots of women—women he wouldn't have to marry, either. He almost chuckled aloud, but caught himself.

He went to work on the safe, his ear pressed close beside his maneuvering fingers. The position was awkward. He drew back, and his elbow knocked against a loose book. The book toppled and thumped to the floor. The sound was actually very slight, yet he whirled, catching his breath. His broad bulk collided with a pedestal.

There was a split-second's vacuum of silence. Then a crash. A heavy piece of bronze statuary banged to the floor along with the pedestal.

Callahan cursed. His gun came out of his pocket. The first instinct was to get away, and he really did lunge half-way across the room. But he paused there, listening. The thought of what lay in the safe, the temptation of it, combined with the hope that he might be able to work the combination, rooted him to the spot.

He was panting, like a cornered bull. Murder was in his heart—red, raw murder. His hand was rigid on the black butt of his blunt automatic. Beads of sweat, alternately hot and cold, stood on his forehead, while his scalp seemed to be undergoing a chilling process of expansion and contraction.

Thus he waited, his legs spread far apart, his huge head sunk between his shoulders, his teeth clamped hard—an immobile, watchful, deadly intruder. He thought he heard footsteps—light, cautious footsteps. He thought he heard a faint click. He thought of turning and breaking out through the nearest window. But he did not. Something held him there—something intangible. Perhaps the desire to see face to face the owner of the footsteps, to kill with the unreasonable madness of a killer's blood.

The door leading into the reception room opened on a crack. Then it slid back a little farther, and a long beam of light flooded in and revealed Callahan in all his raw deadliness. The man in the door, old, gray-haired, hatchet-faced, emitted a gasp. He held a gun in his hand, but made no visible attempt to use it.

Callahan fired. He did not shoot to wound. He sent that leaden slug of annihilation right through the man's heart. The man swayed for a moment, then pitched forward. He was dead before he hit the floor.

Callahan muttered deep in his throat. He bounded for the door, and with one foot over the dead body, he paused, and his eyes narrowed craftily. He drew from his pocket the cigarette case which Dan Sanderson had forgotten to take along, chuckled ironically, and flung it back into the library.

Then he lunged out of the library, on through to the kitchen and down into the cellar. A moment later he was outside. He saw lights springing up in the house. He cursed the misfortune that had made it necessary for him to leave the safe unopened. But he rolled on toward the highway at a mad pace, and slowed down only when he reached the walk.

No one passed him, no one saw him, on his way to the automobile. He leaped into the seat, jammed his foot against the starter, and threw into gear before the motor was well under way. The car jerked forward, coughed, but finally fell into a smooth whir, and in another moment's time he was pounding away for the city.

Before he swung into Westchester Avenue he stopped and changed his license plates. Thenceforth he drove at a moderate pace. He did not take his car to the garage, but parked it in front of the dusty-faced house where he had his rooms. At two a.m. he opened his door and, snapping on the light, dropped into a chair next to the sideboard, and slopped liquor into a tumbler.

There was a stir in the other room, and after a brief interval Nance came in, her forehead puckered quizzically. An emerald negligée hung from her white shoulders about which cascaded her wealth of jet-black hair in alluring disarray.

Callahan paid no attention to her. He lounged in the chair, his mouth drooping, his eyes haggard. He drew his gun from his pocket and wiped the muzzle on his handkerchief, leaving powder stains on the white cloth.

"Bull!" exclaimed the woman. "You—you— What did you do?"

He cackled raucously. "Blew the heart outta a flat-faced butler in Westchester. But don't worry, kiddo. They'll not get me. They'll get somebody else."

"What do you mean?" she breathed, coming nearer.

He whirled in his chair. "What the hell do you think I mean? None of your damn stinking business if you want to know. Go back to bed. Go on! Get the hell outta here!" He half rose, waving his fist at her.

She shrank back, her hands pressed to her breast. A mixture of anguish and terror writhed in her eyes. "You—you don't mean—" He heaved out of his chair, his face flushing with rage. A torrent of vile abuse belched from his curling lips. He ended up by grasping Nance's throat and pressing it until she twisted to the floor. Then he lifted her and flung her into the other room.

"Oh… God!" she sobbed, her scantily-clad body convulsing with each sob.

Callahan fell back into the chair and embarked on a drinking bout that knew no limit. Bit by bit he tore off his clothes, intending to go to bed. But the liquor hit him hard, and by four o'clock he was dead drunk, and did not hear the milk wagons rumbling and clanging through the street. He lay full length on the floor, head pillowed in one arm.

In the other room, Nance was still sobbing.

III

A T ABOUT ten o'clock next morning Dan Sanderson was having a chat with the manager of the shipping department on the ground floor of the Columbian Safe Company's building. Dan had become very popular with the men in all the departments there, and most of them looked up to him because of his uncanny skill in the manipulating of locks. Dan was a patient listener, and a good talker in his line, never hesitating to dilate, when asked to, on the tricks of his trade. The manager was just getting interested when an office boy weaved his way toward them and said:

" 'Scuse me, Mr. Sanderson. Two men outside wanter see you."

Dan left the manager and followed the boy out into the waiting room. The boy indicated two men lounging indolently against the rail. One was tall, raw-boned, hawk-nosed. He gnawed disconsolately on a shaved-down match. The other was short, spare, and looked bored to death with his surroundings. His suit was badly in need of a pressing, and his faded fedora was a wreck. He drew on a rag of a cigarette and did not seem to enjoy it.

"You men want to see me?" asked Dan.

"Your name Sanderson?" droned the small man wearily.

"Yes."

The small man groped in his pockets and finally extracted a cigarette case. He snapped it open and held it up for Dan to inspect.

"This yours?" he sighed.

"Why—yes."

"Humph!" grunted the lank man, deciding to unravel his form and stand erect.

The other said, "It's him, Sam."

"So 'tis, Steve."

The small man actually yawned. He waved his hand at Dan and ordered: "Get your hat if you got one and come along with us."

"We got a few questions to ask you," supplemented the lank man over his partner's shoulder.

"Who are you?" asked Dan, puzzled, of the small man.

"I'm Corrigan." He jerked his thumb toward his companion. "This is Gannon. We're a couple o' Armenians from Headquarters."

"Police Headquarters?"

Corrigan seemed vastly pained. "Don't—for cripes sake—don't act like a hick! Get your hat and let's toddle."

Dan suspected the worst. He went for his hat, apparently calm, casual and collected; but inside he was dazed, dumfounded, and a little sick. They did not put handcuffs on him. One walked on either side. They had a taxi waiting. Corrigan entered first, then Dan, then the lank, shambling Gannon.

"Take it easy, bud," Corrigan told the driver.

The two detectives sat back leisurely. Corrigan lit a fresh cigarette.

"Have one," he offered Dan.

"Thanks." Dan got his light from the glowing end of Corrigan's cigarette and inhaled deeply.

Gannon shaved down a new match and again went to exploring the crevices in his teeth.

"It was tough," Corrigan ventured lazily, "that you didn't get anything outta that job."

"You've got me wrong, Corrigan," was Dan's shot.

Gannon grunted and spat out of the window.

Corrigan said: "Have we? Now, I don't know about that. The butler was killed—plugged through the heart. We found this case in the library—front o' the safe. The safe'd been monkeyed around, but you knocked over a statcher and woke up the servants. It's the kind of safe your comp'ny makes, and you know how the gadgets work. Believe me, buddy, you sure pulled a bone when you went to carryin' this cigarette case around."

"Where was the killing?" Dan asked him.

"Ask me another!" chuckled Corrigan.

"Sweet innocence!" scoffed Gannon.

Dan was not puzzled now. He saw it all. He had intended stopping at Callahan's for the case that night. He knew he had left it there. So Callahan had framed him! A bitterness grew in his heart, and his face hardened.

"You got to come acrost," Corrigan was saying. "We got you neat, guy, and I don't mean maybe. Come on, now, like a nice little chum, and tell Corrigan and Gannon all about it. Better tell us. The Inspector's an egg, if you ask me, and he don't ask much. He asks you once in a nice way, then in a nasty way, and then he uses the good old rubber hose."

"I tell you, Corrigan, you're all wrong," argued Dan. "I wasn't out last night after ten."

"Now, Sanderson," went on Corrigan in a bitter-sweet tone, "tell me a bedtime story. Tell me an alibi. Eh, Gannon?"

"Set it to music," suggested Gannon dourly.

"I was in my room," explained Dan. "I—I haven't an alibi."

"Well… now!" whistled Corrigan, "There's something to write home about. A crook without an alibi!"

"Well, then," put in Gannon, "I s'pose you're goin' to spring somethin' about somebody else pullin' this job?"

Dan bit his lip, and muscle lumps on either side of his mouth bulged.

"No," he replied. "I'm saying nothing—only that I didn't do what you're trying to hang on me, and the Inspector's rubber hose isn't going to make me say different."

"In spite," Corrigan said, "of this butt case o' yourn we found in the room near the stiff?"

"Yes," nodded Dan.

"Hell!" grunted Gannon, a little disgusted.

"Now look here," Corrigan went on, tapping Dan's knee, "you know somethin' about this job, see. We'll say, just for the sake of argyment, that you didn't rod this butler. The point is, guy, this case was there—with your name in it. All right. You didn't rod him. But you know who did. Now tell us."

"I don't know anything," persisted Dan slowly.

"Cripes!" grunted Gannon gloomily.

"Applesauce!" droned Corrigan. "You're stallin', Sanderson. You killed this bird, all right. At any rate, we're goin' to hang the job on you. You won't get the chair probably, but we'll wrap enough circumstantial evidence around you to send you up for twenty years. The district attorney knows his groceries, and he's as tough as they come. So don't think you got a lawn party ahead o' you. The Department ain't much on manners, but it gets somewhere."

"Here we are," rumbled Gannon.

The taxi rolled to a stop beside the curb. Corrigan got out first and grinned crookedly as Dan followed.

"Welcome to our bungalow!" he purred thinly.

Gannon sagged out and stood for a moment taking in a reef on his belt.

Then Dan entered Police Headquarters between them. He somehow felt that doom was closing in around him. The high ceilings, the cold, dull pillars, the echoing corridors, were depressing and not a little foreboding. Some place a man was doing telephone routine with some precinct. His voice sounded monotonous—a hollow, disembodied kind of voice, devoid of animation; a voice like a death-knell.

Presently he was in a room, and the door closed behind him. A man was sitting at a desk, leaning back comfortably in a swivel-chair. He was toying idly with a watch chain that spanned his adipose paunch. He had a bald head, shaped like a bullet. His nose was like a gnarled pine knot, his eyes large and opaque and of a fish-like intensity. His jaw suddenly shot forward.

"Sit down!" he rasped.

Inspector Barrett, a man of indifferent manner, but he got somewhere—

IV

THE CODE of silence—a strange code.

Callahan, reading as many different newspapers each day as he could find, discovered that Dan was holding his tongue. He gloated. Personally, he thought Dan was a fool. He well knew what Dan was undergoing. He knew the mental torture of interminable cross-examination. He could picture Dan, unshaven, haggard, weary-eyed, repulsing the barrage of questions, endless questions, delivered by half a dozen Headquarters men. He could picture, too, in his mind's eye, the third degree, that process of coercion which has driven many an innocent man to manipulate his own downfall.

No less did Nance read the daily papers. She read them with a feeling of stifled horror. A great pain gnawed at her heart. As in a dream she saw the finger of destiny pointing Dan to those grim barred buildings up the river.

One night she said to Callahan: "Isn't there anything we can do to save him?"

"Nope. Save him! Why worry, kiddo? Kind of unlucky that

I lost that cigarette-case, but I ain't going to hang myself on that account."

She lowered her head and stared vacantly at her hands.

"He's really saving your life," she said after a while.

"Rats! It's the code," he gave her.

She shrugged. "I know, but—"

"Aw, lay off! You give me a pain!"

Next day she went to see Dan. The bars were between them. Dan needed a shave, and there were worn lines on his face. But he smiled his old easy smile, and the whimsical twinkle—the brave, gay twinkle—grew in his eyes.

"Dan—I'm sorry," she said, a little huskily.

"Don't be sorry, Nance."

"I am."

"Now, Nance, don't be."

"But they'll send you up."

"I know it. There's just about twenty years ahead of me, but what is a man to do?"

Her eyes were swimming. "But why are you doing it?"

He shrugged.

She might have known why. She half guessed why. He was doing it for her sake. He did not want her to go through life as the mate of a murderer. Hence he had adopted the code of silence.

"Are they through—with you—now?" she asked.

"No. Tomorrow they're going to try again to get a confession. I hope to God I don't weaken!"

Her lips trembled. Her eyes wavered. She sighed tremulously.

"It's hell, Dan!" she murmured.

"Now, Nance," he comforted.

And it was he who needed comforting!

She left him, walking in a daze. She wondered if he would hold out tomorrow. She rather knew he would.

Callahan felt sure of himself now. The lawyer for the defense had been chosen. The date for the trial was being set. This much the newspapers gave out. Of course, they did not give out that the Department was trying for the last time to wring a confession from the prisoner. Callahan got it from Nance.

"Tomorrow they're taking him again," she said.

"How's he feel about it?"

"Oh, he says he'll stick it out."

"Good!" gloated Callahan.

Nance grimaced. The exultant tone of the exclamation made her shudder.

"Don't—talk that way," she urged.

"Bah! You worry about that sap as if he was your own flesh and blood. Lay off the sob stuff, kiddo!"

"But don't talk that way!"

"Why not? It's the breaks. We all get bum breaks sometime."

"With twenty years in the balance."

He glared at her. "Say, what the hell are you trying to do, ride me ragged? Be careful how you talk out o' turn, girlie. I'm like as not to haul off and clout you on the jaw."

She winced, turned away and drifted into the other room. She threw herself down on the bed and wept silently.

Next morning, at about ten, Nance was sitting in the living-room, looking pale and worried, when a rap on the door startled her. Callahan was in the bathroom, putting on a collar and tie. He heard the knock and froze to attention. He listened while Nance walked across the floor and opened the door. Then he heard a lazy, droning voice:

"We're from Headquarters. Where's Callahan?"

For a split-second his entire system was paralyzed. Then he went into frantic action. Coatless, he slid into the bedroom, across to the open window and out on to the fire-escape. He descended to a littered courtyard in panicky haste.

He burst into the cellar below, sped through it and came out on the street. Rapidly he walked down the street. It was warm, and other men were in shirtsleeves. He reached Eighth Avenue and headed north. He had no purpose in mind other than putting as much distance between himself and his flat as possible.

So Dan had squealed on him. Through his brain stormed a great desire to get Dan's throat between his hands and tear it to ribbons. He did not consider the raw deal he himself had handed out. He thought, in his own perverse way, only of himself as a wronged man.

A hunted criminal, he proceeded to lose himself in the back alleys of the great city. That evening he bought a newspaper and stood in a hallway to read it. The police had hit on an altogether new angle. They refused to divulge the details, but they were certain now that Dan Sanderson was an innocent man, and that all along he had been shielding another. They refused to give out this other man's name. But they were in possession of certain testimony that would convict him when caught. In fact the circumstances and the testimony were of such a nature that they had released Sanderson under bond supplied by the company for which he worked.

Callahan swore vilely, crashed the paper and went on losing himself. Then Dan was out, walking the streets a free man. This griped Callahan—griped him to the raw. He felt in his pocket. A gun was there, but not the gun he had used on the butler. That was home—back in the bureau. Damn the luck! They would find it, and a gun expert would prove that it was the gun which had fired the shot that had killed the butler. They would find other things; some masks, his tools, other impedimenta of the shady game.

That night he slept on an East River wharf. Next day he crossed to Jersey and dared to get a drink in a Hoboken speakeasy. By trolley he drifted over to Newark, and spent the night in an out-of-the-way rooming-house. From there he drifted to Jersey City. It was raining, and he bought a coat to match his blue trousers. Through the week he wandered from town to town, and on Saturday turned up in Jersey City again. Half against his will, after much deliberation, he took the tube back to New York. From Church Street he roamed over to the North River, and then down West Street to the Battery. He bought a paper and sat in the park there.

That afternoon Callahan headed uptown, drawn as if by an insidious magnet, toward his flat in the West Twenties. It was in one of the nearby streets that he saw Nance come out of a grocery store and walk in the direction of home. He followed her, from instinct more than anything else.

A few blocks north, just as she was about to enter the street where her flat was located, he saw Dan alight from a north-bound trolley and join her. They stood there, talking. Both seemed very grave. There were no smiles, no laughter.

But Callahan boiled, nevertheless. His reason ebbed away from him slowly, then in great waves. He perspired. His jaw went hard. His huge hands opened and closed spasmodically. He saw them move off down the side street together. He followed, his hand slipping around to his hip pocket. His eyes grew glassy, his breath wheezed in his throat. He almost broke into a run.

He swung into the cross street. Several pedestrians turned to gaze after him with puzzled frowns. He did not notice them. It was doubtful if he saw anyone but the man and woman up ahead. He quickened his pace, while perspiration dripped down his face. He staggered a bit, yet he was not drunk.

Reason, thought of consequence, were thrown to the four winds. Nothing mattered—nothing but the man ahead. An animal-like snarl grated in his throat. He broke into a lunging run. His gun came out of his pocket. He roared even as the gun roared.

Dan keeled sidewise, pivoting about, his face twisted in a grimace of pain. He spun down into the gutter. Nance whirled around, saw Callahan charging toward her and swinging his gun for a second shot.

Then a shot banged out from another quarter. Callahan dragged to a stop. He stood swaying on his feet and gazed about stupidly. Two men were running toward him from across the street. One was lank and raw-boned, the other short and spare, with a cigarette dangling from his lips. Gannon and Corrigan, from Headquarters.

Callahan brought up his gun again and fired at them. The shot went wild, smashed a window on the other side of the street.

"You bum!" snapped Corrigan, and fired.

Callahan collapsed.

The two detectives reached him and stood over him, hard and cold and threatening. Corrigan reached down and picked up Callahan's gun.

Dan was on his feet now. Blood was dripping from his left arm. He looked pale, and he was shaky on his feet. Nance gave him a supporting hand. They came over and joined the detectives. Callahan was passing out, but he was still conscious enough to recognize Dan.

"Damn you, you—you squealed," he choked.

People were crowding about. Two policemen appeared on the scene and drove them back.

"Gawd!" groaned Callahan. A moment later he was dead. "Well," said Gannon, "that's that. I'll go get the morgue bus."

"Yeah," nodded Corrigan. "Gotta butt handy?"

At a nearby hospital they patched Dan's arm and put him to bed. It wasn't very serious. They said he would be out in a week.

After a few days Nance came in to sit by him. She had been crying, and she smiled now, warmly, a little wanly, and ran her hand over his.

"I'm sorry," she murmured, "that he died thinking it was you who squealed."

"Now, Nance." It was just like Dan to say that.

She lowered her head, remained silent for a long moment,

biting her lower lip. Then, in a low outburst, suppressed but none the less passionate:

"I had to, Dan. I couldn't see you go through all that torture any longer. You didn't deserve it. And I couldn't stand the way he gloated. I couldn't stand his brutality any longer. And I didn't love him. How could I? Oh, God, how could I?" She sobbed, and added, after a moment, "When I—love you."

She put her cheek down against his hand. He felt a tear.

"There, there, Nance, darling."

"The code," she murmured in a choked voice, "is a curse. It's not for women. It's not even for men. But I'm strangely—glad—you kept it. It was—my—place to break it!"

A strange manner of a code, this code of silence.

A Gun in
the Dark

*It was an easy way, a coward's
way, with no chance for the
victim and, it seemed, no
chance of discovery—a gun in
the dark, a shot in the back.*

YOU WILL not find Nick Peroni's rendezvous listed in the New York guide books, so don't look it up. You won't find his name in the telephone directory, either. Nor will a pilgrimage aboard one of those Times Square-to-Chinatown sightseeing buses make you any wiser; that goes for Nick's and The Bowery, what's left of it, and Chinatown, too. You can see as much, if not more, by boarding a southbound sub at Grand Central, getting off at Canal Street and walking east. Which is to say, you won't see much of anything, at all; but the subway ride is at least worth a nickel.

Nick's place is not far from Chatham Square. You have to be in the know to get in. It takes up the third floor of a run-down four-story building. Nick owns the building, and many people wonder why he doesn't let out the store below. An alley runs in the rear, and on dark nights, sometimes, trucks pull up there and unload bootleg. A cop around the corner whistles conscience-free, for he has orders from the man higher up, and a wife and three children to support, and a car to be paid for on the installment plan.

The police tolerate the existence of this place as a means toward an end. Those who don't know the inner penetralia of crime, the silent machinery of the law, will immediately rise to condemn this practice. Those who know will nod understandingly. Such a rendezvous is by way of being a net for those who, prowling the city's streets after dark, run athwart the law. How? you will ask, and the answer is simple. Nick knows every gangster and gunman south of Washington Square, and his rendezvous is a favorite hang-out for men of that stripe. These gang-

sters know one another, and not all of them are friendly, even though they commingle on a common ground. A murder—a robbery, and the bloodhounds of the law leap into action. There are stoolies hanging out at Nick's, and Nick himself has been known to come across on the q.t., when hard-pressed. Someone is bound to know when so-and-so was last present, where he is living, or if he suddenly has disappeared from that lodging. The social register of gangdom is high at Nick's, and gossip always leaks out somehow.

Steve Callahan and Tony Valenzo hung out there regularly. They were a couple of detectives from the nearby precinct, and one was as different temperamentally from the other as night is from day. Callahan was thirty-five, rangy and flint-eyed, and hard as nails. He had no illusions, and had fought it out with more gunmen than any other sleuth in that district. Three times within the past five years he'd been in the hospital with gun-wounds. He was a fast and deadly shot, and in gangdom was known for a tough customer to deal with—a good one to steer clear of.

Valenzo was younger—no more than twenty-eight. Dark-eyed, nattily dressed, emotional, good-looking. He had the smooth grace of a tiger—and the fighting courage of one. Two years he had been linked with Callahan—two years of friendship, two years of working and fighting side by side. Brothers were never more closely drawn to each other.

And Callahan, because of his brotherly interest in his partner, cursed to high heaven the night that Rosa Talerio had first sung in Nick's rendezvous. Even so she sang again on that winter night, while wind and snow beat at the crusted window-panes, and Callahan and Valenzo sat at a table in the shadows, drinking Scotch highballs. The room—three rooms that had been knocked into one—was jammed with ex-pugs, case-hardened sporting men, and many others whose business was one of the gun and the streets at night. They sat at a dozen tables, in pairs and groups ranging from three to half a dozen or more. Layers of tobacco smoke hung motionless under the ceiling. A couple of big Negroes drafted from Harlem night-clubs served the drinks and mixed in the crowd with easy familiarity. And Rosa Talerio, rocking her beautiful face, stamping her feet, clapping her hips, sang a moaning, droning melody about muddy water, to the accompaniment of a tin-panny piano hammered by a flat-chested mulatto.

"Ain't she a dream, Steve?" demanded Valenzo, swaying with the syncopated rhythm.

"Forget it!" clipped Callahan.

"Boy, a dream, what I mean!"

"Forget it, you crazy gumshoe! Lay off that broad. I tell you, bud, she spells trouble with a capital T."

"Go 'way, Steve. You're talking through your hat. What's the matter, you jealous, big boy?"

"Jealous my eyebrow! One solitary hair on my wife's red head is worth a damned sight more than all that spaghetti bender put together!"

Valenzo's eyes flashed darkly. "Cut it out, Steve! I won't have you talking about her that way! Who the hell d'you think you are?"

Their eyes held. In Valenzo's was turmoil, like black seas breaking in the night. In Callahan's, ice touched with steel, hard and probing and unrelenting. His brain functioned clearly. There was no doubt about it. His partner was in love with Rosa. And what is reason in the haloed face of love? He backed down like a man.

"All right, Tony, if you feel that way about it," he said, and downed his drink, his brows bent thoughtfully. Inside him a thought pounded, drowning out all else. Ever since, two weeks back, Valenzo had met Rosa, that thought had pounded into his consciousness. A hunch, a canny knowledge of women, or what? At any rate, that thought kept telling him that Rosa Talerio was danger double-distilled, that Valenzo was a blind young idiot, that no good would come of it. Callahan could be bitter, and in his heart he hated the girl, hated her because his partner was head over heels in love with her.

The song ended, Valenzo beckoned her over, and she came swaying as reeds sway by watercourses—dark, satin-skinned, red-lipped, liquid-eyed; sat down while shouts and hand-clapping still applauded her and demanded an encore.

"What'll you drink, baby?" breathed Valenzo, leaning over the table and taking her left hand in his own.

"Well, make it cognac. Hello, Callahan."

Callahan grunted and looked elsewhere.

Valenzo was saying, "Sweet, I've got something for you—later." Out of the corner of his eye Callahan saw Valenzo raise one of her fingers from the others and press it warmly. It was, he noticed with a quick chill, the engagement finger.

"Oh… Tony!" Rosa whispered that, lowered her lids.

They all had drinks, and then somebody yelled for another song, and others followed. Rosa got up, smiled all around and sauntered over to the piano. Callahan lounged in his chair, a sardonic droop to his mouth. Rosa took a fan from the top of the piano. The song was Spanish, and when she had finished a voice called, "Can you tango that?"

Rosa looked around quizzically. Presently a tall, dark man,

with glittering teeth and jet, marcelled hair, rose from one of the tables. "I'd like to tango that with you, Rosa," he said.

"Sure," she laughed.

Valenzo leaned closer to Callahan, nudged him.

"Who's that guy?"

"Dunno. Never saw him." Callahan caught Nick Peroni's eye and motioned him over. "Who's the sheik, Nick?" he clipped.

Nick stared at the table, leaning on his elbows. "Dat's Luis Rodriguez. Chicago. Whatcha call De Madrid Kid."

"Oh-ho," whispered Callahan. "The Madrid Kid."

Valenzo's hands clenched and his lips flattened hard against his teeth as he watched The Madrid Kid swing into step with Rosa. They danced beautifully, and The Madrid Kid looked down into Rosa's eyes continuously, and she into his, as if they were the only ones in the room. At the end of the number thunderous applause greeted them, and again they danced. And when this was over Rose went to sit down with The Madrid Kid, and they drank, each bent across the table toward the other, smiling. Valenzo saw the Kid reach out and press Rosa's hand, but she withdrew it quickly. She had come back to earth and to the realization of the fact that Valenzo was among those present. A little flushed, she feigned some excuse, left the table and retired to her dressing room.

Valenzo stood up. He jammed his hands into his pockets and, crossing to The Madrid Kid's table, sat down. "Guess you know who I am, don't you?" was his first shot.

"Sure," nodded The Madrid Kid blandly. "Tony Valenzo, Rosa's boy friend."

"Then get wise to yourself, guy, and keep your own company."

"Why, what do you mean?"

"Can that stuff. You're from Chicago. You're not dumb."

"For Gawd's sake, can't I dance with the girl?"

"No, you can't, because you're one of these bimboes that thinks he's it with the ladies. I know your breed, guy, and I don't like it. Can't dance with a girl without crawling all over her and making goo-goo eyes. Take my tip, Kid, and lay off."

"Cripes, you're tough!"

"With pups like you, yes."

The Madrid Kid gnawed at his lip. Black hatred smouldered in his eyes. His right hand twitched, for that hand had always been close friend with the butt of a gun. But he caught hold of himself, and essayed a thin smile.

"All right, gumshoe," he ground out. "You win this time. Pick up the marbles." But there was that in his tone and demeanor that hinted of other times to come.

That night Valenzo went home with Rosa.

II

WHAT IRONY—for Callahan—when Valenzo said, while they were lounging in the precinct next day, "And when it comes off, Steve, you'll stand up for me." And when Callahan only shrugged Valenzo continued, a little warmly, "You're a fine guy. You don't even congratulate me."

Callahan picked up a newspaper and spread it before him.

"Look here, Steve!" Valenzo snapped. "Get over it! Rosa's all right, I tell you. What right have you got to stick up your damned nose at her? Because she sings in a greaseball cabaret?"

"I see," said Callahan, "they got one o' the bums pulled that mail robbery in Jersey City."

"To hell with Jersey City! I'm talking about Rosa!"

Callahan sighed, laid aside the paper and lit a cigarette. He regarded Valenzo evenly for a long moment. Then: "Pipe down, Tony. I'm going to stand up for you, ain't I? Well, then, can the comedy. Sure, Rosa's all right, if you say so. Guess I just had a touch of liver. Sure, she's all right. Good luck, Tony."

Valenzo beamed. His dark eyes sparkled. "Thanks, Steve. You bet she's a good kid. You should have seen her when I gave her the ring. She was tickled pink. Say, I'll tell you she's some girl, and I don't mean maybe."

"You off this afternoon," Callahan reminded him

"You bet. I wanted to go to a matinee with Rosa, but she had to go to a doctor about her throat. Got a cold and she can't afford it account of her singing. I'm chasing over to Broadway, though, to get her a pair of shoes. We passed the place Sunday night, but it was closed. Knobbiest pair of shoes you ever saw, Steve."

That reminded Callahan that his youngest, a boy of three, needed a pair of shoes, too, and he arranged to go with Valenzo. They grabbed a brief lunch in a one-arm restaurant, and Valenzo blew to cigars. Afterward they struck Broadway at Chambers Street, and a little later Valenzo stopped before a window and pointed out a pair of ladies' pumps; something new, black patent-leather with slim, red heels. Callahan reflected that his wife would class them among things which she termed as "loud," but he nodded at Valenzo's enthusiasm, and they entered. Presently they came out with their purchases, and Valenzo made for the subway while Callahan, remembering that his wife needed a new plug for the electric iron, strolled in quest of one. He finally secured one, near Park Row, and as he was making for the Cortlandt Street subway station, he was almost knocked over by a taxi-cab. He jerked back, flung a silent oath at the driver, which was clipped short as he caught a fleeting glimpse of the cab's passengers. There was no doubting their identity— The Madrid Kid and Rosa Talerio.

His mouth hardened and his eyes glinted as he gazed after the taxi. He reflected bitterly. Engaged to Valenzo the night before. Out riding with The Madrid Kid today. And on this he kept meditating all the way uptown in the subway.

He drifted down to the precinct that night, found Valenzo making a report on the typewriter and whistling merrily. He stood in the doorway for a long minute, staring at the back of his partner's head. Then he sighed, shrugged, and entered with a, "Hello, Tony."

Valenzo looked around, smiled. "Hello, there, Steve. Soon as I finish this we'll chase over to Nick's."

The night was chill when they left the precinct. Most of the snow had been shoveled from the streets and lay in dirty heaps in the gutters. Under the street lamps the men's breaths could be seen shooting out like silver clouds. A brisk walk of ten minutes brought them to Nick's place, and they found the rendezvous pretty crowded, with Rosa in the middle of a song. Her eyes smiled at them as they moved toward their favorite table. Callahan looked about searchingly, saw no sign of The Madrid Kid.

Afterward Rosa joined them at the table, a worried expression on her face.

"What's up, baby?" asked Valenzo.

"Headache. I'm sick all over. Nick's letting me off early."

"Gee, that's too bad! You better take care of it."

Callahan saw the diamond sparkling on her finger. What a stone! He told himself that a greater portion of Valenzo's savings had gone into the buying of that. His eyes wandered, settled on a string of pearls about her neck. Valenzo saw them at the same time.

"Where'd you get the pearls, baby?" he asked.

"Oh… these. Imitation," she laughed. "Two-ninety-eight on Grand Street."

He pressed her hand. "Some day, sweet, you'll be wearing a real string."

Nick appeared at this juncture, rubbing his hands. "Telephone," he announced. "For you, Tony."

Valenzo rose and followed him out, and when he returned he was frowning. "That guy I nabbed for the Sullivan law, Steve. They want me at the night court for a minute. Will you see Rosa home, Steve?"

"Oh, never mind about that, honey," chimed in Rosa. "I'll be all right."

"Well, anyhow." Valenzo leaned under the table, came up with a package. "Those shoes, baby."

"Oh, honey, thank you so much!"

Valenzo went out, and Rosa returned to the piano to sing.

She finished the song, bowed, smiled, and retreated into another room. When she appeared again she was dressed for the street, and with a nod of the head, a wave of the hand, to old customers, she clicked out.

Callahan got up, put on his overcoat, lighted a cigarette, and with a brief good-night to Nick, followed. Reaching the dark, gloomy street, he looked up and down and spotted Rosa just turning into the next block. The section was a miserable, deserted one, and he could clearly hear the clicking of her heels on the pavement. He quickened his pace, and then he heard a sudden, stifled cry.

For a moment he paused. Then he pulled his gun, broke into a run, and rounding a corner, saw Rosa reeling into the gutter and a dark figure disappearing into an alley. In quick bounds he reached her where she now lay in the gutter, and bending down, put an arm under her and lifted her. The collar of her coat had been ripped aside, and he noticed that there was no necklace about her throat. Quickly he drew the collar shut against the stinging cold.

"Oh-o-o!" she was moaning, and then her eyes opened, saw Callahan's face close beside her own.

"Oh!" she choked.

"What happened?" he clipped.

"Some—man—attacked me! I screamed!"

"I heard you. Lose anything?"

Her hand clutched the collar closer about her neck. "N-no. No."

Callahan relaxed. He almost smiled in his sardonic way.

"I'll put you in a taxi," he said.

"Oh, thanks."

Several minutes elapsed before a nighthawk taxi rolled into view. He helped her in, slammed the door after her, and watched the taxi shoot off. Then he jammed his hands into his pockets and retraced his steps. Entering Nick's rendezvous, he stood just inside the door running his eyes over the gathering. He saw four faces that had not been present when he left. Three of these were in a group. One was alone. Toward this man he strolled leisurely and sat down facing him.

"Hello, Blackie," he said.

"Oh, hello there, Steve. Ain't seen you in a long time."

"No? Not since you got out in October, eh?"

"Nope."

"Living around here?"

"Yeah."

"Minding your own business?"

"Who, me? Sure. Nix on the old game. Workin' on the docks now."

"Not at night, though, eh?"

" 'Course not. What'd I be doin' here if I was?"

"That's right. How long have you been here, Blackie?"

" 'Bout an hour."

"Didn't see you. I was here until a half hour ago."

Their eyes locked.

"You're a lousy liar, Blackie," Callahan ground out. "How'd you come?"

"Why, I got off a Canal Street crosstown and walked over."

"You did, eh. Sidewalks are all cleared, eh, aren't they?"

"Huh? Sure. Why—"

"Close your trap! Look at your feet, you poor sap! Look at the snow half-way up your legs? Did you get that way from walking on clean sidewalks or beating through a snowbank in somebody's alley?"

Blackie's jaw dropped.

"Come out o' your shell, guy," went on Callahan. "Let's go in the next room. Snap on it!"

Blackie rose and with Callahan passed into an adjoining room. Callahan closed the door behind him and bored Blackie with a hard stare.

"D'you want me to frisk you or are you going to save me the trouble and yourself a bat in the jaw?" was his frank question.

Blackie wilted. He said nothing—only reached in his pocket and drew out a string of pearls. Callahan took them, dangled them from his fingers.

"Did she see you?"

"No. I got her from behind."

"H'm. What are they worth, Blackie?"

"Well, about five hundred bucks."

Callahan bit his lip. *Two-ninety-eight!*

"Get out of here!" he snapped at Blackie.

"Huh?" Blackie was dumfounded.

"Get out! And listen, you little bum. Don't breathe a word about this, or I'll fix it so you'll go up for twenty years. And when you see these on her neck again, leave 'em alone! Breeze! Drift!"

Blackie drifted. And Callahan, alone, stared at the pearls.

"Two-ninety-eight!" he muttered. "Damn her!"

III

CALLAHAN FOUND himself harboring an intense desire to wound Rosa's vanity.

A plan took birth in his brain that night and by morning was full grown. He went over to East Broadway, down near the Manhattan Bridge, and entered a small jewelry shop run by a Jew who was a very good friend of his. Berkovitz was his name.

"Morning, Berky," greeted Callahan, "How's tricks?"

"Oi, beezeness is punk, Steve."

"Same old story. Wish I had one tenth the rocks you've got.

But look here." He pulled his hand from his pocket and dangled the string of pearls. "What are they worth, Berky?"

Berkovitz took them, adjusted his eye-glass and held them close under his nose. "Um. Vell, four-hundred berries, Steve, I'd give."

"I'm not selling them, understand. Now tell me what they're really worth."

"Vell, between me an' you, Steve, I'd say six-hundred."

"All right. Now I want you to do something for me, Berky, and sometime I'll do something for you. Make a set of paste pearls to match these—an exact match, get me?"

"Sure."

"Can you do it?"

"Sure, seein' it's you, Steve."

"Good. Give me a ring at the precinct when they're ready."

When Callahan dropped in at the precinct late that afternoon he found Valenzo in high spirits.

"Well, Steve, old timer, how goes the grand old life?"

"So-so, Tony," muttered Callahan. "You?"

"Jake!" He reached toward the desk, picked up a small, flat package and unwrapped it. Presently he displayed a box of dainty lace-edged handkerchiefs.

"Humph!" grunted Callahan.

"For Rosa," smiled Valenzo. "Made in France, Steve. Ain't they the cats? She'll rave about them."

Callahan said, "They're sure nice," and then sat back with a newspaper.

He did not go to Nick's that night, nor the next, though Valenzo managed to drop around on both occasions to see Rosa. Valenzo never spoke to Callahan about Rosa's loss of the pearls, and he took it for granted that Rosa had not mentioned the incident to her fiancé.

The two detectives were sitting in the precinct a few nights later chatting with a reporter from the city news association, when the telephone rang and Callahan picked up the receiver. He said into the mouthpiece, "All right. Be right over," and hung up. Then he rose and shrugged into his overcoat.

"Be back right away, Tony," was his parting shot.

Ten minutes later he walked into Berkovitz's store, and the Jew produced the genuine and the paste strings of pearls.

"Couldn't tell the difference," smiled Callahan as he held them side by side. "All Jake, Berky. I'll do something for you sometime."

He stowed the genuine pearls in an inner pocket and thrust the paste set in his overcoat pocket. Then he went out, hopped a taxi and was driven to Nick's rendezvous. The place was not crowded yet, for it was only nine o'clock. But Rosa was there, and she was sitting at a table with—The Madrid Kid!

Callahan could have laughed outright, the irony of the situation was so perfect. He nodded to Nick and weaved his way nonchalantly toward the table at which the two sat. Rosa looked up, forced an easy smile that was not so easy.

"Hello, Callahan," she jerked.

"Greetings," supplemented The Madrid Kid. He was dressed to perfection. A diamond solitaire sparkled on his tie. His hair was marcelled and shone like black onyx.

Callahan looked from one to the other with his probing, unsmiling eyes.

"Won't you sit down and have a drink?" ventured The Madrid Kid.

Callahan shook his head. "No, thanks. Just dropped around to give you this." His hand came out of his overcoat pocket, dropped the pearls gently to the table.

"Oh!" breathed Rosa.

And The Madrid Kid exclaimed, "Gee, Callahan, that's good work. Who frisked them?"

"That's my business. Some amateur. He didn't know pearls. I trailed him to a 'fence' on Canal Street."

"Great!"

"The fence offered him two bucks for 'em," went on Callahan dully. "I got 'em for nothing. They're selling for two-ninety-eight on Grand Street."

He saw Rosa blanch, saw The Madrid Kid's lips tighten. He could have laughed in the woman's face. Her eyes darted toward her companion, and in them rose a look of lacerating contempt. The Madrid Kid said nothing. He was dumfounded.

Callahan turned on his heel, wandered across the room and sat down at a table by himself. Yet he watched the pair. And he saw them arguing, saw Rosa's lips moving rapidly in what appeared to be hot indignation. To himself he smiled, bitterly. No doubt she was calling The Madrid Kid a cheap skate, a fraud, a dirty tramp. Then she got up abruptly, stamped a foot, strode across the floor and banged into the adjoining room. The Madrid Kid sat staring at the string of bogus pearls.

Callahan called up the precinct to tell Valenzo where he was, but the man at the desk reported that Valenzo had gone off on a job.

"If he comes in, tell him I'm at Nick's," he explained, and hung up.

Then he went back to the table and sat down. When, later, Rosa sang, he could see The Madrid Kid's eyes following her every movement hungrily. There was no doubting that the Kid was in anguish, that he, too, loved Rosa. Later he saw The Madrid Kid draw her aside, talk to her earnestly, imploringly, while she kept shaking her head. Then presently she stopped shaking her head, listened, looked into his eyes and smiled. He pressed her hand.

Callahan walked out a little before the time he knew that Rosa usually departed. But he did not go far. He hung in a black doorway opposite the rendezvous, and when Rosa came out, accompanied by The Madrid Kid, Callahan followed them to Canal Street. There they boarded a taxi, and Callahan got into one that came a moment later.

"Trail that car," he said.

They drove uptown to the West Thirties, alighted in a dark street and entered a small walk-up apartment house. Callahan followed, ascertained Rosa's apartment in the lobby and after waiting there a moment climbed to the fourth floor and put his ear to the keyhole.

The Madrid Kid was saying, "Honest, Rosa, I thought it was real. I thought the guy sold it to me was a friend of mine. He said it was worth five-hundred at least."

"Aw, that's just your story."

"No, Rosa, it's the truth. I'll get you another, darling. You and I'll go and get it on Broadway. Pick any one you want."

"Honest, you'll do that?"

"Anything, darling. Only give up that gumshoe."

"Not yet. This ring—ain't it a beauty?"

"But I'll get you the pearls. And we'll leave New York."

"But I want to keep the ring, too. It's you I really love, my boy. And we couldn't get away. You don't know Tony. He'd trail us—he would!"

"Listen," said The Madrid Kid, and his voice lowered.

Callahan could not catch what he said, but after a moment he heard Rosa exclaim, "Oh, you will! You angel!" And then, "But why must I give up the ring?"

After a long pause The Madrid Kid's voice—"There may be a way."

Then no more talking.

Presently Callahan retraced his steps, reached the street and walked east toward the subway.

What a leech she was! And what a fool Valenzo was! And for that matter, The Madrid Kid, too.

Tony must be told. There was no getting out of it. All the way down in the subway Callahan kept telling himself that Tony must be told.

At the precinct he found Valenzo and the inspector quizzing

a couple of Hester Street roughnecks who'd done some shooting over a crap game. There was no opportunity for a heart-to-heart talk with his partner. At midnight the gangsters were marched to Headquarters, and Callahan went home a little later with his story still untold.

When he reported at the precinct next evening, he had his plan well outlined; how he would lead up to it, how he would tell Tony in the easiest way possible. But the detectives' room was filled with a couple of reporters, the inspector, and some others, and the main topic was a coming heavyweight match at the Garden. And again Callahan was sidetracked from his purpose.

The telephone rang, and as Valenzo was nearest to it, he picked up the receiver. He had to press a finger over his left ear to shut out the din of conversation, and when he hung up he rose and reached for his overcoat.

"See you later, Steve," he called as he breezed out. There was a radiant smile on his face.

IV

AND AGAIN Callahan was unable to relieve his mind, to tell Valenzo what he had seen, what he had heard. It would be a terrific jolt to Tony, yet how much more so if the thing hung fire and he learned of it at a later date. Valenzo would take it hard—no doubt of it. He was that kind. A thing like this would sink him, drive him almost to black despair. But he would get over it eventually. And better now than later. Yes, somehow, before this night was out, Valenzo would get the truth.

The reporters drifted out, and a couple of detectives went with them. The inspector yawned, locked up his desk, grunted a lazy good-night and thumped out.

Callahan picked up a newspaper, tipped his hat over his eyes and planted his feet on the desk. The single window, looking out into a courtyard, was framed in sooty snow a week old. The floor was littered with cigarette and cigar stubs. Ashes covered the two tumbledown desks—ashes and papers. Reward notices were pasted all over the drab walls. The green-shaded electric light glared upon the dust and disorder impartially. The night wind, cutting over from the East River, hooted spasmodically in the area way, plucked at the window, rattling it. But the room was warm, drowsy, and the lieutenant at the desk outside was droning monotonously in the telephone.

Callahan let the paper slide to the floor, yawned, stretched and tipped his hat lower over his eyes. He closed his eyes and dropped off into a contented half-sleep. Sometime later he was awakened by the booming voice of the lieutenant calling—"Hey, Callahan!"

Callahan muttered an oath and drifted yawning into the desk.

"Say, Callahan," went on the lieutenant, "your partner Valenzo is in the hospital. Don't know what it's all about, but he's got a bullet in his guts. Taxi driver picked him up. Better run over."

Callahan was instantly awake. He got the name of the hospital, snapped into his coat and went out of the precinct on the jump. He reached Canal Street and, hailing a taxi, flung out the address as he jumped in and slammed the door behind him.

It took him ten minutes to reach the hospital, and another five to fight and bully his way through to the doctor who was handling the case. But the doctor barred him from the room.

"I tell you, this guy's my partner!" stormed Callahan.

"Never mind. You can't see him now. We've taken out the bullet and he may live."

"Was he conscious? Did he say anything?"

"Yes, he was conscious."

"Where'd it happen?"

"My dear man, you can't expect all the details. He was in pretty bad condition when we received him. He couldn't say much. The taxi driver is still in the lobby, I think."

"Thanks," clipped Callahan, and swung swiftly back toward the lobby.

There was a small man sitting on a bench there. His hair was tousled, his overcoat open, a red sweater buttoned up around a collarless shirt.

"You the guy brought the wounded man here?" Callahan shot at him.

"Yeah. How much longer they gonna keep me waiting?"

Callahan flashed his badge, and the man brightened.

"Where'd you pick him up?" was Callahan's next question.

"On East Nint' Street, near Second Avenue. I'd dropped a couple at the Village Fair Club and was just rollin' along. I see dis lump o' black over de snow in de gutter an' I pulls up. Sure enough it's a guy."

"Was there anybody else around?"

"Nope. Nobuddy."

"Hear any shots?"

"Nope. Nuttin'. I don't know how long he'd been layin' there. So I hefted him in me taxi an' druv over here. Dere ain't no crowds over dat way. It's pretty dam' dark if yuh ask me."

"Listen. Drive me over. You'll get paid."

"T'anks. It's good t' meet a dick what don't expect everyt'ing f'r nuttin'."

"Cut the gaff and snap into it. Come on."

When they reached East Ninth Street the driver slowed down, looking for the spot where he had found Valenzo. Presently he pulled up and got out.

"Right here, chief,'s where I found him. See the blood spots on the snow."

"Got a flashlight handy?"

"Yeah, sure."

With the flashlight in his hand Callahan inspected the snow, saw the blood where Valenzo had lain. He swung the beam across the cleared sidewalk, followed blood spots for almost a block, then stopped.

"Must have been hit here," he said. "Then staggered east. Must have been coming east. What time did you find him?"

"Couple minutes after nine. I remember, 'cause when I dropped that couple at the Village Fair the gent remarked it was nine bells."

Callahan ran his eyes over the darkened, shoddy houses. No sign of life was visible. The whole street, the houses, were dark and gloomy. What, he mused, had Valenzo been doing over this way, far out of his district?

He retraced his steps carefully, swinging the beam of light back and forth across the sidewalk. Finally he kicked a small object, went to pass, then turned, bent down and picked it up.

"Find a clue?" chirped the taxi driver.

Callahan's jaw had hardened. His teeth shone in a breathed snarl. He spun sharply.

"Chatham Square, and step on it!"

"Got a clue, huh?"

"Shut your trap and step on it, I said!"

At Chatham Square Callahan swung out of the taxi, thrust a couple of bills into the chauffeur's hands, noted his number, and told him to move on. Then he jammed his hands into his pockets and strode west. Ten minutes later he opened the door leading into Nick Peroni's rendezvous.

"Ah, hello dar, Steve!" greeted Nick, rubbing his hands.

"Hello," chopped off Callahan.

Nick sensed that something was up, and took a deep breath, pursed his lips. Rosa was singing her favorite song about levees, deltas and muddy water. Callahan crossed firmly to his favorite table, sat down and ordered whiskey straight. His face was granite hard, his eyes narrowed and chill. Nick hovered near the entrance, fidgeting with his fingers, eying the detective obliquely. Rosa finished her song, bowed to the applause, and chose to sit at a table by herself. She favored Callahan with a smile but made no move to join him. He saw that a string of pearls were about her neck—real ones, this time, he told himself.

Nick was edging his way over. He eased down on a chair beside Callahan and forced a smile.

"Pretty cold out, hey, Steve? Whatcha say, good-ah booze?"

"It's all right. Look here, Nick. How long has Rosa been here?"

"Oh, long tam. Her an' De Madrid Kid come in together 'bout ha'-past seven. Dey sit in de room Rosa uses sometams to rest."

"How long?"

"Wal, dey come out about nine-t'irty. Whatza mat', Steve?"

"Oh, nothing. Rosa's been here since seven-thirty?"

"Yeah, sure, Steve."

"Where's The Madrid Kid?"

"He's-ah just run out for some cigarettes. I don't keep-ah de kind he smokes."

"All right."

"Dat's all, Steve?"

Callahan nodded and Nick got up and drifted away, though still troubled. After a moment Callahan went over to the telephone. When he hung up the receiver the muscles at either side of his mouth bulged hard.

"God!" he muttered.

Valenzo had died at ten-forty-five!

Callahan's eyes flung across the room. The Madrid Kid had returned. He was sitting at Rosa's table.

"God!" breathed Callahan again.

Tony—laughing, sparkle-eyed Tony dead! Shot in the back, they had told him.

With a quick movement Callahan slipped into the short corridor that led to several spare rooms. He turned to find Nick coming after him, a little nervous.

"Where's Rosa's room?" he flung at Nick.

Nick pointed, blinking his eyes, moistening his lips.

Callahan pushed open the door, stepped into the small, cozy room where an amber lamp glowed warmly. His eyes swept about quickly, searchingly. A small dresser, littered with cosmetics. A couple of costume dresses. Several pairs of pumps. Nick stood on the threshold, silent, troubled. Callahan pulled open the dresser drawers, rummaged in them. All but one was empty. The one contained soiled clothing. Nick saw him pull out something white and silky and thrust it into his pocket.

"Steve, whatsa da mat'?" he ventured.

Callahan ignored him and crossed to the window. He unlocked the catch, opened the window, stepped out to the fire-escape. For a moment Nick saw his face framed in the window, smiling grimly. Then—

"All right, Nick. Close it."

Nick closed the window, chewed at a finger, backed out of the room and went back to the cabaret. He sat down by himself, thinking hard, wondering, fearing the worst. He hated to have the law ransacking his place. He liked to keep on the right side of the law—and on the right side of the lawless, too. He had a hard, trying life.

He looked up as the main door opened. Callahan strolled in. Nick's heart missed a beat. That deadly look on Callahan's face. Those icy, cutting eyes. Something—something was going to happen.

Callahan's hands were in his overcoat pockets. His mouth was a thin, hard slash. A cold, chill, steady blaze was in his eyes. With measured steps he crossed the room, looking neither to right nor left—crossed, like the march of doom, toward the table where Rosa and The Madrid Kid now sat. Rosa's look was puzzled. Callahan stopped at the table and eyed her evenly.

"Hello, Callahan, how's tricks?" she flung off nonchalantly.

"Rotten," he clipped.

"Have a drink," offered The Madrid Kid.

Callahan's steely gaze shifted to the speaker, bit into him

keenly. Then it shifted back to Rosa. Then Callahan sat down slowly, gently, like a man sitting down in a dark room. He leaned his elbows on the table and his face, his hard, outthrust jaw crept toward Rosa.

"Tony," he said, "just died."

Rosa's face froze. "My God! How? Who? *Tony?* Oh, my poor, dear Tony! No, it can't be, Callahan. It—"

"Practicing for the stage?" sneered Callahan.

"I—I—" She gripped Callahan's arm. "Where is he? Take me to him! Take me!"

Callahan pulled away his arm. His hand closed about her wrist.

"Sister, you always were a damned good actress, but you can't pull the wool over this gumshoe's eyes. Lay off that boloney!"

"Listen, Callahan, go easy!" cut in The Madrid Kid.

"Close your face, you!" snarled Callahan.

Everybody in the rendezvous had quieted down. Conversations had stopped. Liquor remained undrunk. All eyes were riveted on that table. Nick hovered near the wall, his worst fears realized.

Callahan was asking, "Where were you two at about nine o'clock tonight?"

"Here—right here," replied The Madrid Kid. "Say, what are you driving at?"

"Pipe down on the questions, wiseguy. I'm asking. You were here, eh?"

"Why, sure, Callahan," supplemented Rosa. "In my dressing room. Ask Nick. He was standing right where he is now when we came in—a little before seven."

"Yeah?" Callahan chuckled bitterly. "Alibi stuff, eh?"

"Oh, you make me sick!" snapped The Madrid Kid. "What the hell do you think you're doing?"

"You close your jaw, bimbo. You're in bad company right now." Callahan showed his teeth in a thin, hard smile. "And listen, both o' you, while I do a little reconstructing. You and sister here came in at seven-thirty and went into her room where you stayed until nine-thirty. That right?"

"Sure it's right," nodded The Madrid Kid.

"Like hell it is!" barked Callahan. "I'll tell you where you were. After going into her room both of you left by the fire-escape. There's snow on it and two pairs of footprints on the steps all the way down to the alley; and there's footsteps—your and hers—leading out to the street. Maybe you took a taxi.

"Anyhow, you didn't ride far. You got out, and sister here went into a booth and called up Tony at the precinct. I was there when he got her call. He went out to meet you, sister, all about eight-fifteen, I don't know where he met you. Maybe—eh?—you wanted to have a bite to eat and a couple dances. You finally—you and Tony—took the subway to Eighth Street. No taxi, eh, because taxi drivers sometimes have good memories. You, Kid, followed them, by prearrangement with her.

"You, sister, suggested a cellar restaurant somewhere on Ninth Street, east, because it's out of your usual neighborhood. You, Kid, followed. When the street got dark and deserted you used your rod—and silencer. *Shot Valenzo in the back!*"

"Oh, Lord, you're crazy!" shouted The Madrid Kid.

"Guns in the dark, like yellow pups always do! Shut up! You and sister here left Tony in the gutter, walked back toward Fifth Avenue, maybe rode for one station in the sub, hopped a taxi, came here, through the alley, back up the fire-escape and into the dressing-room. Then, at nine-thirty, the two of you stroll casually out into the cabaret!"

"Oh, my God, Callahan, what are you talking about?" screamed Rosa.

"Calm, darling," urged The Madrid Kid. "It's all a dream. He doesn't know what he's talking about. A nice story, but no legs to stand on."

"No?" shot out Callahan. His hand came out of his pocket, laid a pair of white stockings, on the table. "They're wet," he explained, "half-way to the knees. Did they get that way from staying in your dressing-room—*or walking through an alley choked with snow?*"

Rosa snapped to her feet, her breast heaving. The Madrid Kid rose, his face dark. Callahan rose, cold, flickering lights in his eyes.

"You," he hurled at Rosa, "were on East Ninth Street tonight!"

"It's a lie!" she cried.

"The hell it is! I found this near Tony's body!" From his pocket he yanked a slim, red heel that had come from a woman's shoe, thrust it before her eyes.

She shrank back, clapped a hand to her mouth.

"Listen, damn you!" cried The Madrid Kid. "Cut it out! You're trying to frame us. A heel. What about it? Where's the shoe?"

Callahan cut him with a stare like a rapier thrust. "When you told Nick you were going out for cigarettes you dropped the shoes in an ashcan downstairs. Here they are!" He flung open his overcoat, slammed down the shoes—one shy a heel— the shoes that Tony had bought for Rosa! "No legs to stand on!" he snarled. "Dammit, I'll see both of you burn in the chair! My partner you killed! D'you hear? You killed him, damn your souls!"

Rosa reeled backward. The Madrid Kid blanched.

And then the lights went out, for crookdom will stand by crookdom in a pinch, and a woman of the shadows was in a pinch.

A voice yelled, "Beat it, Rosa!"

Chairs scraped, banged. A shot roared—flame slashed through the darkness. More guns barked, hammered. Men hurled themselves savagely in the blackness.

"Turn on those damn lights!" shouted Callahan, and almost instantly fired.

A hurtling body crashed into him, knocked him to the floor. He cursed, groped to his feet. A gun thundered close by his face. He fired again. There was a hoarse scream—a shrill scream. Glass smashed, wood splintered. Shouts. Curses.

And then the lights. Men were milling through the doorway. Chairs, tables, were overturned. Nick stood with his hand on the switch, his face white as driven snow.

Rosa lay draped over a fallen chair, a crimson stain on her breast. Face down lay The Madrid Kid. Callahan stood crouched, cold rage in his eyes, a streak of blood across his cheek.

Only he and Nick remained standing. The crowd had vanished. Rosa and The Madrid Kid lay motionless.

Presently Callahan moved, bent over the woman, nodded, and crossed to The Madrid Kid.

"What—what?" panted Nick.

"Dead—both," muttered Callahan.

He stooped to pick up Rosa's purse. Idly he opened it, poured its contents into his hand. Some change, some bills, a folded slip of paper. This he opened, squinted at it.

It was a receipt for one-hundred dollars, deposit on an order for a five-hundred dollar lady's fur coat. It had been paid by Luis Rodriguez—The Madrid Kid.

Tony's funeral was a pretentious one. Callahan practically buried him. Berkovitz had given him six-hundred for that pearl necklace, and Callahan used all of it and some more toward Tony's burial. Blackie, the crook who had first lifted it from Rosa's neck, saw the funeral go by.

"Cripes, de Wop's ridin' in style," he muttered.

Bitter epitaph for one who had died by a gun in the dark.

Hell to Pay

A crook tells his part in the gangster war from Chicago to New York.

ALL RIGHT, Mister Man, I'll come clean. Remember, now, you promised me a light sentence. No backing out, see. I don't have to spring this. I ain't afraid of no rubber hose. I'm tough. If I wasn't I would have busted my dome when I took that spill. All right, I'll talk. Sure. Only when them reporters take my picture get me a tie and a shave, will yuh? I mean, my appearance now'd go against me in the tabloids. A feller's got to get sympathy from the public.

Aw, hold your hosses. I'm getting to it. I'll begin from the beginning, and the beginning was something like two years ago in Chicago. There was me and Chick Cassidy and Bud Conroy and Nigger Jackson. Chick always was an enterprising young Mick, and it looked like we was drumming up a good bootleg trade. But the big cheese out there was Joe Spinelli, and he had all the night-clubs pretty much sewed up, and he got sore if anybody butted in on his racket.

Well, Chick was a wild Mick, and he always said there was no greaseball living could tell him where to get off. So we crossed Spinelli. We began to under-bid the Wop and we got control of two fast clubs, The Royal Palace, and the Red Rendezvous, and we turned out some of the best gin in the state, and some pretty good Scotch, too.

But, see, we run up against Spinelli, and we run into trouble. Chick was trotting around at the time with a little frail he'd picked up at The Royal Palace. Josie Trent, a wise piece of brass that got on my nerves from the start. Well, we're all sitting in The Royal Palace one night when Spinelli and two of his sheik guns drop in. We're heeled and we sit tight. The Wop comes over.

"You lay off my territory, Cassidy," he says to Chick, and Chick says, "Since when have you bought up any territory, Spinelli?"

Spinelli's a good-looking Wop. Tailor-made clothes, marcelled hair, silk shirts, diamonds, and tough. "I'm telling you to lay off," he says again. "You're just a lousy little tin-horn trying to bust into big business. Lay off."

"You can go to hell," says Chick. "You think you're big, but it's only your head—kind of swelled up. Go tie your little bull outside, you guinea."

"You monkey around my back door, Cassidy, and you'll see how big I am." With that Spinelli turns around, nods to his guns and they walk out. We all take our hands out of our pockets. They are kind of sweaty from gripping our guns. You know how it is.

Well, we don't lay off Spinelli's racket, and one night, about a week later, we get a rotten break. Two of our trucks run into trouble out around Evanston, and a cop gets bumped off. A guy named Kruse, one of our best guns, has to take the rap, and Chick has to dig down in his jeans for the fall dough. Well, Hartman was our lawyer, and Kruse gets off with fifteen years, but we're broke.

Then Josie gives Chick the air and it kind of breaks him up, because he was nuts on that frail. It ain't long after that we see her in a night-club with Spinelli, and we find out a little later that it was her tipped off the cops about them two trucks out around Evanston. Spinelli'd bought her over while she was still living with Chick. Ain't that just like a woman?

Well, Nigger Jackson is for bumping her off right away, but Chick says no, not just yet. We're all broke, see, and can't pull a broad one like that. But you might remember how one fine night a taxi ran into the lake, and when they dragged it they got the taxi and Josie, but no driver. Of course, not. The driver was one of our guns. He headed the taxi for the lake and then jumped. That's how Josie got hers.

Who was the driver, you say? Well, it won't do you no good, but it was a guy named Lefty Bone. He got knifed a month later in a dinge flop-house out on Drexel Boulevard.

We had hard times. We couldn't make a move because Spinelli was a close friend of a couple of aldermen and they was down on us. But then politics took a change and the gang that got in office wasn't so chummy with the Wop. He pulled several bones, and it got so hot for him that he packed up his bags, took his gunmen and trucks and his business here, to New York.

Well, we swing in fine. Inside of a year we're running the whole racket, living in swell joints and piling up a capital of damn near a million. But Chick don't forget Spinelli. He figures the Wop handed him a raw deal, and he aims to pay him back. He talks about New York and wants to shift there, but we're making money where we are, and kinder talk him out of it. But then we get a streak of bad luck. One killing after another—watchmen, mostly, you know. And then one night Nigger bumps off Jerry the Spic, what run a speakeasy and was a half brother to Alderman Sodano. We was in good with the ward till then, but Nigger pulled a bone, and we hear the State's Attorney is going to declare war, and Chick says, "Change of address, boys.

New York—and Spinelli!" Yeah, cripes, we all come, even though we figured there'd be holy hell to pay. Chick and Bud and Nigger and me come in drawing-rooms on the Twentieth Century and we get a three-room apartment at a ritzy hotel. Twelve of our guns come in later by limousines, and there's three machine-guns. Two weeks later six of our trucks pull in loaded with booze and we store it in a warehouse on West Street.

Then we start out to pick on Spinelli. We make the rounds of the night-clubs, and we under-bid the Wop twenty per cent. Inside of a week we've got a dozen of his clubs and we know he's out to see who's grabbing the gold rings on his merry-go-round. We run into him one night in a club on West Fiftieth Street, and he's sore as a boil.

"So you're looking for trouble, eh?" he asks Chick.

"Who, me?" laughs Chick. "No. I'm just in big business. Be a sport, Spinelli. Can't you stand competition?"

"Competition, hell!" says Spinelli. "You're trying to ride me, Cassidy, and when I'm rid I'm dangerous."

"Yeah?" laughs Chick. "Do I look like a Boy Scout?"

Spinelli looks us over, one at a time. He's got a tux on, and a rod in his pocket. So have we. Two of his guns, Charley Goss and Nick Bonno, are sitting at a table opposite. They're keeping up a conversation but they're watching us, too. Nick is cross-eyed, but he slings a mean smoke-pole. Gawd, I figured something was going to blow up then. But it didn't.

Spinelli says, "This means war, Cassidy."

"Start now, you guinea," says Chick. Can you imagine such a crazy Mick! Honest, mister, I was sweating, and I had my rod half pulled, and my eye on the nearest exit. Sure, I still curse the day I ever hooked up with Chick. A square guy, yeah, but looney—you know what I mean? Like putting your head in a lion's mouth. Well, anyways, Spinelli stalls off, and he ain't so dumb.

"When I start my little war, Cassidy," he says, "I ain't handing out formal notices. Get that. And get this, too, you lousy Mick.

I'm swinging this town, and I'm buddies with a lot of swells that'll back me to the tune of five million bucks. You lay off or I'll fall on your game like a ton of brick. That's no boloney, and if you think it is, try getting funny."

"I got a grudge against you, you spaghetti-bending pup," says Chick. "Your talk is just so much stinking gas to me. I'm sitting on top of the world and I've got some of the best guns in the country. And I'm going to swing New York, Spinelli. Plant that in your nut. War, you say? What the hell did you think I'd expect—a lawn party? Tap your head, guy. You've got water on the brain."

"All right," nods Spinelli. "I'm glad we understand each other. Don't go to the police, Cassidy, if you get lead in your pants. Don't yelp when you're licked. From now on it's war, and one of us is going to move out of New York, maybe feet first, and it won't be me."

"Cripes, you talk big for a little guy!" laughs Chick. "This time next year you'll be good fertilizer for daisies. Move on, Wop, and start your ball rolling whenever you damn please."

Spinelli cackles at this. He always had a dry, mean cackle that useter give my spine a shimmy every time he pulled it. He give us the double O as casual as you please—me and Bud Conroy and Nigger Jackson.

"What I said to your boss goes for you guys, too," he tells us. "All right, then. I'll be going now. I got a date. When I see you again, Cassidy, I hope to hell it will be in the morgue among a lot of other stiffs."

"I'll see you there first, Wop. On your way," says Chick.

Then Spinelli and his guns take the air, and we know war has started. Nigger gets tight that night in the club and insults a broad. She bounces a bottle off his head, and when it don't knock him Chick bats him in the jaw and we take him home in a taxi.

"I told you to lay off the rum," yells Chick, mad as hell. "Six drinks and you're cock-eyed. Now lay off. If you want to run with me you got to hold your head. You'll need it from now on. You haul off an' pull another stunt like this and I'll lay you out personal. We're bucking Spinelli's gang, d' you hear? It means a tight lip and a clear head and a fast gun. This town ain't big enough for them and us. Either they pass or it's us, and there's no quarter. That goes for all you guys. Any guy that talks out of turn or gets ambitious on his own hook is slated for lead poisoning. There can't be no hitches. This is war, and when it busts it's going to make a lot of noise. Put that slob to bed, Bud."

CHICK SAID a mouthful when he says it was going to make a lot of noise. I'll say it made a lot of noise.

We go right to work, see. There ain't no stalling. We go on swiping more trade from Spinelli, and there's a carload of booze on the way from Chi in fish barrels with the barrels smelling like a South Street fish market. We get lots of orders, and our rum is good and we make quick deliveries, and Spinelli's outfit begins to feel the rub.

Then one night one of our trucks is rolling up Tenth Avenue with two dozen cases of Scotch for places in Harlem. A touring car shoots by and two guns bust loose. Our gun is killed instant and the driver is wounded bad, and we lose the rum and the truck. The driver dies next day in the hospital, but Bud sees him beforehand, and he gets the number of the touring car and a general description.

Well, you can bet Chick is sore. He raves around the apartment all day, and then towards night Bud blows in and says, "Listen, I got one of Spinelli's warehouses spotted."

"All right," says Chick. "We'll blow it up."

"When?" asks Nigger.

And Chick says, "Tonight."

So along about ten we stroll out of the apartment house, all heeled, and Nigger is carrying the bag with the bombs. Chick's in one of them moods when he thinks everybody but himself is a dumbbell. That's why he come along. Well, we swipe a sedan on Seventy-third street and shoot off, and in ten minutes we're parked a block away from Spinelli's warehouse. We get in through a back alley and run into three guys who's on guard. They're playing poker and we get them cold. We gag and bind 'em and pitch 'em out in the alley.

There's a lot of booze on hand. Cases stacked twelve high and lots of barrels. We lay three bombs and walk out. We get into the sedan and as we're driving by easy-like there's three explosions. Nigger was driving and he stepped on it. We left the car on West Thirty-eighth Street, hoofed it to Broadway and took a taxi. We're lounging around half-dressed and drinking highballs by midnight.

"I wonder if the pup 'll laugh that off," says Chick.

"He might get sore," says Nigger.

"Wait 'll he gets something to be sore about," says Chick.

Spinelli calls up next morning and says, "You'll pay double for that, Cassidy," and hangs up. Chick laughs and rubs his hands together. "It got him sore, all right," he says, and we have breakfast sent up.

Well, that night we tog out and spread ourselves at the Sicily Club on Forty-sixth Street. Around midnight in drifts Spinelli and Charley Goss and Nick Bonno. They're looking mean and they don't talk much. Chick yells out, "How's business, Spinelli?" and gets only a dirty look. They sit down opposite us, on the other side of the two-by-four dance-floor, and none of them sits with his back in our direction. Us, neither. Nigger was, but we all shift until our right hands are free and we can see what's going on.

You know, mister, I felt it in my bones that hell was going to bust loose that night. I kept looking at that Spinelli gang as much as I could. Nigger is aching to get oiled again, but Chick mixes the drinks and Nigger gets dishwater, or damn near it.

Well, there we are, looking like we ain't got a worry in the world, lounging in our chairs with our hands in our pockets and one foot gripping the floor and ready to go. I can see that Wop and his two guns are up to something. They're looking too serious, and they got their heads together and talking to beat the band. I whispers to Chick, "I smell something, Chick." And he blows smoke at the ceiling and says, "I smell the same thing, Dave." And Nigger and Bud nod and make believe at yawning.

Gawd, I was nervous. Not scared, you see. Nervous from waiting, see. I'm all keyed up and my hand is sweating on my rod and I can see Nigger shifting back and forth on his chair and trying to look unconcerned. I can see Bud, the calmest guy I ever run across, playing with his empty glass and shifting his cigar back and forth like he was thinking about his mother or somebody. You know that look; kind of far away and sad-looking. Well, that's Bud. He can do that. He's that kind—good nerves.

Well, suddenly Chick begins talking, low and soft, but quick, while he makes believe he's interested in the design on the table-cloth. He says, "Get ready, boys. I see the greaseball's trick. He's making out he's playing with the little table lamp, but I see him unscrewing the bulb. He's going to take it out and stick a knife blade in the socket. That'll blow out the fuse—and the lights. When they blow duck and scatter and beat the bums on the draw. Each one of you fire a shot and then beat it. Get the door marked. Get them guys marked, too. I know that trick. I pulled it myself once."

Well, we don't budge, and we don't look that way. But my hand freezes on my rod and I start holding my breath. I can see Nigger tense as a drum-head, and Bud is still playing with his glass, though his eyes are on the little lamp on our table.

"He's just got the bulb out," says Chick.

We don't nod. We don't say anything. We just wait.

And then the lights blow. I snap out of my chair like a spring and skid into the next table. Three bursts of flame come from Spinelli and his boys, but they don't come quicker than ours.

There's screams and shouts and yells about lights, and in a minute I'm sailing for the door. My coat collar's up and my hat's pulled down, and when I get outside I see Nigger and Bud strolling calmly toward Sixth Avenue. Chick's behind. "Cross the street," he says. I cross and go on and at Sixth Avenue we all join together. As we're standing there a touring car shoots by and we see it's the same license plates as the one that got our first truck on Tenth Avenue.

Well, Bud has a flesh wound on the side, but that's all. We go home and sit around, and Chick is in good humor, and he patches up Bud's wound and says, "Let him laugh that off." We learn next day that Charley Goss has passed out. "Yeah," Nigger says, "I got that baby neat," and we all drink to Nigger. Nigger hadn't much brains, but you couldn't touch him for gun work. Came natural with him. Like some folks play the piano. See?

Well, anyways, it was a home-run for us, and we're all kind of tickled over it. You know how it is. I mean, there Spinelli was laying a trap for us and we nip it in the bud. Makes a guy feel good. Aw, I ain't saying we mightn't uv done the same. Hell, wasn't we always planning some new way of busting up Spinelli's racket?

During that next week we all walk careful. It was hell. Sure, I'm standing on a corner by a cigar store in East Fifties one day, bothering nobody. I'd just sent some jack home to my widder mother, and am feeling kind of Sunday-schoolish, standing, like I said, by a cigar store, when all of sudden the plate glass window behind me is smashed. I duck but I still can see that damn touring car snaking off and Nick Bonno looking out. Yeah, silencers. The owner comes out and a cop comes out, too, wiping his mouth and smelling after rum, and they ask if I got the number and I says no. Hell, I ain't calling on no flatfoot to settle my arguments.

Then, two days later, Chick and me are sitting in our apartment figuring up accounts—me, I did most of Chick's figuring—when the door opens slow and Bud Conroy stands there, just like he'd strolled in from tea and a good time. He steps in slow, and closes the door quiet. He looks kind of disgusted. And then he makes a face and groans, "Cripes," just like that— as if he was disgusted with something. And then he sags into a chair and we see he's holding his left arm stiff. "Cuh-ripes," he says again, and Chick says, "Winged, Bud?" And Bud nods and we pull off his coat and clean out his cut—the slug didn't go in—and bandage it. That was Chick's job! He knowed his onions that way.

"I was riding in a taxi," says Bud. "It was on lower West End Avenue where it goes into Eleventh. I was just lighting a butt when I'm winged. No noise—silencer. Didn't see no one. Told the driver to get over to Broadway. Asked if I was hurt. Said no. Changed taxies at Columbus Circle."

"Good you wore a dark suit," says Chick. "The blood didn't show up so much on the black coat sleeve."

Bud's pretty weak, but he don't whine—not him. An hour later we're all playing rummy when Nigger blows in looking like he'd found a gold mine. Slings his hat across the room and smacks me on the back, and then he sees Bud's arm, and we tell him, and he rubs his hands together and grins with his false teeth. We can see he's got something on his mind.

"Spill it," says Chick.

And Nigger says, "Sure. Man alive, gang, if we pull this one on the Wop he'll go crazy. Hot dog, there is a Santy Claus!"

"Get started," says Chick.

"Sure, Chick," says Nigger. "I'm sitting in the back room of Greek Tony's, that speakeasy near Canal Street."

"Getting tight again, eh?" asks Chick.

"Do I look like I was tight?" shoots back Nigger. "Don't rub it in. Well, I was sitting in the back room, and the door leading into the front room was open. I seen two guys coming in. One was Nick Bonno. The other was a guy I don't know, but I heard Nick call him Pete. Well, when I seen them I got up and stepped into a kinda closet and they come in and sit down and start talking. Well, here's the dope. Spinelli's getting a new cargo of rum. His trucks come in from Jersey by way of Staten Island but they got tipped some Federal guys was waiting for 'em at South Ferry. So they run the trucks—two of them—down to the beach, and they're loading the stuff on a barge from an old dock where a summer resort useter be. Tonight a tug is going to tow the barge to a pier on the North River. Going to leave Staten Island after dark—Bonno says about ten o'clock. What do you say, Chick?"

Chick doesn't say anything for a while, but we can see he's thinking. Then he says, "Nigger, you said it—there is a Santy Claus. We got to get a motor boat—buy one. You, Dave," he says to me, "go out and buy a motor boat. Any kind of junk, so long as it runs. On the jump, Dave!"

He gives me a fistful of jack and I hike off for the river. I'm back inside of two hours and they all look at me, and Chick says, "Well?" And I says, "I got one for three-hundred bucks."

WELL, MISTER, me and Chick and Nigger pile into the motor boat just after sundown. Nigger has his little black bag, and he knows how to run the boat. We shove off and put-a-put down the river and the stars are coming out when we pass the Statue of Liberty.

It's pretty cold, and we have to button up our overcoats, and even then we get doused now and then when the spray comes over. We're almost hit by a ferryboat, and my heart goes up my throat for a while, and Chick gets mad for a minute but gets over it. We pass Governor's Island and the little tub is rocking like a canoe and I'm waiting any minute to see the engine stop.

Well, we come in close to the shore at Stapleton and slip along past Fort Wadsworth. We follow the shore until we begin to pass the beaches and we can see the New Dorp Lighthouse shining up on a hill. It's raw as hell and Nigger wishes he had a flask along to warm up on. We keep on and it gets lonely. The beaches are deserted, and we can hear the waves breaking, and there's only some house-lights here and there, back inland a bit. It's pretty dark on the water, and when we near the beach where Nigger says the dock is we go out further and throttle down the motor and wait.

"Cripes, a drink 'd go good now," Nigger says again.

And Chick says, "Pipe down," a little impatient.

So there we are bobbing around out there, waving our arms to keep warm, and watching the shore. For a long time there ain't no light, but soon we see some that look like flashlights and then we see a dark shape moving in, and it's the tug, carrying no lights, see.

Well, that makes us a little warmer, and we're watching so hard we kind of forget the cold. It's about a half hour before we see the dark shape moving out and there's another dark shape behind it. Sure, the barge. We wait until it gets way out and then Nigger gets up speed and we start after them.

We sure do go after them. When we're about a mile off shore we get closer and soon we can hear the tug puffing. We're pulling up behind the barge, see. There's nobody in sight then, but I guess they hear us after a while because we can see a couple of figures moving about on the barge, and they look excited. Then they run off, I guess to tell somebody on the tug, and Nigger gives our boat more gas and turns the tiller over to me.

Then he opens his black bag and gets out his three bombs and braces himself. He heaves the first one high and it lands smack in the middle and there's a terrible explosion and glass flying in the air. He heaves the rest, one after the other, and the barge bucks like a bronco and then flames begin to shoot up.

We don't hang around to get a ringside view. No, sir. We shoot off, pushing the boat as fast as she can go. Some guns pop on the tug, but there's no hits because it's pretty dark. We beat it like hell for the shore and pile the boat on a lonely beach. We leave it there and take to the woods. We can see the barge burning like a big bonfire, and Nigger is happy as a kid.

Well, in half an hour we reach the electric railroad, and in ten minutes we catch a train. We get off at St. George and board the ferryboat and half an hour later we walk off at the Battery,

New York. We take a sub north and get off at Times Square. Ten minutes later we walk into our apartment and Bud looks up from his paper and says, "Well, the Army won all right."

"So did we," says Nigger and we all have highballs.

Well, it didn't take long for that barge to go down. She was out of sight long before the fireboat got there and the tug was gone long before that. Sneaked off and docked on the East River. No use hanging around and getting in trouble.

Next morning Chick calls up Spinelli and says, "Laugh that off, you little Wop." And Spinelli says, "Your pot, you lousy Mick."

We don't go to any night-clubs for a while, but Nigger goes out one day and when he come in he has some news. He was the greatest guy for getting news, and he says, "What you think, boys?" And we all says, "What?" And he says, "The Wop's carrying his arm in a sling."

"You mean Spinelli?" I asks, and he says, "Yeah. I met him on Fifth Avenue. I asks him how come, and he says he had the bum luck to get in a taxi crash." Chick asks, "What else did he say?" And Nigger says, "Aw, he just said the next pot was his."

Well, we all get a big laugh out of that, and then that night we go to a night-club in the Forties. Bud goes along, too, carrying his arm kind of stiff. We ain't there an hour when Spinelli and Nick Bonno show up. Spinelli's still got his arm in a sling, all bandaged up, and after a couple of drinks they get up and breeze.

Another day passes with nothing stirring, and then the next night, while we're eating, the telephone rings and the operator downstairs says there's a Mr. Spinelli wants to see Chick. I'm on the wire, see, and I speak to Chick and we all look at each other and then Chick says, "Send him up," and I tell the operator.

We all sit back, then, and Chick says, "You guys heeled?" Sure, we're heeled. "Well," says Chick, "I don't know what the Wop's up to, but we'll see." When the doorbell rings I cross over and yank it open. Nigger has his gat out ready for dirty work, but there ain't no need.

Spinelli's standing there, with his good hand outside his pocket and his bum one in the sling. He smiles and strolls in and says, "Put away the rod, Nigger. Just dropped in to see how you boys are getting on." I close the door and bolt it against a surprise from any of his guns that might be hanging around.

"Sit down," says Chick, and the Wop sits down, sticks a butt in his mug and lights up.

"That was a pretty clever trick you guys pulled the other night," he says.

Chick says, "We're not looking for compliments, Spinelli. If you're looking for quarter you're in the wrong place."

"Oh, I'm not looking for quarter," says Spinelli. "I was just out for a stroll. Doctor says the air 'll do me good. Just thought I'd drop in. Swell dump you got."

"We're sitting on top of the world," says Chick. "Lot different from Chicago, Spinelli. Guess I've just about got you busted here, eh? Well, you busted me in Chicago?"

Spinelli shrugs and grins to himself. I ain't never seen him so easy-going before. It's something don't strike me right, see. "I ain't busted yet, Cassidy," he says.

"Damn near, though," says Chick.

"Well, that last joke of yours—yes, it was kind of a blow," admits Spinelli.

"Yeah?" says Chick. "You know, you got a hell of a crust walking in here to pay a social call."

"Have I?" asks Spinelli.

"Yeah, you have," says Chick. "I don't like you. I don't like to have you paying me social calls. I'm riding you till you're wiped out. That's what I come here for."

Spinelli laughs, like as if to himself. He gets up, pours himself a drink, and stands by the open window, sort of dreaming like. Then he takes a taste of our rum, makes a face and chucks the rest outta the window.

"Hell, what dishwater!" he says, and comes back, putting the glass on the table. "Guess I'll go home and get a good drink."

He salutes us and opens the door, standing there and smiling a dirty kinder smile I don't like. Suddenly I see Bud turn and hop to the window. Then he yells, "Three guys coming up the fire-escape!" We all spin around at the window, and then there's a bang and Chick falls against me. But there's another bang, close by. Nigger gets Spinelli, and the Wop caves in. Bud has his rod out and fires down the fire-escape. The three guys turn and beat it back down. Nigger's dragged in Spinelli and locked the door.

Chick is sitting in a chair, bent over. He's shot through the side, about four ribs below the heart. Nigger is tearing at the bandage on Spinelli's bum arm. But it ain't no bum arm, see. It's just a stall. There's a little automatic inside the bandage, the dirty greaseball! And pitching the drink out the window was a signal!

Chick keeps saying, "Breeze, gang! Out the window, down the fire-escape, to the courtyard. Snap on, it!"

Bud looks at his wound. The bullet went through, but Chick's bleeding like hell. I run into the bathroom and get a big bath towel and we double it and cramp it around his side, to soak the blood, and pin it on tight with our tie-pins.

"The Wop was always a bum shot," says Chick, sarcastic.

"That'll soak up the blood, Chick," says Bud. "Can you walk?"

"Sure," snaps Chick, mad as hell, and Nigger asks, "What'll we do? What'll we do?"

There's people running up and down the halls. They don't know where the shot was, see. They're yelling and calling for help, and we're slamming around the apartment throwing things together for a quick getaway. Yeah, mister, it was a hell of a fix. It's the Wop caused it. Why'd he have to walk in like that and pull such a lousy trick?

Chick is on his feet, kind of pale, and still mad. "Snap on it, you guys," he says. "Come on. You first, Dave."

I shoot through the window and down the fire-escape. It's only two flights to the courtyard. Chick is behind me, then Nigger and then Bud. There's a door leading into the cellar and we bust in there and pound through it. A janitor or somebody gets in our way and Bud socks him on the kisser and lands him in a coal-bin.

Chick is breathing like it hurts and he keeps his hand pressed against the towel inside his shirt. We've all got overcoats on, and in a minute we reach the street. We stroll out casual, and there's no signs out of the ordinary. We walk two blocks and then pile into a taxi. We drive to Times Square, shake this taxi and get in another one a block further. Burning our bridges kind of, yeah.

Chick names an address in the Twenties, west, and we shoot down there. He'd rented a couple rooms in a down-at-the-heels dump just for a break like this, and he gives me the key and we go in. It's on the second floor—just a dump. He's pretty much fagged, and he gets madder, too, and calls Spinelli a dozen kinds of a pup.

"How about a doctor?" pops Nigger, and Chick says, "You damn fool!" That's all. So we do for him what we can. Try to wash the wound and stop the bleeding. We gain a little, and by morning he's resting easy, though he's still got pain. Nigger sneaks out to buy a paper and busts back in with it spread out like a death warrant.

"Cripes!" he says. "They're after us. The police. The net's out and they've traced us as far as Times Square. That first taxi driver."

"And all for a pup like Spinelli," snarls Chick.

"Hell!" says Nigger. "They'll get the second taxi and—"

"Shut up," says Bud.

"Oh, 'at don't worry me," says Chick. "I can stand the news. Read it, Nigger."

Well, Nigger reads it. The papers are flashing a picture of Chick left over from Chicago days. There's big talk about the greatest criminal bootleg ring in the history of New York. Every cop and dick is on the hunt. All the ferries is watched. Every outlet is closed. Chick and three accomplices. You know. They'd make a grab inside of twenty-four hours.

"We've got to get out of here," Chick says.

"But how?" says Nigger. "We can't take a taxi. We can't swipe a car. Hell!"

Sure, we're trapped like a lot of rats. Can't take a chance on the telephone. We know that as soon as the guy that drove us down from Times Square wakes up and recognizes Chick's picture in the paper the bulls 'll be on our necks. And we figure it ain't going to take long for that.

"How do you feel, Chick?" asks Bud.

"Rotten!" says Chick. "Dammit, I should have plugged that slob when he showed his mug in the door. I kind of thought he was too mild for any good. The dirty, rotten pup!"

"Take it easy," says Bud. "Your wound."

"To hell with my wound!" snaps Chick.

"Talk sense," says Bud, a little sore. "If you go on exciting yourself, you'll wind up in a hospital."

"Hospital—" starts Chick, and then he stops, like as if an idea's smacked him square in the eyes. Then he says, "By God!" And we all look at him. We can see he's got an idea, and let me tell you, Mister, it was a bright one.

"Bud," he says, quick and kind of out of breath. "Sneak out the back way to a telephone booth. Call up the hospital—the nearest one. Tell them to send over an ambulance."

"What?" we all bust out together.

"An ambulance!" he shouts. "You heard me! Dammit, we'll get through this lousy police net. Get an ambulance, Bud. When it gets here you meet it at the door. When the guys come in to carry me out you bean 'em and tie 'em up. We'll swipe the ambulance and beat it north. Anything to get out of the city. Snap on it, Bud!"

Well, there's Chick for you. Brains, when he needed 'em. You bet. Bud sneaks out and in a few minutes he's back.

"Be right over," he says.

"All right," says Chick. "Have your blackjacks handy and sock these guys good."

"Hell, Chick," says Nigger. "Ain't you taking a long chance?"

"Sure, I am," he snaps. "What about it? Do you want to rot here and fight it out with the cops that way?"

That shuts Nigger up, and we wait. Soon we hear a bell clanging, and Bud nods to us, and goes down the hall. A couple minutes later he comes in behind a doctor in a white coat and the chauffeur. Chick has his face to the wall. I look at Bud and we nod. Bud yanks his 'jack and socks the doctor. I sock the chauffeur. They go down like logs.

Then Chick is out of bed and he says, "Dave, put on the doc's coat and hat. Nigger, you take the chauffeur's. Come on, gang. Fast."

Well, we truss up the two guys and gag them and drop them in a closet. On the way out we lock the door. There's some people hanging around outside, mostly kids, and we don't waste much time. Bud and Chick get in the back and close the heavy doors. Me and Nigger get in front. He steps on the starter and a minute later we're off.

We go over to Eleventh Avenue and slam north. Nigger keeps the bell going and we get the right of way. When we hit West End Avenue we're doing forty-five miles an hour. There's a crosstown traffic moving at Seventy-second Street, but it stops when the cop hears our bell, and we almost crash into a touring car.

I lean out to bawl the guy out when I see Nick Bonno sitting beside a tough-looking mutt at the wheel. Well, he sees me, too, and he sees Nigger at the wheel. He gives a start, and when I look back I see he's following us. I tell the rest about him, and Chick curses a blue streak.

We hit the Drive and let her out to sixty. Nigger keeps the

gong going like hell, and Chick and Bud keep looking behind. We lose Bonno for a while, but when we're tearing along near Dyckman Street Chick says, "They're still trailing us." We strike Broadway at the end of the Drive, and it's being repaired and this holds us up and gives Bonno a chance to gain. He does, and he's still on our tail when we cross the Harlem River.

"Go through Van Cortlandt Park," yells Chick. "Maybe we can lose 'em there."

Well, we do that at Two Hundred and Fortieth Street and strike the Gun Hill Road. We lose Bonno and then we hit Jerome Avenue and continue north. Then Chick says, "Listen. When you see a powerful car with only a driver pass him and then shut off the ignition. Then get out and stop him and say you've run out of gas and have to get to a dying man. We'll all pile in. Then we'll bean him and keep him in the back and threaten to give him the works if he yells. Pick out a sedan so we can pull down the back curtains. You'll drive, Nigger. You look like a chauffeur."

We're desperate, see. We can't go far in the ambulance any more, because by this time somebody's wise, and police telephones are working. Chick keeps looking back and then he says, "Here comes one now." And then he adds, "Cripes, it's Bonno again." Bud pulls his rod. "They was waiting for this," he says. "Not much traffic here. They're sore and they want to shoot it out. All right by me." But Chick says, "Not if we can help it, Bud. This ain't no time for fireworks."

Bud gets ready for action, though, and he says, "But we can't help it, Chick."

And he's right. We can't help it. The Wop has three more bums in the back with him, and the first shot smacks into the back doors. But they're solid and don't even splinter. We're doing sixty when Bud looks through the little glass window in the door and takes his first shot. We don't see anything happen.

"Step on it, Nigger," says Chick.

"Hell, I am," says Nigger. "This ain't no Mercedes."

More shots begin to smack the door and then they're hitting fast and regular and Bud says, "Machine-gun, or automatic rifle."

"Cripes," says Chick, "if that's the case we're cooked."

"No we ain't," says Bud. "We'll hit traffic soon and that'll stop it for a while. We'll pass through the traffic and they'll be held up. Later on we'll shake this bus and nab a sedan."

Just then a string of bullets crash through the little glass window in the back and bust out through the windshield. My head ain't missed by much, and neither is Nigger's. He hunches down and we almost smack a tree. Maybe it would have been just as good if we had. It's a minute later that it comes.

You know what I mean. Yeah. There we are doing sixty with a village just ahead when it comes. Yup. I'll swear the bus goes up six feet in the air. There's a hell of an explosion. I hear Chick and Bud scream and then I'm sailing through space. I don't hear anything else.

When I wake up I'm laying in a hospital and a police captain is looking at me. I'm dazed, you know, but I ain't so dazed that I don't know my goose is cooked. Yeah, the police captain. He says, "Hell, you were lucky." I don't get him at first, but then he says, "Your playmates got blowed to hell."

I think of Chick and Bud and Nigger and then I asks, "What happened?"

Well, you know what happened then. Bonno and his Wops was using incendiary bullets and they hit our gas tank and the whole works blowed up. The ambulance turned head over heels on the road, and Bonno and his bunch was coming so fast they couldn't duck it. They tried, like you know, but they hit a tree doing forty-five and, well, yeah, every one of them is killed.

That's all I know, Mister. It's the whole story from the beginning. Yeah. I get a light sentence, don't I? Huh? I mean, like you said….

What's that? I'll be lucky if I get off with fifteen years! Cripes, do you call that light? Aw, say listen, you can get me off easier than that. Please, Mister, I got a widder mother, like I said.

Huh? You say that's your idea of a light sentence? Well, say, what in Gawd's name's your idea of a heavy one? Huh? What I deserve. Well, what—what do I deserve?

What? The Chair!

Aw, say, it was only Spinelli, that dirty Wop…. Fifteen years, though? Well— What? Maybe twenty… maybe *life!*

Gawd, life! *Life!* LIFE!…

Street Wolf

The story of "a gangster who might have been a poet."

THIS NAPOLEON DAMIANI was a Corsican, though a lot of guys took it for granted that he was a Wop. Perhaps that is because few ever came to know his full name. They called him Napo, and that was all right by him. He was born in Akron, Ohio. When he was ten years old he robbed the till of a fruit store run by a Greek and got away with it. Call it beginner's luck, if you will, but take a look at Napo fourteen years later, when this chronicle of a gangster, who might have been a poet, opens....

The untimely death of Marino was an accident, in a way of speaking. Spider Link had taken to booze and cracked up. He'd been nailed for swiping a car and got out on bail, but he was afraid to stand trial because he thought that they would try to nail him for something else. And he was afraid of Carmody and Spinoza, a pair of dicks who rated in the neighborhood. So Marino, who was boss of the mob in this eastern seaboard city, and Napo, who planned to be its next boss, got Link drunk, then followed him and plugged him in a dark, wayward street. This, among the street wolves of any great city, is called justice.

The accident occurred a few minutes later when Napo and Marino ran into Patrolman Mandelbaum, who had been drawn on the run by the shots. They met at a corner, and Napo clubbed his gun across Mandelbaum's jaw and knocked him out. Running on, they saw two figures coming from the opposite direction. They crossed the street and dashed back whence they had come; but another patrolman, one Shotzendorf, appeared at the corner. Marino fired, and Napo cursed him.

The other two men were hard after them, and one fired, and

Marino got the back of his head blown off. Napo crashed through a store window, beat it out through the back, and got away. In the papers next day he saw that Patrolman Shotzendorf had been killed.

He lay low for two weeks, and then emerged and assumed leadership of the mob. He was a tall young man, with black hair and smooth dark skin, and a quiet manner of doing things. He dressed modestly and well, and he had ambition. There was not a single mark against him on any police blotter in the country. The girls of the joints said he was a handsome guy, and many said he looked like Rudolph Valentino—and he did. But he always looked above and beyond them, for he had ambition, and beneath his calm lurked a strange romantic urge. Napo even thought that some day he might bust into society, and he carried on a spiritual romance with Joyce Travers, whom once he had met and talked with briefly in Antonio Callineri's florist shop. On the wall of his bedroom was the picture of a society girl cut from *Vanity Fair*....

Napo was glad Marino was gone. As a matter of fact, he had been meditating on a ways and means of getting rid of Marino, for Marino had always been too free with a gun, and Napo loathed the use of a gun unless it was absolutely necessary. Booze was his racket, and hi-jacking the medium, and when he stepped in and told the mob that he was boss, he added that booze would be their one—and only—racket. He said it quietly, passing his dark, steady eyes from face to face.

The man behind—a big political gun—had been worried about Marino for a long time, and after his death, this man met Napo in Antonio's sitting-room and had a long and serious talk with him. He liked Napo, and he told Napo that they could get on fine, so long as no cops were bumped off. Napo, quietly dignified, assured the big man that he would steer clear of cop-shooting.

"I'm glad Marino's dead," said the big man. "He was getting too cocky, and that don't go. And he was crazy with a gun. You used your head when you busted through that window and got away. Any other guy would have tried to smoke off the cops. You play ball nice, Napo, and I'm your friend. When the next elections come off, I'll need a guy like you, and I'll pay you good."

"Okey," said Napo. "I don't think I'm so dumb, Bill. I'm a business man. Some day I'm going to retire and have a nice house and get myself a nice wife. No tart, either."

"You're a comer, Napo!" smiled the big man, and went out.

THEY WERE gathered in the rendezvous in Coke Street. Sam Dvorak. Heinie Dorn. Charley Haas. Bat Price. Spats Pazzo, kid of the outfit—a flashy guy, loud-mouthed. Napo was drinking ginger ale, the others Scotch. Sleek he was, well groomed, his dark face in repose.

"Sam, you and Heinie and Spats and me go out in the touring car. You drive, Sam. Charley, you and Bat go in the truck. We'll park this side of the old brewery and roll along when you other guys come up in the truck. Sam, for crying out loud, stop spitting on the floor!"

"Jeeze, I forgot, Napo!"

Napo went on. "The booze is kept downstairs in the cellar

and there's two guys planted in the office. You stay at the wheel, Sam. You, Spats and Heinie and me, we'll crash the office and put these guys to sleep. I don't want any guy getting free with his gun unless it's necessary."

"Well, hell, Napo," said Pazzo. "It's so far out in the country no one would hear."

"That's all right, Spats. You heard me, and if any shooting is necessary, I'll start it. But if any guy busts loose with his rod before I do he ain't going to be happy. There's three hundred cases out there, or about that, and we ain't going to take a chance on a shot being heard. I'm running a business and not a shooting gallery. Is that clear?"

"You know your stuff, boss," said Sam Dvorak.

Pazzo yawned. "Yeah, I guess you're boss, Napo."

"Kinda keep that in mind, Spats," Napo said softly. He stood up. "Well, let's drift."

The touring car, which Dvorak had brazenly taken out of a public parking ground the day before, rolled out of the back door of the city and struck Woodward Boulevard. Heinie Dorn sat in front with Sam Dvorak. Napo and Pazzo sat in the rear.

Napo thought of Joyce Travers. The picture of her standing in Antonio's florist shop was still clear in the eye of his mind. And even before the memory of her he felt humble and inarticulate. He dared to play with the thought of holding her in his arms. She would be warm and soft and there would be the sweet perfume of her. The thought warmed his blood, and he rose to great heights of mental ardor, but the heights were dizzy, and he slipped back and felt humble again.

Pazzo said, "I'm getting that roadster tomorrow, Napo."

Napo flung away his cigarette. "And you'll probably take some frail buggy riding and try to get fresh."

"I don't have to get fresh," said Pazzo. "They fall too easy."

"You must think you're a John Gilbert."

"Yeah, he ain't got nothing on me."

Dvorak laughed out loud and then spat.

Napo brushed his face. "I wish to hell you'd look out how you spit, Sam."

"Jeeze, I forgot, Napo."

The tires hummed softly on the cement road. Heinie Dorn began to sing *Old Man River.*

"That's lousy," said Pazzo.

Dorn paid no attention to him, but let his voice out like a trumpet.

"Soft pedal," said Napo.

"Yeah, Heinie should hire a hall," chimed in Dvorak.

Pazzo said, "An empty hall, Sam."

"Yeah," laughed Dvorak.

"You guys don't know good singing," growled Dorn. "Listen, when I was a kid I sang in the Lutheran church in Milwaukee."

Dvorak asked, "Was them Lutherans the guys that had a couple wives all the time?"

"Listen," said Dorn, tapping Dvorak on the shoulder, "Lutherans is respectable people."

"Aw, he means Mormons," said Pazzo. "That guy Hiram Young had wives all over the place."

"It was Brigham Johnson," said Dorn. "Ain't you ever studied spelling in school?"

"No. I was always dating up girls."

Napo sat quietly in the shadows, watching the woods roll by. In two years he would make enough to retire. He would keep in touch with Joyce Travers. He would go to some respectable broker and have his money invested. He would make his money work for him. He had been studying the book of etiquette lately, and he knew that when eating soup you should move the spoon away from you, that it was all right to take asparagus in your fingers, and that it was improper to pick your teeth at the table.

Lately, too, he had wandered into a book store and bought all the books on Napoleon that he could find. He tried to read them, but they were too heavy. But the pictures were interesting and the books made nice ornaments for his new flat. He also bought another picture of the Emperor riding on a horse and looking sad. It was the retreat from Moscow. That guy certainly used to get around.

"Here we are," said Dvorak, slowing down.

"Pull up," said Napo.

The touring car stopped. Beyond, and to the right, loomed a large building, dark and silent. Fields and broken timber surrounded it. It was ten miles from the city limits, and two miles from the nearest town. In the days before prohibition men came in buses and brewed beer, and horse-drawn trucks, laden with fat, damp kegs, rumbled in and out on the cobbled driveway. The air then was rich with the smell of hops and malt, and smoke billowed industriously from the brick stacks. Now a prominent bootlegger leased it to store his stock in trade.

They waited in the darkness.

Pazzo lit a cigarette and said, "Napo, this town of Kirkville has a nice bank. Only two miles from here."

"Banks don't interest me," said Napo.

"Hell, they should."

"I'll stick to booze, and so will any guy that runs with me."

"Yeah, that's right," said Dvorak.

Pazzo's cigarette end brightened. "I'd like to bust a bank some day just for fun. You stay in booze and you kinda get in a rut."

"It's a rut that pays well," said Napo.

"Oh, I don't know."

Napo turned and looked at the red cigarette end. "You shut up about banks, Spats!"

The cigarette end described an arc as Pazzo waved his hand. "It's spec—it's spectacular, Napo."

"You heard me, Spats!"

Pazzo shrugged and looked out of the car. "Them guys must have stopped for a drink."

"That truck ain't no Stutz," said Dvorak.

Heinie Dorn stretched his arms and yawned. Dvorak brought up the subject of Lutherans again, but Napo told him to shut up.

Then Pazzo said, "Here they come."

Dvorak started the motor. When the truck drew abreast of them, he pushed into gear and started off. He gained on the truck, passed it, and Bat Price waved. Napo was leaning forward.

"Drift up past the entrance, Sam," he said in a low voice, "and swing in close to the bushes and stop. I'll get off here. Come on, guys."

He opened the door and dropped off. Pazzo and Heinie Dorn followed, and Napo stepped out into the road and motioned for the oncoming truck to pull in. Charley Haas, at the wheel, swung in and Bat Price jumped down and came towards Napo.

"All right, Bat," said Napo. "Tell Charley to stay there. You hang around the entrance. Us three will go in and when everything's okey we'll whistle. Then you and Charley come in with the truck."

"Right, Napo."

Napo pivoted and went briskly towards the wide archway that formed the entrance to the sheds and the old wooden loading platform. Pazzo and Dorn joined him and they clung close to the shadows of the wall as they entered.

They reached one end of the loading platform and stopped. Napo pointed and they nodded. There was a dim square of light in the darkness at the farther end of the platform. They crept along, the platform level with their shoulders. Napo led the way. Behind him was Dorn, and behind Dorn was Pazzo. Napo's hand was in his coat pocket. Pazzo and Dorn had their guns out.

Napo, as he drew closer, saw that the window was open. And then he could hear the low guttural voice of someone in the watchman's office. He reached the flight of six wooden steps that led to the platform and marked the end of it. The office, too, marked the end, and both door and window looked on to the platform. The window was nearer the head of the stairway, and Napo had his eyes glued on it as he cat-footed up the steps. His gun was in his hand now, and his face was quietly tense. Dorn was behind him, at his heels. Napo reached the top and stepped towards the open window as Pazzo stumbled. The sound of his foot striking the step echoed sharply.

Napo's scalp tightened, but he jumped for the window. Dorn, too, jumped, and cursed under his breath. A kaleidoscopic moment followed. Napo saw two men in the yellow glow of a dirty lantern. He saw one of them sit dumfounded while the other swept up a gun that had been lying on the table.

Napo snapped, "Don't—!"

But the gun boomed and the shot turned Napo half-way around. He gritted his teeth but emitted no outcry. A second shot boomed, close by his ear. That was Heinie Dorn. Napo, turning again towards the window, saw one of the men at the table try to get up and then fall to the floor; and a choked, surprised look was on his face.

"You raise 'em, buddy!" Dorn barked at the other.

Pazzo caught hold of Napo's arm. "Napo!"

"You clumsy pup!"

"Cripes, Napo, I didn't mean—"

"Stop broadcasting my name!"

Pazzo was nervous. "Strap on one of my spats caught on a nail."

"You had to wear spats, you cake-eater!"

"Oh, God! Oh, God!" groaned the man on the floor.

Bat Price came running down the platform. "What happened?"

Pazzo said, "Napo's shot. Where you shot, Napo?"

"Right side, little higher than my pants belt." He spoke with an effort.

Price scratched his head. "What'll we do, Napo?"

"Oh, God!" groaned the man on the floor.

Pazzo rasped, "Somebody kick that guy's mouth shut!"

Perspiration dripped from Napo. He felt dizzy. "Listen." He moistened his lips. "Bat, any cars on the road when those shots went off?"

"No."

"All right. Heinie, climb in the window and frisk that other guy. Then tie him up. Spats, run back and tell Charley to drive in with the truck. Tell Sam to keep his eyes open and blow the horn twice if anything goes wrong."

Pazzo said, "Jeeze, Napo, don't you think we better blow?"

"Shut up! You were beefing tonight about how easy it would be to bump these guys off. Well, two shots have been fired. If it wasn't for you, they wouldn't 've been. Do what I told you. Snap on it!"

Dorn was climbing in through the window, warning the man who was standing to keep his hands up.

"Hell, if it ain't Heinie Dorn!"

Dorn squinted. "Huh?"

"Sure, I seen you last year in Indianapolis. You used to hang out in Dutch Weber's place. What a slob you turned out to be!"

"I'll slob you!" He frisked the man and then clouted him on the jaw with the barrel of his gun. The man fell down.

"Oh, God!" moaned the other.

"Can't you be quiet!" growled Dorn. He began tying the man he had knocked down. When he had bound him hand and foot he went to the window.

"Open the door," said Napo.

Dorn went over and threw back the bolt, and Napo sagged in, holding his side. His lips were tight against his teeth. His eyes looked weary.

"I'm sorry," muttered Dorn.

" 'S all right, Heinie. Go out and start loading the booze. Every man on the job."

"We oughter get a doctor," said Dorn.

"Doctor!" snapped Napo. "I don't know one."

"Jeeze!" murmured Dorn.

"Go on, Heinie. Help them guys load up and don't take all night."

Dorn went out.

"Oh, God!" moaned the man on the floor. He was lying face down.

Napo leaned against the table. "Shut up!" he muttered.

He felt the blood coming through his shirt, and grimaced. Damn Spats! The blood was running down his leg. It was warm and crawly. Napo convulsed. If it kept on this way, he would bleed to death.

He looked around the room. There was a cot against the wall and he went over and sat down. The pain caught him and he choked. His whole body quivered. He looked at the pillow, picked it up, felt it. He ripped it open. It was stuffed with cotton.

He took off his coat, his shirt and his undershirt. He looked down at the wound. At first it frightened him but as he stared at it it seemed to become familiar. What was a wound anyhow? But the bullet was in there.

He pulled apart the pillow and packed the cotton over the wound. Then he tore his undershirt in strips, tied the strips together and wound the improvised bandage tightly about his waist. He pulled it as tight as he possibly could. When he finally tied the knot he was scarcely able to move. Then he put on his shirt and his coat and lit a cigarette. He noticed how his hand shook. Little nerves jerked throughout his body. His head ached and his eyes felt heavy. He went to the window. Dimly he could see his men loading cases into the truck.

The man whom Dorn had knocked out and bound up, came to and said, "You'll see, you guys. Yeah, you'll see."

"Pipe down," said Napo, without turning.

"Yeah, you'll see."

Napo walked over and sat down. "You close your jaw."

The man lay back and stared at him. "Who the hell are you, anyhow?"

"What's it to you? I'm nobody. I'm from out of town."

"You better go back where you come from, stranger."

"Yeah, I think I will."

He got up and went to the window again. The cases were banging steadily into the truck.

The wounded man on the floor suddenly screamed. Napo's scalp tightened. He went back and put his hand over the man's mouth.

"Keep shut," he said.

The man still tried to scream. Napo got up and went over and grabbed a handful of cotton. He came back and stuffed it into the man's mouth.

"Hey, he'll choke," complained the other.

"Too bad," said Napo, and went back to the window.

It seemed an eternity before Dorn came back and said, "All in. Three hundred and five cases. Some load."

"Yeah. Let's breeze then."

"Hey," called the man who was tied. "Call a doctor for my buddy."

Napo regarded him for a moment. "You try getting out of them ropes and call one yourself."

He passed through the door and looked with Heinie Dorn down towards the truck.

"That guy knows you, Heinie."

"Never seen him before."

"You sure?"

"Well, hell, I don't remember."

The others joined them and Pazzo asked, "How you feel, Napo?"

"Rotten. Get started. Bat, you and Charley on the truck. You know where to go."

"H-e-l-p!"

Napo cursed under his breath.

"That's the guy thinks he knows me," said Dorn.

"Yeah," said Napo. Then, "Get started, you guys. Spats, you go and join Sam."

"Okey."

The truck started off. Spats hopped on and then alighted at the gate.

Dorn and Napo were still standing on the platform. Dorn looked at his chief.

"H-e-l-p!"

Dorn kept looking at his chief. "Well, Napo?"

"Let's look at that guy," said Napo.

They went back and walked into the little office. The man who had been yelling, shut up and panted heavily. The other was groaning, the wad still in his mouth, blood all over him.

"You know me?" asked Dorn, looking at the man who was not wounded.

"Yeah—I know you. I seen you before. I know you."

Dorn nudged Napo. "He knows me."

"Yeah," said Napo. He took a quick step, raised his gun and brought the barrel down upon the man's head. Blood appeared. Napo stood up slowly. He was gray and drawn. But not from this. From his own wound.

"D' you crack it?" asked Dorn.

"Dunno."

Dorn dropped to one knee, took the man's throat between his great hands and pressed. He pressed hard. After a little while he stood up.

"He's done now," he said.

"All right. Let's go," said Napo.

They went out and walked along the driveway and then out through the gate. Pazzo was sitting in the back. Napo climbed in beside him. Dorn jumped in front beside Dvorak, and Dvorak meshed gears and drove off.

Dorn looked around and said, "Tough, him knowing me."

Napo's voice was drowsy—"Yeah, Heinie."

THE BIG car rolled into the suburbs. Napo leaned forward and held his stomach. Pazzo put an arm around his shoulder.

"What's the matter, Napo?"

"Hell," muttered Napo.

Heinie Dorn looked around and asked, "What's the matter, Napo?"

"Hell," muttered Napo.

He leaned back and arched his neck and seemed to gasp for air. A lot of things seemed to be going on inside him. He felt nauseated. A hammer seemed to be pounding at the back of his head. The wound felt as if it were opening and closing, and the pain was terrible. A groan strained between his teeth.

Pazzo patted his back. "Cripes, Napo—cripes, Napo!"

"You have to slam my back?" asked Napo.

Dorn was peering back into the darkness that enveloped Napo and hid the pain on his face.

"Napo, how you feeling, Napo?"

"Lousy."

Pazzo could feel his body writhing and knew better than the others.

"Don't nobody know a doctor?" he rasped, as if the others were holding out.

"Me and Sam ain't been here long," said Dorn.

"Napo needs a doctor," said Pazzo.

"If you didn't wear them spats," said Napo, "I wouldn't."

"Aw, hell, Napo, that was just a bad break for me."

"For you?" Napo's chuckle was brittle.

The car crept nearer the city. At a boulevard crossing a traffic policeman raised his hand. Dvorak stopped and they watched the cross country cars pass athwart them. Pazzo eyed the traffic policeman tensely. Napo slouched in the corner, feeling very dizzy, very sunk, very rotten.

The traffic policeman blew his whistle and waved his hand. He stood with his hands on his hips as the big car rolled by. Dvorak, at the wheel, looked straight ahead as he shifted into high.

They breathed easier as they sped away. Pazzo even chuckled, but not heartily.

"Funny how I hate a cop's uniform," he said.

"Yeah," said Dorn. "You inherited that from your old man, I guess."

"Hell," grunted Napo.

Pazzo snapped, "Cripes, you guys, we got to do something about Napo!"

"Well, Jeeze!" said Dorn, helpless.

Napo sat up and held the side of the car. "Listen. I need a doctor. I'm bleeding, and that bullet's inside. Listen. Peel your eyes for a doctor's sign."

"But, Gawd, Napo," exclaimed Pazzo, "you can't go right in—"

"Will you shut up?" asked Napo quietly.

"Well, I thought—"

"You thought! You forgot how to think when you was born and you never got back in the habit again. Now listen. Find a sign that says Doctor on it. Drive up. Don't park right in front. We ring the bell. We all put handkerchiefs on our mugs. We don't take 'em off. We make the doc go over me."

Pazzo demurred. "But, hell, Napo—"

"Shut your trap! Sam, drift along slow and keep your eyes open."

Napo fell back wearily and closed his eyes. He closed his teeth, too—tightly, because that pain was raising hell again.

The black car roamed through the streets. Presently Dvorak pointed. They were in a sedate residential district. The street was dark and deserted, and elm trees rustled softly.

"Good as any," said Napo. "Pull into that next block, Sam."

Dvorak nodded and swung right into the next street. He pulled up beside the curb and shut off the ignition. They all got out. Napo came last, drooping. Heinie Dorn held his arm.

"Let go," said Napo. "I can walk."

They walked up the elm-lined street, turned and ascended a short flight of cement steps. Dvorak rang the bell as the others tied handkerchiefs about their faces. Then Dvorak put one on. The masked faces looked at one another. Napo was swaying. Dorn reached out a hand. Napo moved away from it.

The door clicked open and a woman looked out. Her mouth opened.

Dorn had his gun leveled. "No noise, missus. We just want some medical attention."

He pushed in. The others followed and stood around in the hall. The woman kept opening and closing her mouth.

"Call the doc, missus," said Dorn.

She took several breaths. Then she cried, "Henry!"

A voice drifted down, "Yes, Alice."

"Come down a minute."

Napo sighed and slumped down upon a chair. Dvorak took up a position beside him. Pazzo and Dorn stood on either side of the woman, holding their guns.

"We ain't looking for trouble, missus," said Dorn. "We just want medical attention."

They heard footsteps. An old white-haired man appeared in a bathrobe. He saw the masked faces and blanched. He shuffled to his wife and put an arm around her. He assumed some measure of dignity.

"What is the meaning of this?"

Dorn said, "Our buddy here has a bad wound. You clean it and take out the bullet."

"I will not!"

Dorn and Pazzo moved closer, their guns leveled.

"We ain't got much time, doc," said Dorn. "We ain't fooling."

"Snap on it, pop!" clipped Pazzo.

The woman cried, "Henry—please!"

"This is an outrage. I'll—"

Dorn's tone was dull— "You'll do what you're told."

"Henry—please!"

Pazzo took a quick step and jabbed his gun in the doctor's stomach. "You hear!"

The doctor inhaled tremulously. "Well, come along."

They took Napo into a small, white room. He looked suspiciously at a lot of instruments that gleamed behind glass doors. Dorn took off his coat and shirt. They laid Napo down.

"You'll need an anesthetic," said the doctor.

"Like hell," said Napo. "Go ahead to work."

He groaned and writhed and ground his teeth together while the doctor worked over him. Sweat poured down his face. His fingernails dug into his palms. The others stood around stolidly. The woman was crying softly.

The doctor extracted the bullet and held it up.

"I'll take that," said Dorn, and it fell, blood-stained, into his hand.

The pain began to numb Napo's senses. It didn't seem real, this pain. He was dreaming. Soon he would wake up and laugh. Funny, how you dreamed about pain....

Soon he would be sitting in a limousine, with a chauffeur riding in the open. Joyce Travers would be sitting beside him. He would be holding her hand....

The doctor was putting in stitches. Napo knew nothing about it. He didn't care. He thought he smelled flowers. Antonio's flowers. No, Joyce was holding an armful of flowers and they were standing in a summer garden, beside a fountain. No, it was Antonio's palace of flowers....

Then a voice was saying, "Come on, Napo. You're all fixed. We got to go."

That was Dorn's voice, but it was blurred.

"We—got—to—go, Napo!"

Napo remembered. The pendulum of other thoughts swung slower, then stopped and hung motionless. Napo remembered. He blinked. He looked down and saw a clean white bandage around his waist. Dorn and Dvorak helped him to his feet. They put on his shirt and coat.

"No exertion," said the doctor.

They led Napo into the hall. His feet dragged.

"Thanks, doc," said Dorn. "Now you keep out of sight for five minutes."

The doctor and his wife stood side by side. They said nothing. But the doctor's face was bitter.

They took Napo out into the street, Dorn and Dvorak supporting him, and walked slowly towards the corner. Slowly because Napo's feet dragged. His eyes were still blurred, and his mouth felt like blotting-paper.

They eased him into the car. He lay back and sighed and closed his eyes. Pazzo climbed in and put an arm around him.

Dvorak started the motor, shoved into gear, and the black car rolled on into the city.

SERGEANT AUERBACH was snoring. The telephone bell jangled. Sergeant Auerbach grunted, sniffed, rubbed his nose and then went on snoring. The telephone bell jangled again. The sergeant grunted, made a motion as if he were brushing a fly from his face, and moistened his lips. Then his eyes blinked open. He looked around after the manner of a man awaking amid strange surroundings. He looked at the telephone. It jangled.

He yawned and said into the mouthpiece, "Fourth Police Precinct."

Then he listened, and kept grunting and nodding his head. He made some notations on a slip of paper.

"And your name is Dr. Henry Pennell. Uh, yes. Five-nine-two Vine Street. Uh, yes. Telephone Western three-one-eight. Right. Uh, yes. Well, doctor, we'll probably get in touch with you again. Thanks."

He hung up and scratched his head, reading what few notes he had written down. He thumped his hand on a desk bell. A reserve appeared, and Auerbach said:

"If Carmody is sleeping, wake him up and tell him he should come here."

The reserve disappeared. A moment later Carmody strolled in, yawning. His tie was off, his collar open and his hair more disheveled than usual.

"Me, Otto?"

"Yeah. A Dr. Pennell just called up, Jake. About ten minutes ago four guys rang his bell and came in wearing masks. One of them was shot in the right side and weak from loss of blood. The other guys made Pennell take out the bullet and fix up the wound. They never removed the masks, not even the guy was shot. Then they went out."

"H'm."

"H'm. He didn't hear no car starting, so they must have walked away. Two of the guys were about five feet ten and kind of broad and husky. The wounded guy was taller and slimmer and kind of dark. The other guy was thin, too, but a little shorter, and he wore gray spats. That's all the dope."

"H'm."

"H'm. Looks like a couple of gangs been playing Fourth of July."

"Yeah."

"Here's the doctor's address and telephone number."

Carmody copied them and strolled off into the back room. He kicked the chair upon which Spinoza was sleeping. Spinoza woke up and stretched his arms.

Carmody said, "Gang fight again, Mike. Four guys walked into a doctor's house and made him take care of a guy was shot."

"Yeah? Ain't they got fun these days?"

"A tall, slim, dark guy again, Mike. Two heavy birds. A guy with spats, I wonder if the tall, slim, dark guy could be the one was with Marino when Shotzendorf was killed."

"You trying to pull clues out of the air?"

"Well, there ain't been any other kind lately."

"Well, suppose I finish this sleep."

Carmody lit a cigarette. "A tall, slim, dark guy. H'm."

"Why don't you go out and pick up all the tall, slim, dark guys you know?"

"H'm," mused Carmody.

The sound of voices breaking suddenly in the central room made him turn and listen. A reserve appeared in the doorway.

"Hell, Jake, come out and get an earful of this!"

Carmody went out.

An elderly man, well dressed, was speaking to Sergeant Auerbach.

"Yes, he was crawling on the road. My headlights picked him up. Oh, I'd say it was about two hundred yards this side of that old brewery on Kirkville Turnpike. Of course, I stopped. I got out and found the man just soaked with blood, all over the stomach. He was groaning terribly. I tried to talk to him. He was pretty glassy-eyed, but for a brief moment he seemed to realize that I was talking to him. And he said, 'Listen, they choked a friend of mine—back there. They shot me. My friend knew one of the guys because when I was laying on the floor I heard him say Heinie Dorn. You get me? *Heinie Dorn!*' And then he screamed and I felt him stiffen. He died there on the road. His body's outside in my car. I thought I'd better bring him in."

Carmody, without saying a word, took a flashlight from the desk and went out. When he returned he said, "Bennie Kline."

Sergeant Auerbach wrote down the name.

"My name is Philip Burnside," said the man. "I live at the Hotel Redstone. I'd visited my brother in Kirkville and was driving back here to the city."

Auerbach wrote that down, and then said to Carmody, "I'll call the morgue and have 'em put the stiff on ice."

"Yeah," said Carmody. "I'll shoot out to that brewery."

He picked up Spinoza and explained briefly as they went out to get the police two-seater.

Half an hour later they stood in the little office on the loading platform and stared down at the man who had been choked to death.

"Sure," said Spinoza. "Hi-jackers came out here and Bennie and this guy talked out of turn. Well, Jake, things are looking up."

"This guy was choked, Mike, because he recognized that guy called Heinie Dorn. They mustn't have thought the other bird heard."

"Guess they figured he'd just go and bleed to death kind of nice and quiet."

They entered the brewery and found some doors forced.

"But they got what they wanted," said Spinoza.

Carmody strolled back to the office. "This guy goes to the morgue, too."

"Yeah. Big business for the morgue." They drove to the morgue, and from the morgue to Police Headquarters. They went into the Bureau of Criminal Identification and investigated the files.

"Ah, yes," drawled Carmody.

"Got something, Jake?"

"Picture and everything. Heinrich Dorn. Wanted three years ago in Boston for a drug-store hold-up. Got off on that because the clerk failed to identify him. Served six months, he did, five years ago, in the Michigan State Penitentiary, for holding up a restaurant in Lansing. Suspended sentence a year and a half ago for beating up a cop in Akron, Ohio. Mike, we get copies of this picture made and we spread the net for Heinie Dorn."

When they returned to the station-house Sergeant Auerbach said, "Hey, Mike, that girl friend of yours called up again."

Spinoza chuckled and wagged his head. "Ain't women funny?"

But he took the telephone and called up Rose.

"Sure I'm all right, Rose…. What's that?… Oh, forget it, honey. Yeah, go to bed. Jake and me are playing cards. It's slow down here…. Yeah, sure, go to bed."

He hung up and poked Carmody in the ribs. "Damn funny, them women. Rose had a dream I was being shot at. Picture me getting shot with the wedding coming off soon. Funny!"

"Yeah," said Carmody.

"And how!" said Spinoza.

NAPO LAY in bed. His face was wan and yellow against the white pillow, and he stared at the wall.

Carrie Noll sat in a rocker. She had just finished reading the morning papers.

"Them dicks know something, Napo," she said.

"Hell, I never thought that guy would he able to crawl out and be picked up. It don't say what he said, does it?"

"No, Napo."

"I wonder if he said anything."

The rocker creaked. "Don't think about it, Napo. That's just paper talk about them having a clue. It's boloney."

"You just said they knew something."

"I was just talking."

She came over and stroked his forehead. He moved his head. "Cut it out, Carrie."

She smiled down at him. "Poor Napo."

"Shut up!"

She sat down again and rocked. "You just stay in bed, Napo, and take things easy. I'll look after you."

"You won't."

"Don't be silly, Napo."

He frowned. He didn't feel like talking. Why the hell couldn't she leave him alone? He turned his face to the wall and closed his eyes. He felt like a wet rag. Must have lost a lot of blood, and that damned wound either stabbed him in the ribs or itched until it almost drove him crazy.

The doorbell rang and Carrie let in Pazzo.

"You read the papers, Napo?"

Napo nodded.

Pazzo said, "We should have finished that guy."

Napo looked at Pazzo's feet. "See you're still wearing spats."

Pazzo shrugged and fumbled for a cigarette. "Well, hell, Napo."

"Yes, hell!" Napo's eyes seemed darker.

Pazzo fidgeted and then said, "Well, the booze is stored away okey. No hitch at all."

Napo merely grunted. The atmosphere was strained, and Carrie motioned for Pazzo to go.

"Well, hope you're better, Napo," said Pazzo, with an attempt at nonchalance.

Napo said nothing and Pazzo went out.

Carrie rocked. The window shades were mostly down, the room cool and shadowy. Napo narrowed his lids, as though he were drowsing, but he could see Carrie, and she looked beautiful there in the half-light. It felt good to have a woman looking after you, mused Napo, but he must never let Carrie know that. He didn't want to have anything to do with her beyond friendship. He'd pay her well if she insisted on taking care of him. Napo's ambitions did not include a broad who had been mamma to half-a-dozen racketeers and a former Assistant State's Attorney.

He moved his head and looked at the picture he had cut from *Vanity Fair*. He liked to look at it because it reminded him of Joyce Travers, even if it did not resemble her. It was the idea, the symbol.

He closed his eyes and wondered that if he could concentrate steadily on Joyce Travers, would he fall to sleep and dream about her? The idea bore possibilities, and he was concentrating assiduously when Antonio came in and spoiled everything.

Antonio wore a smart gray suit, an immaculate white vest, a polka-dot tie and a winged collar. Antonio was some tomatoes when it came to clothes, decided Napo. And he was clean. Napo had a liking for Antonio.

"I am sorry, yes," said Antonio, patting his hand. "It is too bad, Napo. I will send you some flowers by, yes. The papers do not look bad this morning, no."

"What I was telling Napo," said Carrie.

Antonio looked at her benignantly. His liquid brown eyes sparkled. "You are a good girl, Carrie, to take care of Napo."

"I don't need taking care of," said Napo.

"There, there," soothed Carrie.

"Listen, Antonio," said Napo, "you take Carrie out to eat."

"It would be the pleasure," smiled Antonio.

"No," said Carrie. "You need somebody here, Napo."

"I don't. You go ahead. I want to be alone. Go on, now. Don't hand me an argument."

"Well"—Carrie sighed—"then I'll come back, Napo."

"You don't have to. Heinie'll be in."

Antonio took off his pince-nez and polished them with his silk handkerchief.

Carrie got up and put on her hat.

Later in the afternoon Heinie Dorn and Sam Dvorak came in with some more papers. Napo read them and found nothing new. Dvorak spat on the carpet and was sharply reprimanded.

Dorn said, "Papers don't worry me, anyhow, Napo. Them guys ain't got a leg to stand on. Saw Pazzo at Joe's."

"Yeah, him and his spats," said Dvorak.

Dorn leaned back. "He was getting boiled on Dago ink."

Napo muttered.

Dvorak walked up and down and then stopped and said, "Spats drinks too much. If he could hold it, he'd be all right. But he can't. Soon as he gets a' edge on he starts shooting off his mouth."

"About his women," nodded Dorn.

Napo breathed deeply. "Heinie, you look after that Wop while I'm laid up. I don't want him getting soused too much. He gets plastered sometimes and wants to play Fourth of July. And that second-hand roadster ain't going to do him no good."

Dvorak said, "Seems we ought to be able to get along without him."

"We got to take it easy now," said Napo. "When I get out of bed and on my feet again I'm going to talk plain to Spats."

"Him talking about banks," said Heinie Dorn. "Cripes!"

Dvorak started to spit, but remembered, and whistled instead.

Carrie came back at four, and after a while Dorn and Dvorak went out.

"I said you didn't have to come back," growled Napo.

"There, there," said Carrie.

She made dinner for him, and he ate in silence. It was good to have a woman cook for you and wait on you. But Napo rebelled at this pleasant thought. He ignored Carrie, and finally fell asleep.

She stood by the bed, looking down at his dark, quiet face. A handsome guy, this Corsican, and something magnetic about him. She bent down and kissed him. Then she went into the living-room and curled up on the sofa.

"JAKE," SAID Margaret, "I wish this case was over."

Carmody shrugged. "They all get over sooner or later. We'll get this Heinie Dorn, and then it won't be long. I've got a hunch that we're beginning to smell the trail of the guy that shot poor old Shotzendorf. It's funny, Margaret, how things work out. A gunman gets caught most times on just a little bit of a clue."

"But there are others besides Heinie Dorn, and you know how these gunmen fight. Jake, with all these killings lately, and with you in the worst district in the city, I'm becoming a nervous wreck. Can't you ask them to shift you?"

"I couldn't do that, Margaret. Besides, it's not as bad as you think, and I have a good time. I'm careful, Margaret."

She shook her head. "Were you careful four years ago when you were shot in the leg? It was suicide, dear, to jump through that cellar window when you knew two killers were in there."

He grinned. "Think of the medal I got, honey."

"Jake, don't laugh. I mean it. You are not careful. Neither is Mike, and Rose knows it as well as I do. What do you get out of being a detective, anyhow?"

"Well, I get my drinks free, and my cigars. I get a percentage off on my clothes—"

"Jake, do be serious!"

Inwardly he knew how his wife felt, but there was no sense in encouraging her. He used a smile, a bland, carefree attitude, as a shield.

He left the flat and boarded a trolley car. He sat alone and meditated and felt sorry for his wife. It was rotten to have her worrying all the time, but there was nothing he could do. He had joined the Force fifteen years ago, and now he was part of it, and it was part of himself. Habit is not an easy thing to shake off. He had gradually woven himself into the network of law and crime. The game interested him, and habit had minimized in his mind the danger to which his calling exposed him, much the same as a novice's second airplane flight lacks the thrill of the first, even though the danger of a crash is no less great. The habit of natural courage becomes as inconsequential to the individual as the natural habit of cowardice. Neither thinks anything of it.

Well, the net for Heinie Dorn was spread. Carmody was optimistic. All the known speakeasies were being watched. Patrolmen were on the lookout, and a young plainclothes man, drafted from an outlying district, was eating his meals regularly in Mag Haggerty's boarding-place known to be shady.

When Carmody reached the station-house Spinoza was already there, and he had news.

"Jake, Flemming just phoned in. He was sitting like usual in Mag Haggerty's, having lunch, when two guys came in and went in the back room. They stayed in there about fifteen minutes, then they came out again. Mag said, 'So long, Bat,' to one of them. Flemming saw 'em get into a black touring car and drive off. The car had Delaware pads—four-two-one-six. They drove off. Then about an hour later Flemming was walking past Joe Latanzio's Spaghetti House when he saw the car parked there. He drifted past as the two same guys came out and piled in and drove off. There ain't much in that, Jake. Flemming's a young guy thinks he's cut out to be a great detective, and he did by luck get a break here.

"I checked them pads up. They were lifted from a sedan in a public garage two weeks ago. Now Ted Gilford, who was on traffic at Woodward Boulevard and Southfield Road the other night, suddenly remembers a touring car going by with Delaware pads towards the city. It came from the direction of Kirkville and that brewery. Flemming explains what the guy looks like he saw at the wheel leaving Mag Haggerty's. Ted has an idea he saw the same sort of guy the other night at the wheel. Jess Mulligan, the bootlegger, owned that stock at the brewery, said them hi-jacks got off with three hundred and ten cases of the best Scotch in the country. He's burying them two guys good."

"It means," said Carmody, "that maybe Latanzio, like Mag Haggerty, is being supplied by these hi-jacks. Latanzio ain't been in trouble much. He might get that way, though. No other news?"

"Nope. Cassidy picked up a guy at the railroad station he thought looked like Dorn. The guy turned out to be a Polack fish dealer who was waiting for his mother-in-law."

"Did the Polack get sore?"

"No. But his mother-in-law did. She said he was probably trying to duck her." Spinoza looked at his watch. "Look here, Jake. I got to run down to Izzy's and try on that new suit. I figured my gray one was good enough to get married in, but Rose wanted a blue one."

Carmody grinned. "Won't be long now, Mike."

"I only hope we get this case over with before Rose and me go on our honeymoon. We're going to the mountains, Jake. Paddling a canoe and that stuff."

"Lucky dog!"

"What I think, Jake!"

SPATS PAZZO was drunk. He was terribly drunk. He had been drinking most of the day. He sat in Joe Latanzio's Spaghetti House. Latanzio refused to give him another drink.

"But I want one, Joe."

"No, listen, Spats," said Latanzio. "You've had enough."

"I tell you, Joe, I want a drink. I want a drink. Say, do you mean to tell me I'm drunk?"

"Eat something, Spats. Better you eat something."

"But first I want a drink."

Latanzio shook his head. Six other diners were in the place, and all were listening.

Pazzo banged the table with a spoon. "You get me a drink, Joe."

"No, Spats. You're drunk now."

Pazzo picked up a plate and broke it.

Latanzio frowned. "Spats, stop that. It ain't right."

"Then get me a drink."

"No, Spats."

Pazzo sat back. "Listen, Joe, did Napo tell you not to give me no more drinks?"

"Napo didn't say nothing."

"You're a liar!"

"Spats, be a good guy. Go in my back room and lay down a while and sleep it off."

"Sleep what off?"

"You're drunk."

Pazzo broke a glass. "I ain't drunk!"

Latanzio put an edge on his voice. "Spats, you listen to me. If you go on like this you'll spoil my business. Them glasses and plates cost money. Now cut it out, Spats. I ain't standing for it, I ain't."

"Joe, I want a drink or I'll bust this joint up!"

The screen door banged. Latanzio looked around. Dvorak and Dorn came towards the table.

Dorn said, "What's the matter, Joe?"

"Spats is drunk. He's busting up all my stuff."

Dorn and Dvorak looked at Pazzo coldly.

"Spats, you go home and sleep," said Dorn.

"Like hell I will!"

Dorn and Dvorak sat down and lit cigarettes.

"You're plastered, Spats," said Dorn. "You're going home and sleep it off."

"Yeah, am I?"

Dorn said to Dvorak, "Sam, take this mutt home."

Dvorak stood up. "Come on, Spats."

Pazzo shook his head. Dvorak caught him by the collar and heaved him to his feet.

"You leave me alone!" snapped Pazzo.

Dorn stood up. With his tongue he rolled his cigarette from one side of his mouth to the other.

"Spats," he said, "you go home with Sam. Napo is sick in bed and we ain't going to have you getting in trouble. You get fresh now and I'll punch in your mug. I'll be waiting here for you, Sam."

Dvorak dragged Pazzo out and threw him into the roadster which Pazzo had recently acquired. Dvorak sat behind the wheel and drove off.

Latanzio said, "Heinie, he is bad when he gets drunk. He can't stand drinking."

"Yeah," nodded Dorn. "Bring me a steak, Joe, and a bottle of ink. I'm hungry."

Latanzio shouted the order into the kitchen and then stood behind the little cigar counter, by his new cash register. He smoked a cheroot.

The door opened and Carmody strolled in. "Hello, Joe," he said.

"Hello, Jake."

Carmody put his elbows on the cigar case and said, "I feel like smoking one of your cheroots, Joe."

"Sure, Jake." Latanzio slid a box on to the counter. "Take a handful."

"Thanks. I ain't been here for a long time. How's business?"

"Not so good, Jake."

Carmody chuckled. "You always say that, Joe. Getting some good booze these days?"

"Yeah, kind of. You want a couple bottles, Jake?"

"Not tonight, Joe. Maybe some other time."

"Any time, Jake. You know me."

Carmody lit up. "Yeah, you're a pretty good guy, Joe."

"Sure. Well, excuse me a minute, Jake. I got customers."

"Okey."

Latanzio moved from behind the counter. Carmody smoked the cheroot and stared thoughtfully into the small mirror behind the counter. Latanzio went back to the table at which Dorn sat, moved around some plates and said a few low words. Dorn sat motionless. Latanzio came back to the cigar case and leaned on it.

"How's your spaghetti, Joe?"

"Pretty good."

"Think I'll have some." He turned and looked around at the tables.

"All full just now, Jake."

"Yeah. But maybe that guy back there wouldn't mind if I sat down with him."

He strolled back and stopped at Dorn's table. "Mind if I have something to eat here, buddy?"

"Go ahead," muttered Dorn.

Latanzio hovered behind, breathless.

Carmody sat down and sighed "Warm these nights."

"Yeah," said Dorn.

Latanzio went off and then brought back Dorn's steak and Carmody's spaghetti. Carmody started eating. A slab of sandy hair lay down across his forehead. He seemed tranquil and benign.

Dorn ate, too. He stared hard at his plate and chewed his food slowly. Latanzio stood by the cigar counter, watching them. His face was shiny with perspiration.

"Good spaghetti," said Carmody.

Dorn grunted.

Carmody finished and shoved back his plate. He took a drink of red wine, then relit his cheroot and sat back.

Dorn ate faster. He gulped his wine. He finished by wiping his plate furiously with a piece of bread.

Then he called, "Joe, my check."

"Mine, too, Joe," said Carmody.

Latanzio came over and said, "That's all right, Jake."

"Thanks," said Carmody.

Dorn put down a dollar bill, got up and took his hat.

Carmody rose, too, and they walked towards the door. Dorn waited for Carmody to go out, but Carmody held the door open.

"Before me, buddy," he said.

Dorn rolled out and Carmody fell in step beside him as they walked down the street. At the next corner Dorn waved his hand and, "Well, I go this way."

As the hand came down Carmody caught it. "No, this way, Heinie."

Dorn stood stock still.

Carmody grinned. "It's a pinch, Heinie. Come on."

IT WAS hot. Napo lay in bed, with nothing more than a sheet over him. He was drowsing, and Carrie Noll sat on the edge of the bed, fanning him. The window was open. Somewhere a radio was playing jazz music, muffled and far away.

The lights in the bedroom were out, but moonlight came in through the open window and the fringe of it touched Carrie Noll's head gently. It lay softly on her pale cheek. Her lids were lowered. She was looking at the dim face of Napo. It was beautiful to be alone with him.

A knock sounded on the door in the living-room. Carrie rose carefully from the bed, so as not to disturb Napo. She went into the living-room, asked who was there, and then opened the door.

Dvorak walked in and walked right past her into the bedroom.

She closed the door and hurried after him. She gripped his arm and whispered, "What's the matter?"

"The cops got Heinie."

"Sh! Don't tell Napo. It'll disturb him."

Came Napo's quiet voice from the darkness—"I heard it." Carrie sobbed.

"Turn on the lights," said Napo. She pressed the switch. Dvorak's eyes jerked about the room. His jaw was set.

Napo did not move. "How'd happen, Sam?"

"Heinie and me went into Joe Latanzio's for supper. Spats was there, plastered to the eyebrows. He argued. Heinie told me to take him home. I took him and locked him in his room. When I come back Joe told me Carmody got Heinie. Carmody come in and sat down at Heinie's table and ate supper. Then when Heinie went out Carmody went with him, saying nothing. Joe looked out and watched them walk down the street. At the next block Heinie started to cross the street. Then Joe says Carmody took his arm and walked off with him."

"God!" murmured Napo; then, after a moment, "Well, it's good you got Spats off. Carmody might have picked you guys up, too, and Heinie can stand the gaff better than Spats. I wonder what they got on him."

"You got me, Napo," said Dvorak.

"I got to see the big fella first thing in the morning. Sam, you go over to Antonio's and tell him to get in touch with him. Tell him he should meet me in Antonio's tomorrow morning."

Carrie said, "You can't get out of bed, Napo!"

"Got to."

"You can't! I won't let you!"

"Shut up," said Napo.

Carrie turned on Dvorak. "My God, Sam, why did you have to tell him, in his condition?"

"Well, Jeeze," mumbled Dvorak.

"He'll kill himself!" cried Carrie.

"Lay off," said Napo. "Go ahead, Sam. Tell Antonio tonight. I'll be down there at nine."

"All right, Napo," said Dvorak.

IT WAS a well-groomed, clean-shaven but very weary Napo that walked into Antonio Callinari's living-room next morning.

"Ah, Napo, you look bad," said Antonio.

"I feel lousy."

"Take this big chair, Napo. It is more comfortable, yes."

Napo sat down slowly, pressing his lips together. Then he relaxed with a faint sigh and lit a cigarette.

"It is too bad, yes, about Heinie."

"He's got the guts, anyhow," said Napo.

He leaned back and closed his eyes. The cigarette hung motionless in one corner of his mouth, and the smoke rose in a thin, gray column.

The big man was on time. He rocked in wearing a Norfolk jacket and knickerbockers.

"I'm in a hurry, Napo," he said. "I've got a date to play golf at the country club. What can I do for you?"

"You know about Heinie," murmured Napo.

"Yes, Napo, I do. How much do you suppose they've got on him?"

"As far as I know, nothing. There's no witness. That guy they picked up on the road couldn't have said much because he was shot right off the bat. He's the guy gave me mine. We didn't start the shooting. He's dead now, and I don't know what them guys can hold Heinie on."

"The chap who died on the road might have mentioned his name."

"Yeah," nodded Napo. "But that ain't enough to hold a guy on. Except the bulls down there'll use it as an excuse to whale hell out of Heinie."

The big man took a turn up and down the room. "Tell you what I'll do, Napo. First of all you'd better get a lawyer. Get Max Aronstein, and tell him I sent you. As soon as you get Max he'll apply for a writ to get this Dorn out of the cops' hands.

I'll see he gets the writ. I'll review the case personally, and perhaps the evidence which the cops have is so slight that I'll be able in a short time to throw the case out."

"Thanks, Bill."

"Don't mention it, Napo. This accident seems to have been unavoidable, and so long as no cops have been hurt, only a couple of bums, it's all right with me. But remember me when election time comes around, Napo, and I'll see a lot of campaign money goes your way."

Napo smiled. "Bill, we'll get on all right."

"Sure thing. I like you, Napo. You're not loud-mouthed, and you carry a head on your shoulders. If you play right with me, some day you might be a ward boss, and let me tell you, Napo, that there's more gravy in being a ward boss than in being mayor. Only play ball, Napo, and don't shoot any cops."

"I'll play ball, Bill."

The big man grinned and came over and patted Napo on the shoulder. "Well, I hope you get better, old man. I've got to run along and play golf with the president of the Society for the Prevention of Crime. And this afternoon I've got to make a speech at the summer school to the little kiddies on the Reward of Honesty. I'm a pretty busy man, Napo, but I'll always have time to lend you a hand. Well, so long, old man."

The big man went out and Napo smiled to himself. Good guy, the big fella.

Antonio was smelling his flowers. "Napo," he said, "Carrie Noll is a nice girl."

"Yeah, she's all right."

Antonio removed his pince-nez and polished them with his silk handkerchief. "I would never think you thought that way, no, Napo."

"Well, hell, can't I think a broad's all right without going nuts over her? Carrie's all right, but that's as far as she goes with me."

"I like her, yes," said Antonio wistfully.

Napo looked at him. "You want her?"

"I was thinking, yes, I'd ask you."

Napo chuckled. "Why ask me? I got no strings on her."

He rose slowly and put on his hat.

Antonio, smiling graciously, put on his pince-nez and rubbed palm over knuckles. "Be careful of your hurt, Napo, yes."

"Sure. Now I guess I got to see this Max Aronstein."

HEINIE DORN reeled across the room and slammed down into a chair. His collar was ripped away from his neck. His hair was sweaty and plastered down to his brows. A glazed look was in his eyes, and there were welts on his cheeks. His jaw stuck out like a snow plow.

Officer O'Leary had his sleeves rolled up, and he was perspiring. Spinoza had his sleeves rolled up, too. He was leaning against the wall, holding a length of rubber hose in his hand. Carmody had reversed a chair and straddled it. His arms were folded on the back, and a slab of sandy hair lay down across his forehead.

Dorn glanced from one to the other with a grim, determined look.

"Go ahead, you tough guys! Go ahead!"

O'Leary came over and banged Dorn on the jaw. "We're having fun," he said.

"Yeah, so am I," gritted Dorn.

Spinoza snapped, "You killed them guys at the brewery, Dorn! By God, you killed 'em!"

"Yeah? You'll get over that, Dago."

"Heinie," drawled Carmody, "we're after the big guy mainly. We know you ain't the big guy, and if you give us a break we'll give you a break."

Dorn had a short, hard laugh. "A break don't interest me, Carmody. I don't know a thing. I wasn't out at the brewery. I'm a stranger here. I been looking to get in on some good bootleg racket, and I don't know any big guy. I sure wish I did."

"You lie like a rug!" clipped Spinoza.

"That's all you know how to do, Dago, is wisecrack."

Spinoza hit him, and drops of sweat snapped from Dorn's face. A vicious, cold fire burned in his eyes. For two hours last night he had undergone this inquisition of the law. And this morning, another two hours were rolling by. Dorn was a case-hard. He had met with this sort of thing for most of his life, and he had learned to play it as a game. There was something savagely philosophical in his attitude. He realized that such measures were inevitable, and he experienced a savage satisfaction in being able to withstand each onslaught.

Spinoza went to the door at sound of a knock. He opened it and spoke with a policeman. Then he turned.

"Jake, that Dr. Pennell is here," he said.

Carmody stood up. "Tell him we'll see him in a minute."

He picked up Dorn's coat. "Heinie, put that coat on and fix your collar and tie."

When Dorn had done this, Carmody took a handkerchief and tied it over Dorn's face. "Now stand right here," he said; and to O'Leary, "Pat, go down and bring in Dr. Pennell."

Dr. Pennell came in a moment later and said, "Good morning, gentlemen."

"Doctor," said Carmody, "take a look at this guy. Does he look anything like one of the guys broke in your house that night."

Dr. Pennell peered through steel-rimmed spectacles. He coughed behind his hand. "Well, now. Well, as a matter of fact, he does. Same build, dark suit—and of course, the handker-chief— But, then, it would be difficult to swear by it."

"Naturally," nodded Carmody. "But you admit that he does look something like one of the men."

"Oh, yes—something."

Carmody pulled off the handkerchief. "We believe he's one of the four."

There was a streak of blood on Dorn's cheek. He laughed shortly.

Dr. Pennell peered keenly. "Has he been fighting?"

"Oh, yeah," chuckled Spinoza.

"Yeah," said Dorn. "We been playing games. I stand up and these babies knock me down. Like a circus. Yeah."

Dr. Pennell coughed behind his hand. "You know, Mr. Carmody, I've heard a lot about this so-called third degree. And, do you know, I don't exactly approve of it."

"That's too bad," said Carmody, with a half-smile. "But then a lot of people don't understand it. We only use it on tough eggs. This man you see standing here has a record, and a bad one. We start in by asking him certain questions, and he tells us to go to hell. He expects to be rough-housed, and he gets it. Do you suppose we could get anything out of him by conducting a nice quiet conversation? Not on your life. These guys only understand a certain kind of language. Well, sorry to bring you down here, Doctor, but every little bit helps. Thank you."

The doctor left, his attitude hinting that he was still unconvinced.

O'Leary rolled his sleeve higher. Spinoza hefted his length of rubber hose.

Carmody straddled the chair again and said, "Well, Heinie."

"All set," snarled Dorn.

O'Leary leaped across the room, his fists clenched....

An hour later Carmody said, "Well, recess, boys."

Dorn's laugh rattled. "You guys ain't even began to hurt me yet."

Spinoza said, "We ain't even started, guy."

"Yah, you're a lot of lousy pups. Why don't you go drag in the whole force? This kindergarten ain't even funny. You guys ain't got a thing on me, and you can all go to hell. I'll be out of this side-show damn soon, and then you can play marbles to pass the time away."

Carmody said, "We'll exercise this truck-horse again this afternoon."

"You guys are just trying to ride me."

"Yeah," nodded Spinoza, "in a chair with electric fixtures."

I WANT to tell you something, Spats," said Napo. "You lay off the booze while Heinie's in this jam or you ain't ever going to grow up to be a man."

"I didn't do nothing, did I?" snapped Pazzo.

"You heard Napo," muttered Sam Dvorak.

"Yeah," said Bat Price. "You lay off."

And Charley Haas said, "Or me, I'll cave in your mush personal."

"Well, cripes," snapped Pazzo, "I ain't done nothin'. It wasn't my fault if Heinie got pinched. Hell, if Sam didn't take me home, maybe him and me'd be in the catch, too."

"You heard me, Spats," said Napo quietly. "You lay off the booze and watch your step. Too much booze knocked the hell out of Spider. If he was sober that night he would have seen that he was being fixed to get the works."

"Listen, Napo, there ain't no guy ever going to give me the works. I don't rate in Spider's class. He was a tinhorn. But all right. I meet you guys half-way. I'll cut out drinking if it'll make you happy."

"That's all I ask," said Napo.

Days of waiting followed. Max Aronstein, seeking a writ of habeas corpus, was blocked when Carmody, determined to keep Dorn inside the walls of the law, charged him formally with the possession of a gun and demanded that he be held on such evidence as had been accumulated.

The man behind them had to play a tactful game and could not come out in the open. However, he assured Napo that if Dorn kept his mouth shut, as he had admirably done so far, the case would come up quickly and Dorn would be released on suspended sentence. He cited the lack of positive evidence. The doctor could not identify Dorn with any measure of assurance, and no one had actually seen him commit the crime. Max Aronstein could shatter Burnside's story of how Bennie Kline had babbled Dorn's name while dying that night on the highway. They had clear sailing, said the big man—if Dorn kept his mouth shut.

Napo was able to get around better. He quietly told Carrie Noll to stay out of the flat, and made her a present of five hundred dollars. She threw it back at him, raved and cried, and then, having discharged this emotion, assumed a determined air.

"I'm going to be Antonio's girl friend," she said bitterly.

"Good," said Napo. "He's a nice guy."

"God, Napo, you ain't got no heart at all!"

"Didn't I offer you five hundred?"

"Do you think that's what I wanted?"

Napo shrugged. He looked past her and regarded the picture he had cut from *Vanity Fair.* And he thought of Joyce Travers.

And a day later he saw her again in Antonio's palace of flowers. She wore a blue sheer dress and a blue hat, and her teeth sparkled when she recognized him.

"How do you do, Miss Travers?" said Napo.

She must have noticed how slowly he walked, and how thin his cheeks were.

"You have been ill?"

"Yes," he said. "Little."

"Oh, that's too bad. It was so good of you to send me those flowers."

"It was nothing," he said. "I liked to."

"Flowers are beautiful."

"Yes, flowers are beautiful."

He wanted to say that she, too, was beautiful, but there was nothing of the wiseacre about Napo.

Then she was saying, "I am making arrangements for a social

benefit to be held at the Garden Pavilion. It is for the sick children at the City Hospital. We are to have little booths where souvenirs will be sold. There will be refreshments and dancing. Perhaps you would like to help these poor little dears by subscribing."

"I'd like to," said Napo.

"The tickets are ten dollars, and of course many people subscribe a little more. But then that is not necessary. The ticket will admit you."

Napo glowed. "I'd like to subscribe—well, say, a hundred dollars."

"Oh, that is so kind of you!"

"It is nothing," said Napo.

"Here is my card. If you will mail your check sometime soon, I'll send you the ticket. And I shall be there, Mr. Damiani, and if you feel equal to it we'll have a dance."

Napo spent the rest of the afternoon in his flat, alone. He was weary, the wound was hurting, but his spirits were high. He would dance with Joyce Travers! He looked at her neat white card. He would hold her in his arms and dance—yes, by God, no matter how much this wound pained! He had never anticipated a stroke of luck such as this. They would be close together. He danced well, and he would ask her if maybe sometime they couldn't dance at one of the classy night-clubs.

How drab and cheap and tawdry Carrie Noll seemed by comparison! Thank God, he had never fallen for her! She would have dragged him down to the level of a lot of other mutts. Funny, that Antonio wanted her. Napo began to feel superior to Antonio. It occurred to him that Antonio was just a cheap Wop dressed up. He took a walking stick from the closet and looked at it. He would carry it to the Garden Pavilion.

The next day was mild and sunshiny, and Napo went for a solitary stroll in the park. The perfume of flowers was sweet here, and great trees arched over the quiet paths. He followed a narrow path through luxuriant shrubbery and past sparkling pools; over a Chinese bridge, quaint and wooden, that crossed a gurgling brook. On down the shady path, and past cosy summer houses.

Turning a corner, he saw Pazzo sitting on a bench with a girl. A little child played in the grass nearby. Pazzo saw him and looked a little startled.

"Oh, hello—" he jerked out.

Napo nodded, paused for a moment, and then strolled on.

"Oh, who is that good-looking fellow?" asked Fanny.

"Him?" Pazzo expanded. "Why, he's a friend of mine."

"Gawd, ain't he swell?"

"Yeah. I know a lot of swell guys." He turned and pinched her cheek. "Baby, I'm crazy about you. My roadster's just aching to take you for a spin."

"Now, Johnny, be a nice boy now!"

"Aw, Fan!"

"Well, maybe, Johnny, some night this week. But you musn't get fresh."

"Baby, I never get fresh!"

THEY SAT in the rendezvous in Coke Street. Napo. Pazzo. Sam Dvorak. Bat Price. Charley Haas.

It was raining out. The rain thrashed against the windows and drummed on the roof. The men sat like so many images. Price and Haas stared at the floor. Sam Dvorak stared at the ceiling. Pazzo lounged on the bed, regarding his new spats. Napo stood by the window, lean and silent, his hands behind his back, his eyes gazing down into the drab, wet street.

Presently Pazzo yawned. "Well, I guess Carrie and Antonio are playing house these days."

Nobody moved. Nobody said anything.

Pazzo got up and strolled around the room, whistling. He jangled loose change in his pocket. He stopped and looked at a bottle on the table. He laughed.

"Hell, guys, I been on the water wagon for damn near two weeks."

He looked around for some show of applause. Seeing none, he jangled the change in his pocket and whistled softly. Then he yawned again and stretched his arms. He sat down on the bed.

"Guys," he said, "it's funny, the way I been having a lot of ideas lately."

"Yeah," said Dvorak, "that's sure funny."

Bat Price laughed out loud.

"I mean it," said Pazzo. "I don't think we're taking full advantage of our talent."

"Bet he's thinking of banks again," said Dvorak.

"Yeah," nodded Pazzo, "and other things."

Napo turned. "Spats, what did I tell you?"

"Aw, hell," growled Pazzo. "A guy can't even have ideas in this mob. I'm getting sick and tired. I ain't going to have my style cramped all my life."

Dvorak said, "Yeah, you're liable to get cramps in the stomach from lead poisoning if you don't lay off."

"Aw, tie that noise outside," snapped Pazzo.

CARMODY MEDITATED. He picked his teeth with a shaved-down match. He sat on the small of his back in the swivel-chair, one leg dangling over the side, the other jack-knifed against a drawer of the desk.

Spinoza was in high heat, pacing the room. "If we can't hold a lousy bum on evidence, I don't know how ever the hell we can hope to get at the mob. With shyster lawyers and some big guy in the works and a lock-jawed Assistant State's Attorney, we got a fine chance—a fine chance.

"Look here, Jake. I'm just as sure that Heinie Dorn is one of this mob as I am of my own age. That palooka is crooked, and if he was less tough he would have sprung a yarn. And that smooth-tongued kike Aronstein, he could convince some guys that black was white. But he can't convince me! Why the hell is it that all the brainy lawyers take the stand for crooks and killers?"

"We got a bad break, Mike," drawled Carmody. "I know that we didn't have much evidence, and the possession of a gun nowadays is considered a cheap technicality. A guy not as tough as Dorn would have cracked up under what we gave him. It was just too bad that we ran up against a man of iron. If we'd got our hands on Spider Link again that time, but...." He shrugged.

Spinoza smacked fist into palm. "We're taking the count, Jake, but I'll be damned if I'll throw in the sponge. We've been made a lot of jackasses of. Why, damn it, if that Assistant State's Attorney ever gave birth to a bright idea he'd die of pain. I never saw such a blockhead in all my life. Aronstein literally spanked him. The Jew just looked at him as if to say, 'You're a nice little boy, but don't talk out of turn or papa'll spank.'"

Spinoza snorted. His dark eyes flashed with anger. He boiled all that day, but at night the sight of Rose cooled the troubled waters.

She was small, dark as Spinoza, a warm armful of Italian girlhood. She had straight black hair pulled down over her ears and knotted on the nape, and her eyes were liquid brown.

"Michael, you look worried," she said.

"No, sunbeam; just sore. Dorn got off on a suspended sentence. What a break!"

"Oh, Michael, don't let it worry you!"

"Sunbeam, it don't—not tonight. I got you right here and I shouldn't worry. I ain't!"

He kissed her and his eyes sparkled. "What did you do today?"

"I was buying things, Michael. Towels and pillow-cases and tablecloths and napkins. I stopped in the flat, too. I like to go there, Michael, and just look around. It makes me so happy."

"Yeah?"

"M-m-m! It's so new and nice and clean, darling. I can just

picture us there." She snuggled up under his chin. "We'll be so happy, you and me alone there, Michael."

"Yeah, sunbeam, we sure will."

"You and me—alone."

"Yeah," he whispered near her ear, and then kissed it.

She looked at him with her wide, round eyes. "I love you, darling."

"Love you, sunbeam."

"How much?"

"Lots."

She snuggled closer, and he kissed her dark head. Then she sighed. "Well, my man, I suppose I'll have to put the supper out." It tickled her to say that. Spinoza watched her go into the kitchen. His thoughts were amorous. Couldn't help it.

He stretched himself, lay well back in the big chair and smoked after the manner of one at ease with the world. Good to have a wife and come home and sit around and hear her singing in the kitchen. Good to have her kiss you as though she meant it, and, yes, even worry about you. You made believe you resented her worrying, but, honest, under it all you really felt pleased, as if you were somebody. Hell, if she didn't worry, you'd resent that, too.

Spinoza whistled. He felt like a married man already. He felt like somebody. He could see Rose in the new flat, small and neat and pretty—hell, prettier—as a picture. Jake and Margaret would come over sometimes for supper, and they'd sit around talking or playing cards. Yes, sir—that was the life, after all! And a kid—say, a daughter like Rose would be something to write home about. Boy would be okey, too. Only he'd never get on the cops—no, sir!

"Michael!"

"Yup?"

"Supper's ready."

"Coming, sunbeam."

Great life! A week hence—Mrs. Michael Spinoza!

SPATS PAZZO weaved his sport roadster precariously through traffic. Precariously because he was drunk again. He had fallen off the water-wagon with a bang. He was maliciously happy. Whenever he saw a traffic cop he thought how nice it would be to run the big bum over.

He felt capable of doing great things. He felt capable of swaggering up to Napo and telling him where the hell he got off. Napo was cramping his style.

The sun was shining brightly, many cars and people were out, and Pazzo was sure he cut a ritzy figure in the robin's egg blue roadster, with the top down. His imitation Panama hat was set at a rakish angle, and his left arm was crooked smartly on the top of the door. All the girls looked pretty, and he was certain that all of them favored him with smiles.

Presently he was riding through the park. The atmosphere brought up recent memories, and he slowed down, peering across the lawns and shrubbery that separated the vehicular drive from the pedestrian pathway. Suddenly he jammed on the brake and stopped. He shut off the ignition and reeled across the lawn.

"Hello, Fan!"

Fanny looked up from the latest copy of sex secrets, and set her face.

Pazzo flopped down beside her and grabbed her hand. She pulled free and slapped his face.

"I told you I didn't want to see you no more!" she said.

"Aw, baby."

"And don't call me baby. After what you tried to pull the other night I don't want never to see you no more. I told you I wasn't one of them kind of girls, and you sure have got your nerve with you to come here again."

"Give us a kiss, Fan."

"Will you please don't do that!"

"Aw, baby."

"Mr. Pazzo, stop it!"

He grabbed her hands, held them, and kissed her. Color burned in her face as she tore herself free. Pazzo slouched back and laughed. He slapped Fanny's knee. She slapped his face.

"Look here, kid, cut that out!" he snapped, suddenly dark.

"You're drunk," she said. "And you're nothing but a low common Wop. You're like one of these sheiks I been reading about. You think all girls are the same. If I tell my motorman friend he'll squash your nose."

Pazzo's lower lip drooped malevolently. His eyes narrowed and a dull gray look crept into his face. He saw the girl through a quivering haze, saw the whiteness of her skin and the warm, luscious crimson of her lips. A common Wop, eh? A sheik, eh? His fist doubled and struck out. It struck the girl between the eyes. Her body jerked and then slumped and her head fell back.

Pazzo's eyed widened. She was unconscious. He jumped up and looked around. He saw the little girl Joan sitting in the shadow of a bush, a dozen yards away. He sucked in his breath and moved towards her.

"Joan, you want to go for a ride in my nice automobile?"

The little girl clapped her hands. "Goody-goody! Where's Fanny? Where's nursey?"

Pazzo took Joan by the hand. "She's sleeping. See?"

"I want nursey."

"We'll go for a ride first. No use waking her. Just come along with me."

He picked up the little girl and carried her across the lawn. He put her in the roadster and climbed in himself. He started the motor and drove off.

His rum-fogged brain formulated vague plans. Kidnaping paid well, and the girl's folks were swells. He looked down at her. Pretty kid. Her blond curls were blowing in the breeze and she was laughing and clapping her hands.

He chose roads that did not bite into the heart of the city. He would reach his rooms in Murdock Street by a roundabout but inconspicuous route. That was all that was necessary. He'd show that broad. He'd show everybody—Napo included. There was no guy could cramp his style!

He felt grieved. Everybody was picking on him lately. Napo, too; and the other guys. And that frail. A common Wop, eh? Well, she could laugh this off. Fifty thousand dollars—that's what he'd ask, and by God they'd pay it or he'd bash the kid's brains out!

He drove with a vengeance. He had been wronged all his life. Nobody had given him a chance. He'd show them. He was a big timer, and he'd sure show them.

The first thrill of the ride having passed, the little girl began to ask for Fanny. Pazzo told her to be quiet. She shook her head.

"I want nursey."

"She's sleeping. Well get her soon."

"I want nursey."

"Now be a good girl. Be quiet."

Joan stood up and whimpered. Pazzo pushed her back down and cursed under his breath. She cried and waved her hands.

"Be quiet!" snapped Pazzo.

"I want Fanny. I want nursey."

She squirmed and waved her hands. Pazzo tried to hold her still, but she clawed at him.

"I don't like you," she said. "You aren't a nice man."

"Sit down! Be quiet!"

He hurt her, and she screamed. Pazzo became enraged and slapped her face. He swerved to avoid hitting a car parked at the curb. A man looked out of the car as he swung by, and heard Joan scream. The man opened his mouth and frowned.

"Hey!" he shouted.

Pazzo's blood chilled. He looked back and saw the car lurch

away from the curb. He pressed down hard on the throttle and crouched over the wheel. The other car was howling in pursuit.

Pazzo almost crashed into a truck at the next intersection. The truck-driver cursed and a policeman standing on the corner blew his whistle. The sound cut through Pazzo like a knife. He had the throttle down flat against the floorboard. Looking into the mirror on the mudguard, he saw the policeman swing on to the running-board of the pursuing sedan. He struck the wheel savagely because the car would not go faster.

Joan was screaming, and he gave her a back-handed crack on the mouth. Behind him the police whistle was blowing. Ahead, a policeman came running out of a side-street, stopped, looked up and down and saw the speeding blue roadster. He shouted and pulled his gun.

Pazzo ducked. But the policeman did not fire because he saw the head of blonde curls. He jumped into the street and caught the sedan on the fly.

Pazzo weakened. The law was on his heels, and he was in danger. He remembered what they'd told him had been done to Dorn. They would beat him too. Once he had had a taste of the rubber hose in Buffalo—just for bouncing a bottle off a cop's head. No limit to what they would do in a case like this. They'd accuse him of being another Hickman and beat him to a pulp. His heart ached and hammered against his ribs.

Why had he done this? Whatever had prompted him to do such a thing? That broad—yes, that broad, damn her! He didn't want this little kid anymore. He wanted to escape. He wanted to creep back into the fold, to be under the cool steady wing of Napo. God, why couldn't he be like Napo?

Rum and stark fear rattled him, blinded all reason, made him shake in every limb, in every nerve. If he'd stayed sober he would never have done this. Napo was right. Rum was no good. Look what it did to Spider Link.

Booze was good to trade in, but not good to drink. He would creep repentent back to Napo and tell him he was right. Damn those whistles! He looked back. The sedan was nearer now and a cop was on either running-board. They had their guns out.

"Oh, dear God," groaned Pazzo, "don't let them get me!"

Pedestrians jumped out of his way. The street seemed to be full of obstacles. Pazzo cursed and raved and prayed. He struck the little girl. She screamed and tried to climb over the door. The whistles blew. People swarmed from doorways. More policemen appeared.

"I got to get away!" cried out Pazzo.

He gave the little girl a shove. She slipped over the door and fell from the speeding car. A woman screeched.

"Oh God! Oh God!" choked Pazzo.

He saw that the sedan had stopped and that people were crowding in the street. He crouched over the wheel, kept the throttle flush with the floorboard. Then he heard a siren and saw a low, black car in swift pursuit.

He opened his mouth as if gasping for air. He shook the wheel. He writhed in his seat. He moaned.

The siren screamed.

A shot barked.

It carried away one corner of Pazzo's windshield. He bent lower, and his face turned the color of dough, his eyes widened with horror.

Another shot barked.

The blue roadster heaved. They'd hit a tire! The wheel spun viciously in Pazzo's hand. The car struck the curb and keeled. It hurtled across the sidewalk. Pazzo threw up his hands and screamed, as the roadster cannoned through a plate-glass window.

NAPO STOOD by the open French windows in Antonio Callinari's sumptuous living-room and looked down into the traffic of Broad Avenue. It was six o'clock, and shop girls and clerks were hurrying home.

Carrie Noll lay in the comfortable depths of a large sofa,

polishing her fingernails. Sometimes she raised her eyes and looked at the neat, slim back of Napo. And sometimes she sighed—softly, tenderly, as one sometimes sighs over a broken illusion or a lost hope.

Antonio came in, beaming. He crossed to the sofa, bent down and kissed Carrie. She did not seem particularly interested. Antonio sat down beside her and reached for her hand.

"Don't you see I'm cleaning my nails?" she said.

"Excuse it, flower," murmured Antonio.

"Get me a drink."

"Yes, flower."

Antonio went to the sideboard and mixed a drink. He said to Napo, "You had a good talk with the big fella, Napo?"

Napo turned around and leaned against the wall. "Yes. He's starting a new bootleg racket, and I'm going to run it. It's big, Antonio, and inside of a year I'll be worth a fortune. We're going to run booze straight from the Canadian Border. Guys will smuggle it over at night on horses and hide it in the woods. We're getting six trucks to run it down in."

Carrie said, "I'm glad to hear that, Napo. Boy, you're sure rising in this little old world. The big fella thinks the world of you."

"He does, yes," nodded Antonio, and took a drink to Carrie.

He started to sit down beside her, but Carrie said:

"Turn on the radio."

"Yes, flower."

He crossed the room and turned on the radio, and a clear, resonant voice said:

"…and Patrolman Albert Marks leaped aboard the sedan at Grove Avenue and Twelfth Street. The chase was spectacular and exciting and drew people from houses and stores. At Grove and Fifteenth Patrolman George Moran joined the sedan and the chase continued up Grove. It was at Twentieth Street that the kidnaper threw little Joan Monterey from the speeding roadster; and the child is now in the West End Hospital suffering from a fractured skull. She is not expected to live.

"A few minutes later a police car from the Fourth Precinct joined the chase. In it were Officers Burke and Mandelbaum, Detective-Sergeant Jake Carmody, and Detective Michael Spinoza. It was Carmody who fired the shot that blew the roadster's rear left tire, causing it to swerve across the sidewalk and crash into the huge window of Cohen & Cohen, Hardware Merchants, at 250 Grove Avenue.

"John Pazzo was killed in the crash and is now at the City Morgue.

"About half an hour later Police Headquarters were notified by Mrs. Monterey of the disappearance of her little daughter. They were able to tell her that the child was at the West End Hospital. Mrs. Monterey, who lives at number 6 Park Court, is in a state of collapse.

"Detective-Sergeant Carmody and Detective Spinoza went to interview Miss Fanny Hale, who was nurse to the child, and from whom the child had been stolen in Green Park. It was she who told them Pazzo's name. It seems that Pazzo had been seeing her in the park for several months. Lately she had consented to take an automobile ride with him, but an incident occurring during the ride caused her to resent any further attentions on Pazzo's part. This afternoon he appeared in the park again, quite drunk, and a scene ensued because she told him that she did not want to see him again. Enraged, he struck her. When she came to, the child and Pazzo were gone.

"This daily news summary is broadcast each day at six o'clock by the *Evening Chronicle,* through the courtesy of Station XYX—"

Napo clipped, "Shut it off, Antonio!"

Antonio shut it off.

Tall, lean, dark—Napo stood against the wall. His fists were clenched and a dark scintillating fire burned in his eyes.

"I knew it!" he murmured. "I knew Spats would end this way! Damn him!"

"Be calm, yes, Napo," urged Antonio softly.

"Calm?" Napo chuckled briefly. "That dirty Dago! He would soak himself with booze! He would play around with women! He knew women! Why, that puppy didn't know his elbow from a hole in the ground!"

Carrie said, "Take it easy, Napo. He's dead and dead guys tell no tales."

They had never seen Napo's rage come to the surface before. His dark, lean face was deadly, his mouth a tight line, his jet eyes two small points of black fire. His fist quivered.

Carrie Noll came over and put an arm around him. "Please Napo, take it easy. You ain't well."

He shook her off. "Sit down!"

He picked up his hat and strode towards the door. He walked too fast. The pain bit at his side, caused a wave of sickening heat to rush to his head. He gritted his teeth.

"Nap," cried Carrie Noll.

He opened the door and went out. He had to grip the banister on the way down, and a chill, nerve-wracking blast followed the rush of heat.

Napo felt sick—at heart and at head.

POLICE COMMISSIONER STEARNS was a rock-built, hard-jawed man of fifty. His gray eyes had the penetrating power of a steel rapier, his hair was short and gray and bristling. He had a voice like the crack of a gun.

"Jake, these gangster outrages have gone far enough!"

"What I was saying," drawled Carmody.

"Get me, Jake. I want this city turned upside down. I don't care if you guys get no sleep for weeks. I want this city taken by the slack of the pants and shaken hard. I want every man on the Force to cut loose. Round up every known gangster and scour the speakeasies and round up every man who looks the least bit like a gangster. Treat 'em rough. Load up the jails. The newspapers are razzing hell out of us, and the public is razzing us too. And we deserve it.

"Jake, you've got a little girl of your own. Think of it—think how you'd feel if she was taken off by a soused Wop and then kicked out of a machine going sixty miles an hour. I've kids too. God, Jake, I'm no sob-artist, but this thing has hit me smack between the eyes. It's made me realize that my kids aren't safe, that no kid is safe, with mutts like Pazzo at large. There's been a reign of terror in this city for the past year. We've got to terrorize these gangsters. They don't stick to booze. They try everything, from stealing kids to ripping them open. Jake, I want a reign of terror. Sweep up the speakeasies. Terrorize the men who run them and make them speak.

"This Pazzo—you say you've got a hunch he was with the four guys who made that Dr. Pennell attend to a wounded man that night."

"Yeah. Pazzo had spats on. Dr. Pennell, when he viewed the body at the morgue, said this Pazzo was about the same build as the guy who wore spats that night, and he thinks this Pazzo was wearing the same kind of suit. He said Dorn looked like one of them, too, but he wasn't ready to swear by it. Harry, Dorn got off by the skin of his teeth. He's one of the guy's I'm going to try getting back again. He's one of the gang, or I don't know my tomatoes."

"Then get him!" roared the Commissioner. "Land on this city like a ton of brick, Jake. I'm giving the same talk to every precinct, and I want action. This is no time for Sherlock Holmes stuff. We've got to be rough and act fast and raise hell. All right. On your way and start the ball rolling!"

Carmody walked back to the station-house. He walked no faster than he usually did, and his face was still bland and tranquil. In the back room were six detectives. He sat down and told them in plain and unhurried words what was to be done.

They paired up and started off. Spinoza came in and Carmody took him by the arm and walked right out with him.

"Mike, we are going places to collect people and ask questions. The Commissioner is all hot and bothered, and I don't blame him."

Spinoza rubbed his hands together gingerly. "That's what I've been waiting for, Jake—general orders to get nasty. I feel nasty as hell and I'm going to get lots of exercise."

"First off," said Carmody, "we'll drop in on Joe Latanzio."

They found Latanzio standing beside his cash register, and Carmody said, "Joe, will you come over to the house with us?"

"Me, Jake? But why?"

"Little get-together party."

Latanzio spread his hands. "But, Jake—"

"I know, Joe. Put on your hat and coat. Or go as you please."

"I ain't done nothing, Jake. You need warrants—"

"Yeah, I know. We got pockets full of warrants we fill out as we go along."

Spinoza walked back to a table at which were sitting two men, drinking chianti.

"Who are you guys?" he asked.

"Huh?"

"What's your names?"

"Mojeki," growled one.

And the other said, "Bonno."

"Where do you work?"

"We're out of work. Looking for jobs on the railroad."

Spinoza said, "Meantime drinking high-priced chianti. You birds come along."

"Why?"

"We want to look up your family tree," said Spinoza.

"Pinch, eh?" chuckled Bonno.

"What a bright boy!" sneered Spinoza.

They stood up and Mojeki said, "Well, we got time to spare. Come on, Jack. This dick's got a brain-storm."

The two of them, along with Latanzio, were marched to the station-house. Four others were there, brought in by one of the pair whom Carmody had sent forth. Two policemen were on guard.

Carmody said, "Come on, Mike. Now Mag Haggerty."

On the way out Sergeant Auerbach put down the telephone and said, "Boys. It's terrible. That little girl just died."

Carmody stopped short and stared into space. He remembered the still white face, the blonde curls stained with blood, the stricken mother. His eyes blurred. He sighed, and breathed, tranquilly but sadly, "Ah, God!"

Sergeant Auerbach said, "What?"

Carmody said, "Come on, Mike."

Spinoza said nothing, but his face was deadly. They walked down the street. As they turned the corner Spinoza exploded:

"Jake, why the hell can't they leave the kids out of it?"

Carmody walked on beside him, and after a while said, "Mike, by nature a wolf preys on the weak. From what I've read in books, a wolf in the woods will never attack anything his equal. They go around in packs, and when one does go on his own he picks on something that don't stand a chance. There ain't much difference between a woods wolf and a street wolf, except the street wolf is supposed to be human, but he ain't."

"Well," said Spinoza, "when a woods wolf preys on chickens or sheep or something like that, the man who owns these things, he shoots the wolf. Lays for him in the dark and shoots him dead. Right?"

"Yeah, Mike."

"But," went on Spinoza, "if you or me ever laid for a street wolf and shot him in the dark, we'd have hell to pay. A lawyer would say that ain't honorable and we should be broke and kicked in jail. Right?"

"Yeah, Mike."

Spinoza spat. "Hell, there ain't no justice. Let's cross here."

They walked into Mag Haggerty's.

"Hello, boys," said Mag.

"Hello, Mag," said Carmody. "Put your bonnet on and come over the house for a while. It's cooler there."

"I ain't hot, Jake."

"But we are, and we want to go where it's cool."

"But—" She stopped and seemed to see light. Her jaw fell. "What's the matter, Jake?"

"Nothing. We'll sit down and wait."

Spinoza helped himself to a doughnut, but grimaced and put it down. "That thing's left over from the war!"

Mag was saying, "But, Jake, what have I did?"

"Nothing. We just want to have a chat with you. Be nice, Mag."

Dumfounded, she shuffled into the back room and came out a moment later wearing a hat and a black shawl.

When they reached the station-house again the crowd of pick-ups had grown to twelve. Carmody and Spinoza took Latanzio and Mag Haggerty into another room.

"Now," said Spinoza to Latanzio, "as one Wop to another, spring what you know."

"Gawd, boys, I don't know nothing!"

Carmody reversed a chair and straddled it, leaning his arms on the back. "Joe, as far as I know, you've never been dragged in on a police quiz. Let me tell you something. We mean business. When a man buys booze from hi-jackers he's taking a chance. You took a chance. We want you to talk, and if you don't we'll lick hell out of you."

Latanzio looked frightened.

Carmody said, "This John Pazzo. You knew him?'

"He—he used to come in, that's all."

"That's not all. Who used to come in with him?"

"Some other guys, I don't know."

"Joe, we mean business."

"Honest, Jake, I don't know nothing. Them guys came in and et there. Could I help that?"

"You knew Dorn, too," said Carmody out of a clear sky.

Latanzio started, licked his lips. "Well, Jeeze, Jake, he used to come in, too."

"With Pazzo, eh?"

"Well—" Latanzio gulped and closed his mouth.

"Sure," drawled Carmody. "And you bought booze from them, didn't you, Joe?"

Latanzio pulled at his collar. His voice cracked. "Jake, for Gawd's sake, I ain't hurt nobody!"

"Well, all right, then, you bought booze from them."

"I had to buy it from somebody, Jake," pleaded Latanzio.

Carmody suddenly turned on Mag Haggerty. "You, too, Mag."

She looked startled. "Me!"

"A dick planted in your place saw two guys go in your back room. He saw these guys later come out of Latanzio's. They were using a car with Delaware pads that looked mighty like the car a traffic cop saw coming in from that brewery the night two guys were bumped off out there. Now listen, both of you. You've been playing games with a bad mob, and we're after that mob, and we're going to make it hard for you if you don't spring something. We want to know the name of every guy in the hi-jack crowd that's been supplying you with booze. I've been decent to you, Joe, and you, too, Mag, as long as I've known you. But if you don't play ball with me now somebody is going to get hurt. All we want is the names of the guys. We intend to get 'em."

Spinoza took a length of hose from the desk and hefted it. He looked at Latanzio. Latanzio shrank back.

"Gawd Almighty, don't use that!" shouted Mag Haggerty.

"Joe," said Carmody, "how about it?"

"I don't know! I don't know!" yelled Latanzio.

Spinoza went to work on him. Mag Haggerty screamed. The room was sound-proof.

Latanzio fell on the floor, kicked, heaved, yelled.

Mag Haggerty shouted, "Joe, tell 'em! Don't be a fool!"

Carmody gripped her arm, "Don't you be a fool! How about it?"

She blanched.

"They'll kill me! They'll kill me!" screamed Latanzio.

"Mag," said Carmody, "come clean. You know."

She glared at him. "Let the Wop up!"

Spinoza sat back. Latanzio, sobbing, lay in a huddle.

Mag Haggerty put her hands on her hips. "Joe," she said, "we can't be fools. We're business people. Tell 'em and I'll okey it."

Latanzio stammered, "Well, Dorn and there was Spats Pazzo—him that's dead—and Sam Dvorak and Bat Price and Charley Haas and—and—" He gulped and looked at Mag.

"And?" drawled Carmody.

"Jeeze, he'll kill me!"

"Who, the main guy?" asked Carmody.

Spinoza swung his length of rubber hose.

"Aw, cripes, a guy named Napo," said Mag Haggerty.

"Napo, Mag? Napo who?" said Carmody.

"You don't know him. He ain't ever been mugged. A young guy. That's all I ever heard—Napo."

"Tall and slim and dark?"

"Yeah, kinda."

"Where's he live?"

She shook her head. "I don't know. Them guys ain't telling even customers where they live."

Carmody stretched and smiled. "Mike, what did I tell you? Tall and slim and dark. Mag, give me those names again, so I can write 'em down."

With the list of names he went to Police Headquarters, and from the files in the Bureau of Criminal Identification he discovered that James "Bat" Price had served two years in Sing Sing for robbery; that Charles Haas, alias Charley Hasbrouck, had served short terms in the penitentiaries of Missouri and Illinois; that Samuel Dvorak, alias Sam Devore, had done time in Atlanta for mail robbery and another term in Massachusetts for house-breaking. These bulletins, with pictures accompanying, had been sent out by the various states during the past seven years. There was nothing concerning a man named Napo.

But Headquarters, on the advice of Carmody, sent out alarms for the old offenders, and these alarms spread not only throughout the city, but to cities beyond, in other states.

"Through them, or one of them," said Carmody to Spinoza, "we ought to get this guy called Napo."

"Looks," said Spinoza, "as if this case is going to postpone my wedding."

Carmody stared into space.

DORN STABBED a broad finger at the newspaper. "And this—hell, the cops are out for blood! Yesterday they started cleaning up. Guys, they're after us! They're after us, and in the meantime, cripes, they accidentally pull in two guys wanted for a bank stick-up in Providence. In Latanzio's—ah, Gawd that Carmody and Spinoza again! Them guys are sure poison. And—oh, my Gawd, here's our pictures! It looks like me, too. You, too, Sam—and you and Charley, Bat."

"How'd they know?" asked Bat Price.

Napo said, "Latanzio."

"But it don't say so," said Dorn.

"It wouldn't. The dicks gave Latanzio a break."

Bat Price got up and paced the room. "Damn Spats! Damn Spats!"

Dorn said, "And you, Napo. But just Napo. That gives you a good break."

"That's the only name Latanzio knew me by. That's the only name a lot of guys know me by."

Charley Haas said, "We should have took Spats for a ride long ago."

"Never mind what we should have done," said Napo quietly. "It's what we have to do now. You guys better blow this town. It's not safe. This jam's a bad one and the big fella can't help us. I've had a talk with him. He was nice about it, but he made me understand. We didn't kill this kid, but Spats was one of us, and that'll go against us along with killing them two guys at the brewery, and I'll have another count against me because I was with Marino when he bumped off Shotzendorf. You guys have got to breeze. But right now you guys are in worse danger than me, because your mugs are in the sheets and mine ain't. All they got on me is a name. It's too bad, boys. We been doing nice until Spats pulled that bone. I'll give you all what jack's coming to you, and then it's so-long."

It was the longest unbroken speech they had ever heard Napo make. He stood against the wall, lean and dark and cool. They all looked at him a little sadly.

"It's tough, Napo," said Dorn. "We been good buddies. You come with us, Napo."

Napo shook his head. "No. And you guys better split up, too. In this case there ain't safety in numbers."

Dvorak said, "Napo, you ain't well yet. It ain't right to leave you alone."

"Hell, I'm all right, and I'd rather be alone. If you hit Akron, look up my friend, Tom O'Rourke. He'll hide you. Don't worry about me. I'll get out of this. They got nothing on me yet. I'll blow the town in a few days."

When they left that night, Napo felt a great loneliness descend upon him. To him they were good men, all of them, and he hated to see them go. He sat in his flat, smoking one cigarette after another, staring at the picture he had cut from *Vanity Fair* and thinking of Joyce Travers.

His dreams, his hopes, his tower of ambition, were toppling. He felt sad and depressed. He felt like the Emperor Napoleon looked in that picture of the retreat from Moscow. He wondered if he were in any way related to the Emperor.

It was a damn shame. Here he had climbed the road to success, had been in well with the big fella, had steered clear of liquor and women and rough joints.

And he hadn't caused much killing, either. Only a few guys. And then Spats—that Dago—had to go and get mixed up with some broad and then run away with that kid. Napo felt the sharp pinch of Fate keenly.

He had tried to be a nice guy, reading up on etiquette and wearing good clothes and acting like a gentleman. He had tried to make something of himself. Now he would have to start all over again, and it wasn't easy to get guys as good as Sam and Heinie and Charley and Bat.

He took a bath and felt refreshed. He put on clean clothes. He worked up some measure of spirit. Why, say, they hadn't anything definite on him. He would shake this town and go back to Akron and start all over again.

Next morning he went down to see Antonio and Antonio looked troubled.

"It looks bad, Napo, yes."

"Not so bad," said Napo. "The boys have breezed."

"But you, Napo."

Napo shrugged.

Antonio removed his pince-nez and wiped them with his silk handkerchief. "Napo, I don't like to say this, no. But, look, I have a business here, and you being looked for, it's bad for my business, yes." He looked miserable.

Napo's scalp tightened. He looked down into the traffic of Broad Avenue.

Antonio made motions with his hands. "Of course, Napo, we are friends, yes. I would do anything for you, but—"

"I heard you the first time," muttered Napo.

"Napo, you ain't mad, yes?"

"Why the hell should I be mad?"

Antonio replaced his pince-nez and sighed, "Such a dumb thing that Spats did!"

Napo remained silent. Antonio turned and went to the table and put his nose down among his beautiful flowers. Then he left the room.

Napo sat down and stared at the carpet. He scarcely heard Carrie Noll come in. She stood looking at him for a long moment. He seemed so drawn and sad and alone.

"Napo."

He did not look up.

She came over and sat down beside him. "Napo, boy, it looks bad. Why don't you get out of this town?"

"I'll go when I'm damn good and ready."

"Go now. You look rotten, Napo. You ain't well."

"I'm all right."

"You're not. For God's sake, listen to reason. Go away. Listen, boy, take me with you. You need someone to look after you. I want to look after you, Napo. I love you. I'll do anything for you. I don't want money, Napo. I don't want anything. I only want to be with you. I've known a lot of guys, Napo, but you're the first I ever loved like this."

She grasped his hand. She bent over and sobbed and kissed it.

Napo sat rigid, staring straight ahead. His nerves vibrated. There was a thumping in his heart. Carrie frightened him. He was afraid of her. There was danger in women—in this kind of woman. He had avoided and evaded her for months. He would not let her break through the wall he had built around himself.

"Don't be a fool!" he muttered. "Cut out this mush."

"Napo, boy, it ain't mush. My heart's busting for you. I love you, Napo. Let me take care of you. Let's go away—together. Oh, Napo!"

Her arm went around his neck and she put her head on his chest. She held him tightly.

"Don't, Carrie!"

"Napo, Napo!" she sobbed.

He became furious. He took hold of her arms and wrenched them from his neck. He pushed her off and stood up. She fell back into the chair. Tears were streaming down her cheeks, and she looked broken.

He turned his back on her, put on his hat, and walked to the door. He opened it and went out quietly. But he was trembling, and beads of perspiration were on his forehead.

THE GARDEN PAVILION was strung with many Chinese lanterns, and a full moon looked down through the trees. There were many little booths containing merchandise and novelties contributed by the merchants of the city. There were men in white flannels and girls in light summer dresses, and there was laughter and conversation and gayety.

A band played on the circular dance-floor. The floor was like a veranda, open to the night and the stars, and vines grew on bits of lattice-work. Beyond the railing were many people who could not afford to pay admission. But they looked on, some of them wistfully. Around the dance-floor were many little tables at which sat people drinking refreshments. Others danced to the syncopated rhythm of the orchestra. The saxophone warbled, the drum rolled, cymbals clashed and the trombone hooted and was then silenced by the clear, keen challenge of the cornet.

Napo leaned against a veranda post, smoking a cigarette. He wore a neat blue flannel coat, gray flannel trousers and russet shoes. His black hair was slicked back. He stood serene in all his lean dark smoothness. He cut a figure that was to be envied, and he carried himself like one to the manner born.

He was pleasantly thrilled. It was the first time he had ever been in an atmosphere such as this, and he drew it close to his heart. All the girls were clean and pretty. They danced grace-fully, and so did the men. The Chinese lanterns, the cool breeze, the light liquid laughter—all put into Napo's heart a longing for undefined things.

This was what he wanted. This was what he would get. He would begin all over again, choose new men carefully, run a racket in some other city. Akron was as good as any. The passing of Spats along with the chaos he had caused, was a thing of the past. Napo mused that he would join whatever big gang there was in Akron and then slowly work toward the lead. A few men might have to be killed, but such things are inevitable if you ever hoped to win success.

The music stopped and the dancers drifted off the floor. And Napo caught his first glimpse that night of Joyce Travers. She was crossing the floor, slim and regal and beautiful to behold. Napo stepped out to cut her off. She saw him and smiled, and he went up to her and bowed slightly.

"So glad you came!" she said.

"Yes," said Napo. "It is a nice place."

"Isn't it *beautiful!*"

"Yes," said Napo.

"And how are you feeling? I remember you were ill—"

"Oh, I'm feeling fine."

"Well, I'm so glad to hear that!"

"Yes. Will you dance with me?"

"Of course! I'll meet you right here for the next number."

"Thank you very much," said Napo.

She laughed in that soft way of hers, tilting her head slight-ly, and then went off. Napo returned and stood by the veranda post. He felt like somebody.

And when he danced with Joyce Travers, he felt as if he were in what some people called paradise. She seemed to melt in his arms. She moved with him as if she were part of him. He could smell the perfume of her hair. Her hand felt soft in his, and at times he felt the elusive touch of her breast.

He did not mind the pain in his side, nor the way the effort of dancing sapped his energy. He was sick and weak; he knew that; but he was happy, too, and would have danced with her all night, until he dropped from exhaustion. For months he had hoped for this bit of ecstasy, and neither pain nor the ominous thunder of the law could rob him of it.

There were two encores, and at the end Napo smiled and said, "You dance fine."

"You do too, you know."

"Will you sit down with me and have a drink?" he dared.

"I'd love to, Mr. Damiani, but I am so busy."

Napo was at a loss. He wondered if he had overstepped himself, and groped for something to say.

But Joyce Travers said, "Perhaps later we might have another dance."

"Yes, yes," said Napo, his eyes lighting up. "I'll look for you."

"Do!"

He watched her walk away. He ached for her. But he wore a mask again as he went back and stood by the veranda post. His breathing was jerky, and his stomach trembled, and his side pulsed with pain. He looked around for a chair. He was moving towards one when a man approached him and said:

"Pardon me, but somebody wants to see you outside."

Napo recognized him as the man who had taken his ticket at the entrance.

Puzzled, he followed the man to the gate, and saw a uniformed policeman standing there. The policeman beckoned. Napo's scalp tightened, but he went forward.

The policeman said, "There's a little summer house over there. Come along a minute, will you?"

The policeman took his arm, but Napo shrugged off the hand

and went along. He stepped into a small summer house and saw a girl and a man sitting on a bench.

"Is this the man?" asked the officer.

"Yes, that's him," said the girl.

The policeman said, "This young lady claims that one day in the park you passed her while she was sitting with that guy Pazzo. She says Pazzo said he was a friend of yours."

Napo recognized her, and caught his breath. But he said, "She's mistaken."

"Oh, no, I ain't," said Fanny. "Me and my motorman friend here were looking up at the dance-floor and we saw you dancing. You're the man. I got a good memory for faces."

The price of a dance!

The policeman was holding his arm. "Well, anyhow, suppose you come along to the station-house. You, too, miss."

"I sure will," said Fanny.

They walked out past the pavilion. The band was playing. People were dancing. Napo saw Joyce Travers swing close to the railing, in the arms of a tall, blond man. They were smiling.

Napo looked away, and a lump caught in his throat.

CARMODY SAT in the back room of the station-house, picking his teeth with a shaved-down match. Napo sat facing him, but looking at the floor. "So your name is Napoleon Damiani," said Carmody, and regarded a number of small white cards he had taken from Napo's pocket.

"Yes," said Napo.

"Napo for short, eh?"

"Never heard of it."

"H'm." Carmody looked at his watch.

They waited in silence. After a while the door opened and Latanzio was shoved in by Spinoza.

Napo sat rigid.

Latanzio bowed his head and fidgeted with his hands.

Carmody said, "Joe, is this Napo?"

Latanzio was unable to utter a word, but he nodded his head.

Carmody jerked his thumb. "All right, Mike. Take him back. Mandelbaum come in yet?"

"No. But I phoned him, and the other guys."

"Good."

Spinoza took Latanzio out and Carmody creaked his swivel-chair.

"Well, Napo, this looks bad."

Napo asked quietly, "Why?"

Carmody shrugged. "Several stick-ups, killing of Shotzendorf, killing of two guys at a brewery in the country. And Link's death."

"What's that got to do with me?"

"That's what we're going to find out. You know, Napo, crime is a bad thing. It doesn't pay. You can beat the racket just so long, but in the end you walk into a trap. You stumble over something you hardly notice and the whole works come down on top of you. Like this thing tonight."

"I'm still in the dark," said Napo.

"Light will come."

Mandelbaum came in next and looked hard at Napo.

"Take a good look," said Carmody, "and tell me if you think this was the guy was with Marino that night Shotzendorf was killed."

"Jake, it looks like him. By God, it looks like him!"

"What I thought."

"It is him, Jake!"

"You're crazy," said Napo.

"Am I?" snapped Mandelbaum. "Listen, guy. I couldn't have described you, but now that I see your face again I know it!"

Napo chuckled. "I still think you're crazy."

"All right, Mandelbaum," said Carmody. "You can go."

"*That's* the guy," clipped Mandelbaum as he went out.

Napo was holding himself taut as a bow-string, while trying to appear outwardly calm. It seemed incredible that he should be in the hands of the law. It had all happened so casually, so smoothly, that there was about it an air of unreality. No chase, no fight. Merely a trap set by nothing but circumstances—a trap that had closed down gently upon him and was now pressing tightly. He, Napoleon Damiani, a man of vision, in the hands of the law!

Dr. Pennell came in, and Napo recognized him immediately. Spinoza also entered, and a policeman.

"Doctor," said Carmody, "we believe we have here the man you treated that night when four gangsters entered your house."

"Oh!" exclaimed Dr. Pennell.

"Take your shirt off, Napo," said Carmody.

Napo closed his lips tightly and did not move. They were closing in on him! His eyes flashed.

Spinoza and the policeman came over and took off his coat, then his shirt and undershirt.

Dr. Pennell bent down. "Yes, that is the wound. And the man is not well. He has not been taking care of himself."

"Thank you, doctor," said Carmody.

Carmody stood up and put his hands on his hips. "Napo, you've been identified by Mandelbaum as the guy was with Marino when Link and Shotzendorf were killed. Dr. Pennell says he fixed your wound. That girl identified you as a friend of Pazzo's. Latanzio says that you and Dorn and Pazzo and Haas and Price and a guy named Dvorak all ran together. Now what the hell have you got to say?"

Napo pulled on his undershirt and said, "Ask Max Aronstein, my lawyer."

NAPO, BEING a man of vision and therefore of imagination, foresaw doom. The possibility of actual extinction was not yet entirely comprehensible, but the sequence of events that would lead up to it inundated him. He visualized the trial, the grilling, the days and weeks and months behind bars, the legal gymnastics of the state, the wear and tear on his system, which even now was run down and hardly equal to the task. He did not visualize these details correctly, since he had never gone through a similar experience before and knew next to nothing about the machinery of the law.

Max Aronstein came to see him at eleven that night in the station-house lock-up and Napo told his story, interrupted often by quick, sharp questions on the part of the lawyer. Aronstein was a small, beady-eyed man, prematurely bald, and hard-boiled.

"Well, Napo," he said, when Napo had finished, "you're in hot water, aren't you? Yes, yes, indeed. Now get me, kid. I'm no genius, but I'm a damned good lawyer, and when a client is in bad, I tell him straight to his face. You—are—in—bad, Napo."

"Hell, I know that."

"Good you do. You've also been caught at a time when press and public and the whole damned police department are shouting for blood. If these guys had only one-tenth of the evidence they've got on you, they would still try to burn you. See what sentiment against a string of killings does? As it is, they've got enough evidence to burn you and any guy that's ever been associated with you.

"I'm not an optimist, Napo. I'm a tough nut and I'm out to prevent guys from going to the chair who rightfully, according to all laws, should go there. The Almighty Dollar is my lord, and nothing else matters. How much have you got, Napo?"

"About fifty thousand."

"Well, that isn't so much, but a friend of yours has promised to add to that. He's standing by the best he can, but he can't do anything besides shell out money. I hope you realize that, kid."

"The big fella is okey."

"You said it. Now, Napo, there's nothing to do but plead guilty. Absolutely nothing else we can do. Then I'll have to warble a long yarn in your defense, along lines that you did not commit actually any of the killings, that they were done over your head. We'll have to rake up some character witnesses and that will cost money, too. You don't look tough and you must at all times act like a gentleman. I'm not the guy to paint a rosy picture for you, and I want to tell you right now that you have just one chance out of a hundred of getting out of this. You have ninety-nine chances of winding up in the chair. It's my business to pick the one chance, and I'm not saying I can do it. I can only try. Frankly, kid, I've never had a tougher case."

Many things combined to shatter Napo; his poor health, his brooding nature, his imagination, and the crushing evidence against him. The little cell was a fit place in which to brood; and alone, in the dark, away from watchful eyes, he let himself wallow in despair.

He saw no possibility of his ever getting out of the net. Success now seemed far beyond his reach. Joyce Travers, about whom he had spun romance, was a lost hope. The limousine with the chauffeur riding in the open, was another hope that paled and was lost in the darkness of what lay beyond. Out of all the hodge-podge of illusions, nothing remained. And one reality grew in his mind—Carrie Noll.

When illusions have died, regret creeps in. So with Napo. If he had gone with Carrie that day when she wanted him to go, when she told him she loved him, surely he would not be sitting now in this tomb-like cell. But he had built a dream around Joyce Travers, and he was paying the price of a dance and a few moments of ecstacy.

Pity follows regret, sometimes even in the strongest men; and pity grew in Napo's heart, throughout the night. And when the well of pity is drained, the underlying nature of a man bites to the surface. And the underlying nature of Napo was naturally and essentially vicious, otherwise he would never have been a wolf of the streets.

In the morning he was told that Antonio Callineri had been taken into custody. Joyce Travers had been interviewed by detectives, and had said that she had met Napo through Antonio. She was shocked and mortified, and hoped that Napo would get the death penalty. That was bitter gall for Napo. Antonio, who had a big business at stake, confessed freely that he had permitted Napo to store liquor in the buildings at his country hot-houses and was wheedled into telling how Napo and Marino had killed Spider Link.

Close upon this staggering information came the news that Bat Price and Charley Haas had been picked up in Cleveland at almost the same time that Sam Dvorak and Heinie Dorn had been picked up in a roadside restaurant by state troopers near Harrisburg, Pennsylvania.

The last ounce of hope was squeezed from Napo, and he became sullen and morose and uninterested even in death.

An officer came for him and took him into the back room of the station house, Carmody and Spinoza were there, and the officer went out. Napo slumped into a chair, a drawn, sick and weary man, with a droop to his mouth and a dark, sullen look in his eyes. A bird was singing in the alley back of the station-house, the sun was shining brightly, and a warm summer breeze puffed in through the window.

"Well," clipped Spinoza, "your goose is cooked, Napo. Your boy friends are being brought in on fast trains, Callineri is a witness for the State, and the great Napoleon has about as much chance as a rat in a trap."

Napo thought of the picture of Napoleon's retreat from Moscow.

"Worlds of evidence," went on Spinoza. "Mandelbaum, swears you were with Marino. Fanny Hale and Callineri turning State's. We've had a nice cell cleaned out for you in the county jail, and we're taking you there this morning. This trial won't take long, Napo. It's open and shut. You're as good as dead now."

It might have impressed Napo, if he hadn't known as much before he entered the room.

Carmody was placid. "It's always the way, Napo. I've seen

others like you before. You all rise and then you fall, and we go around picking up the pieces. You guys, all of you, think you're smart. You think everybody else, including us cops, are dumb. Maybe we are dumb, Napo. But ain't it funny how in the end you get yourself licked? Fact. Why, say, we ain't as responsible for landing a gunman as he is for landing himself. We ain't smart, Napo; we ain't got a lot of brains. Brains pay more than a cop gets for his salary. But it's the system, Napo, that gets a criminal—not one man, but the whole Force, the system. Ain't you ever heard a wise gambler say that he can't beat a system? And after all, Napo, the law is *some* system."

An officer looked in through the doorway and said, "There's a broad to see Napo."

"Tell her to go places," said Spinoza.

"No, let her in," drawled Carmody.

Carrie Noll came in and stood in the center of the floor. Her eyes were red-rimmed. She was sad, and sadness always makes a beautiful woman look more beautiful.

"Napo," she murmured.

"Hello," muttered Napo.

"Napo, is there anything I can do?"

He shook his head and stared bitterly at the floor. He did not want to look at her. She was a woman and she represented softness, and if he could have fallen into her arms it would have been a paradise far more profound than the haloed one in which he had bathed during that dance with Joyce Travers. But beyond Carrie's paradise there would be barren darkness. He would not stoop to her now. For months she had tried to bend him to her charms and he had resisted. A compromise at this late stage was not in keeping with his ego nor with the bitterness of his mind. He turned his back on her. She wilted and sobbed.

Spinoza said, "This guy don't want to see you, sister. You better breeze."

"Napo—Napo!" she pleaded.

Napo was unmoved.

She turned slowly and went out, crying.

"Ain't he a mutt?" said Spinoza.

Carmody sighed and stood up. "Be right back, Mike."

He strolled out of the room and Spinoza sat back in the swivel-chair, his arm on the desk and his hand on his gun.

"You ain't human, Napo," he said. "Didn't you see that girl was all broke up?"

"Dry up," muttered Napo, because he had seen.

The telephone bell rang and Spinoza picked up the receiver.

"Hello.... Oh, hello, sunbeam.... What's that? Am I all right? Of course, I'm all right. Listen, sunbeam, forget that. We're taking this guy Napo over to the county jail in a couple of minutes, soon as the wagon gets here.... I know, I know, but stop worrying. The wedding comes off tomorrow as planned. Yes, and how! Sure. What's that?..."

He chuckled and kept creaking in his chair.

Napo's scalp tightened. In the short space of a second an idea swung around in his head, then stopped and pointed in one direction: escape. It was not a plan, for a plan is in some measure hinged on reason. It was merely an idea, born to full maturity in a split-second.

He shot from his chair and caught Spinoza's gun-hand as the latter tried to jerk up the gun. Spinoza and the chair crashed to the floor and Napo ripped the gun free, reeled backward and fired blindly, without judgment, without necessity. The instinctive blood of the killer roared through his veins.

He turned and leaped through the window, down into the alley.

Carmody burst into the room followed by two policemen.

"My God!" he cried.

Spinoza was sitting up, holding his leg. "That way, Jake! The window!"

"Where you shot?" asked Carmody as the two policemen went out through the window.

"Leg! Here! Never mind. Get him, Jake—get him!"

Carmody shot through the window.

Spinoza crawled over to the desk and reached for the telephone. He heard Rose yelling.

"It's all right, sunbeam. Everything's all right…. No, no, I'll call you later—later!"

He hung up and groaned. "That pup had to postpone my wedding!"

FROM THE alley Napo ran into a street, and he heard the call of police whistles. There was no time to walk and appear like an ordinary pedestrian. He ran, and when he was half-way down the block he saw a policeman appear at the next corner. He stopped and looked back. Carmody and two policemen were rushing out of the alley.

Napo rushed into a drug-store. He ran past a number of people having ice-cream sodas, past a drug-clerk, into a room filled with a lot of bottles, and through to a door. He yanked open the door and came out into a courtyard. Beyond this was a wire fence. He scaled it and crashed through the back door of another building. Then he was running through a grocery store. A fat man stood in his path, mouth agape, unable to move. Napo struck him aside and cannoned out into the street.

His resolve was narrowed down to a hot, burning point. He was ready to kill anybody who tried to stop him, man, woman or child. The innate vicious nature of his being was fully on the surface. The will to live was equal to the will to kill. All other emotions, thoughts of past, present or future, were dimmed by the one fierce craving of the moment.

He covered two blocks, his gun in his hand. He passed many people, who stood like images, transfixed and shocked at the sight of a man with a gun. They as well as Napo heard the call of the police whistles. And that sound, along with the fleeing picture which Napo presented, held them frightened and spellbound.

As he crossed the next street Napo saw two policemen coming up it with their guns drawn. He ran faster and was almost to the next corner when a policeman appeared there. Blocked, Napo chose the nearest means of escape. He dived into a hallway and pounded up a staircase. Before he reached the top he heard a whistle blow at the door below. He turned and fired two shots down the staircase.

Then he ascended another staircase, and at the next landing a woman opened a door. She caught one glimpse of the man with the gun, screamed and banged shut the door. Napo cursed and climbed a third staircase, breathing hard. His whole insides shook. His side pained, his legs wobbled and dragged, and perspiration oozed from his skin.

He heard feet pounding up the stairs which he had left behind. Furious, he fired two shots downward, to keep them back. Up he went—climbing six flights of stairs, and then a seventh that brought him out upon the roof. He staggered, closed the roof door and stood swaying.

When he heard a thump against the door he fired at it. The cool Corsican was no longer cool. His hair was disheveled and his dark face gleamed. His lips writhed against his teeth and his eyes were two small points of black fire, burning with desperation born of stark fear.

After a moment he backed up, step by step, then turned and ran across the roof. There must be a fire-escape. He would go down it, in through a window, killing anybody who got in his way. He reached one end of the roof and looked over. There was no fire-escape. He turned and ran to another side. No fire-escape there. Desperate, he ran to still another side. And found none.

One of these new-fangled fire-proof buildings! A chill swept over him. He turned to retrace his steps, when he saw half a dozen policemen running across the roof.

"Oh, God!" moaned Napo.

They did not fire at him. They were spread out, holding their guns, but they did not fire. They knew they had him cornered.

He bent over the edge of the roof. Directly below was an awning. He shoved his gun into his pocket, slipped over, held his breath, and let go. He knew he had to be quick, and he was. The canvas broke his short fall even as he caught hold of and held one of the supporting rods. That side of the awning broke away from the base, but the other side held.

Napo could do nothing but hold on. As it was, he was below the window ledge, and had not the strength to draw himself up the steel rod and so to the window. His body turned slowly, from side to side, six stories above the street.

He looked up and saw the heads of policemen out over the edge of the roof.

One said, "All right, Napo. We'll get you. Just hang on there a bit."

He hung on. Some of the heads disappeared, but two remained. Napo's thoughts were not in any way concentrated. He was tired, and energy of mind and body were being consumed towards hanging on to the steel rod. He felt like going to sleep, and he did close his eyes. There was no chaos of mind, no keen straining to the future, no welling up of the past. His brain, so weary because his body was weary, seemed to function dully.

Then the window was open and he saw Carmody there. The picture of Carmody and all that he represented, accelerated Napo's brain. Thoughts, but a moment ago dying off, now roared through his consciousness. He saw Carmody lean out, and he looked up into the tranquil face.

"Just a minute, Napo—just a minute."

Carmody was muscling out over the sill, his arms extended.

And then Napo took his eyes from Carmody and looked at his own hands. One was gripped above the other on the steel rod, and the knuckles were white. His eyes widened and stared, not with horror, but with that fixed intensity of one about to die.

He saw Carmody's hand creeping down the steel rod. It almost touched his own—but not quite.

Napo let go.

The Kill

A private dick is sent to clean a town and finds someone else with the same idea.

HAGGERTY WAS a tough burg.

The Agency sent me down there from St. Louis. The Boss gave me a rough idea of what I was to do. But he gave me a letter to Elias Starkhurst who, he said, would give me the same idea polished and trimmed to perfection.

I packed the Gladstone and caught a southbound bus.

It said *Attorney-at-Law* on Starkhurst's shingle.

"So you're Polk," the old boy said.

"Polk," I said.

He was a big man, old, white-haired, brown-faced, powerful in a bony way. He had a voice like a fog horn. He had a long, square jaw. Bold eyes.

"Polk," he said, as if trying to get used to the word. Then he grinned like a kid, waved a big hand. "Sit down, Polk. Have a stogie?" He knocked open a box.

I shook my head and said "Thanks," showing him the cigarette I was smoking.

His face got grave, then grim, then it mellowed a bit and became meditative.

"Polk," he said, "I hope to God you're the man we want."

"We?"

He started a cheroot. "We," he repeated, nodding. "Myself—and the committee of reputable merchants and landowners. I don't have to tell you what put Haggerty on the map. She's a tough town. You know that. She's the headquarters for a beer and alky clique that we are trying to break up. I'm sick to death of this bald-faced lawlessness. And besides—farmers and those living in the country are going to Baxter instead these days. They say it's not safe to walk the streets of Haggerty. What's the result? Merchants are beginning to feel the pinch. The sheriff is powerless. Likewise his deputies."

I had to laugh. "And what am I supposed to do?"

"You," he said, pointing the red end of the cheroot at me, "are to find the books of the Poo-bah of the outfit. He must keep books. Trouble is, we don't know where he lives. This is a town of only a few thousand people. Still, we don't know where he lives."

"Who is he?"

"His name's Bill Herrod."

"And—why the books?"

"We want to get him up on Federal tax charges. We want to find out where he banks. We reckon that when we start proceedings he'll disappear. We don't particularly care whether he pays taxes or not. We just want to get him out of Haggerty."

"Not bad. Where could I pick him up?"

"There's a speakeasy down near the river which he frequents pretty regularly. I have here a picture of him—clipped from a year-old newspaper. You can't miss him."

"And you want his books."

"Yes—and his bankbook, if possible."

"Okey," I said.

His eyes twinkled. "I hope you're the man, Polk."

"Don't I?"

He laughed. We shook.

THE HOTEL was a two-storied frame building with a sagging veranda. I had a room on the top, and I could look over some shacks and see the Mississippi, broad and flat and ochre-colored. There was no private bath, but I had running hot and cold water and two towels with holes in them. It was beginning February, and raw.

I got second-rate fried chicken in the smelly dining-room,

and smoked a butt in the lobby afterwards. The floor of the lobby had no rugs. Six rocking chairs faced the big plate-glass window that looked out on the veranda and the street. The sill was low, and scarred from many feet that had jammed there while men rocked.

It was dark when I put on the overcoat and went out. I walked down the shabby main street that was cold and dusty, past the

stores that weren't doing a thriving business. I turned right and walked down another dusty street, and when it bent slightly I could see the lights of a steamboat on the river.

I turned right again and walked along a street that was near the river. It had some trees on it, and some telephone poles, and some wooden houses that needed paint.

I had no trouble getting in the speak. It was a long, low room, with a bar against the back wall. There were two tables at either side of the door which I entered, and the door faced the front of the bar. At the left end of the room was a door that had *Toilet* over it.

A couple of worn-down janes sat at one of the tables. Three men stood at the bar. I had a gin fizz that wasn't so hot. One of the janes got up after a while and went to the telephone. She bawled out some boy friend. The telephone was in the corner beside the door leading to the toilet. It stood on a triangular shelf where the front wall and side wall met, and the girl had to get on her toes to talk. It was funny, her line.

A crummy joint. I hung around till closing time. I didn't see Bill Herrod. I went back to the hotel scuffling cold dust in the wind. I wondered how long I would have to drink that bath-tub gin before Herrod showed up.

I went there every night for three nights. On the third night the beef-faced bartender got curious.

"Stranger?" he said.

"Yeah."

"Selling?"

"Trying to," I said; and then said, "These merchants aren't buying much."

"What you selling?"

"Farm implements. Haven't sold any yet."

He sighed. "Hard times."

I agreed with him, and he gave me a drink on the house. I hung around till closing time again, but there was no Bill Herrod. I wondered if he'd got wise to a tail.

I told Starkhurst about it. He was patient.

"He'll come," he said. "I don't see how he could possibly have found out."

That was all right by me. Starkhurst was paying.

Saturday night the joint was a little lively. When I drifted in at eight the four tables were crowded. There were two girls and a man at one, three men at another, a girl and a man at the third, and two girls and two men at the fourth. There were six guys at the bar. The bartender was calling me Jack.

The gang was making whoopee at nine o'clock when Bill Herrod came in.

The bartender said, "Well, well, hello, Bill."

"Hello, Hen."

The big beer-and-alky boss wore a big tan coat, a wide-brimmed hat and yellow gloves. There was a diamond in his tie. He didn't look like a pansy. He was one of the toughest-looking babies I ever laid eyes on.

I ordered Bourbon and ginger ale and mulled over the drink. There was nothing to do now but wait till the big boy went out and then tail him. I was standing at the end of the bar, with the toilet door behind me. The joint was stuffy with smoke, and one of the janes was trying to sing.

Herrod drank alone, and sometimes he looked at his watch. I figured he was waiting for somebody. He didn't look at anybody. He looked mostly at his drink, or at his reflection in the mirror. Some guy went to the telephone and tried to get a number. He didn't get it and he called the operator a name. He was tight.

The soused jane was trying to sing again. One of the guys with her shoved a drink in her face, and she drained the glass. But that didn't stop her. I was taking a long look at Herrod. I saw the bartender eying me, and I looked at my watch.

The drunk in the corner tried the phone again and another argument. He slammed the receiver into the hook. He leaned against the wall. The jane switched to another song and tried the high notes. The guy gave her a dirty look and tried the phone again.

The door opened and a tall, lean guy came in. He looked swanky and had one hand in his pocket. The other—gloved—held a cigar.

The door hadn't swung shut yet when the lights went out.

Somebody cursed. I don't know, but I had a hunch something was wrong, and I stepped away from the bar towards the middle of the floor.

I heard a stifled groan, then— "Jeeze…. Oh, Jeeze!" And the sound of a body falling. I heard a door bang shut.

"Hey!" shouted the bartender.

There was the crash of glass and a table going over, and the scuffle and scrape of feet. I stood rooted where I was, my hand clamped on the rod in my pocket.

"Lights!" some guy yelled.

"I heard somebody—" began a girl's voice. Then a shaft of light speared the room. It was the bartender holding a flashlight, and it swept around, stopped on my face, swept around some more.

"Who's hurt?" the bartender asked.

The beam, swooping downward over the bar, showed me a man's leg on the floor. Somebody else saw it too.

A girl yelled, "The man in the tan coat—"

"Gawd!" croaked the bartender.

He climbed on the bar and threw the light's beam down on the horizontal body of Bill Herrod. In Herrod's back, between the shoulder blades, was a horn-handled knife.

"He's been stabbed!" screamed a girl.

I went towards him and knelt down. I didn't touch the knife. I ran my hand beneath's Herrod's coat and felt his heart. There wasn't a murmur. I looked up at the bartender.

"This guy's been croaked," I said.

The bartender had a queer look in his eyes. He didn't say anything.

I stood up. "Well," I said, "you better get the sheriff."

He didn't say anything again. He set his jaw and walked along behind the bar. He shoved the drunk away from the telephone. He turned the crank.

The drunk said, "Ah, 's no use. Central's a bum."

But the bartender cranked and cranked. Finally he gave it up, walked behind the bar again and lit some candles. The joint looked crummier than ever in the candle-light.

He said, "Somebody run over and get the sheriff."

"Okey, Hen."

"Thanks, Johnny."

A guy beat it out.

The bartender came around front and looked down at the corpse. He bent down towards the knife.

I was lighting a butt. "Hey," I said.

He looked up at me. "Huh?"

"I wouldn't touch that knife."

"Why?"

"Fingerprints."

He said, "Oh," as if he didn't quite get it. But he left the knife alone.

THE SHERIFF said, "So they got Bill Herrod." He looked around at us with tired gray eyes. "Who did it?"

One of the janes said, "A guy came in the door as the lights went out. And I heard a door bang a minute after."

"Where's the guy?"

"He ain't here," said the bartender. "He disappeared."

"Know him?"

"Barney Allan."

The Sheriff exclaimed softly, "Um! The gambler, eh? I didn't know he had a grudge against Herrod. I'll have to get the coroner over. Where's the telephone?"

The bartender pointed.

The drunk cried, "I tell you it ain't no use."

The Sheriff looked at him. "What?"

"The telephone. I been tryin' to get a number for the last hour. Central's a bum."

But the Sheriff tried. He didn't have any luck, and he grumbled in his beard. He asked Johnny to run over and get the coroner out of bed. When Johnny had gone the Sheriff assumed a heavy official look.

"This," he said, like a guy revealing a mystery, "is murder!"

It wasn't news, but it made the janes sit up and take notice anyhow.

The Sheriff said, "Did anyone see the man who came in the door stab Herrod?"

"The lights were—"

"I know the lights were out. But somebody might have been standing or sitting near the door. Was Herrod standing alone?"

"Yeah," the bartender grouched. "Nobody was standin' near him. This guy"—me—"was at that end o' the bar. This guy was at the other end. These two guys were six feet to one side, and these other two guys were six feet t' other side. Everybody else was sittin', and this guy was tryin' to get his number on the phone. It was Barney Allan! That's who it was."

I put in, "The knife hasn't been touched, Sheriff. If you can grip it just below the hilt—"

He drew it out that way, careful not to touch the handle.

Then he began taking down names and addresses. When he got mine he looked at me quizzically. I made a motion with my eyes. He wrote down my name and turned away. He knew me, but he didn't let on.

The coroner came in with a bad cough and did his duty. The

blade had reached the heart. Death was practically instantaneous. They began to wonder what they should do with the body.

The bartender said, "I'll call a buddy of his." He added, "If I could get a telephone that worked." He set his jaw. "I'll go around to the cigar store."

He gave me a queer look on the way out.

The Sheriff looked around. "Remember, you—all of you—this is murder. If I have to summons you, I don't want any backin' out." He turned to the coroner. "Well, Jess, I guess I have to get hold of Barney Allan."

The door swung open.

Barney Allan stood there. His eyes took in the Sheriff and the crowd with one look, the dead man with another.

"So that's what happened," he said.

"Barney," the Sheriff said, "you're under arrest."

Barney looked startled, then amused. "Me?"

"Everybody saw you come in the door. You were gone when the lights went out."

Barney chuckled. "Yeah, that's right. When the lights went out I ducked back. I didn't know but some guy was sore because I beat him at cards. I ran." He shrugged. "I'll admit it wasn't the manly thing. As a matter of fact, when I got outside I felt ashamed of myself. That's why I hesitated about coming back."

"You always were a brazen guy," the Sheriff growled.

"Do you want to look at my gun?"

"No," the Sheriff said. "It wasn't a gun, Barney. It was a knife."

"Oh, I see."

The Sheriff was jangling manacles. "And the prints are still on the handle. Put your hands out."

"Well, if you feel that way about it...."

Barney smiled and put out his hands. Both of them were gloved.

WHEN I walked out into the street, it was drizzling. I walked along beneath the trees, looking up. I stopped. I saw a couple of wires hanging where they had been cut.

I went around and woke up Elias Starkhurst. He appeared in a big bathrobe.

"You've got them?" he asked.

"There's no need now. Herrod's dead."

"Dead!"

I gave him the lowdown, and he dropped into a chair and was speechless for more than a minute.

"But—who did it?"

"The Sheriff's got Barney Allan. They say he's a gambler."

"Yes, I know of him. Do you think he did it?"

"No."

Starkhurst squinted. "Do you know—who?"

"No. But it was somebody in the speak. They'll find out maybe when they photograph the fingerprints on the knife. Everybody in the speak was without gloves. Barney had gloves on. But I don't think he did it."

"God, this is—a shock!"

"Yeah," I said, "you might telephone Central and tell her a wire's down in Front Street. Tell the light people they have one down too."

"I wonder who killed him," the old boy mused.

"I wouldn't wonder," I said. "It was a neat job. The Boss will send you a bill when I get back."

"But you're not going?"

"What should I stay here for? The job's over. The big gun is spiked. No, thanks. I might have been in worse tank towns than this, but I can't remember."

"Well." He stood up and gave me the old smile. "Thanks for coming down."

When he shook my hand he gave me a kind of strange, mystified look. I went out thinking that he might have thought I put the knife in Bill Herrod.

I got in bed and stayed awake an hour figuring things out.

IN THE morning the guys in the lobby were talking about it. I brought the Gladstone down from the room and told the clerk to keep it behind the counter till I came back. I ate breakfast in the moldy dining-room, and left it wishing I hadn't. I had that after-the-gin feeling in the stomach.

Besides, it was still drizzling. And maybe you've heard of midwestern mud. Anyhow, the Sheriff looked down at the mouth.

"I took it over to the County Attorney's office," he said, meaning the knife. "Not a thing on it. One of the guys in the speak swears Barney wore gloves."

"Going to hold him?"

"Yes. Hold him? Of course! That guy's smooth tongue don't get across with me."

"The wires were cut, eh?"

"Yeah. Where they pass through the tree near the speak.... Say, don't you think Barney killed him?"

I shrugged, said, "I wouldn't know."

"But, anyway"—he shook a finger at me—"the guy that swung that knife wore gloves! And nobody but Barney had gloves on when the lights went out!"

"Okey." I stood up. "Well," I said, "I'm driving back to civilization." I hesitated. "Mind if I talk to Barney?"

"Go ahead."

I went in the cell and sat and gave the gambler a butt.

"Thanks," he said, and I gave him a light and he said, "Thanks," again.

"You're in a tough spot, aren't you?" I said.

He laughed to himself. "Seems so. But—what the hell—I'll get out of this. I didn't rub that guy out. Me—use a knife?" He laughed again, and let smoke dribble from his nostrils.

I liked his guts.

I said, "Anyhow, you're in a tough spot. Even if you get out of the Sheriff's hands, there's Herrod's playmates."

That changed his face. "Wasn't I the fool?" he said. "I mean, to run out when that happened?"

"Hard to say. I might have done the same."

He thinned his eyes on me. "What the hell are you, a shyster looking for a job?"

"No," I said, looking at my butt. "I'm a private dick."

"Oh-o, so that's what you are."

"And I don't believe you killed Herrod."

He got wary. "What's your game, stranger?"

"Business. If you've got any jack, I'll go after the guy that killed Herrod."

"Who killed him?"

"Listen," I said, patient. "I don't use a Ouija Board. I've only got a hunch you didn't. You don't have to fork over now. Fork over if I find the guy."

"How much?"

"I'll have to talk with my boss on long-distance."

He leaned back. "Okey."

The Boss was no piker. He said two thousand. Barney said that was all right, but I said how did I know he was a good debt. He said if I didn't think he was I should go to hell. I thought he was.

I went walking back towards the hotel to engage the room again. I heard a big car's cut-out behind me, and I looked around. It was a Packard, and I know an armored touring car when I see one. Just to be safe I swung into a cigar store.

I was three steps inside the door when I looked around and saw the muzzle of a Tommy-gun sticking through the curtains. I dived into a recession in the wall as the fireworks opened. I heard the beat of the gun, and I saw the glass showcase disappear. I saw the cash register kind of fold up and then the little sheet-iron stove. It happened and was over in less time than it took me to tell that.

I heard the car's cut-out dying away.

I heard the little tobacconist gibbering on the floor. I went over and looked at him. He wasn't scratched.

I went out into the street and looked up and down. I heard men exclaiming—other shopkeepers. I tramped on to the hotel. It figured that the guns thought I was in league with Barney Allan. Maybe that beef-faced bartender had started the rumor. And maybe they'd seen me come out of the jail.

The hotel clerk and some other guys were on the veranda.

"What happened?" the clerk choked.

I pulled a grin, though don't you believe it was from the heart. "I guess some guy was playing with a gun and it went off," I said.

I didn't start to shake until I got to my room. Then I flopped to the bed, and found it hard swallowing. The sweat was hot, too—and then cold.

I tried a shot of gin, spiting the stomach to soothe the nerves. I looked at myself in the mirror. I looked like some other guy.

WHEN I was fairly steady again I made a plan of the speakeasy on a sheet of paper. I marked down the bar, and the tables, and I put an X down to indicate each person as he or she stood or sat at the time the lights went off. I studied this thing a while, and then I went around to the telephone office.

I told the manager who I was, and he shook my hand. I said I'd like to speak to the girl who was on duty the night Herrod was killed and the wires cut. He took me to the girl.

I said, "Now, Herrod was killed at ten. The lights went out then, and the telephone was out of commission for some time before that. Do you remember when the last call came in or went out over that line?"

She said, "I remember some drunk arguing with me. It must have begun about twenty to ten. He wanted to speak to a girl named Agnes Mullaney. He didn't know the number. He said she lived in St. Louis. I told him he'd have to have the number. This kept on, from time to time, until ten—when it suddenly stopped."

"That was when the wire was cut," I told her.

I thanked her and went out.

Everybody who was in the speak at the time Herrod got the works was still in town. That is, I took it for granted everybody was in town. The Sheriff had warned each and every one of them not to go places. It meant that if they did before he lifted the ban, he would get another suspect.

This helped matters.

So I took a Brody that was not hallmarked by common sense.

I went to the speak.

The beef-faced bartender got a start out of that, and his freckled fat hand shook when he poured me out a tot of Bourbon. There were six other guys at the bar, three of them in a bunch, the others stray numbers.

I took a drag at the Bourbon and decided to get tough. I addressed the glass.

"Some wiseacres," I said, "took it into their heads to try out a Tommy-gun on me. I suppose you heard the racket. Well, they've got one hell of a nerve." I gave the bartender a dirty look. "I happen to be after the guy that got Herrod. If any dirty stumble-bum gets in my draft I'm going to hurt him. Have a drink, bartender."

"Uh, thanks."

"And you might broadcast that last load I gave you."

He looked innocent—about as innocent as the dog that stole the meat. The six other guys shot me some sidelong looks. I finished the Bourbon and smacked down the glass. I hung around a couple of hours and four of the guys who'd been in the night Herrod got it, turned up and had some drinks and talked about it.

That night I wandered around town, finding that I'd suddenly got the habit of using side alleys. I didn't stand in front of lighted store-windows, either. I drifted into a pool-room and found another one of the guys.

The drunk who'd been struggling with the telephone. He wasn't drunk now. He was shooting billiards with another guy. They didn't look up, and I stood back in the shadows and watched them spear the balls. They were pretty good.

I said, "That's a nice shot," once.

The guy who didn't get Agnes Mullaney looked up. "Thanks—" And then he squinted, then grinned. "Oh, you were there." He looked at his cue. "Too bad about Barney Allan."

"Oh, I don't know," I said.

"He's in a tough spot, though."

"I don't think so. Hell, he didn't kill Herrod."

The guy laughed. "Well, if he didn't—" He wagged his head. "Well, if he didn't, he'll sure get a bad break. Because they're gonna nail that guy."

"Who?"

"The State, of course."

Then I laughed. "Don't you believe it."

The guy's friend looked at me once and then looked everywhere else.

"Be seeing you," I said, and strolled out.

I ducked into an alley up the street and watched. The drizzle had stopped but the cold hung on—windless but penetrating. I went over the plan of the speak in my mind, checking up and wondering if I had the right hunch. I was still wondering when the two guys came out.

I tailed them through six different alleys until they came to a dark street near the coal yards. The rows of houses there were gloomy and I suppose in the daytime they would have looked sooty. I could smell the soft coal that was still damp from the recent rains, and I could smell soft coal smoke.

The two guys entered a three-story frame house, and I went

along in the shadow of the board fence on the other side of the street. There were about three lighted windows in the frame house, and then there was a fourth—on the top floor at the right. I leaned against the board fence.

I leaned there for an hour. Then I saw the light go out, and a couple of minutes later I saw the two boy friends come out and head back towards the center of town. When they had disappeared I crossed the street and entered the house, and I climbed the stairs, getting my bearings. I reached what I figured was the door to the room in which I had seen the light go off.

It took me ten minutes to baby open the lock. I used a little pocket flash, keeping the beam away from the windows. I saw two bags on the floor, both packed. I searched the room—bureau, closet—and found everything cleaned out. Then I busted open the bags.

I looked at the size in the collar of one of the shirts. It was fourteen and a half. That would be the little guy's—the guy who was soused the night of the kill. I dug deeper. I found a big oiled envelope with a rubber band around it. It was soiled and contained a couple of time-tables, some old letters, all addressed to Peter Hawes. Hawes was the little guy. I found some pictures too. One was of Hawes standing in athletic tights with arms folded. On the back of it was written, "Marble Circus, Kansas City, Mo." I slipped that back in the envelope, snapped back the rubber band.

Then I went after the other bag. There was no identification here. I found a couple of radio tubes and a pair of ear-phones, a switch and some wire, and a pair of rubber gloves. I put all the junk back and closed the bag. I'd broken the locks on both bags, so it was impossible to lock them. I didn't care much.

I left the place and went back to the hotel. I made a long-distance call and talked for ten minutes. I hung up and looked at my gun. Then I went around to the speak and found the joint fairly crowded. Hawes and his pal were there, and they gave me a funny look which I pretended not to notice. I had a drink alone at the bar.

I was having another when Hawes and his pal paid up and went out. I waited until the door banged, and then threw a dollar and a half on the bar. I beat it out the door and saw the two men hurrying up the street, about twenty yards away.

I yelled, "Hey!"

I didn't expect the next move. The two guys started to run. I ran after them, and yelled again, and I had my hand on the gun in my pocket. They swung into another street, and when they were midway to the next block I saw Hawes turn as he ran. I jerked behind a pole as his gun boomed. I heard the whistle of a bullet, and I leaned out and fired. The .38 jumped in my hand, but Hawes went down, sliding on his face.

The other guy hesitated, and I could see him hefting a gun. I fired over his head, and he took it into his head to skin out. I ran after him and fired another shot, over his head. He disappeared around the next corner.

As I reached Hawes, who was crawling, he turned and fired. I got a jolt in the left leg and skidded. He fired again, but the skid saved me, and I landed him, bearing him to the sidewalk. He groaned, "Oh, cripes!" hopelessly, and his gun rang on the walk. I was sore, and I belted him on the head with mine, then rolled off and tried to get up. I yelped. It was the leg.

"Where you hurt?" I said.

"Leg," he muttered.

"Oh," I said. "A leg for a leg."

He heaved and tried to use the gun again. I straight-armed his gun-hand and slammed him again with my gun. This time his head hit the sidewalk, and I reached over and took the gun from his hand.

It was cold sitting in the street, but I couldn't get up. In a few minutes I saw some men up at the corner and yelled to them. They came down the dark, cold street, but they came warily.

"What's up?" one of them called.

"Is that you, Sheriff?" I said.

"Yeah."

"This is Polk."

As he came closer I could see the big gun in his hand.

IT WAS kind of funny, Hawes and me sitting in the Sheriff's office, each with a bandaged leg resting on a chair. The Sheriff was there and he had a deputy with him. Hawes' face was drawn and bitter, and he had that look in his eyes that talks louder than a confession in words.

The Sheriff was kind of hot and bothered. "But look here, Polk. Why did you shoot this man? What right have you to shoot a man?"

"None," I said. "Except that I shot in self-defense."

"Yah," snarled Hawes.

I looked at the two bags that the deputy had brought over from the rooming house near the coal yards.

I said, "I hate to see an innocent man get it in the neck. I was sure Barney Allan was innocent. I was sure these guys were guilty until a little while ago. It's up to you to get the other one. But you've got the main squeeze right here. It's my contention that this is the guy killed Herrod."

The Sheriff said, "But everybody says this guy was on the phone. Besides, there were no fingerprints on the knife."

"Of course not," I said. "Will you open that yellow bag and drag it over?"

The deputy opened it, and I fished out the rubber gloves, the ear-phones, and a pair of heavy scissors.

"These scissors." I said, "cut the wires. These ear-phones were used to tune in on the telephone line coming out of the speak. This palooka's buddy was in the tree in the street through which the wires passed. He heard this guy talking to Central, and he waited for the key word. When that came he cut the wires, and Hawes killed Herrod."

"But," the Sheriff said, "how could he get from the phone—"

"He didn't. He stayed right there. He'd been in that corner for at least twenty minutes. He was waiting for Herrod to shift to a desirable position. When Herrod leaned against the bar with his left side. Hawes said the key word. As soon as the light went out he—threw the knife."

The Sheriff opened his eyes wide.

Hawes swallowed hard but said, "That's a dirty lie!"

I said, "It will be up to the State to break that story down. I called Kansas City tonight and got in touch with a guy named Swanson, who owns the Marble Circus. He said that a year ago you had an act with him. A knife-throwing act. It was a very good act. You used to get a line on an object, then a helper would blindfold you and you'd throw the knife. Now deny *that*."

Hawes turned gray and I saw his lips shake.

"Besides," I said to the Sheriff, "he wasn't drunk. The bartender swears he came in sober, and then he took only three highballs all the time he was there. The bartender says there were other nights when he drank as high as ten and never showed it. I demand his arrest, and it's up to the State to make him come across."

"Gosh, Polk," the Sheriff said, "you've done a lot for this here community."

"Sure," I agreed.

But I got Barney Allan's check for two thousand two hours before he was released, and I went right around to the bank and cashed it.

It took a week before the County Attorney got Hawes to squeal on his pal. It was this way. They told him that if he stood trial alone the State would want a death penalty. They promised him twenty years if he came across, and he came across.

Hawes had found it hard to get a job and he'd slid into the booze racket under Tony Chico, a big gun in Kansas City. Tony studied the situation in Haggerty and figured he was bigger than Bill Herrod. He sent Hawes and his pal after him.

Hawes had imagination, and instead of using a Tommy-gun he got fantastic.

He told about Tony too. But Tony denied everything, and a clever lawyer he had, proved that Hawes was a liar. Of course, Hawes wasn't. But Tony was a big gun.

They still think down in Haggerty that I turned Hawes in because I had the community's interest at heart.

The Spot and the Lady

It is altogether a different matter when the killer is made the victim.

BUTCH WOKE with a start and his big body creaked the springs of the cot when he moved. His hand settled on the .45 in his pants belt and his stomach grew rigid against his sweat-soaked undershirt. He raised himself on one elbow, his shaggy eyebrows bending over bitter eyes that fastened on the door.

He drew the big automatic and released the safety.

He put first one foot, then the other, on the floor. He rose slowly from the dirty bedclothes and stood with big feet planted wide apart. Beads of sweat stood out on his huge face. Sunlight stabbed through the blinds of green shutters, and the smells of a Dago street came in with the sluggish heat.

Butch had been in that room four days.

Cables in his neck tightened when the second knock sounded on the door. His gun steadied on the door, the base of his hand close against the right side of his waist.

Who the hell could have found him out?

He licked his lips and his Adam's apple oozed up and down his throat.

He was afraid. Butch, the killer, was afraid. That knock had sounded so gently, so casually, as if the one who had knocked was calm and at ease and self-assured.

Besides, Butch was weak, for his stomach felt like a hollow tomb. No food had passed between his lips in four days. His head ached from the lack of it.

And they'd come to rub him out.

He was not a patient man. The four days in the stuffy, sweltering room had almost driven him crazy. The smells of Dago food from the flat beneath had magnified his hunger.

This was the end. The mob's guns were outside the door.

For the third time that gentle knock sounded.

Butch snarled: "I warn you guys, it's smoke if you bust down that door!"

He moved on his big feet and pushed the big gun in front of him.

"Ah, Butch," droned a nasal voice, "don't be that way."

Butch felt his scalp tighten. That was a familiar voice. But not the voice he had expected.

He choked, "Cassidy?"

"Sure."

"What the hell do you want?"

"Oh, I just thought I'd come around. The frau that runs this joint said you ain't been out in days."

"What's that to you?"

"I hear you're on the spot, Butch."

Butch brought his feet together and his forehead wrinkled with thought. He shoved the gun into his pants belt, crossed the room and opened the door.

Cassidy strolled in, wearing a droll smile. The precinct dick was a small man. He had a hard straw hat slanted over one eye and a rag of a cigarette drooped from his lips. He closed the door and leaned indolently against it.

"Hot, ain't it, Butch?"

"Jeeze, it's terrible!" Butch mopped his face, his neck, his hairy chest.

Cassidy droned, "I seen some guys hanging around. Gus Strom… Lefty."

"What! In *this* street!"

"Yeah… up and down."

Butch heaved to the shuttered windows. His big palm massaged the butt of his gun. He wheeled.

"God, Cassidy, can't you get me out o' this?"

"Why should I?"

"I been on the up and up with them guys, Cassidy. They ain't got no right to put the cross on me."

"Then what the hell are you scared of?"

Butch looked hopeless. "The spot is the spot, Cass. I'm on it. My moll warned me. She's been a regular pal, that broad."

Cassidy shrugged. "I should walk down the street with you! Ixnay on that, Butch. The frau here just said that a guy took a room and wouldn't let nobody in to make up the bed. Said the guy didn't go out since the night he took the room."

"I'm starvin', Cass—so help me!"

"That's too bad, Butch." Cassidy took off his hat, mopped the sweatband, and put it on again. "Well, I'll just poke along then." He turned and put his hand on the knob.

Butch rolled across the room and grabbed his arm. His thick voice pleaded.

"For God's sake, Cass, help me! Pinch me, Cass! I'll be safe behind the bars. I gotta eat. I'll go crazy here!"

"Can't do, Butch. What am I going to book you for?" He spread his palms and arched his sandy eyebrows. "You see how it is. It's really too bad, but—well, no can do. I'll get you a sandwich, Butch."

"Jeeze, Cass, that's swell. But look—I gotta get out. Get the patrol, huh? Ride me to Headquarters or some place where these mutts can't get me."

Cassidy looked crestfallen. He shook his head slowly, sighed. "Can't be done, Butch. You'll just have to stick it out here or meet your hot grease out in the street. I'd like to. But, you see, we ain't got anything on you. Want that sandwich?"

Butch stared with wide eyes in which horror welled. Four days in this room had been a nightmare. He couldn't stand four more. Not two more. Even if he could, those guys would be waiting in the street. What had he done? He didn't know. He'd got plastered to the eyebrows last week in a speak in Little Italy. Had he spilled something to a copper-heart? And had the mob got the copper-heart before he got to the cops?

Butch wanted to land in jail. He would be safe there. Safe behind stone walls and iron bars, with three squares a day. And if you slipped a guard five bucks he'd get a pint of alky. Slip him ten and he'd let the moll in for ten minutes. Butch had a couple of centuries in his pockets.

Cassidy was lighting another cigarette. Cool guy, Cassidy. Never got excited. And it was common gossip up and down the pike that a gun thought twice before making a grandstand play for that copper. They said he had brains, too, and a swell line of stoolies.

"You see," Cassidy was saying, "I can't do a thing, Butch. It's the breaks of the racket. You've always been a pretty tough guy. Hell, take it on the stand-up. It'll be over in a couple of minutes. I'll send flowers."

Butch rubbed his throat. "You—you saw Gus—and Lefty—out here?"

"Sunning themselves up the street. Gus gave me a tip on the races."

Butch began to shake all over. You went out—walked up the street—looking straight ahead, your belly at a standstill, your heart in your throat. Suppose they plugged you in the belly—Butch had seen many a man plugged in the belly. Or if—if Big Joe Palanzio took it into his head to pull the stunt he'd pulled on Snifter. They gagged Snifter and then began cutting him up bit by bit. It took three hours. Butch groaned. He'd made a couple of slices himself! Snifter had two-timed....

"God Almighty, Cass!"

"Huh?"

"Take me, Cass! I ain't got a show this way. I can't let them guys get me. You don't know what them guys are liable to do!"

Smoke dribbled from Cassidy's nose. He patted Butch on the shoulder. "There, there, Butch. That's just an idea you have. It'll be over before you can say boo."

"Cass, for God's sake—give me a break—just once like this! Chuck me in a cell for a week so I can feed up and get my strength back. Then I'll take a chance. But I'm weak now, Cass—weak as a cat."

Cassidy opened the door, smiled wearily. "It's really too bad, Butch. I don't suppose I'll be seeing you again."

"Cass," choked Butch, "take me! Get the wagon!"

"I can't, Butch. Don't you see I can't?"

Butch stared with glazed eyes. His lower lip fell down and hung shivering and gleaming. He made motions with his mouth as though he were choking.

Cassidy backed away, saying, "Anyhow, I'll get you that sandwich—if you want it."

"Cass!"

"Huh?"

"Come here—in."

"Now, Butch, no use going over all that—"

"Cass, come in!" Butch choked.

He almost dragged the precinct dick in. He closed the door. He gripped Cassidy's arms and stared blindly at Cassidy's cool sallow face. His big body trembled.

"You got to take me, Cass. Because—you got a reason."

"Ixnay."

"Yes, you have, Cass! Look—I—I was in on that Willow Roadhouse job."

"Be yourself, Butch."

"You gotta take me, Cass. I swear I was in on it. Me—and Massa. We got Higgins out in the garage and let him have the fog in the guts. You know that job, Cass. You—you—hell, you was workin' on it!"

"What the hell kind of a song and dance are you trying to hand me?" Cassidy chuckled good-humoredly.

Butch's eyes blazed angrily. "Song and dance, my eye, Cass! I'm tellin' you—see. I'm tellin' you I and Massa fogged out Irish Higgins. He was on the muscle in the wrong neighborhood for too long—see? We don't mean to fog him when we get him out there. We're just gonna beat him up. But he makes a crack about my moll and then he starts to feel for his smoke. You get me, Cass—I—we fogged out, that baby!"

Cassidy showed polite interest. He looked down at the butt

he held in his hand and idly knocked the ash off with his little finger.

"You want me to give you the ride in, Butch, and when you think you're safe you'll give me the razz. You're in a tough spot, all right, but you ain't taking too many chances on getting out. You'll have to make it sound more reasonable, Butch."

Butch shook him. "You hear, Cass! We did it—me and Massa. And you gotta get me off this spot and book me and put me in jail!"

Cassidy dropped the butt. "And Massa. I didn't know about Massa. Guess we can work up something between the two of you. Okey, Butch. Come on."

Butch shook his head. "The wagon, Cass. I gotta go in the wagon. I ain't gonna walk up no street."

Cassidy chuckled and casually drew the gun from Butch's belt. He hefted it and smiled at it.

"The wagon's right around the corner, Butch."

"Huh?"

"It's been there for twenty minutes." Butch scowled. "The wagon—" Cassidy was pointing the gun at him, smiling. "I ran across that moll of yours, Butch. A raid. I was going to pinch her—but I made a proposition instead. She went copper-hearted."

"Forget it! She told me I was on the spot—"

"I told her to tell you that. Come on, you gofor."

It's the Live Ones That Talk

A nervous bank president, a few killers and a private dick.

WHEN KNOX came into the office muttering to himself about the rain Alvin Johns looked up from a typewritten sheet and said: "How would you like to go to Maine, Chet?"

"You've always had a grotesque sense of humor," Knox said, hanging up his wet slicker.

Johns gushed smoke through his nostrils and dropped his eyes to the typewritten sheet. He was a weathered-looking man.

"You could take the roadster," he said, "and make Bridgeboro in six hours, easily."

Knox, burly, well-groomed, came to the desk, picked up a sheaf of letters, shuffled them, ignored his senior partner.

Miss Winterborne said from the next office: "Your call, Mr. Johns."

Johns picked up the telephone on the desk and said: "Hello, Bridgeboro Tavern.... This is the Eastern States Detective Service, Mr. Johns speaking. A Mr. Terry, one of our operatives, checked in there at six last evening. He telephoned me shortly afterwards, said he would phone again either from there or from Loon Lodge. I'd like to know if he got away from your place.... I see.... H'm.... Oh, yes.... No, that's all, thank you."

Johns put the receiver gently on to the hook. Knox had stopped opening letters and was looking down at Johns curiously.

Johns, picking up the typewritten sheet again, said: "That Coastal Mercantile and Trust trouble. You were out yesterday. I sent Jack Terry to Bridgeboro."

Knox darkened. "What the hell did you want to monkey with the Coastal Mercantile for?"

"Have you looked at our bank balance lately? Jobs are not dangling for the taking.... Kallow, the president, went to Maine a week ago to ease his nerves. Link, his attorney and close friend, went with him. They're staying at Loon Lodge, owned by Hector McAleer, loaned to them for several weeks as a friendly gesture. Here in Boston Kallow's life was threatened by an anonymous depositor who believes Kallow swindled and caused the run on the bank."

"I shouldn't wonder."

"Let me finish. Kallow's nerves were run ragged by the state of the bank. It is said the anonymous threat precipitated a complete breakdown. Link urged Maine, went with him. Three days of calm were good for Kallow. Then a face at the window, the sight of a gun. They think Kallow's been trailed to Maine and murder is on the make. Link phoned for an operative yesterday morning. I sent Terry."

"You call the lodge?"

"Can't get 'em. Terry phoned from the Tavern shortly after he reached Bridgeboro, said he was held up because he couldn't get a car to take him the four miles to the lodge. He said he'd get there somehow and phone me again when he did. The man at the Tavern said he finally managed to hire a flivver and went off himself. The bed wasn't slept in last night. I can't get the lodge. I'm worried about Terry."

Knox made a fist and thumped it slowly on the desk. "You know damned well Kallow was to blame for that bank muddle! Why did you take the job? Are we going to be like any other lousy cheap gumshoe agency or—"

"It looked like easy money, and I thought that they were exaggerating the danger anyhow. We're hard up, Chet—"

Knox slapped the letters on the desk, crossed the room and put on his slicker. "Anybody but Terry—and you'd go yourself, old timer."

AT TWO that afternoon Knox rolled his dripping roadster down the main street of Bridgeboro. He pulled up before the Bridgeboro Tavern, climbed out and entered a small lobby littered with easy-chairs and brass spittoons and a half dozen men watching the rain that had threshed down for three days.

Knox stopped at the desk and said to the old man there: "Are you the proprietor?"

"Yes," the man said, turned the register around.

"I want to talk with you," Knox said, and strode into the adjoining room.

The proprietor followed, wearing a puzzled frown.

"I'm from the agency," Knox said, "that phoned you this morning. Any word of Mr. Terry?"

"No, nothing. The man down the garage who rented him the flivver, the man was in this morning asking about it. Because Mr. Terry said he would bring it back again last night, or send it back with someone."

"Use your phone?"

The old man nodded, and Knox entered a booth, dropped in a nickel, asked for Loon Lodge. After two minutes he hung up, came out and shrugged.

"Operator can't get the lodge."

The old man gulped, said: "The man is sure worried about his flivver and—"

"There's a friend of mine worth more worrying about than a flivver," Knox said. "How do I get there?"

"There are two ways, one shorter than the other but hard to follow. You better take the long way. I'll try drawing you the roads. They're bad. Lots of rain."

Knox went with him back to the desk, and the old man drew a rough map on the back of an envelope and supplemented it with explanations.

"I'll find it," Knox said. "Thank you very much,"

He paused to stuff and light a battered old briar. Men came down from regions above. A few came in out of the rain. Some went out. There was talk of rains and bad roads and freshets. With his pipe drawing, Knox went out and climbed into the roadster.

Two hundred yards farther on he left the black state road

and took a dirt one that looped back of a sawmill, crossed a covered bridge and then became treacherous with ruts and mud and burrowed narrow and winding into drenched, strong woods.

At the fork, he took the left road rather than the shorter one which cut over the ridge and joined the shore road two miles beyond. He caught glimpses of the lake through gaps in the trees, but his eyes stayed mostly on the road and he could make no more than fifteen miles an hour. There were many forks, many cross lanes, and he had to stop frequently and refer to the map.

Bone-weary from the long drive, he drew on a cold pipe, cursed the road, the weather, the job Terry had been sent on. Half an hour after leaving the Tavern he braked at an intersection of three lanes and looked for signs.

Two shots clapped in the noisy rain. Knox's pipe was shattered, ripped from his mouth, stinging his teeth. He knocked open the left door, flung himself downward and half out of the car, bracing his left arm on the running-board, clawing with his right hand for the gun in his armpit.

A third shot pierced the right door and rang against the emergency. A fourth shattered the windshield, and by that time Knox landed on his hands in the mud, pulled his legs down after him and settled on his toes, turning and crouching behind his car. The gun's safety unlatched, he crept to the rear of the car, raised the gun, listened. His nape bristled, there was a savage twist to his lips, and green fire burned in his deep-set eyes.

Presently he heard the muffled roar of an engine. He darted around the rear of the car, lunged long-legged across the road and started up the steep intersecting road. Before he reached the hump in the road he heard the engine fading away beyond in the trees. He stopped, cursing, and looked around. He saw where a car had come down the hill, backed into a small clearing, turned around and waited while a man had come down to the crossroads. After a minute Knox hefted his gun, closed the safety and slushed back to his car.

He roared the motor, meshed gears violently, and slewed from side to side on the getaway. A mile farther on he left the dirt road, turned sharp left into thick pine woods and rolled on soaked pine-needles. Paths diverged at frequent intervals, but signs showed him the way.

He landed in a clearing back of a rambling lodge that set on a knoll overlooking the lake. He parked the car in front of a large barn and climbed a stone path toward a screened porch at the rear of the lodge.

He rattled the screen, crowded it with his body to dodge the streams of water pouring from the porch eaves. A woman's face appeared in the window of the house door; eyes peered hard for a moment.

"Open up," Knox called huskily.

The face disappeared. Knox tried to force the screen door; it was bolted, not hooked, and resisted.

The house door opened abruptly and a gaunt, bony man in boots and blue jumper, stood there holding a rifle.

"What you want?"

"Eastern States Detective Service— This is Loon Lodge, isn't it?"

"Yeah."

"Well, sweetheart, maybe you think I came here to stand out in the rain all day!"

"Here, here," said another voice. "What's this, what's this?"

A corpulent, red-cheeked man crowded in the doorway.

"Hello," he chirruped.

"Hello," growled Knox. "Are you Mr. Link?"

"Yes, yes."

"Open up, then. I'm Knox from the E.S.D. Is Terry here?"

"Terry?"

"Terry—Terry! Sweet suffering gods, snap out of it and open this door!"

Link said: "Rupe, open the door."

The bony man shrugged, clumped across the porch, slid back the bolt. Dripping, Knox ducked in out of the rain, stamped mud from his shoes, stopped before Link.

"Terry—Terry," he said in a low rumbling voice. "The man we sent here yesterday."

Link opened his small full mouth; his eyes widened. "Why—why, no man came here. We wondered—we've been waiting—"

"That's enough," Knox chopped off.

He stood with his big fists knotted, his burly shoulders lowered, his big feet spread wide. He turned by fits and starts, stared down Rupe. He walked the length of the porch, heavily, his shoulders rolling; came back and stopped and stared so long and so levelly at Link that Link became uneasy.

"I beg pardon, Mr. Knox—but what you have just said—"

"I know, I know," Knox said dully. "Pardon me. I'm all steamed up. Terry's disappeared."

"Good grief!"

Knox's fists swung at his thighs. "And some baby took a few pot shots at me down the road."

Link convulsed and swallowed hard, his moon face blanching. Then he gripped Knox's arm.

"Mr. Knox," he said softly, nervously. "Please—please keep the news from Mr. Kallow! Don't tell him! He's frightfully upset, worried, worn to a frazzle! Just say you—just pretend you were the only man sent—say you were unavoidably delayed—"

"Wait a minute," Knox said flatly. "I didn't come here to play watch-dog for Mr. Kallow. I came here to find my friend. He happens to be the best friend I have, all the more invaluable to me because I haven't many."

"But my dear sir—"

"Quit it. I'll handle this mess the way I see fit. If you don't like it, hire another agency. Where's Mr. Kallow?"

Link bristled pompously. "Sir, my client—"

"And my friend, Mr. Link, is—missing. Which is more

important to me than the state of your client's mind or liver. Now don't hand me any of your courtroom dramatics. You haven't hired me. You hired Jack Terry, and he's vanished. And I'm looking for him. If I help you and your client incidentally that will be just your good luck."

Link fidgeted, started to say something several times, then made a hopeless gesture.

II

KNOX WAS a candid, plain-spoken man—often too much so for his own good. Obsequious overtures were not in his make-up. He went straight to a point without frills. He was a cop from the ground up, a little jaded, a little tired of crime and the lying and viciousness that went with it.

"You saw the face at the window, Mr. Kallow," he said. "Had you ever seen it before?"

"No."

"Would you recognize it if you saw it again?"

"No. I would say I saw a hat, soaked with rain, shadowing a face—and perhaps the glint of a gun. We had just finished dinner night before last."

"Did you see it, Mr. Link?"

"No."

Kallow was a charred clinker of a man, with bony fingers, a slack mouth and ghosts in his eyes. He sat huddled in a big chair, hardly able to speak. The rain threshed against the roof and the logs in the fireplace crackled and snapped.

"No shots fired," said Knox.

Link said, "No. But last night—we heard someone on the front veranda. Rupe, the caretaker—came down with his rifle. We had all gone to bed. We found no one. It was only this morning that Rupe called our attention to—" He stopped, crossed the room and raised one of the shades. He pointed to a large X chalked on the outside of the window. "These marks—they're on all the front windows."

Knox, standing before the fireplace, nodded, did not move.

"Rupe was here when you came?" he said.

"Yes," said Link. "He looks after things all year around. Lives during the winter in a cabin down near the lake. General factotum around here. Just now he helps Miss Fairway with the housework."

"She been here long?"

"No. Mr. McAleer doesn't open the lodge until July first. His servants come up with him and Mrs. McAleer. They couldn't spare even one. Mr. McAleer wired Rupe to get the place ready for us and told him to hunt us a cook. Miss Fairway arrived the day before we did. She's been quite nervous—with all these goings-on. I doubt if she'll stay. You can't blame her."

"Did Rupe try to follow any footprints?"

"He says he can't. The ground is covered with pine-needles and they take no impression."

"Any threats by telephone?"

"The telephone has been out of order since yesterday afternoon. The storm, I guess."

"Or cut wires." Knox lit a cigarette. "Keep the shades drawn and the doors locked. Don't answer any knocks. I'll be back."

"Where are you going?" Kallow cried, startled.

"Look around," Knox said, leaving the room.

He went out the back way, his slicker buttoned up to his neck, his hand in his pocket, gripping his gun. He descended the knoll to the clearing where his car was parked and walked on, taking the path he had driven in on.

He came to an intersection, where a pine tree had two signs on it, one indicating Loon Lodge, the other Camp Wildway. He took the latter lane, the pine needles sopping beneath each solid footfall. He came to a fork, one lane leading on to Camp Wildway, the other marked Gray's Landing. He paused and looked around with sharp, searching eyes. He went on to Camp Wildway, found it to be a large cabin, locked, vacant, overlooking the lake. He returned to the fork and took the lane leading to Gray's Landing.

A few yards beyond it descended abruptly, slippery and treacherous because of the wet pine needles. A hundred yards below he saw a small dock jutting into the lake. Half-way down he stopped short and stared at a hat lying in the bushes. He picked it up, looked inside. The initials J.T. were stamped on the sweatband.

Knox's eyes narrowed. He stood and looked round and round. Then he went down to the dock and stood on it looking at the water. The rain was lashing it and he could not see beneath the surface. He found a long stick and poked it in the water. It was deep. He could not touch bottom. He climbed into a rowboat moored to the dock by a generous length of rope and pushed the boat out till the rope was taut. He probed beneath the water with the stick.

Five minutes later he hauled on the rope, climbed to the dock and stood somberly in the rain—a burly man, hard as nails in his business, roughshod in his dealings. His face looked suddenly white and sullen, his upper lip lifted wolf-like, clenched teeth bit off an oath.

He climbed the slope slowly, deep in thought, his greenish eyes glazed and his palm sweating on the gun-butt.

RUPE LET him in the back door. Knox went hard-heeled and somber through the kitchen, through the pantry, down the short corridor, into the living-room.

He sat down on a straight-backed chair, ground the heel of one hand slowly into the palm of the other. The surface of his eyes was dull, lustreless; but their depths were ablaze. In the dim uncertain light he must have appeared, to Link and Kallow, merely pensive and sunk in thought.

"If—if I thought there would be no danger," Kallow muttered, "I'd leave—go back to Boston. But now I'm here! I can't leave! There's death in the woods!"

He crouched back in the chair, the light of the flames lapping his fear-ridden face.

Link coughed, rocked on his heels. "Just be calm—be calm. Mr. Knox is here."

Knox rose suddenly, towering. "Rupe!" he called, so fiercely that Kallow cried out in terror.

Slow footfalls brought Rupe into the room.

"Get a length of stout rope, Rupe, and come with me."

Rupe didn't move.

"You hear me!"

Link said: "But, Mr. Knox, you can't leave us in the house alone—without even Rupe. You can't!"

"Stay," Kallow quavered. "Money is no object. For —— sake, don't leave us here!"

"Rupe," said Knox, "get that rope."

"I got to stay here," Rupe said unemotionally.

Knox said in a low roar: "You know where Terry is? *He's in that flivver—in the lake!*"

"My ——!" Kallow cried.

"Now get a rope," Knox said. "The flivver is off the end of Gray's Landing. Terry went down with it. Shot right off the dock."

"But you can't pull the car up with just a rope," Link said.

"I don't want the car up. I want to get Terry's body up."

Kallow cried: "I will not be left alone in this house!"

"Besides, Mr. Knox," Link said, "of what value will the body be?"

Knox sighed. "Get me that rope, Rupe. You don't have to go with me. But get it."

"I'll look," Rupe said.

Knox went into the bathroom, stripped, put on his slicker. Rupe came in with a coil of heavy rope and Knox took it and went out. He reached the dock, climbed into the boat, tied one end of the rope to the boat. Then he took off the slicker, grasped the free end of the rope and dived into the water.

Three times he rose, snorting out water. The fourth time he climbed back into the boat, hauled it to the dock, climbed to the dock, put on his slicker. Out of the water he raised a body to which he had attached an end of the rope.

"That was tough, kid—tough," he murmured.

He examined the body carefully, found no bruises, no wound. He heaved the body over his shoulder and toiled up the slope with it. He carried it into the big barn and laid it on a work table. Over it he threw some old burlap bags. He went into the lodge, rubbed himself down, dressed and strode into the living-room.

"I got it," he muttered. "Put it in the barn."

Link said: "Were there any signs of violence?"

"No."

"What a frightful accident!"

"Accident, eh?"

Rupe said slowly: "He must have got off our road. He must have gone down that hill. It'd be slippery."

"That sounds simple," Knox said. "To have taken that road he would have had to make two errors. There are signs at all the forks. He might have missed one, but he wouldn't have taken a second. Not when there were signs."

"What then?" Link asked.

"Somebody gave him directions. Somebody rode with him and Terry took it for granted he was being shown the way, so he didn't bother looking at signs. Going down the hill, the other man jumped out. Or got off at the top of the hill, this side of the slope."

"But who?"

Knox said: "You telephoned us from here, didn't you?"

"Why, yes," Link said. "I phoned right from this room. We've three. There is one on the writing-table over there in the corner, one in the hall upstairs, and one in the pantry."

"All on the one line?"

Knox said: "Where were you, Rupe, when Mr. Link phoned?"

"I don't know when he phoned."

Link said: "Ten o'clock yesterday morning."

"Guess I was moppin' your bedroom out."

Knox crossed the room and looked at the telephone. "It's one where you have to turn the crank, I see. When you turn the crank a bell rings here, doesn't it?"

"Why—yes," Link said.

"Could be heard in other rooms. Get Miss Fairway, Rupe. No, never mind."

III

KNOX WENT into the kitchen and found Miss Fairway peeling potatoes. She was a straw-blonde, plump, thirtiesh and quiet in a mouse-like way.

Knox said: "Mr. Link telephoned on long-distance at ten yesterday morning. Where were you?"

"Here, I guess."

"You guess."

"Either here or out on the back porch. I washed some of my things yesterday. It might have been about then."

"Your left hand, Miss Fairway."

"What?"

"Let me see your left hand."

He took it and looked at it, dropped it.

"How did you manage to get this job?"

"There was an ad in the Portland *News*."

She smiled. She was pretty in a sort of wan, lazy way, and there was a subtle languor in her gray eyes.

"I never bargained for all—all this," she said. "But I need the money. Jobs are hard to find."

Knox drifted back into the living-room, said to Rupe: "You hired Miss Fairway, I believe. She have good credentials?"

"Yeah. I put an ad in, and she had the best out of about twenty letters I got."

"How long have you been caretaker here?"

Link broke in: "Surely you don't suspect Rupe and Miss Fairway?"

Knox didn't reply. He took a slow turn up and down the room. Presently he said: "Neither Rupe nor Miss Fairway were out at seven last night?"

"No," Link said. "We were at dinner. Rupe eats with us, helps serve too."

Rupe said: "Mr. Terry must have just got lost. There's nobody around these woods yet. It's early. This is the only place open. Camp Wildway and Beaver Lodge and Camp Heather, they don't have caretakers."

"That's good to know," Knox said. "It's good to know because somebody else met Terry, or he gave somebody a lift. Somebody gave him wrong directions. Somebody knew of that hill with the lake at the bottom."

"But how," Link said, "could that somebody have known who Terry was?"

Knox looked at Rupe. "Somebody knew you phoned for a private detective."

"I'm gettin' tired o' this," Rupe growled. "You're hintin' I got a hand in this."

"Keep your pants on," Knox said. "Can't I ask a few questions? Somebody's got to take hold here."

"Of course, of course," soothed Link. "But all this— Really, Mr. Knox, you're treating all of us as if—as if—"

"I'm just trying to get things straight," Knox rapped out. "My buddy's had a raw deal somewhere. I don't believe it was an accident that bounced him and the car into the lake. I've got a healthy hunch some bird was expecting him, and that bird steered him down that hill. You've got to take me—and like it.

Understand, I'm here now to solve a murder—not to prevent one. Rupe, call Miss Fairway in here."

Rupe went out and Miss Fairway came in with her languorous eyes and at word from Knox sat down quietly and folded her hands. Rupe appeared and stood scowling resentfully at Knox.

Knox said to Miss Fairway: "How old are you?"

"Thirty-one."

"Married?"

She looked puzzled.

"I know, I know you're Miss Fairway. Have you ever been married?"

"No."

"You're sure?"

"I ought to know, oughtn't I?"

Kallow interrupted fretfully: "Damn it, Knox, I sent for a bodyguard! I didn't send for a man to come here and disrupt this entire household!"

Knox looked at him stonily. "You will please be quiet, Mr. Kallow. I'm not on your payroll. The man you sent for is dead. I didn't come to replace him."

"Then you have no right here!"

"Haven't I? Oh, yes I have, I have!"

"The next thing, Miss Fairway will leave and we shall starve!"

"Will she? No she won't. Nobody will leave here.… Miss Fairway, go over to that desk, sit down and write out your full name."

She rose obediently, gave Knox a half-smile, sat down at the desk and wrote.

Knox picked up the sheet of paper. "Rupe," he said, "have you got the letter Miss Fairway wrote asking for this job?"

"Got it in my room upstairs."

"Get it."

As he tramped out, a hissing sound came from the kitchen.

Miss Fairway rose, said: "Something's running over."

"Go ahead," Knox said, staring at Miss Fairway's handwriting.

Kallow complained irritably. Link began tramping up and down, tightening his mouth. The rain hit the roof in great sheets, lashed the trees. Link clapped his hands to his head.

"You're making a muddle of everything, Knox! So help me, you are!"

Knox, unimpressed, said: "So I imagine. Not half the muddle your client made of the Coastal Mercantile."

"Look here, sir—" Kallow began hotly.

"Don't tell me."

Link made fists, set his fat jaw. "What I am going to do, Mr. Kallow—what I am going to do is—engage another agency. We might as well have no protection at all, with this man."

"I'll stay here while you drive to the village," Knox said, laughing shortly.

Link shook, his face reddened. "Confound you!"

Finally Rupe came down, looking puzzled. "I can't find it. I thought I saved it. I tore the others up. Maybe I tore it up too. I donno."

Knox took three fast steps, gripped Rupe by the arm. "Listen to me, you! What's the truth about it? You're not as dumb as you act!"

"Let go my arm!"

Rupe wrenched loose and fell back, his bony fists knotted, his brows meeting darkly over his nose.

"You stay right here!" Knox clipped. "I'll get that girl. I'll settle this."

He strode into the corridor, through the pantry, knocked open the swing-door leading to the kitchen.

"Miss Fairway—"

He stopped. The kitchen was empty. His glance flicked to the rear door. It was open. He drew his gun and ran to the back porch, yanked open the screen door, stood on the top step. His mouth twitched, hardened. He ran down the stone path to the clearing by the barns.

His car was gone. He ran part way up the path, stopped, listened, peered ahead. He heard nothing but the rain and the wind, saw nothing but the gloomy woods. He turned on his heel, ran back to the lodge, stalked into the living-room and grabbed up his slicker.

"Well, she's gone."

"What!" Link exclaimed.

"Gone. Flown. Beat it." Knox had the slicker on. "And in my car!"

"Good grief!"

"Got a car here?"

"Rupe's Ford—in the barn—"

"Not that girl—not that girl!" cried Kallow. "And she's been in the house all along—and I've been eating the food— My —— I wonder if I'm poisoned!"

"Girl is she?" rapped out Knox. "Not that baby. She's a married woman or I'll eat my words. I saw the groove on her finger where she used to wear a wedding ring. How'd she get here to the lodge?"

Rupe muttered: "I called for her in the village. She phoned she was there. Judas Priest, she had all kinds of references—"

Knox started out, stopped, turned and jabbed a forefinger towards the men. "You'll find this before you're much older: you'll find that Miss Fairway disappeared. I don't mean that jane that was here, either."

Link dropped heavily to a chair, raised his hands, dropped them hopelessly.

"Don't leave us, Knox!" Kallow cried, rearing up, his eyes bulging with horror.

But Knox was on his way, banging doors.

IV

KNOX BACKED out the Ford sedan, swung it around, choked it and went bouncing up the lane. He had both hands on the wheel, and in his right hand, too, he held his gun. At the first fork he turned right, rolled along level on the soft needles, his eyes keen, darting from side to side.

He reached the dirt road and swung right, stopped the car and looked back up the dirt road. He got out and found fresh wheel tracks in the mud, climbed back in the car and continued whence he had come earlier that day. He remembered the crossroads where he had ducked four bullets. Turning a bend, he saw them. He accelerated at the risk of a bad skid, reached the intersection and, with one hand on the wheel, the other holding his gun raised, he veered left and pounded up the ridge road from which he had been fired on.

Half-way to the top of the steep incline, he braked sharply with his foot, yanked on the emergency. He saw his car—the rear end of it protruding from dense thickets through which the front of it had plowed. It was almost keeled over. Its right rear wheel was free of the ground.

He ducked out of the Ford quickly, waited several minutes, watching the back of his car. Then he dived to the side of the road, crashed through the thickets and saw that a stump had stopped his car's progress. The side-curtains were smeared with mud—had been since a detour on the road from Boston. He couldn't see inside. He pulled open the door and thrust in his gun. Its muzzle stopped against the woman's arm. She was slumped side-wise.

She was dead. Her chest and throat were bloody.

Knox opened his mouth. It stayed wide open for a full minute, while he remained motionless, staring. Then he stepped back, grimaced, brushed the back of his hand across his eyes, across his lips. He stood with his burly shoulders sagging. Water fell in streams from his down-turned felt hat, glistened on his face. He slushed through the wet thickets to the roadway, his feet lagging, a weary droop to his shoulders.

He got into the Ford, climbed the remainder of the hill in first gear, shifted to high and rattled along the top of the ridge, slowly. The rubber windshield wiper moved monotonously back and forth, the small space it cleared limiting his outlook.

Coming to a fork in the road, he stopped. He looked around for signs, saw none. It was a desolate region of sparse woods and rock-strewn fields. He took the right-hand road and jolted over rocks, splashed through ruts filled with water. The road narrowed. He passed a weatherbeaten farmhouse, went on and finally came to a dead-end. He turned around and headed back, stopped in front of the farmhouse, walked to the rickety porch and knocked.

No one answered. He went around to the rear, saw wheel ruts. He knocked at the rear door. He shrugged. No answer. He half-heartedly tried the door. To his surprise, it opened. He entered a kitchen and stood looking around at the bare shelves, a rusty sink.

He moved through other deserted rooms. He started at sound of a thump, looked at the ceiling. His hand tightened on his gun. He found a narrow staircase and went up softly for a heavy man. He heard a bed-spring creak. He spun around, fastened his eyes on a closed door.

He reached the door, turned the knob, whipped it open. Shades were drawn, but he trained his gun on something that moved.

"Steady!" he growled.

The springs creaked again. He heard a muffled whimper. He crossed to the nearest window and raised a shade. He saw a woman bound hand and foot, lying on a cot. He put his gun in his pocket.

"You're all right," he said.

He sat down on the bed, drew a penknife from his pocket,

hesitated. He laid the knife aside and untied the knot of the cloth that gagged the woman.

"Oh, oh," she panted.

"Take it easy. You're all right."

"—— ——! get me out of here!"

"Sh—sh. Get your breath. Be a good girl. I'm a friend."

He sat with his big hands hanging between his knees.

"Been harmed?"

"No—no. But—"

"That's all right then. Who are you?"

"Anna Fairway."

"This is great. How did you get here?"

She blew at strands of hair that had fallen over her eyes. Knox brushed the hair back from her forehead.

"I—I answered an ad—to cook. I live in Portland. A man wired me to come out. I came out on the narrow gauge and got off at the depot. I'd wired back I'd come on the bus, but I took the train instead because I missed the morning bus. When I got off at the depot I asked the agent how I got to the Tavern, where the man was going to meet me. He said it was a five minutes walk. I left him and went out, it was showering, and a woman asked me if I wanted a lift. I had my new spring hat on, and I got in. I was brought here and there were three men, and then I was tied up like this. I could have near died."

"Did you tell the woman where you were going?"

"Yes, kind of. I only asked for a lift to the hotel, and I said a man from Loon Lodge would meet me there. I remember she looked surprised. Then she said she was going that way. They said they wouldn't harm me and I'd be let go in time, but it's been days!—and I never saw the woman again!"

"Did the men come back?"

"A couple of times a day. They brought me milk and sandwiches. I begged them to let me go. I cried and one of them cursed and struck me. Please, please untie me! They've been getting nasty. I'm sure they're criminals, and something's gone wrong and I don't know what they might do."

"Get any names?"

"Only once, when one of the men struck me: one of the others called him Massa. He had black shiny hair and looked Italian. He was always playing with a gun. It frightened me. He was tall like you, not as heavy—and good-looking but he looked vicious too, with the gun and the snarly way he'd talk. The others were evil too, but they always seemed nervous because he handled the gun so much."

Knox patted her arm. "Good girl, Miss Fairway. I'd be able to pick that guy out in a crowd. Do you remember the car you came here in?"

"I think it was a Buick. Anyhow, it was a dark red sedan."

Knox began slicing at her bonds. "I'll take you to the hotel, Miss Fairway."

"But they took everything I had—my valise—my handbag—money—all my references!"

"I'll see your room is paid for. You stay in the room. In a little while you'll have your job. When we get out in the car, lie down in the back, in case we pass the boy friends."

He found her valise in a closet downstairs. He carried it to the car, looked up the road, called to her. She came running and climbed in the back, curled up on the floor.

KNOX WALKED with her into the Bridgeboro Tavern. The proprietor looked curious. Without a word the woman signed her name on the register and when the proprietor took down a key from the rack and started to take her bag, Knox said: "I'll take it." He accompanied the woman to her room, set down the valise.

"Now remember," he said, "stay in here. Keep your door locked and"—he looked at the door—"bolted. I'll have a word with the man downstairs. I'll need you to identify those men, perhaps. And—your job, you know."

"Yes, yes. Oh—I'm so grateful to you, Mr. Knox. You're simply wonderful. I don't know how I can ever—"

"Then I'll be seeing you." Knox was at the door. He ducked his head slightly, said, "Until then..." and went out.

Downstairs, he motioned the proprietor into the little sitting-room.

"When I left here this afternoon," he said, "did you notice anyone go out in a car shortly afterward?"

"Well, there were men coming in and out. I think—yes, there were three men went out and drove off. I didn't think anything of it."

"I'd like to see their names."

"Well, they weren't stopping here. Lots of folks come in and sit around and listen to the radio for baseball scores. The man about the flivver, he was in again. Did you find Mr. Terry?"

Knox finished lighting a cigarette, flicked the match into a cuspidor. He said: "I'll appreciate it if you'll send meals up to Miss Fairway. Let no one but me see her."

"Is—is there anything wrong—?"

"Thank you very much," Knox said, and went out.

V

RUPE PROWLED from window to window, drawing the curtains aside, peering at the drenched woods.

Kallow sat nearer the fire than before, a blanket wrapped about his legs.

Link paraded up and down, throwing his chest out, appearing hearty and unconcerned. Yet his mouth was tight, and his eyes flicked nervously at Rupe. He puffed too furiously at a cigar to give a complete impression of nonchalance, and his strides were overlong. Kallow seemed to have aged during the day. He kept locking and unlocking his bony fingers.

"I dread another night here, Link. I dread it! My nerves are gone. I'll never be the same again."

"Tut, tut."

Link made an elaborate gesture with his cigar.

"I plunged heavily, Link. I didn't mean to. How could I have expected that run on the bank? ——! how could I foresee that some crazed depositor would take it into his head to kill me for—for a little thing like that. I'm too old—too old a man to stand this persecution, this horrible suspense." He clenched his fists. "And—and that impossible detective! He barges in here like a bat out of hell, roars around the place, insults us—"

"He was right 'bout the woman," Rupe grumbled. "I thought she was a rotten cook."

"Now are *you* going to start?"

Link said: "They must have known we were coming here before we left Boston. How did they find out?"

"You, my attorney, should ask *me!*"

Link sighed: "Yes.... Knox was right about the woman. We must humor him, Mr. Kallow. We must humor him so that he'll stay here. I—I—by gad, I *have* got confidence in him. If he leaves us—"

"If he leaves," rumbled Rupe dourly, "me, I leave. I'm only the caretaker here. I been cookin', I been makin' beds, I been moppin' floors—"

"For which," said Kallow, "Mr. McAleer pays you."

Rupe thumped the butt of his rifle on the floor. "But he don't pay me to get killed!"

"Now, now—please," said Link, acting as buffer again. "Please don't let us argue. It's the strain—the strain. This weather—these sinister woods— Please!"

Kallow swallowed, licked his parched lips, writhed in his chair.

"Night is—coming," he said scarce above a whisper. "Suppose—suppose Knox doesn't come back! What's keeping him?"

Link stiffened, gasped, "What was that?"

Rupe gripped his rifle hard.

Through the threshing of the wind and the rain they heard—

"Help! Help!"

Rupe started for the front door.

"Don't!" cried out Kallow.

Rupe bent his head, cocked an ear. "Somebody yellin' for help—a man."

"Let him yell!" Kallow screamed.

"Rupe—Rupe—" Link acted as if he didn't know what to say.

"Help! Help!"

"Rupe," cried Kallow, rising, shaking, "don't open that door! I command you! Don't go out!"

"Sounds like on the lake. Maybe a man's drownin'—"

"Don't open that door!"

Kallow jerked a small automatic from his pocket, held it in a shaking hand, pointed it at Rupe.

"By ——! Rupe, if you open that door—if you open that door—"

Link made vague, nervous gestures. "Mr. Kallow—please—put away that—that gun." He went towards his client with jerky steps, on thick legs that trembled.

A shadow fell the length of Rupe's face. "A man's yellin' for help. In the woods here when a man yells for help—"

"If—if you open that door, so help me—I swear—I'll—"The gun wobbled.

"Help! Help!"

Rupe cursed and lunged for the door. Kallow's gun exploded. The bullet sank in the wall, far wild. Link, with a hoarse outcry, fell on his client, struck at the gun. It flew from Kallow's hand, skidded far under a bookcase.

Rupe had the door open. He leaped to the veranda, looked towards the shrouded lake. He unbolted the screen door, jumped to the wet pine-needles.

A masked man jumped from behind a tree, thrust a gun against Rupe's ribs. Rupe swung on him. Another masked man jumped from behind another tree and grounded Rupe with a blow on the head. The first man bounded up to the veranda, leaped through the door, his big automatic steady.

"Mitts up, you guys!"

Kallow was falling back into a chair.

Link said: "Now, sir, please—"

"Pipe down! Up with those mitts, fat boy!"

The second and a third man joined him. Masked, inimical, they stood rooted to the floor.

The spokesman was tall, wore a black raincoat, had a snarly, rasping voice.

"Who else is in this place?"

Link said: "Only—the two of us—here."

"Quit stallin'." He went to Link and thrust his gun against Link's stomach. "I'd hate to blow your guts out. It'd make me sick at my stomach for a week. You got servants here, ain't you?"

"The—the cook—we had—she left—suddenly. There are only us two."

Trembling, lips hueless, Link nevertheless stood straight, in front of Kallow, who crouched in a chair gnawing at the knuckles of his right hand.

The black-coated man jerked words over his left shoulder— "You boys shake this joint down, top to bottom, first. Snap on it."

The stocky man and the small man started off, disappeared. The black-coated man remained rooted to the floor, his black hat-brim pulled well down, his hands gloved.

Kallow said nothing; sometimes whimperings stirred in his throat. Link held his breath for long spells. The sound of feet tramping around upstairs reached his ears. His eyes fluttered to the ceiling.

The two men reappeared. The stocky man said: "Ixnay. Nothin' doin'."

The black coat crackled as the tall man tramped forward. "Where's the cook was here?"

"I tell you—she left," Link said.

The tall man struck with his left hand. Link staggered. The tall man reached for Kallow, caught him by the throat, heaved him up and shook him.

"Maybe you know, daddy!"

Kallow's mouth writhed. Inarticulate sounds ached in his throat. He could not speak. The tall man threw him violently back into the chair, and Kallow cringed, holding his hands in front of his face.

"I say, sir, he's an old man," Link said.

The tall man swivelled. "But you aren't!" He struck Link again, between the eyes, and as Link toppled the stocky man struck him in the back of the neck, straightened him. Link held up his hands awkwardly. He was not a man used to rough fists. He looked baffled and ashamed.

The tall man jabbed him with his gun. "You get this, you fat boy: I want the truth outta you. Or it's daisies for you. What did you do with that jane was here?"

"I have told you—"

"I know what you told me! I don't want a lie! Damn your guts, I want the truth! You hear me!" he cried stridently. "What did you do with that jane?"

"She ran away. God's truth, she ran away!"

The tall man struck with the barrel of his gun and Link went down heavily, lay flat on his back, groaning. The tall man stood over him, vibrant with rage, pointing the gun at his stomach.

The stocky man said: "Jeeze, kid, take it easy. There ain't nobody else here. Maybe she double-crossed us. I know women, I do, and ten to one—"

"Shut up!" rasped the tall man.

Unabashed, the stocky man said: "Well, why the hell don't you look? You know. We'll see if she lammed on us. We can't hang around here all night."

The tall man cursed the stocky man. Then he looked down at Link. "Did a woman come here this afternoon?"

Link shook his head weakly. "No. Nobody came here."

"Go ahead, kid," said the stocky man. "You and Skinny take a look. If she double-crossed us we'll know then, and I'll nail her personal, and to hell if she is your jane."

The tall man stepped over Link, said: "Come on, Skinny."

The little man joined him and they went through the pantry door. Their feet could be heard thumping up the stairs.

Link sat up, felt gingerly of a bump on his head, winced. He got laboriously to his feet, felt for a chair, dropped to it with a groan. He looked woebegone, dazed, rattled. There was a lot of noise upstairs.

The stocky man looked at the ceiling. He stood solidly on wide-planted feet, whistled a few bars, looked at the two broken men, chuckled hoarsely.

Dusk was falling rapidly.

Kallow started in his chair, gripping the sides. His mouth flung open.

The stocky man tensed, scowled.

"Drop it, honeybunch," Knox said from the doorway.

VI

THE STOCKY man heaved around, dragging his gun with him in a short, tight arc, the butt close to his right side.

Knox's gun crashed, red flame belching from the black muzzle. The lodge shook. The stocky man took a few lagging steps and then dived to the floor as his gun went off and drove a bullet through the head of a bearskin. The gun bounced from his hand as hand and gun struck the floor and he lay deathly still.

Knox clipped: "How many more?"

"Two!" Link gasped. "Upstairs!"

"Okey."

Knox came in, stooped quickly, heaved the stocky man over on his back.

"So," he said.

Link was on his feet, trying to get out a lot of words and getting out none.

"Quick," Knox muttered. "Take Kallow. Beat it. Go down in the bushes or the boat-house. Stay there."

The noise upstairs had stopped. Link stood like a man stricken.

"Get out," Knox muttered.

Link turned as Kallow was rising. Link gripped his client's arm, hurried him to the door, outside. They went along the front of the lodge, cut into the bushes, disappeared in the trees.

Knox did not hurry. His eyes were hard and green, his big face somber. He picked up the gun the stocky man had dropped. He found one bullet in the breech, five in the magazine. He added a bullet to the magazine of his own gun and hefted a gun in either hand. He laid one down long enough to get out of his slicker, which he dropped to the floor.

Then he crossed the room, kicked open a door, went down a short corridor to the foot of the stairs. He listened. Not a sound came from the regions above. The stairway turned at right angles half-way up. Knox waited for a moment, then turned on the nearest light switch. He went quickly through all the lower rooms, turning on lights, pulling up the shades. When the entire main floor was lighted and all the shades raised, he made sure that all the windows were locked, took the key from the locked rear door, went to the front door, locked it from the outside and stood for a moment on the veranda, nibbling his lip in thought.

Then he stepped from the porch, saw Rupe stirring. He motioned Rupe into the woods, and after a moment Rupe crawled out of sight, dragging his rifle with him. Knox slid along the front of the veranda, darted from tree to tree, joined Rupe.

"How're you?" Knox said.

"Bum. They jumped me. It was a trick."

Rupe sat on the wet ground stolidly.

Knox said: "I got one of them. Two more in there. Upstairs. Lights downstairs. They shouldn't dare come down. If you see anybody moving downstairs fire through the windows."

"What about Mr. Kallow and—"

"They're off in the woods somewhere, hiding. You stay here. Watch the front. I'll go around and watch the back. If in doubt, shoot, because these guys are killers. Everything straight?"

"Yup."

"Okey."

Knox left him and weaved through the trees, worked around to the rear of the house and hid near the base of the stone path, with a view of the back of the house, the back porch, and the left side. Rupe was in a position to watch the front and the other side. Knox could see the kitchen, the light hanging from the ceiling, to douse which a man would have to walk to the center of the room.

Five minutes later he heard the crack of Rupe's rifle, heard shattered glass. Then silence. No reply from inside. He saw the swing door from the pantry to the kitchen open slowly. He raised the .45 he had taken from the dead stocky man. It convulsed in his hand. Echoes hammered his eardrums. Glass shattered and the pantry door closed.

A little later all the lights went out. The men inside had located the main switches. Darkness had come in the woods, the lodge became a bulking shadow. Knox crept nearer, until he felt the streams from the eaves striking his hat. He pressed close to the lattice-work beneath the back porch. Presently he heard a window scrape open. The dampness had made the windows stick. He ducked back into the trees, saw a window open above the back porch; a dark frame in which no face appeared.

Minutes passed. Then he heard a dull thud on the earth. He ran towards the side of the house, looked around the corner, saw a body rolling down the slope of the knoll towards the thickets.

"Stop, you!" he barked.

The form rolled into the thickets as Knox lunged towards it, both guns raised. He crashed through the thickets, fell upon an inert man. In an instant he cursed. It was the body of the stocky man. It had been carried upstairs and dropped from a window aloft.

He spun and ran towards the back of the lodge. Through the young saplings he saw a man dropping from the roof of the rear porch. He fired. The bullet clattered among the trees, was deflected. Two muzzles blazed from the corner of the porch, and two bullets richocheted off the wet trees. Two men raced down the stone path, firing sidewise.

Knox felt a bullet pass through his hat without budging the hat. He flung against a tree, raised his .38, fired twice. One of the running men took a header and cried out and the other kept running, fleet as the wind. He reached the clearing and sped across it towards the path out.

The man on the ground lifted his gun. Knox threw himself into the bushes as the gun exploded. The bullet snicked past close to his head. Another buried itself in a tree with a wet smack. A third crackled through branches over his head. Knox fired twice with the .45, one gunclap interlocking with the other. The man on the ground jerked twice and lay still.

Knox vaulted over him, landed heavily beyond and lunged along the side of the clearing. He emptied the .45 up the path. The muzzle blasts drew two shots from ahead, but Knox was behind a tree, heard the bullets strike. Then he darted up the side of the path, heard feet pounding on the wet needles. He caught a fleeting glimpse of a diving shadow—fired—heard a body threshing through bushes.

Knox jumped back of a tree, breathing hard. He shoved fresh cartridges in his .38. He waited for another sound. Heard none. He waited five minutes. He felt around on the ground, caught hold of a big rock. He heaved it a matter of ten yards, heard it rattle through bush, thump to the earth.

He saw two jets of flame, heard two explosions. The bullets hit well up the lane, roundabout where the rock had fallen. Knox fired at the flashes, sweeping four shots back and forth. Four times the gun beyond belched flame. Knox fired one more. Another shot came from the bushes.

Knox jumped out to the path, gained the low bush on the opposite side, lunged up the slight grade. He saw the shadow of a man trying to run. He heard the sound of cartridges being thrust wildly into a magazine.

He dived for the man as the latter turned and jacked his gun. Before the man had the breech closed Knox was upon him, striking with the .45. The man staggered with a scream as the .45 crashed against his gun-hand. He dropped his gun, kicked at close quarters. Knox struck him across the side of the face, and as the man raised his hands to his face, Knox jabbed the muzzle of his .38 against the man's stomach. "If you want more, you heel—start something!"

"Take it easy! You have to bash my guts in?"

"I'll bash more than your guts in! Get in front of me. Try any hocus pocus and I'll wreck your spine. Get going. Back to the lodge."

He hustled the man down the path, came to the clearing, saw the gaunt shape of Rupe start and raise his rifle.

"Me—Knox," Knox said.

"Oh." Rupe lowered his rifle and waited stolidly. "I didn't know where to go, it happened so fast."

Knox stopped the skinny man by the body that lay on the stone path. "Who's this?"

"Massa—Nick Massa—"

"Leave him there, Rupe. Here's the key. Go in and light up."

Rupe took the key and stalked up the path, entered the lodge through the rear. The skinny man stood sniffling in the rain.

"Up the path, you," Knox said.

The lights went on as they reached the back porch. Knox prodded the man into the kitchen, on through into the living-room. He frisked him, found nothing but a pocket knife, took that.

"What's your name?"

"Skinny."

"You had a father, didn't you?"

"Huh? Sure."

"Well, maybe he had a name."

"Burch."

Knox turned to Rupe. "Get Kallow and Link if they haven't started walking back to Boston."

Rupe went to the front porch and called. Link's voice answered, and in a few minutes Link and Kallow came in, soaked to the skin.

Kallow quavered: "This is the end of me. Link, you'll have to give me an alcohol rub. Rupe, turn on the electric heater for the hot water. Rupe, get me my big flannel bathrobe. I'll catch my death of cold."

He tottered to the fire, hugged its warmth.

Knox was toeing the spot where the stocky man had bled badly. He looked at Burch, said: "Who was this guy?"

"Sam Korn."

Knox chuckled bitterly. "A fine bunch of gunmen!"

"You wasn't doin' such hot shootin' yourself," Burch said.

"You poor fathead, I got two of you! And I could have got you. But it's the live ones that talk. It's tough on you that you're left to tell—and take the rap."

"Jeeze, I didn't kill anybody!"

"Just an innocent young sophomore, I suppose, playing Fourth of July—"

"Rupe," cried Kallow, "do get my bathrobe! Make me a hot toddy—before I get pneumonia."

Knox sighed. "Rupe, wet-nurse Mr. Kallow so he'll shut up."

Kallow looked indignant, started warm words. Link silenced him with a placating gesture.

Rupe went out, growling an oath.

KNOX SAID: "Now, Skinny, spring the lowdown or I'll turn you over to the cops in pieces."

"I ain't killed a soul ever in my life. It was Massa started all this—Massa, ——! he used to lay awake at night playin' with his gun."

"Who was the woman?"

"Massa's. She was married once to Toddy Sloane, but Toddy got the heat in his belly a month ago in Providence. It was Massa hooked up with her a couple o' weeks ago. She used to be his moll down in Philly four years ago before she married Toddy Sloane. I warned Massa. But he fell nuts over her again, and she had somethin' on the ball.

"Sam and me didn't trust her. And we was right. She gypped us. The wren gypped us! Her and Toddy was in on a deal two months ago. They stuck up a jewelry store in Hartford and got away with a lot of ice. They had to lam it north in a car, and they kept switchin' cars, duckin' the cops on the way up. They get up in the woods and it's stormin'. They lose the road and land here and jimmy a window and spend the night here.

"They figure they're tailed close, so they bunk the ice here and beat it in the mornin'. They get over in New Hampshire, duck the cops all around and work south again. Then Toddy gets drunk and is shot down in a fight with bootleggers.

"Kitty hikes up here to get the ice, and she finds carpenters around and beats it back again, worried. We meet her in Boston. After a while she springs her story and we come as far as

Portland. We read in the paper an ad for a cook at Loon Lodge. That bungs up our plans, because we figure this joint is occupied. We come up and hang around Bridgeboro. Massa wants to gun right in, but Kitty's afraid.

"We holed up in an old farmhouse, and one day Kitty comes in with a broad—the cook that was comin' here. So Kitty goes. Then the telephone line is out. We can't get in touch with her. Massa's hangin' around up the path one night when a guy comes in a car and asks the way to Loon Lodge. He says he's a private cop after Massa tells him he's from the lodge. Massa steers him—"

"Just what I thought," nodded Knox.

"And Kitty—what does she do? Lams on us! Like we warned Massa: look out for broads!"

"The trouble with you guys," Knox said, "is that you empty your guns and then run. You knew my car. You treated it to a shower once. You did it again when it started up that hill."

"Massa couldn't help it. He was—"

Kallow broke in: "Then—then it's something else altogether! They were not after me!"

"The first time," Knox said, paying no attention to Kallow, "I got a lucky break, Skinny. The second time I got a lucky break, too. Because I wasn't in my car."

Burch chewed on his lip, his eyes popped. "What was the name of the store in Hartford that was robbed?" Knox asked.

"Linderman's. Thirty thousand in ice. And the dame—after gettin' us all steamed up—what does she do? Lams—like that! Flooey! I ain't takin' this rap alone. That dame is gonna take it, too."

Knox smiled. "No, she isn't, Skinny. You're going to take it all by your lonesome. The jane was in the car you and those other two hoods sashayed with lead."

"What!"

"She beat it out of here in my car. She was on her way to join you birds. I was nailing her. I figured she was a fluke. She was on her way to that farmhouse—with the ice, my boy—and you let her have the heat good and plenty!"

Burch choked, began to bite furiously at his fingernails.

Knox said: "So you'll take the rap, honeybunch. You'll take it and you won't like it. While I"—Knox drew a pouch slowly from his pocket—"call on Linderman's."

Skinny clutched at his throat, gasped.

Knox held out a palm, poured diamonds into it from the pouch. "On the way back from town," he said, "I tried to haul my car out of the ditch. So then both cars got ditched. These were in Kitty's handbag. Pretty, Skinny?"

"____!"

Knox said: "Out of the reward I'll take a few dollars… and send you flowers."

GETTING PERSONAL

"**A**H—GOOD MORNING, Mr. Nebel. Glad you're back. Been vacationing?"

"Tramping it around the Caribbean a bit."

"Rest?"

"That—and for a change of scene, new atmosphere and more philosophy."

"And did you acquire any?"

"Surely. I get it in strongest doses in the raw. Down there, in the out-of-the-way, God- and man-forgotten places, you'll find the dregs, stranded flotsam; never made any effort to stem the tide, just drifting with the current and finally cast up on the first handy reef and the husks left to dry out. You don't have to ask their story; their faces and mostly the look in their eyes tell volumes. I don't believe in maudlin, indiscriminate sentiment over such wrecks; but it's a bit pathetic to see these human derelicts bound for the port of Hell. Still, they provide the shadows that give clearer relief to the good things of life. I've always hunted them out, knocking about for some of my twenty-three years in this place and that. It's given me an understanding of contrasts. Can't write a story of all high lights, you know."

"So that's how you get such punch in your Underworld stories, Mr. Nebel?"

"I expect so."

"You take your writing seriously?"

"No one more so. You have to if you want to make the grade nowadays, and you're impelled to if you have ambition to go away, 'way up. To sit in a comfortable chair and tap a typewriter is easy exercise; to make those keys bring out a satisfactory story is about the hardest work going. If you do your work right, energy just oozes out of you and gets into the story. If it's there, it must come from somewhere, and you're the source. Why—night after night, when I'm not reading or working on a plot, I

write just for practice and exercise—anything, a scene, action, character. I may tear it up afterward or, if it happens to please me, file it away to use later. It's all work. A writer, like an artist, always has his eyes open, observes what he sees, makes his comparisons, his notes on odd bits of true scene and character, and files them away in the back of his head for future reference."

"Been much of a student, Mr. Nebel?"

"Of life—not at school. I walked out of public school at fourteen and have never set foot in a classroom since. I've studied people where they live and work and play and fight. That and men like Conrad have helped me a lot."

"Something like Jack London?"

"Don't josh me, Mr. Editor."

"That's all right, Mr. Nebel. You've come a long way in a short time, and the world's before you. It's all up to you. Come in again. *Black Mask* is always glad to see you."

Publication History

renewed by Popular Publications, Inc., 1955. From *Black Mask* Vol. 10, No. 11 (January 1928). Reprinted by special arrangement with Keith Alan Deutsch, proprietor and conservator of the respective copyrights, and successor-in-interest to Popular Publications, Inc.

A GUN IN THE DARK by Frederick Nebel. Copyright © 1928 by Pro-Distributors Publishing Company, Inc. Copyright renewed by Popular Publications, Inc., 1955. From *Black Mask* Vol. 11, No. 4 (June 1928). Reprinted by special arrangement with Keith Alan Deutsch, proprietor and conservator of the respective copyrights, and successor-in-interest to Popular Publications, Inc.

HELL TO PAY by Frederick Nebel. Copyright © 1928 by Pro-Distributors Publishing Company, Inc. Copyright renewed by Popular Publications, Inc., 1955. From *Black Mask* Vol. 11, No. 6 (August 1928). Reprinted by special arrangement with Keith Alan Deutsch, proprietor and conservator of the respective copyrights, and successor-in-interest to Popular Publications, Inc.

STREET WOLF by Frederick Nebel. Copyright © 1930 by Pro-Distributors Publishing Company, Inc. Copyright renewed by Popular Publications, Inc., 1957. From *Black Mask* Vol. 13, No. 3 (May 1930). Reprinted by special arrangement with Keith Alan Deutsch, proprietor and conservator of the respective copyrights, and successor-in-interest to Popular Publications, Inc.

THE KILL by Grimes Hill. Copyright © 1931 by Pro-Distributors Publishing Company, Inc. Copyright renewed by Popular Publications, Inc., 1958. From *Black Mask* Vol. 14, No. 1 (March 1931). Reprinted by special arrangement with Keith Alan Deutsch, proprietor and conservator of the respective copyrights, and successor-in-interest to Popular Publications, Inc.

THE SPOT AND THE LADY by Grimes Hill. Copyright © 1931 by Pro-Distributors Publishing Company, Inc. Copyright renewed by Popular Publications, Inc., 1958. From *Black Mask* Vol. 14, No. 3 (May 1931). Reprinted by special arrangement with Keith Alan Deutsch, proprietor and conservator of the respective copyrights, and successor-in-interest to Popular Publications, Inc.

IT'S THE LIVE ONES THAT TALK by Frederick Nebel. Copyright © 1931 by Pro-Distributors Publishing Company, Inc. Copyright renewed by Popular Publications, Inc., 1958. From *Black*

Mask Vol. 14, No. 9 (November 1931). Reprinted by special arrangement with Keith Alan Deutsch, proprietor and conservator of the respective copyrights, and successor-in-interest to Popular Publications, Inc.

www.ingramcontent.com/pod-product-compliance
Lightning Source LLC
Chambersburg PA
CBHW061035030726
47504CB00002B/383